Rupert Legge is the son of the 9th Earl of Dartmouth and Countess Spencer, and the grandson of bestselling novelist Dame Barbara Cartland. He was educated at Eton and Oxford, where he read Chemistry and spent a year researching the Philosophy of Science. He was called to the Bar in 1975 and practised as a barrister before joining a city firm as a maritime lawyer.

For his first novel, *The Children of Light*, published in 1986, he made a special study of the persuasion techniques of contemporary religious cults.

He now lives, with his wife and two children near Bath.

*Also by Rupert Legge*

The Children of Light

For my grandmother,
Barbara Cartland,
with love

# Chapter 1

1964
*Conningsby Park, Gloucestershire*

'Think he's forgotten?' The brown-haired boy tipped back his head and squinted up at the stone columns above him. They were as tall and thick as trees.

'Nah.' His brother, squatting on the steps next to him, was blond, finer featured than the other boy, slightly taller and thinner. 'He's busy, that's all.'

The two boys looked very small beneath the massive Palladian portico of the great house. On either side of them stretched yard upon yard of Portland stone glistening in the warm golden light of the midday sun.

The brown-haired boy tapped his foot impatiently. He reached in the pocket of his jodhpurs and drew out a conker. He dug his nail into it to test its hardness. 'Daddy's always busy.'

'Daddies usually are,' the blond boy replied knowingly.

'Says who?'

'I have it on the best authority.'

'You mean Nanny?' sneered his brother.

'No, not Nanny.'

'Mummy, then?'

'It's just a well-known fact. Everyone in the cosmos

1

knows it . . . everyone, that is, who's not a pig-ignorant —'

'Why you . . .' The brown-haired boy's mouth set. His fingers clamped harder around the conker. Already his arm had gone back. Then, suddenly, it froze. Above the distant rattle of the lawn mowers, they heard the great door behind them open and close with a slam.

Both boys stood quickly to attention, turned. Before them on the portico stood their father, a stocky figure in a tweed jacket. His fleshy cheeks were slightly flushed. A matted tangle of hair fluffed out of his open-necked shirt. He hitched up his tan corduroy trousers and stepped forward, sniffing and testing the air as if he were nosing a fine claret. A broad-palmed hand reached out to each boy. He took hold of their quailing fingers and squeezed them like a vice.

Both boys looked up at him, squinting, watching intently the movement of his eyes. He turned to his brown-haired son first. 'So what have you learnt, eh? Can you do it now?'

The boy's eyes flicked momentarily towards his brother. 'Trying, Father.'

The three of them trotted down the long flight of steps towards the Land Rover. 'So you're going to show me, are you?' boomed the man's voice.

'Yes, Father.'

They drove through the park with its deer and old oaks, past the folly, past the lake, until they reached a paddock set out as a showjumping course. There were five-bar gates, walls and a water jump. To one side stood a low row of bales and posts propped up on tin drums, the children's course.

By the gate leading to the paddock stood a lean white-haired man with a red-spotted handkerchief tied around his throat. He set to work straight away, checking bridles and saddles on the boys' two New Forest ponies.

'Everything ready, Perkins?' their father asked as he swung out of the Land Rover.

'Yes, Lord Rudlow,' nodded the groom. 'Which of the young masters would you like to see in the ring first?'

'Oh, I don't know.' His Lordship's gaze followed the blond boy climbing the fence. He smiled. 'All right, Anthony. You go.'

Perkins helped the blond boy up into the saddle and adjusted the stirrups. 'There you are, Master Anthony,' he said softly. 'You're not going to let me down now, are you? Or your dad'll have my guts . . . No need to be nervous.' He checked the girth. 'Just show her who's boss and remember what I taught you, right?' He winked, led the pony towards the ring then let her go.

The boy bit his lip. He clicked his tongue and squeezed the mare's sides with his knees. Soon he was cantering around the ring.

The groom turned to Lord Rudlow. 'Boy's got a natural seat — we'll make a fine horseman out of him, I'll be bound. Figure of eight now,' he called to Anthony, and immediately the boy pulled on the inside rein, coaxed the pony on with his outside leg and easily executed the manoeuvre. Perkins and Lord Rudlow looked on with pride as the pony was effortlessly quickened into a gallop, as it was walked backward, turned in tight circles, and finally put at the rows of hay bales and posts which it cleared without a hitch. 'Bravo!' they called.

When Lord Rudlow's other son took the ring, his pony at first refused to move then sauntered forward at a lazy walk. The boy scowled and whipped it, but the pony only

3

took a couple of paces before it stopped in front of a loose bundle of hay. It neighed and lowered its head, forcing the reins down out of the boy's hands.

'Get off with you,' yelled Perkins, running over. He whacked the pony on. 'Now sit back a bit, Master Hugh, and a bit straighter. Don't slouch and don't be so hard on the mouth or you'll never learn.'

The boy, blushing miserably, nodded and struck the pony again on the flank. He managed the figure of eight somehow, but the reluctant pony's lagging hooves set one of the tin drums clattering.

Back with Lord Rudlow, Perkins sighed. 'I've tried, Y'r Lordship, but he's pulled her mouth to ribbons. It just don't seem to come naturally to him, not at all. But he's improving . . . little by little. The will's there.'

Lord Rudlow flicked a fly off his cheek. 'Don't worry. It'll come.'

They watched Hugh over the little set of jumps. He managed the hay bales but both sets of posts fell, bringing the tin drums with them.

'OK,' called Lord Rudlow, 'that'll do. Back for lunch.'

Hugh turned and saw his father standing with one arm resting lightly on Anthony's shoulder. He saw his brother's smug expression, and breathed in deeply. His jaw clenched. 'If it's all right, Father,' he called, 'I'll try the jumps one more time.'

Already he was cantering around the paddock, gaining speed. Perkins quickly stepped forward and propped up the poles. Hugh did another circuit then wheeled the pony swiftly round. Perkins drew in his breath. 'No,' he shouted. 'No!'

The line that Hugh had taken was not that leading to the pony jumps. He was heading for the five-bar gate on the showjumping course. 'No!' the groom shouted again.

But the boy's gaze was fixed on the jump. He flicked his whip and forced back the reins. The pony sprang forward. Its front feet lifted. For a second it looked as if it might just clear the fence, but the effort was not quite enough. The gate clattered down. The pony lurched.

Hugh had dropped the reins and his whip. His body was sliding off to the left but somehow he was still hanging on to the mare's mane.

How Lord Rudlow laughed! His fist drummed the fence. A second later he had jumped it, leaving Anthony standing. He ran forward and lifted Hugh off his pony. 'That's my boy,' he chortled, raising him in the air. 'That's my boy.'

From his vantage point, Hugh sighed with relief and wiped the sweat from his brow. He looked beyond his father, across at Anthony. He cocked his head slightly and smiled.


1973
*Queens, New York*
The little girl lay in bed staring out into the grey darkness of the room. She was intensely aware of every sound from below. She had been listening out for the ring of the doorbell for over an hour now, but all that she had heard so far was the drone of the seven o'clock chat show and her mother's footsteps, moving ceaselessly back and forth between the kitchen and the dining area at the far end of the living room.

It was going to be a very special dinner. After school, Ma had driven Loretta down to the supermarket off Fairview Drive. For once, they did not stand outside the window checking out the special offers that week, or stop to fill the basket with the bumper bundle of frozen misshapen cuts. Ma went straight to the fresh meat counter, chose prime Florida rib, then went on and picked up some soft shell crabs. She always said they weren't given enough protein and fresh fruit in the American Army Airforce, not for fighting men. And abroad — well, foreigners just didn't eat like the folks back home.

It wasn't fair of her to send Loretta to bed, though. Not tonight. Not before he arrived. Some of the other girls at Fairview Elementary did not go to bed 'til eight or eight-thirty and they saw their papas all the time, not just once or twice a year when he came home on leave.

Loretta pulled her teddy bear to her. The soft fur brushed her cheek. She sighed. He was a very superior bear. He had real suede pads, limbs that actually moved, and the sweetest of expressions — a rather sad, lost look. Pa had given her the bear the last time he was over. There was only one other like it in the world, Pa said, and that one belonged to the Queen of England.

The smell of sizzling beef fat came up the stairwell and through the crack beneath the door. She heard the judder and whizz of Ma's new mixer making the mayonnaise for the soft shell crabs. Then suddenly she heard the short sharp ring of the doorbell.

Her heart leapt. She slipped out of the sheets and slid down the side of the bed on to the fluffy mat. Its nylon hairs tickled her toes. She crept across and quietly opened the door . . .

'Victor, how I've been missing you . . . I ask you, who'd be an army wife?'

'It's great to be back home. Just great.'

6

A pause, then Ma again: 'Honey, you OK?'

'Tired, that's all.'

'Hammered more like.' A shrill laugh. 'I don't mind. I just hope you'll be able to enjoy your dinner, that's all. I've got all your favourites.'

'I'm sorry, babe. I'm really sorry. The boys laid it all on. Insisted on sending me off in style. Nothing I could do.' A pause, then: 'How is she?'

'Loretta? Fine, just fine. Tucked up safe. I wasn't sure when you were coming.'

The little girl opened the door wider and slipped out on to the landing. Through the banisters, she could just see her father's shiny black shoes and the turn-ups of his grey twill trousers. 'I'm not quite asleep, Pa,' she called. 'Not quite.'

'Lorie, Lorie, Lorie – let me see you!' Already he was bounding up the staircase, sending vibrations through the floorboards. Then she was up in his arms, the evening bristles on his cheek scratching her soft skin. 'How you've grown!' Adults always said that – and very annoying it was too – but coming from Pa it was fine. She hugged him and basked in the closeness of him. She felt the slight tremble that passed through his body, and closed her eyes and hugged his broad shoulders, sighing.

The moment didn't seem to last long enough. Already he was holding her away from him. 'Let me have a good look at you.' His breath carried a strong smell of something like sourballs. 'As pretty as anything,' he crooned. True, she had chestnut hair as soft and fine as strands of silk, and wide sapphire eyes. Then he hugged her again and put her down gently on the floor.

She did not want to let go so soon. She moved a pace towards him, took hold of his legs and felt the hardness

7

of his calf muscles through the rough twill of his Army Airforce uniform.

Her room looked very small with her father standing there. A frieze of Disney characters ran around the skirting board. A cluster of dolls filled the only spare chair. A collection of postcards were jammed into the frame of the mirror. She still had every postcard which her father had sent her from England – the guardsmen outside Buckingham Palace; Tower Bridge; Trafalgar Square; the Norfolk Broads.

Her father ran his fingers affectionately through her fine silky hair and she quivered at his touch. 'I've got something for you,' he said teasingly.

'Not now, Victor,' interjected Ma. She patted her bouffant hair. 'It's late and she's got to go to school tomorrow.'

'Oh, please, please, please,' Loretta pleaded. Her hand went up to his and squeezed it as tight as she could. She looked up and felt the warmth in his smile, in his eyes.

He glanced across to Ma for a moment, then knelt down. 'OK,' he whispered, 'provided you promise that afterwards you'll go straight back to bed and go to sleep.'

She bit her lip and nodded.

It seemed a long time then before he came back. Ma helped her on with her dressing gown, squeezed her feet into pink furry slippers and brushed her hair, but all the time she was listening. She heard Pa's heavy, rapid steps on the staircase, the lock on his suitcase clicking open, and then there was an interminable pause until his footsteps sounded once again and he re-entered the room clutching a package wrapped in gold paper with a squashed, roughly tied bow.

'Here you are, Lorie.' He handed it across to her, eyes glinting.

'Thank you, Pa.' It was about the size of a shoe box. She felt along the side, rattled it, then almost reluctantly untied the bow and ripped off the paper.

Inside was the most exquisite doll she had ever seen. It had fine sculpted hands, and a porcelain head with sparkling glass eyes and fine red-brown hair, not unlike her own. The doll wore a cream dress covered in gold lace and over her shoulders was a burgundy velvet cloak trimmed with speckled fur.

'Oh, Victor,' Ma crooned. 'That must've cost you.'

He shrugged and said without looking at his wife: 'Yeah, but she deserves something special. You like it, Lorie?'

'Like it?' She clutched the doll to her. 'I love it! It's fantastic. No one at school . . . thank you, thank you!' Still holding the doll, she gave him a big kiss.

Her fingers swept over the doll's velvet and ermine cloak. 'Who's it of, Pa?' she asked. 'The doll, I mean.'

'It's a Lady of the Court.'

As he bent down inches from her, she smelled the sourballs on his breath again. 'And what's a Lady of the Court? I thought everyone was a lady?'

'Yeah, true, but these are different. They're married to Lords and they live in huge old houses. Real big.'

She looked up. 'How big?'

'Well, let me see — as big as Grand Central Station.'

'Oh,' she sighed, 'they must get very lost, then. And . . . and what do they do all day?'

'They — er — dress up and look beautiful and go to balls. Yeah, and every Thursday they go and take tea with the Queen at Buckingham Palace and eat cucumber sandwiches. Tiny cucumber sandwiches, no bigger than postage stamps.'

The little girl's eyes opened wide. 'Are they allowed seconds?'

'Oh, yes,' Victor smiled, warming to his theme, 'but most of them only take one, because they are so slim and elegant and have waists so small you can put your hands around them.'

Loretta sat down on the floor, put her arms around her knees and hugged them to her chest. 'What else do Ladies do?'

'Hmm.' He sucked in air through his teeth and turned to Ma. 'Marsha, can you help me out here?'

'I can tell you one thing they *don't* do — they don't push trolleys around Safeway, that's for sure!'

'Yeah,' Pa nodded, 'they have cooks to do the cooking, maids to dress them, butlers to wait on them, chauffeurs to drive them. Some even have a man who does nothing all day but clean their jewels.'

The little girl sighed wistfully. She sat silently for a while, then said very quietly: 'When I grow up, I think I'd like to be a Lady.'

Pa chuckled. Ma leaned forward. 'Loretta, I thought you were gonna be a nurse.'

'Well, yes,' she bit her lip, 'I think I'll be a nurse on Mondays and Tuesdays, but the rest of the week I'll be a Lady. How about that?'

'I think that's swell, Lorie,' replied Pa, still laughing. 'Real swell.'

'But right now,' Ma added lightly, 'it's time for Her Ladyship to go back to bed.'

'Do I have to — really?'

'You promised.'

10

Reluctantly, Loretta gave her pa one last hug, then he lifted her up in his arms again and carried her over to the bed, still clutching her doll.

She slept between the doll and the bear that night, excited but peaceful. She wondered what treat her pa had in store for tomorrow. Again and again she wished that he could tell her stories every night and would never have to leave them.

1973
*Eton College*
'Best of luck,' whispered the tall, gangly boy with a prominent spot on his chin.

Anthony patted his shoulder, and smiled. 'Thanks.' He stood up and walked slowly towards the lectern. His hard starched upright collar dug into his neck and the collar stud was tight against his windpipe. The creak of the floorboards at each step was very loud. There seemed to be creatures crawling and gnawing inside his stomach, his mouth was dry, his palms wet – he only hoped his panic did not show.

He pressed his hands against the sloping sides of the lectern to stop his fingers trembling and gazed out across the crowded hall of Upper School. Most of the audience was a blur: a mass of flowery hats, balding pates. Then there were figures in black; other Eton boys with their stiff collars, narrow white bow ties and black tail coats, and gowned masters – the beaks.

In the centre of the third row, he spotted first his father and then his mother, sitting next to his tutor. She was looking up at him expectantly beneath the broad brim of her bright yellow hat, silently egging him on, feeding

11

him with her strength. His father, head bowed, was studying the programme.

Anthony tried to clear the lump in his throat. He swallowed. He breathed in. '*Ad Augustissimum Principem Georgium Tertium* . . .' The vibration of the words echoed inside his skull. The first line. What the hell was the first line? Then in a rush the words came back. He was away.

Lord Rudlow sighed and scratched his temple. As the long Latin recital continued, he nodded at the few familiar phrases and words. They spurred his memory back to his own school days, and a trancelike glaze covered his eyes.

He looked up at the marble busts of the eminent Old Etonians which stood on plinths between the deep-set window ledges: Wellington; Chatham; Gladstone; Shelley; Fox. He saw the layer of dust on Fox's prominent nose and chuckled at this unintended slight. Then his gaze switched to the leaded lattice windows and the bright warm June day on the other side of the double-glazed panes. He sighed wistfully.

'Bravo! Didn't Anthony do that well?' Lady Rudlow turned to him with sparkling eyes. Her fine-boned, handsome face was flushed with pride.

'Yes, splendid.' Lord Rudlow rubbed his hands over his trouser legs and said with a half smile, 'And tell me . . . which bit did you enjoy most?'

'Don't mock, George!' There was a sharp note of reproach in her voice. 'Of course I didn't understand a word of it — that's hardly the point, is it? It's the honour.'

Anthony's tutor leaned across. He had a full head of black hair slicked back on his skull, and sharp brown eyes. A hood lined with fur hung from the back of his gown. 'You must be very proud of your son, Lord Rudlow. Very proud. It's not every day we have a boy in the sixth form who is also in the first eleven: "*Mens sana in corpore sano*".'

Lord Rudlow nodded sagely. He remembered that one: 'Sound mind in a sound body'. 'I know, I know. Bright boy. Never in sixth form myself. Or, for that matter, in the first eleven. This is all very well . . . but do you really think it makes much sense for him to go on and read Latin and Greek at Oxford? In this day and age, what?'

'Greats?' The tutor bristled. His fingers fastened defensively on one edge of his gown. 'The best training for the mind. Incomparable!'

'Don't doubt it. But someday the boy will have to join me in the rough and tumble of the aircraft business. Can't say that a familiarity with Latin and Ancient Greek is something I really look for in prospective employees. I wonder whether something of a more practical bent wouldn't serve him better?'

'Your son is a scholar, Lord Rudlow. A scholar of some distinction. After finding his way through the intricacies of Plato and Aristotle, he should not have the slightest difficulty with − dare I say it? − the more mundane preoccupations of the commercial world.'

The veins in Lord Rudlow's cheeks turned purple, but, to his annoyance, the beak had timed this last sally perfectly. The next boy was already standing at the lectern, announcing the title of his monologue: *Ode on a Distant Prospect of Eton College*, by Thomas Gray.

'Ye distant spires, ye antique towers,
That crown the wat'ry glade . . .'

Lord Rudlow exhaled forcibly, crossed his legs, and returned to his study of the two fat pigeons on the window ledge.

Privileges, he mused, sometimes had to be endured.

When finally they were released into the sunshine, Lord and Lady Rudlow made straight for the Parade Ground where Hugh was leading a squad of the school corps. The grey tarmac reverberated to the sound of tramping feet, to the pipes, to the sudden hoarse orders of still immature voices.

The pipe band were positioned at the rear of the Ground just in front of the brick mass of the Drawing Schools. In the sunlight, the pipes sparkled like freshly polished silver. The red, green and purple checked kilts fluttered in the wind. Toes tapped beneath white, pasted spats.

Lady Rudlow smiled. She brought out a canvas stool and sat down next to a large woman in a loose printed silk dress. She fanned herself slowly with the school magazine, then turned around casually to have a word with her husband – to find him gone.

She saw that he had pushed his way to the very edge of the Parade Ground to stand in the front row of the spectators. He was stood to attention, head craning forward, eyes fixed on his son's every movement.

Hugh's squad wheeled and turned and were marching towards them now. Young innocent faces flushed with colour peeped out between the dark green of the berets and the sludge green of the uniforms. The *de rigueur* stiff movements were like those of only partially articulated mechanical toys.

Hugh was on the extreme left. A white leather strap ran diagonally over his stocky chest and an officer's sword clattered against his leg at each step he took. His jaw was set. His eyes flicked across constantly to check his men. He looked to be totally in control.

Suddenly he shouted, 'Squaaaad halt,' and the boys stopped instantly. They made a movement as if pulling their feet out of mud, then pounded the tarmac with their boots.

Lady Rudlow glanced across at her husband. She caught a broad grin crossing his face in response to Hugh's shouted command. Then he was off, moving back and forth in the crowd, strolling up to the other fathers, joking with them, pointing out his son, suddenly standing to attention, mimicking Hugh's erect stance.

'Boys!' Her Ladyship shook her head ruefully, and smiled. 'They never, ever grow up.'


## 1979
*Queens, New York*

They were fighting again. It happened almost every day now that her parents were together again. The brief period of elation when Pa had first returned home for good a year ago had lasted no longer than the blooming of the white roses in the garden.

Loretta sat in the armchair by the table in the living room, trying to block out the sounds coming from the kitchen. She took hold of the hem of the dress arranged across her lap and carefully drew the needle through the fine blue net. Today was meant to be her day. She had been asked to her first teenage dance, but no one seemed to care.

Through the door came Ma's high-pitched whine: 'Don't speak to me like that!'

Then Pa's deep voice: 'I'll speak to you any goddamn way that I like, you bitch!'

Loretta heard the crack of a chair as it fell on to the linoleum floor, the creak of the kitchen table as it was brushed aside. Then she heard the smack of Pa's hand against Ma's cheek.

A shiver went down her spine. She felt a stabbing pain in her stomach. She closed her eyes for a moment and breathed in deeply. She felt the pressure mounting around the bridge of her nose; despite herself, she was ready to cry. Loretta tried to concentrate on the dress, on her sewing, but she could not steady the trembling in her fingers.

Another dull crack from the kitchen.

'How dare you!' screamed Ma. 'How dare you!'

The needle slipped from Loretta's fingers.

She swallowed. Her body shook. She felt so impotent, so futile, so betrayed. She rose slowly and walked across the living room.

Through the open door she could see them: Pa, eyes bloodshot and raw, slouching over the pine kitchen table; Ma, pressing a wet kitchen cloth to her face, pointing at him, screaming.

Pa swivelled around slowly, leaning against the table for support. Fragments of a broken glass and a pool of golden liquid lay on the floor beneath him. A whisky bottle stood on the table by his right arm. As he swivelled around, his hand moved to protect it.

Loretta felt she must try and do something. She took a step forward. She was standing in the doorway now. Pa must have seen her but his eyes remained distant and unfocussed.

'Stop it!' cried Loretta. 'Please!'

Pa turned away. 'Get out, Lorie,' he growled without looking at her. 'Go to your room.'

It was not as easy as that. He could not just order her out and pretend that none of this was happening. She took another step forward. 'It's my home . . . my home too, you know.'

Ma's eyes narrowed. They flashed accusingly at Pa. 'Now look what you've done.' Then, her mouth still trembling, she turned to Loretta. 'Maybe Pa's right,' she sighed. 'Go to your room, Lorie. Your Pa and I were . . . were . . . ' She waved her arm despondently. 'We were having a private talk.'

'Please, please, please!' Loretta blinked away the tears, but still they came. 'Can't you . . . why do you have to . . . ?'

'Shit,' groaned Pa. His eyes closed for a moment, then flicked open again. 'I'm sorry. Shit! OK, I'm sorry.' He glowered across at Ma. 'I just wish you'd see it my way once in a while. It ain't easy, you know.' He picked up the whisky bottle and stuck it into his pocket. He barged past Loretta without looking at her.

'Where y'going, Victor?' Ma called.

'Where do you think? Out of this rat hole.'

'When are you coming back?'

'When I'm ready.'

Loretta saw only anxiety in her ma's face when the door slammed. She felt it in her body too as she hugged her. 'There, there, now,' Ma soothed. 'Nothing to be worried about. Things aren't always as bad as they seem.' She ran a trembling hand through Loretta's hair. 'Adults sometimes lose their temper but that doesn't mean —'

'You mean you still love Pa?'

'Of course I do, and you must love him too.'

17

Loretta nodded, moving her head ever so slightly against the soft contours of Ma's breasts. 'I do. That's why —'

'I know.' Her mother swallowed. 'I know. Everything's going to be fine. All we got to do is wipe away those tears and get you ready for the dance. The Slingers will be here in less than an hour and you want to look your best for Bob, don't you?'

'I don't want to go any more.'

'Don't be silly, of course you do. You want to wear your new dress?'

'Yeah, but . . .'

'But, nothing! I tell you . . . everything's gonna work out fine.'

# Chapter 2

'She's ready for you, Mr Hugh,' called the plump blonde groom.

Hugh curled and uncurled his fingers about the leather hunting whip. He opened the door and strode down the tack room steps to where the mare stood waiting.

She knew it was a hunting day. Already she danced with excitement, eager for the chase. Hugh patted her neck. 'Easy there, Zola,' he soothed. He took the reins from the girl groom, put his left boot into the stirrup and swung himself up into the saddle. 'Thank you. My father left yet?'

'A couple of minutes ago. On Zilpah.'

Hugh nodded. He tightened the left-hand rein and guided Zola through the stone archway leading off the stable block.

The rain had stopped only an hour before. The mare breathed steam like cigar smoke in the cold air, as her hooves crunched lazily over the well-rinsed gravel.

The sounds of the meet grew louder: the yapping of hounds, shouted commands, manoeuvring of horses, convivial chatter.

Horse boxes were parked in rows in the paddock before him. Women in bottle green huskies, green wellington boots and silk head scarves leaned against cars. They

19

chatted idly, drank from thermos flasks and polished the lenses of their binoculars. Beyond, as far as the eye could see, stretched manicured parkland improved and reconstructed by Capability Brown; whole hills had been moved, lakes dug, woodlands planted, follies built.

Hugh passed through a second archway and was now at the front of the house. A broad sweep of Portland stone led up to a Palladian portico of twenty towering columns surmounted by Corinthian capitals.

Without warning, the reins slackened in his hands. The front of the saddle pressed against him. He heard the screech of brakes, the ricochet of flailing gravel. His legs gripped tighter. 'Whoah there,' he soothed.

A battered green van pulled up just inches from his mount. A bearded man in a black jacket leaned out of the window and spat out the match he held between his teeth. 'Fascist pig,' he sneered. From somewhere inside the van a woman shrieked, 'Murderer!'

For a moment Hugh stared at them, then casually he increased the pressure on the reins, and without a word moved off at a slow walk towards the other riders. He was not going to give them the satisfaction of provoking an incident, especially with the Joint Master.

Hounds yapped all around him now, a continuous moving mass of cream and tan furry bodies, floppy ears, keen eyes and long wagging tails. The field was about a hundred and fifty strong. He nodded and greeted everyone he knew with a cordial smile and a murmured pleasantry. It was the usual crowd; bowler-hatted farmers from the neighbouring land, a few tenants, a few local friends, and the London crowd — some trying hard to look more country than the true country folk; others just a shade too well turned out, their coats too new, their appearance too studied.

He drew up beside his father who was dressed in an identical Hunting Pink coat. Despite the years that separated them, there was a distinct family resemblance. Both men shared the same strong jaw and deep-set hazel eyes.

At the sight of Hugh, Lord Rudlow's lip curled. 'You were late down for breakfast this morning, boy. Cutting it a bit fine, what?'

Hugh shrugged and smiled. 'Sorry, Father. Late night. Belated thirty-fifth birthday drinks.'

'Hmm,' mumbled His Lordship, then changed the subject. 'See the antis are out in force today. Heard they were out this morning with their damned aniseed, laying trails, unblocking the earths. Damn nuisance, but it'll take more than that to spoil our day, what?'

'Quite. Bet they go home after a day protecting the fox, and stick knife and fork into a battery chicken.'

Lord Rudlow smiled. 'Move off in ten minutes, OK?'

Hugh nodded. As he turned away from his father, he noticed a slim, dark, elegant girl on a sleek black hunter. He eyed her surreptitiously as he rode forward, scooping a glass of port off a drinks tray as he went. He drew Zola to a halt a few paces on, next to a redheaded man of about his own age. The man's skin was very sallow, his eyes bloodshot. 'Henry,' Hugh greeted him, 'thanks for last night. Good party. Amusing crowd.'

'You seemed to be getting on very well with the Cummings girl. Very well indeed, if I might say so.' He rested his hand on his saddle and leaned forward. 'I hear that she's quite talented.'

Hugh grinned. 'You'll have to do better than that, old

boy, if you want any details. You know me. No stories out of school – the discretion of a monk.'

'About the only thing *you* have in common with a monk. Come on!'

But Hugh's attention was directed elsewhere. He was looking beyond his friend towards the girl who had caught his eye. 'To change the subject slightly, have you any idea who that girl is over there? The dark one on the black colt?'

Henry twisted around in his saddle and followed Hugh's gaze. 'Over there? That's Mrs Prendergast.'

'No, not her, you idiot. The one next to Simpson.'

Henry smiled as if he had just scored a point. 'Oh, her – no. She's new. I think she's Simpson's guest.'

'Think he's going out with her?'

Henry sighed and looked at the glass of port in his hand. He winced then drained it in one. 'Hugh, you're incorrigible! It's some god-awful time in the morning, you hardly got a wink last night, and already you're lining up some poor innocent –'

'So what do you think?' Hugh cut in impatiently. 'Is he or is he not going out with her?'

'Think he wishes he was.' Henry twisted around again and studied the scene. 'He's given her a cigarette and now he's searching for a light. The boy's fumbling, looking worried . . . distinctly worried. She's giving him a fake smile.' He laughed. 'Oh, he's spilt his port! Simpson's spilt his port all over his nice clean coat. Black beauty doesn't think it's funny. She doesn't think it's funny at all. She's turning away, pretending she's not with him.' Henry smirked. 'No, a hundred to one Simpson hasn't got lucky. Ninety-nine to one he won't get lucky. Sorry, old boy.'

Hugh grinned. 'So the field's wide open? If you'll excuse me Henry, I'm going to put my name down. Just do me a favour, will you? If I give you the signal, look after Simpson.'

'Hey, what about me?'

'As you so rightly pointed out, after last night we're in no fit state for a war of attrition.' He nudged Zola forward. 'Next time I'll babysit for you. Promise.'

He weaved through the field until he was a yard from Simpson, a gaunt, long-necked man in John Lennon glasses. Hugh steadied the mare. In order not to appear too keen, he turned to the girl and casually touched his cap, then almost at once returned to Simpson. He forced a smile. 'Hello, William,' he said smoothly, 'pleased to see you out with us.'

Simpson seemed to have guessed the game. Rather than introducing the girl, he employed the diversionary tactic of immediately embarking on a long and involved story about a hunt saboteur and a policeman.

Hugh gave him his head for thirty seconds, whiling away the time by studying the port stain creeping down Simpson's coat. Then he interrupted: 'Manners, William! You haven't introduced me to your guest.'

'Oh, sorry.' William Simpson flourished a hand in the general direction of the girl and mumbled a name incoherently. Deliberately so, thought Hugh.

'I didn't quite catch that . . .?' He turned to the girl.

She lowered her eyes, but there was nothing shy or demure about her straight-backed posture, her relaxed holding of the reins or the easy command with which she controlled her horse. Her skin was olive and unflawed apart from a beauty spot on her right cheek; her features fine but strong. Her black hair was netted above the long smooth nape of her neck.

'Marie-Louise Vosse,' she purred, then looked straight at Hugh, shooting him a glance with her wide dark eyes. There was ice behind those eyes, Hugh thought, but probably only the ice of pride, a thin self-protective coating just waiting to be melted into tears.

'First time out with us?' he asked.

'Yes,' she tilted her head and smiled, 'but I hope not the last.'

Before he could reply, a horn sounded three quick successive blasts.

The dogs barked and scampered between the horses' legs, out and off through the first gate. Hugh wheeled Zola round. 'After you, Miss Vosse.'

'No.' She smiled disarmingly. 'I should follow you, Master.'

He touched his cap again then urged his horse forward, trotting after the hounds.

Once through the first gate, he looked around. Marie-Louise was close behind. She sat well, her balance near perfect. The horse must have been a hireling but from her poised, unflurried air she could have ridden it for years. The smile was still on her lips.

A shout of 'Bastards! Capitalist murderers!' carried towards them on the wind.

Two hours had passed without a find. The hounds were well out in front now, covering the high ground to the right. Their tails were bobbing as they worked, but for some minutes they had been almost silent.

Simpson had shown a dogged persistence in his pursuit of Marie-Louise and now, true to form, was heading in her direction, seemingly oblivious of her strong preference for Hugh's company. Henry was trying to engage Simpson in conversation, but he kept moving away, his eyes slavishly fixed on Marie-Louise.

Suddenly, one of the hounds gave tongue. A moment later they all raised their heads and bayed in answer. There was rustling in the undergrowth and they were gone, up and away. Hugh smiled at Marie-Louise and urged his horse forward at a canter. 'They're on to something.'

His pulse quickened. The balls of his feet pressed down hard on the stirrups. He shortened the reins, leaned forward and kicked his horse on.

Zola jumped to his touch, moving effortlessly into a gallop. Her front feet kicked up the turf as she went. The wind smacked against his face and ruffled his hair.

The first hedgerow loomed before him. Seven, six feet to go. 'Now, my girl.' He leaned further forward, giving Zola her head. Her powerful hind quarters pressed down and kicked. Up and over they went, gliding through the air. Then down, carefully now, on to the soft earth.

He felt the mare's hooves slide as he landed. A foot, maybe more. Zola momentarily lost balance. Hugh steadied her and they were away again.

His father was just in front of him, coaxing his mount on with low murmurs. The rest of the field were far behind.

When Hugh reached the high ground, he saw the pack two fields below. He crossed three fields, three more fences, and still the hounds before him were in full cry. On and on they went — over the brow of a hill, across another meadow and into a copse.

The low branches snagged at his coat and ripped at his skin. He neither noticed nor cared. Nor did he turn to see whether Marie-Louise was following. His blood was up. All that mattered now was the chase.

He fought his way through until he reached a small dell surrounded by limes. The pack was collected there, sniffing and searching.

A black horse came up by his side: Marie-Louise. Her olive skin glowed from the fresh air. Her eyes were bright with the thrill of the chase. 'I've been watching you,' she said, 'you've done this before.' She paused and ran the reins through long elegant fingers, smiling impishly.

This was one of the things that Hugh loved about horses – they did so much of the seduction for you. He chatted to her idly about the hunt, about Conningsby, but he knew that what he said was not really important. It was the body language which counted. And he could tell from the way her hands played with the reins, the way she smiled and tossed back her head when she laughed, that his message was getting through. Already that icy look in her eyes was softening.

Slowly the rest of the field was catching up with them. Even Simpson was just visible in the distance. Still the hounds sniffed and searched without a find.

'The scent's gone cold,' called a man in a green coat.

Suddenly the air was filled with a cackling sound that grew louder and louder, to be followed by a strange nasal hum. 'Death to all huntsmen,' yelled a rasping voice. 'Death to the murderers,' cried another. A horse neighed and shied at the shout.

And there they were – twenty silhouettes on the skyline not fifty yards away. Each wore a black cloak and a mask depicting a grotesque painted skull. Wind swelled their cloaks and sunlight shone behind them, framing their bodies with a ghostly aura.

Apart from the neighing of the horses, there was silence. Everyone stared. Hugh blinked, uncertain at first that his mind was not playing tricks on him after a sleepless night, then his bewilderment changed to anger.

The saboteurs vanished as suddenly as they had appeared. When Hugh looked again, only a lone bare oak broke the skyline.

'That's right, get off my land!' shouted Lord Rudlow. 'Sod off and do your amateur dramatics somewhere else.'

At that, a couple of huntsmen laughed, someone said, 'How about some Gilbert and Sullivan?' and the spell was broken. Horses turned. The pack was mustered.

Hugh turned to Marie-Louise. 'I'm sorry.'

She shrugged. 'There's no need to be. It's all part of the times we live in.'

The bearded man threw back his head and laughed. He peeled off the skeleton mask and replaced his spectacles. 'Well, that showed them, didn't it? Did you see their faces? Did you? Shaken to the skin, the bastards!'

'What I can't stand is their bloody arrogance,' said a lean man with a Mohican haircut, brandishing a can of beer. 'The sooner they learn that we are a force to be reckoned with . . .'

There was a party atmosphere in the camp as they laughed and bundled up their capes. A very thin blonde girl poured coffee out of a dented thermos.

Only the bearded man appeared too preoccupied to join in the general mood of hilarity. He crawled up to the brow of the hill and surveyed the scene through his binoculars. 'The hounds have lost the scent,' he chuckled. 'They're moving off at a walk.'

'Should I take the costumes back to the hire shop, Jack?' asked a gangly boy in his teens. 'They've got to be back by six.'

'Later,' replied the bearded man without lowering his binoculars. 'The hounds are grouping. They're heading off towards Beeches Bottom.' He stood up suddenly, signalling with his arm. 'Quick! Back in the vans. We'll cut them off at The Point. Move it, can't you? For Christ's sake, this isn't some damn Sunday school outing . . . *move it*!'

Already he was running towards the three vans parked in a muddy siding on the neighbouring field. By the time the others had arrived, the engine was revving. Fifteen of them squeezed in the back. 'Ready,' said Jack, and slammed the van into gear.

While he had been with the rest of the field, Lord Rudlow had laughed off the incident with good-humoured indignation. Now that he was riding side by side with his son, his mood had changed.

Hugh's attempts at lighthearted conversation had all met with a low grunt or stony silence. His father's face was sullen. Eventually, Lord Rudlow turned to him and said, more in sorrow than in anger, 'See, my boy? It's what I was saying. Conningsby and the surrounding countryside will be secure for only so long as we own it. The old country families are being supplanted everywhere by people who don't understand our traditions. Hedgerows pulled up. Housing developments sprouting like mushrooms. Progress, they call it. Hah!'

He sighed. 'The worst of it is, that pack of saboteur

idiots is the least of our worries, it's the politicians, the urban planners, the developers and the bloody Department of Transport that are the real problem. Remember that, boy. It's up to us to preserve the country traditions and the way of life here. Like it or not, we are the custodians of the English heritage. Once it has gone, it'll never come back, what?'

'Absolutely,' Hugh nodded agreement. There was no point in arguing but, in Hugh's view, his father's obsession with maintaining the Conningsby estate in the old style had become entirely divorced from financial realities. The estate workers were looked after from the cradle to the grave. All two hundred cottages were let on peppercorn rents. His father had consistently refused to rent any of them lucratively to London week-enders or to sell any land for housing. The bulk of the profit from the Rudlow Aircraft Company was now spent on subsidising the estate. His father's grand vision of a rural idyll was a very expensive luxury indeed.

A horn sounded. 'Ha, ha! Some sport at last,' Lord Rudlow barked with glee. He kicked Zilpah on and was away.

'Come on.' Hugh urged Zola forward. The hounds were tightly knit and racing across the field before them. They were on to something. He was not going to let his father beat him to the next fence.

He struck the mare's flank with his whip. She was galloping by the third stride. He felt a new urgency in her. 'You can do it, Zola, my beauty. You *will* do it!'

Jack slammed his foot down on the brakes. The Mohican was thrown against the partition in the back. Beer cans rolled. 'OK, five of you out here,' ordered Jack. 'Go for the hounds. Got your sprays? The rest stay with me.'

His fingers tapped impatiently against the dashboards while they disembarked. Immediately the back door crashed to, he drove on. The windscreen was splattered with mud. With the sun in his eyes, the verge and the mud track met in an indistinct yellow blur.

The van bumped and jolted and swayed. There was a hissing sound. 'Oh, Christ!' he shouted. 'A bloody flat.' He struck the steering wheel hard with one fist, then winced at the pain as he pulled the van to a halt.

'Shall I get out the jack?' asked the gangly youth. 'We've got a spare, haven't we?'

'Of course we've got a spare, berk! You stay behind and fix it, OK? We've got men's work to do.'

'I resent that,' snapped the thin blonde in the back. '*Men's* work! By what right . . . by what Godgiven right do you assume that the job which you are about to do is the exclusive preserve of the male species? It's a flagrantly sexist remark. I mean, what makes you think that you need a dick to do it, huh?' She folded her arms. 'I for one am not budging until you retract.'

Jack sighed. 'No sexist connotations intended, OK?'

The girl stamped her foot. 'No, I demand a full unqualified apology.'

'For Chrissakes, don't you understand there's a war on?' The muscles around his neck tightened. He swung out of the driver's seat. 'I apologise. I'm sorry, really sorry. Just a temporary slip due to my sexist, racist, imperialist, fascist education, OK?' he shouted over his shoulder. 'Now, move it!'

Jack jumped over a barbed wire fence and pushed through a gap in the hedgerow. As he gazed across the valley, his skin broke out in a cold sweat. 'They're coming this way,' he yelled. 'They're in full flight. Murdering, murdering bastards! Everyone to their stations.'

He felt for the canister of 'Antimate' in his pocket, then, without waiting for the others, headed down across the field, hugging the hedgerow for cover.

It was tough going. The bastards had ploughed up the earth and his feet kept sticking in the mud. There was a deep ditch to cross, too. He jumped that, but as he landed on the other side, the bank gave way under him. Slowly, he started to slide back.

He grabbed for a twig. It was blackthorn and cut deep. He winced at the pain but did not let go. Every second the sounds of the hunt were getting louder. He could hear the yap of the hounds, the callous cries of the death dealers. His glasses were all steamed up and he was still halfway up a muddy bank, slowly slipping into the ditch.

He must make it! He kicked his feet into the bank and somehow gained a purchase. He wrapped his handkerchief around the thorn and pulled himself up. He stopped then, panting for breath, took off his glasses and wiped them.

When he put them on again, he saw the hounds speeding past on their deadly mission, oblivious of him. He stared at his bleeding, aching hand, bit his lip, and sighed.

He might be too late for the hounds, but the main field was still some way off. Beyond the plough, he saw the first of them coming this way: two specks of red – like globules of blood – bobbing up and down, bringing suffering and death in their wake. He could hear their war cries, their yells of delight in the scent of slaughter. His blood boiled.

He looked quickly about him then, head down, ran

31

along the hedgerow. His glasses were steaming up again now, his hand was throbbing, but he did not care. Nothing worthwhile is ever achieved without sacrifice.

The hedgerow ended in a drystone wall that was crumbling in places. Yes, that was where the bastards would jump, if they had the guts. He gasped for breath, straightened slightly and peered over the wall. They were coming . . .

'A decent point at last!' cried Lord Rudlow, his eyes alight with the thrill of the chase.

Hugh gave him a nod in reply. They had taken the last three fences at a flying gallop. He was not going to waste energy on talk. Though a good horseman, it was as much as he could do to keep up with his father when the thrill of the chase was on him.

A hedgerow. He shortened the reins and leaned forward. Zola was ready. She took it effortlessly as she had the others.

'Ha!' cried Lord Rudlow as Hugh landed neck and neck with him. He glanced contemptuously at the rest of the field behind them and raced on.

The wind seemed stronger now. It pounded on Hugh's face, freezing the sweat as it formed. The sun was in his eyes. He blinked and half lowered his eyelids. The green-grey haze of the earth beneath and the yellow-blue haze of the sky had merged into one.

The thud of the hooves was a drum beat. Ever louder and louder.

A stone wall.

Panting, he shortened the reins. He was still neck and neck with his father.

Suddenly, Zola's ears went back. A high-pitched whinny filled the air.

She shied. Her body twisted and rose.

His mouth went dry. Hugh gripped the reins and held hard. He felt them bite into his skin, felt Zola's weight strain against him.

They were airborne now. It must only have been for a second, but everything seemed to happen very slowly.

He saw a man standing upright behind the wall. He saw the skull mask with its bulging red eyes.

He saw the flaring nostrils of his father's mount. He saw her stop short, forefeet planted square, body frozen.

He saw her slide towards the wall, gouging out furrows in the soft mud. He saw the sudden panic on his father's face.

Immediately Hugh had landed, he pulled Zola up short and wheeled her round. Stupid bugger! he thought. He looked for the man in the skull mask. He had gone.

Then he looked down and saw his father. Lord Rudlow lay on the grass, flat on his back. His velvet cap had come off in the fall. All around him were loose stones from the crumbling drystone wall.

Another rider was approaching fast. Hugh cried out. The hooves missed his father by inches.

It was Henry. 'For God's sake, stop the others,' called Hugh, dismounting. 'Father's taken a purler. Needs a few minutes to recover.'

He scrambled back over the wall to where Lord Rudlow lay. 'Are you all right, Father?'

There was no reply. No sign of recognition in the staring, vacant eyes. Blood trickled from his mouth. Blood bubbled from his ears.

Hugh felt a cold sensation of terror creep over his body.

'Call an ambulance, someone!' he shouted. 'And notify my mother. A green Range Rover. She's following with the weekend guests.'

He took off his coat and laid it over his father's chest. 'No, nothing to worry about,' he repeated automatically again and again as the riders passed. He smiled at Marie-Louise but waved her on.

Eventually he saw his mother making her way over the field. The quilted paisley jacket dwarfed her slender form. Her grey-tinged hair was pinned back beneath a trilby. She walked boldly up to them with a no-nonsense air.

'Not a bad day until this,' she remarked. 'Zilpah all right?'

Hugh nodded. 'I think so.'

She knelt down beside Lord Rudlow and clutched his limp hand in hers. 'Damn careless of you, George,' she whispered. 'But don't worry, you old soak, we'll sort this out.'

She stared down at him and stroked his hand with nervous little movements. 'You'll be back in the saddle, right as rain, in no time. Do you hear me? Do you hear me . . .?'

# Chapter 3

The muscles around her eyes tensed as she craned into the mirror and flicked her lashes with mascara. She blinked twice, then leaned back on the dressing table stool and admired her handiwork. Her wide sapphire eyes were enhanced by the faintest black line and mushroom beige eye shadow. The hint of powder on her lightly tanned skin hid the hairline scar on her left cheek. Her long dark chestnut hair shone with a natural brilliance. Yes, she would do.

She rose and sidestepped between the bed and the wall. Only a small single bed, it almost filled the olive green-painted room. She reached the built-in wardrobe and struggled with the sliding louvred doors. They snagged twice before opening.

Dresses, trousers, skirts and jeans were all jumbled together. Some were wrapped in polythene. Others strained on wire hangers from the bent pole above. She combed through the rack and peeled them apart as best as she could. She inspected them all, arranging half a dozen possibles on the bed. These she held up before her in turn and studied in the mirror. After much hard thought, she decided on a pair of black silk slacks and a matching top. They both bore a little square of pin pricks where the cheap labels had once been.

She dressed quickly, glanced in the mirror again then checked the contents of her bag: a run-down lipstick, compact, hairbrush, purse, diary, blemish stick, eye drops, keys and lip gloss.

She walked through to the kitchenette across the passageway. Dirty plates, old pizza cartons and lipstick-stained cups covered the draining board. The flip-top bin did not shut. The waste-disposal gurgled.

A key turned in the latch.

'Julie,' she queried, 'is that you? I spent hours yesterday clearing up, but every time I come back it's just the same. It would really make my day if just once I came home and this place didn't look like it had been raided.'

The short fat girl with a moon face dropped her keys into her voluminous shoulder bag. 'Sure. I'm sorry, but you know housework and me just don't seem to get along. I'm constitutionally unsuited to it.'

'But you could try, couldn't you?' Loretta pleaded.

The fat girl sighed and walked straight past the kitchenette through to the small sitting room. A dusty yellow glow striped the half-drawn blinds. Julie picked up the television control, grabbed a handful of peanuts and puffed up the sofa.

Loretta stood in the doorway, watching her, 'Julie, you know what's happened?' She tried to sound casual.

'What?' The fat girl opened her mouth and threw a peanut in the air. It landed on her chin, bounced off her stomach and rolled down behind the sofa cushion.

Loretta blushed slightly. 'I've been offered the job.'

'No kidding?' Julie stared up at her for a moment. 'That's terrific,' she whooped. 'That's — I'm so excited for you! This calls for a celebration.' She sprang up from the sofa with surprising agility. 'What's in the fridge?'

'But I haven't decided if I'm going to take it. I mean . . . it's quite a step.' Loretta pressed herself against the kitchen units as her room-mate squeezed past her.

Julie caught her breath. She fixed her gaze on Loretta and frowned. 'What do you mean? You can't be serious. It's a gift from heaven.'

'I know, but . . .'

The fridge door opened, bathing them both in blue light. Julie sighed. 'Nothing but *vin très ordinaire*.' She pulled out a half empty bottle of Californian white. 'But what?'

Loretta shrugged and smiled. 'It'll be such a change, that's all. I don't know, I really don't.'

Julie poured a glass of wine for each of them. 'Look, Loretta, you'd be a fool not to take it. I'll miss you like hell, but you've got your career to think of and − hell − there's really not much to keep you here, is there now?' She sipped the wine. 'Yuk!' she spluttered. 'How long has this stuff been fermenting in here?'

The entryphone buzzed.

'Bob?' queried Julie.

Loretta nodded.

'Uh. Huh. He'll be gnawing the tablecloth when he hears. Promise you won't listen to him? Don't, whatever you do, let him sweet talk you out of it, you hear? His motives will be entirely selfish. Entirely dishonourable.'

Loretta walked the two steps to the door. 'Don't be ridiculous, Julie. Bob's not like that. He's my oldest friend. We are just like − well − brother and sister.'

'Ha! That's what you think. I bet you anything he's crazy about you.'

'But not in that way.'

'For men, sweetiepie, there *is* only one way.'

Loretta shook her head. She picked up the entryphone receiver. 'Yes, honey . . . no, I don't care if you've got a cab waiting or not, you come up here like you always do. I'll meet you on the landing, OK?'

She was not going to go down there alone. Not at this time of night. She nodded to Julie. 'He's coming up.'

'Have a good evening — and take the damn' job!'

Loretta smiled and nodded. She picked up her bag, checked it again, then walked out on to the landing.

She hurried past the rows of numbered doors, past the incinerator chute. From the low whine of the motor, the lift was in motion. She shuddered as she stood in front of the two dull metal panels of the lift door.

It had happened over two years ago, but still she heard the echo of the rapid scramble of footsteps rising from the dusty stone stairwell as clearly as she had on that cloudy October evening. Two years of analysis and group therapy had not served to ease the pain or dull the fear . . .

The elevator slowed down just before the fifth floor. The gates opened. For some reason the landing was in darkness. The only light came from the mirrored panel behind her.

Two black youths stood outside. The one on the left had only the beginnings of a pubescent moustache. His staring, frightened eyes flicked over her in nervous little movements.

The other was much taller. He wore an expensive leather jacket and a stained yellow sweatshirt. He stuck out his foot to stop the lift doors from closing. His small, piercing eyes met hers. He smiled.

Loretta clutched her shoulder bag strap tight to stop

her fingers from trembling. 'Excuse me.' She smiled back diplomatically and made to step out.

A leather-clad arm barred her way. She could smell the leather and the sweat. She could also smell her own fear.

'Don't like riding with us, eh?' said the tall one.

This is the time to be cool, she thought. Mustn't show you're frightened. Set your mind positively that nothing is going to happen, and nothing will.

They moved so fast she was not sure what happened next. Suddenly she felt the weight of their bodies against her. There was a pain in her chest. She spun through the air and crashed into the side of the steel box. Hands pressed down on her shoulder blades. She was losing her balance.

The lift juddered as she landed. Her head smacked against the floor. The single spotlight above her turned a circle.

For a second she wished that the fall had just knocked her out so that she wouldn't have to face what she thought was coming next.

'Want my bag? Take it!' she panted. She tried to scream, but heard no sound.

Every time she had taken any lift she feared something like this might happen. She had dreamed it so often ever since she had left home and moved in to share with Julie. She knew that her looks made her especially vulnerable. But here? In her own apartment block?

They were not interested in her bag. She felt her legs rise and stretch, her back scrape along the nobbled lift floor. She felt them pulling and heaving, trying to drag her out.

In her dreams she had been terrified, frozen, immobile. They had had their way with her — or at least she had woken up screaming and dripping with sweat before the moment came. Now to her surprise all she felt was anger, disgust, and a overwhelming sense of self-preservation which overcame physical fear.

She slammed the palms of her hands hard against the lift wall, clutching desperately for something to hold. She found the sides of the lift door and pressed her palms against them. Still the young men pulled. Welts rose at the pressure. The heels of her hands turned purple. Her legs clicked at the joints as she felt herself being stretched like a wishbone. 'My God!' she moaned.

'Tough bitch,' muttered the tall youth.

His full weight landed on her chest then. He held her down. His bloodshot eyes were inches from her face, the pupils dilated.

She turned and squirmed and tried to wriggle free, but hands the size of dinner plates reached out on either side and grabbed her wrists. She felt the sweat pouring down her face as she realised that she had lost control of her own limbs. Her legs, though free, kicked the air vainly. Her hands seemed to curl into his as if they had no substance.

The younger one stood on the landing just out of range. He looked furtively around him. His long knuckly fingers unbuckled his belt, unzipped his fly.

Julie had done judo classes, Loretta recalled. Why in the hell hadn't she?

She gasped for air. Each breath was so shallow. She was losing control of her lungs too. She tried to steady herself, tell herself this wasn't happening. She closed her eyes. She took four more breaths, deeper this time. Then she tried to scream. It was loud. It was good.

The tall one snarled. He let go of her left wrist and

the palm of his hand came down hard, smothering her mouth, flattening her lips on to her teeth. All that mattered, just then, was to free them. She wriggled her jaw back and forth, chewing, using his palm as a lever, then with her two front teeth, she caught a centimetre of salty flesh. She bit hard. She tasted blood.

He yelped and pulled his hand away. 'Bitch!' he yelled, then called to the younger one: 'Gimme the fucking gag.'

Someone . . . someone must have heard her scream. Why did no one come?

She shouted out again. The hand came down instantly, smothering her, cutting her short.

With her free hand she tried to grab the man's hair but she could not get a hold. Her hand flailed then tightened around his ear. She twisted it, dug in her nails. He did not even flinch.

But the head was still there above her. Above her and in range. Getting her bearings now, she straightened two fingers and held them in a V. She could get his eyes. But at the last minute, she hesitated. She couldn't do it.

'Dumb bitch.' He rode her like a horse. He squashed both her wrists and arms under his knees, and however much she twisted and turned, she could not buck off his weight.

With both hands he prised open her jaw. The younger boy stuffed a handkerchief into her mouth. However fast she breathed, there did not seem to be enough air coming through. Her throat was very dry. She was fighting for air. Only the rapid pounding of her heart reassured her that she was still alive.

She felt the will to resist leaving her. She was so helpless. Each time she tried to move, she felt his crushing weight pinning her to the swaying lift floor.

The other youth stepped off the landing into the lift. He pressed the button and the steel doors wheezed shut. With a low thud, the motor began to turn. The floor dropped a few feet, then the boy jammed a steel wedge between the doors and the lift stopped.

'Easy,' said Loretta's captor. His lips blew onion and hamburger scented breath into her ear. 'My little brother, you see, it's his birthday. He's never done nothing before. I promised him one big treat. Now you just lie back and enjoy.'

She mouthed helplessly. Already she could feel the younger one getting to work on her lower regions. Her knickers and tights had gone. Her skirt was up around her waist. A blast of air rising up from the lift shaft froze her buttocks.

A hand came down then, delving deep with sandpaper fingers. She clenched her teeth, shaking, sweating. Sickly sweet bile filled her mouth. A wave of nausea showered her brain.

God, this isn't happening. I'm imagining it, aren't I? Just got to be strong, that's all. Somehow rise above it. Somehow – oh Christ! – go on living.

She had said the same thing to herself when, some two weeks after the day of her first teenage dance, she and Ma had finally realised that Pa was not coming back.

This time though, whatever happened, she wasn't going to cry. She no longer had any tears left for herself. They had all been spent many years ago.

The gag was real, though, and so was the pain.

The tall boy prodded his brother in the back. 'Hey, what the hell you doing? Skip the fucking foreplay.'

Why had no one come . . . somebody . . . anybody? And why wasn't she struggling any more?

Loretta felt the muscles strain as her legs were prised apart. She felt crouching naked legs rub against hers, nails biting into her skin.

She had never had a real boy friend, a serious relationship. The offers had been there in legions, of course, but something had always held her back. Commit yourself to someone and you open an express line to your heart, a line where betrayal rides buckshee. She had never expected it to happen like this. She had always imagined freshly laundered linen sheets, birdsong, a big old-fashioned brass bed and a lot of good champagne.

The tall one flicked his head round. 'Hey, what you playing at, brother?' he shouted. 'We ain't got all night.'

'Just gimme a moment.' The younger one shuddered. 'A man needs time!'

'Hey, what you saying? For Godssakes, can I believe my eyes? You ain't got a fucking hard on!'

The other boy kneaded himself. 'It's coming, I tell you. I'm almost ready.'

'Christ! You make me real sick, man. Get a hold of yourself!'

The boy's hand movements were more frantic now. 'It's coming. It's coming.'

'Jesus Christ will be here sooner. And after all the trouble *I've* been to – '

'OK,' the boy pronounced. He bit his lip and crouched before Loretta, still holding himself. 'I'm ready.'

Then, suddenly, there was a shout outside. The bang of a fist on the outside of the lift door that sent an echo up and down the lift shaft.

The younger boy's anxious eyes swivelled around towards the door, then back down to himself.

43

He rose slowly, kicked the wedge from the door and pressed a button. The motor of the lift clunked into action. They were moving again. 'I'm sorry. Hell . . . ' he shrugged, '. . . it ain't working for me, man.'

Loretta closed her eyes and gulped. Her mouth filled with the taste of gag.

'What you mean?' The big guy's eyes blazed, bulging out of their sockets. 'You chicken?'

His brother shuffled forward, his hands dug deep in his pockets. His mouth twitched.

She could hear the commotion outside now. Steps in the corridor.

The lift stopped. The doors were opening, admitting a spreading wedge of light from the landing outside. The boy moved back, knelt and grabbed Loretta's arm. She thought at first he was trying to kiss her, but his eyes had the same fixed look as when his hand had first gone inside her. He peeled back his lips, showing teeth clenched in fury and humiliation. 'Remember me,' he said as his hand passed across her cheek.

Then, immediately the doors were fully open, they were gone. She heard them racing along the landing. She heard their whoops and guffaws, their heavy footsteps as they swung around the banisters, barging into walls.

Only after she had pulled the gag out of her mouth did she notice the blood trickling down and staining her dress. At first she thought it couldn't be her blood, then she checked her nose for bleeding. It was dry.

She summoned up the courage to raise her hand to her cheek and there she felt the warm tacky wetness of her own blood. She shuddered as very slowly her finger went down the open cut. She lifted her hand away from her

face and stared with unblinking eyes at her crimson finger
tips.

It seemed a long time before the lift doors opened.
Loretta saw Bob's broad mouth turn down, a look of
concern in his warm chestnut eyes. 'Anything wrong?'

She snapped herself out of it. 'Oh − no.' She smiled,
moved forward and pecked him on the cheek. 'Nothing
at all.'

They stepped into the lift just before the doors closed.
They started the descent and passed the fifth floor without
stopping.

Loretta turned, calmer now, and glanced at her
reflection in the mirrored panel at the back of the lift.
The lighting was so unflattering, it was enough to drive
a girl into a fit of depression. Did she really have green
skin? Did she really have those bags under her eyes? And
she noticed to her dismay that her scar was showing. All
the time that she had been standing waiting and thinking
back to that night, she must have been running her finger
up and down its line: the dusting of powder had gone.
She turned towards Bob but made sure that her scarred
cheek was closest to the wall. 'Where are we going?' she
asked him. 'Hamburger or pizza?'

He shook his head smugly. 'A surprise.'

She knew that meant somewhere expensive and really
did not want Bob spending all his hard earned dollars
on her, especially since they were just old friends going
out for something to eat. She knew what they paid him
at Wendheimer, Frink and Crindle and it wasn't nearly
enough. 'Nowhere expensive,' she ventured. 'It's not
necessary. I'm really just as happy with − '

He cut her short with a dismissive shrug.

45

Bob was good-looking in a macho kind of way. He had broad, clean features, thick short-cut brown hair, and despite his sedentary job, weatherbeaten skin. He could easily be mistaken for an Ivy League jock, but in fact his parents were far from rich. They ran an office cleaning service from their home close to where Loretta's mother lived in Queens.

The surprise turned out to be an Italian place called Zefforelli's on East 67th and Park. The restaurant was all polished steel, leather and whitewash — like a designer laboratory. It was full, though not with the kind of fashionable glitterati that Loretta had expected when she first sniffed the expense of the place. The clientèle seemed to be businessmen, planning or closing deals.

From the other side of the room there was a raucous outburst of laughter that was taken up and imitated by each of the eight men sitting at a round table. The sound bounced around the whitewashed walls and made her wish she was someplace else. She shuddered. There was something about businessmen's jokes she hated.

She thought that Bob must have been brought here once by one of his richer clients and that was how he knew of the place. It was his idea of the very best. For all his easy good looks, which could open most doors, he was surprisingly short on imagination sometimes.

The maître d' abandoned them when a stout balding man arrived with his entourage and Bob was left to help Loretta into her seat.

She picked up the menu. It had a David Hockney drawing of the proprietor on it but no prices.

No one came near them for a full twenty minutes. Bob twisted round in his chair and tried to catch a waiter's eye. After a few unsuccessful attempts, he resorted to waving his arm. At that the waiter turned and gave him a look of such condescension that Loretta wanted to say 'Shall we leave?' She gulped back the words. This was Bob's evening.

When the waiter finally came over, she ordered *tagliatelle verde* which she guessed should be the cheapest thing on the menu.

Embarrassingly, Bob asked: 'Are you sure?'

She nodded and added as a concession, 'With a green salad.'

Bob ordered the same for himself.

The waiter stubbed his pencil against the pad. The slight sneer on his lips said that if you are that poor, you should be at the pizzeria down the road, not soiling the linen napkins up here. 'The *bella Signorina* must look after her beautiful figure.' He gave a little bow. 'But *Signor*, maybe, would like a main course as well? The special today is *Fagottini di Vitello leccabaffi*.' He looked pointedly at Loretta and kissed his fingers. '*Delizioso*.'

Out of embarrassment, Bob hesitated, then finally shook his head.

'Oh, Bob,' Loretta sighed once the waiter had left. 'I've got such a difficult decision to make.'

He picked the glistening bottle of Clos du Val Chardonnay out of the ice bucket, wetting his cuff as he did so. 'Have a glass of wine. It will help you relax.'

'Thanks. Now, listen – ' the words came out in a rush ' – I told you that André was planning to expand. Well, it's gone through. He's going to open a new jewellery showroom and today he asked me to be part of it. He's offered to double – yes, double – my salary.'

Bob smiled. 'So what's the problem? Grab it before he changes his mind.'

'I'm just not sure . . .'

The waiter returned at that moment, setting down the *tagliatelle* with a flourish. Loretta doused a forkful in the creamy sauce. She was so preoccupied and, by now, so hungry that she was barely conscious of its taste until she glanced and saw Bob's questioning look. 'Delicious.' She nodded and smiled, then patted the corners of her mouth with the linen napkin.

'You see,' she sighed, 'there is one small problem. The shop is in Bond Street. Bond Street, London, England.'

His eyes widened. 'Jesus!' He gulped down a mouthful of pasta and reached hastily for his glass. 'So say you take it, just say you take the job, how long are you going to have to spend over there?'

'Dunno,' her voice grew doubtful, 'probably only a year, but it all depends how it goes. In the jewellery business London's one of the places you've got to be if you want to establish an international reputation. And, frankly, right now, I think I could do with a change from New York. It's just that I get so nervous. You don't know what it's like for a girl alone in this city. Sometimes I feel like a perpetual victim, just waiting for something terrible to happen. You try to be master of your own destiny. You tell yourself, "This is the age of the liberated woman. You can do anything," but it just ain't so. Whether you like it or not you've got to make yourself toughen up, mentally and physically, if you're going to survive in this jungle.'

Bob sipped his iced water and preened himself. 'Yeah,' he said lightly, 'a girl like you should have a permanent body guard. Remember, I'm always there, any time you need me. On the spot legal advice thrown in, too. All part of the service.'

'I appreciate that, Bob, really I do.'

He leant back and threw his crumpled napkin on the table. 'I'm gonna miss you.'

She reached for his hand. 'Me too, Bob. Me too.'

He was much quieter than usual throughout the rest of dinner. Entering the cab for the journey home, he moved closer to her than normal and casually draped his arm over the back of the seat. As they moved off, he let it fall on to her shoulders. Smiling all the time, he tightened his grip. 'Loretta, how long have we known one another?'

'As long as I can remember. Dunno — fifteen, seventeen years. Why?'

'Yes, well,' he gulped, 'in all that time we've been really good friends, right? Really good friends — it's not easy to find people that you really want to spend time with like that, is it? — and all this time, we've never — well — I've never pushed myself on you . . .'

'Yeah, and I respect you for that.' At first she had found the grip of his hand reassuring, comforting. Now she was no longer so sure. She could tell exactly where this conversation was leading. She tried to edge away from him, but at that moment the driver turned a corner and she found Bob sliding back towards her.

'Time after time I've kicked myself . . . hell, I can't expect you to be a mind reader. How can you guess what I've been thinking? How can you know how deeply I care? Loretta — hell, why don't I just come out with it? — I'm crazy about you. You are the only thing in my life that makes it all worthwhile. If only I can extend my hand to you . . .'

The hand was already extended. It was cupping her left breast. She felt a shudder of recoil go down her spine, a wave of nausea as the forefinger scraped against her nipple.

'Bob!' It was almost a scream. She struck out, pushing his hand away, digging her nails into the skin of his hand. Her eyes were wild. Perspiration formed on her upper lip.

'I'm sorry,' he said, pulling away from her. 'Is there someone else? Someone you keep locked away?'

'No, there's nobody else.' She struggled to regain her composure. 'It's just . . . just . . . Please, Bob. Cool down.'

'If there was someone else, I could understand it,' his eyes clouded, 'but as it is, I just don't know what to think.'

Loretta did not reply. The cab was approaching home territory. She just sat there, staring silently ahead of her. The last thing she wanted to do was to hurt Bob, but there was no way she could explain.

As soon as the cab drew up outside the apartment block, she leapt out. 'Thanks a million for dinner . . . and I'm sorry.' From the safety of the sidewalk, she leant into the cab and kissed him, then shut the cab door after her and waved him goodbye.

As the car moved away, she took three deep breaths. She could still feel the imprint of his hands on her body. She tugged at the front of her silk shirt to let the cool air cleanse her.

# Chapter 4

Hugh stood underneath the Victorian archway at Swindon station. He looked at the clock again, tapped his foot, sighed.

Two Japanese tourists had already taken half a reel of film of him in his red hunting coat, and now they were making little oriental gestures at him, asking him to smile. He did so in the hope of getting rid of them, then quickly mumbling an apology, walked through on to the platform.

There were only a few people waiting. A loudspeaker hissed static at him: 'For your own safety you are requested to stay behind the white line on the platform . . . For your own safety . . .'

The 4.15 from Paddington slowed down and drew into the station. A gust of air from the oncoming train smacked his face. He screwed up his eyes and tried to peer through the dirt-encrusted windows of the first-class compartments, then, remembering, ran down the platform to where the second-class carriages were coming to a halt. The engine juddered and stopped; the steel couplings clanged.

A girl with black hair down to her shoulders and a white, clear skin alighted from the third carriage along. The words SAVE THE WORLD were emblazoned across the black teeshirt which she wore beneath her open coat. She heaved a small holdall on to the platform.

Hugh rushed forward. 'Camilla, you made it.'

The girl turned towards him. Her eyes were pale green flecked with brown, their lids red with weeping. 'Yes, thank God, I was just going out when you called.' She put a hand on each of his shoulders and kissed him on the cheek. 'Do we know how serious it is yet?'

He shook his head. 'He's still in a coma. No news, I'm afraid.'

Her fingers tightened on his shoulder blades. She looked away. 'But Daddy'll be all right, won't he?'

'I'm sure he will,' he quavered. He picked up the grip. 'Come on.'

Camilla sat in silence for several miles during the drive to the hospital. Her fingers nervously picked at the stitching on the seat belt. Twice her mouth opened as if she was about to say something. Each time she gulped back the words.

At a set of traffic lights, Hugh pulled on the handbrake and turned towards her. She did not look at him but stared fixedly ahead at an old woman pushing a trolleyload of shopping across the road. 'Want me to tell you how it happened?' he asked softly.

She gave the barest nod.

As he explained, her lower lip began to tremble and she clutched the bridge of her nose between finger and thumb. 'Oh, Christ,' she said, closing her eyes, 'to think that I used to support those — those bastards!'

A car hooted behind them. Hugh released the handbrake, engaged gear.

'Hugh, you know I'm anti-blood sports? Well, in the past I've helped the Animal Liberation Army. Even

. . . been out with them.' She swallowed painfully. 'Do you think . . . do you think Daddy will still want to see me?'

'Don't be so silly. You're still his daughter, damn it.'

She swept back her hair. 'Are you sure? Blood sports were always more important to him than any of his children.'

Hugh breathed deeply and tried to control his voice. 'Camilla,' he said softly, 'we all know what Father's priorities were, but for Christ's sake do you have to bring them up now? The man's ill.'

Hugh was not surprised to hear that Camilla had supported the Animal Liberation Army. She was a friend to all 'good' causes.

At seventeen she had announced that she had become a vegetarian. To her credit she had put up with their father's remorseless teasing and, throughout the school holidays, a diet of tepid overcooked greens sprinkled with peanuts. Only a year later, when her vegetarianism had no longer been an issue, had she slipped quietly back to her old carnivorous ways.

True to form, though, she was now working for Friends of the Earth. After being active in the campaign to stop bleached disposable nappies, her latest hobbyhorse was loo paper. At their last meeting, she had expounded at some length on the subject to Hugh. According to her, most loo paper was made out of wood pulp or 'high-grade' waste paper when in fact it could be manufactured out of old newspapers and other 'low-grade' waste. Only last month, as part of a 'Recycling Day of Action', Camilla had paraded around a shopping centre in Slough dressed as a giant loo roll. It had achieved some publicity for the cause. The *Sun* had carried a 'photo-exclusive' under the heading: PEER'S DAUGHTER SAYS NO TO BOTTY WIPES. Their mother had thought it hilarious. Their father had not been amused.

They drove on in silence for the next five minutes. Hugh thought he must have taken a wrong turning somewhere. They were in a shopping mall. The street was crammed with cars, some double parked, others manoeuvring in and out of the parking places.

Camilla stared out of the window. She did not seem to notice their lack of progress. She was still plucking at the safety belt when eventually she said, almost dreamily: 'It's an unimportant detail, but I suppose this means we'll have to cancel my dance.'

'Well, postpone it maybe. But I doubt we'll cancel it altogether.'

She sighed. 'Ah, well, I never wanted the thing anyway. It was all Mummy's doing.'

He leant towards her and said with a half smile, teasing her, welcoming the light relief: 'But who knows who you might meet?'

'Huh!' she exclaimed. Her voice became almost haughty. 'At twenty-two, I'm quite capable of making my own friends, thank you very much.' She flicked back her hair. 'I just don't see the point of filling the house with a whole lot of freeloaders just because it's the done thing.'

'It will get you asked around.'

She gave an exasperated sigh. 'Don't you understand? I have met, or at least seen, most of the so-called deb's delights,' she imitated their mother's tone of voice, ' "all those properly brought up, nice young men", at the other dances.'

'And?'

'They do absolutely nothing for my ovaries. They're just not my speed. The whole exercise is nothing but an inordinate waste of time and money.'

Hugh suppressed a smile. 'By the law of averages, they can't *all* be white-fleshed, yellow-livered wimps!' He tilted his head to one side. 'I mean, I used to go to quite a few of the things myself.'

'That was a long time ago,' she said almost hurtfully. 'And you're still single. You see! Point made.'

'I don't want to pry,' he began hesitantly, 'but you never seemed quite so vehemently against it before. Why now? If the deb's delights do nothing for you, is there perhaps someone . . . ' he checked himself '. . . er, — someone else you'd like to ask to the ball? If it is still going ahead, that is.'

'No. There's no one else I'd like to ask,' she said quickly, and turned her head away.

Hugh watched her right cheek redden. He grinned.

Lady Rudlow sat straight-backed on a grey plastic hospital chair. A fluorescent tube flickered above her in the tiny waiting room. She stared at a crack on the grey linoleum floor. Her hands were neatly folded in her lap. Her fingers, though, were continually moving, manoeuvring the large sapphire and diamond engagement ring on her third finger, round and round. Her greying hair was drawn severely away from her white face. Her jaw jutted beneath a small pursed mouth which suddenly widened into a warm smile as Camilla entered the room.

She stepped forward hesitantly, then almost ran the last few paces. 'Mummy,' she cried, and smiled as Lady Rudlow opened her arms wide. Camilla kissed her, then rested her head on her shoulder.

Lady Rudlow patted her gently on the back. 'There, there,' she soothed. Then her eyes swivelled around. Her hand dropped away. For a moment both of them looked surprised, shocked almost, by their physical closeness.

'Let me look at you.' Lady Rudlow took one pace back. 'You haven't been down to see us for ages.' She pursed her lips again. 'Just a moment. I think I have a comb in my bag.'

Camilla pushed back her hair with her hands. 'Mummy,' she sighed, 'you know what trains are like — '

'Camilla dear, combs are environmentally friendly and not at all dangerous, you know?' Her Ladyship's eyebrows rose an inch. 'When did one last come in contact with your hair?'

'Mummy, please!' Camilla shook her head in frustration. 'What does it matter at a time like this? How is Daddy?'

'No news as yet.' Lady Rudlow sat down again and sighed. She picked up her brown crocodile bag from the floor beside her chair. 'I've been in this ghastly place for five hours now. They've been very kind — "ever so" kind. Enough tea for a garden fête, but not a word. Now where is it? You really can't let people see you like that.'

Her nervous fingers burrowed deeper in her bag. 'I know it's in there somewhere. The things one has to carry about with one! Everything has been taken care of. A specialist has been sent down from London, a Mr Robinson. He seems frightfully young to me, but I have been assured that he knows what he is doing. And Hugh has alerted Sir Arthur. I don't really see the necessity of his coming down, and on a Saturday too, but apparently he insisted.'

'Has Anthony been told?' queried Camilla.

'No, darling. We thought it best not to. He's got enough problems of his own right now. Ah, there we are!' She brandished a small black comb decorated with a gold band. 'All I have to find now is the mirror. You know how funny they are in hospitals about mirrors.'

Camilla sighed again as she took the comb and pocket mirror from Lady Rudlow. 'All right Mummy, if you insist.'

'Yes, darling, I do.' Lady Rudlow watched as Camilla tugged at her hair, trying to disentangle the knots. 'You must take more care of yourself, darling. This wild scarecrow look of yours is most unbecoming. If it ever was the fashion with your age group, surely it must be *passé* by now?'

'I like it,' Camilla said defiantly.

Lady Rudlow looked at her nails. 'Obviously dear, as you seem to adhere to it with such devotion, but I can't believe it holds much attraction for the opposite sex. Men – decent men, that is – don't like dirty girls. You will make a big effort for the ball, won't you, darling?' she pleaded. 'It's not much to ask, and as it's costing us a small fortune, I do so want you to look your very best.'

Camilla's hand checked halfway through a stroke of the comb. 'But, Mummy, aren't you forgetting something?'

Lady Rudlow paled. She nodded slowly and said in a quiet voice, 'That is . . . if there still is a ball. It'll be such bad luck on your cousin Cynthia, though, if not. I don't know what we'll do. It was to be her ball, too.'

There was a metallic rattling. The door swung open. 'Anybody like a cuppa?' called the tea lady, a plump woman with red cheeks. As she manoeuvred in, her trolley clanking and clattering, she only narrowly missed colliding with the wall.

Lady Rudlow smiled. 'You're looking after us so well. Yes, I am sure my daughter would like some. Too kind.'

'They are taking their time aren't they? So bad for the nerves, I always say. And you, Your Ladyship? I've made a fresh pot.'

'Yes.' Lady Rudlow smiled again. 'Maybe just half a cup.'

Immediately they were alone again, Lady Rudlow beckoned to Camilla to sit next to her. She reached out and took her daughter's hand. Neither touched their tea. 'Zilpah, you know, will have to be destroyed after all.' She shook her head distractedly. 'So sad. It will break George's heart.'

Camilla nodded slowly and blinked. She said nothing.

'George was always prepared to take calculated risks in business and in the field,' Lady Rudlow continued vaguely. 'He was never frightened of danger. That was one of the reasons I loved him, I suppose. He was a real man.'

'Mummy, stop it!' Camilla shook her head and twisted round in her chair. 'You're talking in the past tense.'

Lady Rudlow's hand tightened over Camilla's. Her voice faltered. 'Oh dear, what's going to happen to us?'

There was a knock on the door. Her Ladyship turned like a startled deer, lines of anxiety etched deep in her face. For a moment there was silence, then she drew a deep breath and called: 'Come in.'

The man who entered was well over six feet tall and broad to match. Iron-grey hair was slicked back over a broad high brow. A gold watch-chain strained over the voluminous waistcoat of his black suit. Hugh followed him in.

'Arthur . . . how good of you.' Lady Rudlow smiled gratefully.

'Elizabeth.' He bowed slightly and took her hand. 'I came as soon as I could. My sympathies. I trust that George . . .'

'Still no news.'

He looked around the small waiting room and sniffed. 'I thought I should be here just in case I could render some assistance. If − and I very much hope not − but if circumstances take an unfortunate turn, then we must act swiftly.'

Camilla pushed the hair back off her brow and stamped her foot. 'Christ! What is happening here? Stop behaving as if Daddy was dead!'

Sir Arthur drew a red polka-dot handkerchief from his pocket and coughed loudly. 'We must be prudent. As trustee of the Rudlow settlements, I would be neglecting my duty if − '

'Of course, Arthur, we understand,' soothed Lady Rudlow. 'We understand. Would you like some tea?'

Mr Robinson was in his early forties. He had horn-rimmed glasses and crinkly red hair. He walked straight up to Lady Rudlow, unsmiling.

'Well?' she asked, and breathed in deeply.

'I wish I had come with better news. I'm afraid that the prognosis is not encouraging.'

Lady Rudlow nodded slowly. 'What exactly do you mean, doctor? Please do not try to spare our feelings. We would like to know the truth.'

'The scan shows that the ventricles are full of blood. There are massive head injuries, severe swelling of the brain, and respiratory depression. We wanted to make sure of our findings before we spoke to you.'

Lady Rudlow pressed the nail of her forefinger hard into the palm of her hand. Her tone of voice, though, was calm and controlled. 'Can't you operate?'

The surgeon sighed. 'I'm afraid that would be futile. So far our tests have been unable to detect any response from the central nervous system . . . or find any sign of cerebral activity. None whatsoever.'

'Steady, Mummy,' whispered Camilla.

Lady Rudlow sniffed once and very deliberately folded her hands on her lap. She looked down at them, shook her head and blinked twice. 'You mean his brain is dead,' she said quietly.

'I'm afraid so,' said the doctor. 'All we can do is try to keep him stable and comfortable.'

Sir Arthur stepped forward. 'Mr Robinson, it is imperative that you understand something – I am Lord Rudlow's trustee and executor, and I must ask that you keep him alive. At any cost, do you understand me? He must be kept alive.'

'Of course, we will do everything we can, but once all cerebral activity has stopped, nature – '

'Yes, yes,' Sir Arthur's jowls shook, 'we understand all that, but nonetheless . . . he is still breathing, isn't he?'

'With the help of a ventilator.'

'Then he is alive, and he must stay that way. Whatever happens, the ventilator must not be disconnected. All we can hope for now is that clinically, legally, he can still be classified as alive. Use whatever means you like, doctor, any means – no matter what the expense – but

Lord Rudlow must be clinically and legally alive. A great deal depends upon it.'

Mr Robinson glanced at Lady Rudlow. He frowned. 'Is that your wish, too?'

She turned wide wet eyes on him. A tremor shook her shoulders. 'Yes,' she said. 'Yes. My husband must remain alive.'

# Chapter 5

As the plane flew over the Atlantic, Loretta reviewed the last few days. They had passed in a frenzy of packing and moving. She had never realised she had collected so much stuff, so many little mementoes. There were the matchboxes from all the restaurants she had visited, hats from Florida and Texas, little dolls she had been given years ago, her fashion designs and artwork from college, and clothes which she could now hardly believe she had actually worn. She had given these to the local thrift shop, but the rest of her things she had packed neatly into cardboard boxes and taken down to her mother's house in Queens where she had secreted them in the attic.

Despite two Alka-Seltzer, her head still ached from the farewell dinner that her mother had held for her the night before. Julie and Bob had been there, together with Stanley, her step-father, and Matt, Stanley's son from his earlier marriage. They had toasted her in champagne and wished her luck. There had been tears, of course.

The stewardess leaned over her. 'Last orders from the bar?'

Loretta smiled and shook her head.

'And you, sir?' the stewardess asked the man sitting in the window seat.

Loretta turned towards him, too. He was smartly if eccentrically dressed in a light grey frock coat. His hair was blue-white and bouffant. Traces of powder were just visible on his flushed cheeks.

'What?' He looked up at the stewardess without smiling. 'No. No alcohol. Nothing at all for me, thank you.' He sighed and dabbed his forehead with a fine lawn handkerchief.

'You OK, André?' asked Loretta.

'Who, me? Whatever gave you that idea? I'm suspended above the ocean in a tin box with several hundred madmen, and I have a bomb site in Bond Street, costing me thousands of dollars in rent each day, which I run as a builders' soup-kitchen. Apart from that I'm fine, absolutely fine.'

Loretta grinned and patted his hand reassuringly. 'Don't worry, André, we'll get everyone moving. Everything will be just hunkydory in time for the opening.'

He let out a sigh. 'You know, I just don't think that's possible. Guess who rang me yesterday? The marbleiser who's meant to be doing over the showroom. Running late, of course. He poured his heart out to me all about some unfaithful little boy. As if I need his problems, too! I couldn't get him off the line — well, what do you expect? It was collect. He told me categorically that right now he was just too upset to work.'

'Don't worry,' Loretta soothed. 'Don't even think about it. Just leave it to me.'

'Problems, problems, problems!' He shook his head. 'And to think I could be in Florida now, in my condo. Why do I subject myself to this? Why? It's not as if

I need their money. All the people who matter in the States wear my stuff . . . well, all those with taste anyhow. Who needs Bond Street?'

Loretta had played this game with André so many times. She knew that he would never rest until he had swept Cartier, Boucheron, Van Cleef and Tiffany off the map, so the chances were that, good though he was, he would still be at work for a while yet.

'But the fashionable women of the world need you, André. Europe needs you,' she replied, just as she had on the other occasions.

'You really think so?'

'I know so.'

It did the trick. André preened himself. Calmer now, he drained the last of the mineral water in his glass, adjusted the air vent on the panel above him, then turned back to Loretta. 'Oh, by the way, my dear, did I remember to tell you to bring a ball gown?'

'Yes,' she said. 'You know the red and black one? The one I wore when you took me to the party at the Met.'

André swallowed. 'Oh, that thing!' he replied, rather hurtfully. 'Yeah, well, you can always hire something. I think Veronica mentioned fancy dress anyway. I want you to look your best, your absolute best. Real class. As you know, the jewellery business is all about getting to know the right people.'

'There's our opening party . . .'

'Yeah, yeah,' he flapped his hand dismissively, 'but I'm talking real parties now, society parties — not press and trade and rent-a-crowd. If all goes well, in a fortnight's time Lady Rudlow is giving a ball for her daughter's coming-out, and it's definitely the place to be. You must have heard of the Rudlow Aircraft Company? Megabucks.'

'Oh!' exclaimed Loretta. The name meant nothing to her, but André was clearly so excited by the prospect, she did not want to disappoint him. 'You mean we're going to *that*? Great.'

He nodded. 'We mustn't set our hopes too high, though. The ball has been on and off twice already this week. Seems poor old Lord Rudlow had an argument with a hedge and has been cut up real bad. Touch and go. They called the dance off . . . then it was on again but only as a small party for Lady Rudlow's niece . . . then off again.' He twisted his head from side to side like a spectator at a tennis tournament as he related each turn of events. 'Then they decided that Lord Rudlow would have wished the dance to go ahead. So for the moment, at least, it's still party time!'

'I had no idea that Lady Rudlow was a friend of yours,' Loretta added with, she thought, a suitably admiring expression.

'Strange that you should ask,' he answered casually. 'As it happens, we've never met.'

'Never met? I don't quite follow . . . so how come she's asked us, then?'

'Through some small oversight, she hasn't, my dear,' his ringed fingers patted her hand, 'but when has such a small technicality ever stood in the way of André Swert? I know just how to fix it. Remember Veronica Wellingham?'

She tried to put a face to Veronica Wellingham's name. Grey hair. Pinched features. Divorcee. She nodded. 'Yes, she's the one forever borrowing our jewellery. On so-called "approval", right?'

'Right. Well, she's giving a weekend house party for the dance at her place in Gloucestershire.' André's eyes narrowed conspiratorially. He nodded slowly as if somehow this snippet of information should make everything clear.

'So?' asked Loretta, still confused.

André sighed. He puffed the air out loudly and shook his head from side to side. 'So, my sweet *ingénue*, she's gonna call Lady Rudlow on the Friday night, right? And say that her oldest and best friend and asset at any party, the world famous André Swert, has just flown in from the States, and just happens to be staying with her, right? And, seeing that all her other guests are heading off to the ball, as a special favour could he and his beautiful escort possibly come too, right? Do you see it now? Do you see it? How could the gracious Lady Rudlow possibly refuse?'

Loretta nodded, marvelling at the lengths André was prepared to go to secure an invitation to a party given by people he did not even know.

In New York, he was the regular walker of a couple of well-known society dames whose husbands were either too busy or too uninterested to attend the innumerable events which formed the non-stop calendar for those with seriously social disease.

Together with the parties he was asked to in his own right, André had the New York scene stitched up pretty tight. He did not just confine himself to the grander parties either. There was hardly an opening of a dress shop or a gallery to which he did not go, however briefly, to scrutinise the canapés and cast his expert eye over exactly who was there.

Even the best laid plans, though, can sometimes go

awry. He scanned the gossip columns daily on his way to work, and if one of the big society names was giving a party and he had not been asked, he was in a wretched mood all morning. All Loretta could do then was feed him camomile tea and keep out of his way.

Occasionally, one of the society dames would cancel at the last minute. It would be then that the telephone would ring while she and Julie were seated in front of the television, eating something which had just come out of the microwave. André's voice was invariably feverish: 'Loretta, dear — what a relief! You're in! I just can't begin to tell you what's happened. Drop everything. Run to the bathroom. Green dress with spots will be fine. I'll bring the jewellery. Pick you up in twenty minutes, OK? Byeee.'

She really did not mind how many times he had been through his address book before he called her. It was always fun, and André — well, he was as safe as they came.

Her invitation to the ball at the Met had been preceded by just such a call. It was strange, though, that just now André had been so dismissive of the lowcut red and black dress. It was less than a year old and she distinctly remembered that on the night of the ball he had said how nice she looked in it.

Very occasionally André asked her to something in advance, but these were the parties where, she suspected, his more regular escorts would not feel entirely at home — like the League of Goldsmiths and Allied Trades Barn Dance and Barbecue, for instance.

The wing flaps rose. The tone of the jet engines changed. The aircraft's walls vibrated like the panels of a spin dryer.

'We are now beginning our descent into Heathrow.

You are kindly requested to return to your seats, fasten your seat belts and refrain from smoking until you are inside the terminal building. Thank you.'

André gritted his teeth. Beads of sweat broke out on his brow. 'Oh, God, how I hate landings. Terminal. Oh, God! *Terminal*. Why do they always say that? The last resting place of the vain creatures who thought they could fly . . .'

'Relax, André,' soothed Loretta. 'Just don't think about it.'

His ringed fingers gripped the armrests. The whites of his knuckles showed. 'Oh, vanity, vanity! Come friendly dentists with thy drills, with thy pincers, with thy needles . . . anything, *anything* . . . just get me out of here alive!'

The loudspeaker pinged again. 'Would the passenger in the rear toilet kindly return to his seat?'

André glanced out of the window at the matchbox houses swaying in the mist. He gulped. 'Hey, what's happened to the pressurisation in this plane? Loretta, are your ears popping too? Mine feel like a couple of Sumo wrestlers are using them as punch bags. Stewardess! Stewardess!'

They drove straight to Bond Street from Heathrow. The showroom was a mess. The builders, who were meant to have finished a fortnight ago, were still putting the finishing touches to the paintwork. The floorboards were up. Lengths of bare flex ran everywhere. Every available surface had some sign of past eating or drinking: a plastic cup here; a Mars bar wrapper; a hamburger carton; a dirty spoon. There was sugar on the floor which crunched at each step they took.

The strain of the aircraft landing had been too much for André. He had no energy left to berate the workmen. He just sat down in a corner and buried his head in his hands, mumbling to himself incoherently. The few sentences which Loretta could make out while she comforted him seemed unusually florid even for André.

Surprisingly, though, one of the builders seemed to understand what he was saying. He said it was a passage from King Lear.

Half the workmen downed tools and just stared at André as if he were an extraterrestrial. The others just kept on working, drawing their paint brushes over the wooden surfaces with studied slowness as if engaged in some arcane Zen ritual.

'I want to see the foreman,' demanded Loretta.

'He's off,' came the predictable reply.

She crossed her arms. 'I don't think you understand me.' Her voice was calm but firm. 'I want to see the foreman. And the architect. The daily work sheets. The architect's progress reports. I want to see them all. Now!'

It was only at nine o'clock that evening that Loretta finally arrived outside the terraced house near South Kensington where she was to stay. Plane trees rose at intervals from the pavement, breaking the regimented sweep of the creamy white stucco buildings. A couple of the houses in the terrace had been made into hotels, but she was pleased to see that there were no twinkling neon signs to keep her awake at night.

So far, so good. She had not known what to expect. All she had been told was that one of the girls that André had engaged as a sales assistant was looking for a lodger to help out with the rent. Without further ado, André had booked Loretta in.

The cab driver offered to help her with her three suitcases and she eagerly accepted. She felt slightly guilty, however, for not telling him that the flat was on the third floor.

She found the name 'Wishbone' stuck with Sellotape across the entryphone, pressed it, and at the answering buzz pushed open the heavy front door. The hall was in darkness. She fell against a bicycle before finding a switch which ticked back ominously at her and turned the textured paper walls a musty magnolia.

They had only puffed and panted up to the first landing before the ticking stopped and they were plunged once more into darkness. Loretta sighed. The landlord here, she thought, must either be extremely mean or extraordinarily fit.

Her flatmate came to the rescue, switching on the lights from above and running down the stairs to meet them.

Shona Wishbone, a roundfaced, pretty if somewhat overweight brunette, seemed friendly enough, and the flat, when they finally reached it, was just fine too. It had two bedrooms, both small but still substantially larger than Loretta's box in New York, and a white-painted sitting room-cum-kitchenette which looked over the road. The furniture throughout was basic but quite new. Not bad, thought Loretta. Not bad at all.

The next four days were work, work, work. Unbelievably the first of the three previews of the collection was now ten days off. The invitations had already gone out, and André took the brave decision not to cancel. Three times as many men were working on the site now, the curtains and show-fittings were all ready for installation, and the jewellery was all packed and waiting in New York, ready for the signal for dispatch by armed guard.

Already Loretta was beginning to feel the excitement of being in a foreign city. On Sunday afternoon, when André finally allowed her a few hours off, she made her way to the dusty, dirty heap of Victoria Station and boarded a tourist coach to take her round the sights.

She knew New York pretty well, of course. She had also been to Florida, Maine, Texas, and once to Los Angeles and San Francisco, but this was the first time she had been outside the States. Almost all the other places in the world were nothing but names on a map to her, those sort of weird, distinctly foreign places which fill the pages of the *National Geographic*. The exceptions, of course, were the couture centres: Paris, Milan and London. While at the New York College of Art and Design, Loretta had studied all the fashion magazines and seen videos of the shows. Although New York was up there in the pack, she had marvelled at the audacity of the European designers, their sense of fun, their sheer decadent absurdity.

England, though, to her mind, had always been different, always special. Throughout her childhood, her father had always come back on leave with stories of the strange goings on there. She had sat on his knee and listened wide-eyed as he had told her about the Queen who always went to bed with her crown on over her curlers; about the guardsmen who wore extraordinarily high furry hats, so they could keep their lunchboxes inside; about the Lords and Ladies who ate grouse and jam for breakfast dressed in their ermine robes.

As the coach swept around the corner of Buckingham Gate and she saw the gleaming white mass of Buckingham Palace for the first time, she was amazed how little had changed from the postcard that her father had sent her all those years ago. Metal barriers encircled the fountain and the pavements now and there were a few street lamps that were not in the postcard, but otherwise all was the same. She marvelled at the sheer scale of it − at the wrought iron gilded finials, at the Victoria Memorial − but to her mind what made it really extraordinary was that this was not some long defunct monument carefully preserved to titillate the tourists but a real palace, and inside lived a real queen.

The coach moved off down the grand wide sweep of the Mall. Flags were flying from tall posts bedecked with little wooden crowns. They got caught in the traffic then, and it was a good five minutes before they passed through Admiralty Arch into Trafalgar Square.

It was now a lot cleaner than the Square in the postcard. In the card, all the buildings had been black with grime. The starlings were still circling Nelson's column, though, filling the air with their hungry impatient squawking.

How eagerly she had waited for those postcards. How she had scanned them for any news, any hint that her father might be coming home. Ironically, those years held the happiest memories of him because then she had still been able to look up to him, imagine him from afar as a dashing, fearless pilot ready to risk all for his country. She did not know then about the dark side of his character, the way his enthusiasm and zest for life, his infectious gaiety, would suddenly evaporate and the long, unrestrained bouts of drinking begin.

The coach was now circling Parliament Square. The card of the Houses of Parliament and Big Ben her father had kept for last. It was the signal that he was coming home for good. She was just twelve then. She remembered her whoops of glee the moment she had seen that card in the mail and the way that she bragged to the other children at school that, like them, she would now have a father at home, too. She also remembered vividly the time, only a month after his return, when she had seen a bruise on her mother's cheek, its faint blue outline only just visible under heavy foundation and powder. She remembered the way that she had looked up at her mother with wide, shocked eyes and had asked her what was wrong, and the way her mother had answered almost casually, 'Nothing, darling, I tripped,' and then had hugged her so hard that Loretta felt her mother's heart pounding through her breast bone.

She knew now how brave her mother had been; about how she had tried to keep him away from the booze; about how she had taken him again and again to Alcoholics Anonymous; about how, at every little knock, he would weaken and once more reach for the Bourbon. Her mother had said that it was not really his fault, that something had happened when he had been flying — an accident of some sort — but she would never tell Loretta more.

She shook herself. All that was behind her. Her mother had re-married and seemed happy enough with Stanley. And she, Loretta, had wasted too much of her life living in the past, living with the guilt that even then, young though she had been, there might have been something she could have done to stop her father from leaving.

She was in a different city now, a city where a girl was free to walk alone in comparative safety, a city where people still had the time to be polite to strangers, a city where the old ghosts of her past were not waiting around every street corner to haunt her.

All she needed now was courage.

# Chapter 6

The flat empty scrubland of Salisbury Plain stretched on
for mile after mile. Only the occasional hillock or copse
broke the barren monotony of the countryside. The wind
hissed and whistled, flicking the rye grass in its wake. No
birds sang. A burst of gunfire from a distant army
exercise sent the hares scurrying for shelter.

Where the road dipped, there was a group of ruined
houses still smoking from their most recent
bombardment. The grass was scorched, the gorse and
juniper burnt. Craters gave the area around the houses
the look of a mud-washed lunar landscape.

Hugh changed gear at the bottom of the dip. A long
compound of green chicken wire appeared on the
horizon. As he drove on, the hangars came into view,
then a long low brick building. He slowed down in
front of the gates. The sign read 'Rudlow Aircraft
Co. Authorised Personnel Only. Strictly no admit-
tance'.

A man in a portakabin nodded and raised the metal
barrier.

Hugh drove on past another checkpoint, past the three
vast grey hangars to the administration building. There
was a little well-tended lawn outside with a bed of
regimented red tulips. The flags around the forecourt

hung at half-mast. Hugh swallowed and sighed as he drew the car to a halt.

Despite the sound of voices within, the clatter of typewriters, the roar of heavy machinery, this place now seemed like a wasteland: a kingdom without a king. His father had been the Rudlow Aircraft Company. Now, without him, there seemed no breath of life in the place, only the remorseless wind off the plain beating against the corrugated iron of the hangars like a messenger of death knocking to come in.

Hugh shook himself, pushed open the swing doors and walked into the lobby. Framed paintings of the Rudlow fleet covered the walls: the Rudlow Eagle, the small four-seater tourer that had made the company's name; the Rudlow Scimitar; the Rudlow Scorpion. No one could take away these achievements, though now they were museum pieces, enthusiasts' memorabilia.

'Morning, Carter.'

The uniformed commissionaire clicked his heels and saluted in return, but there was a dead expression in his eyes. The short grey moustache on his upper lip bristled as his lips tightened and he muttered his condolences.

'Yes,' Hugh replied. 'Thank you. Yes, it has been a great shock.'

It was the same with the receptionist and the members of the design team whom he met in the passage. Half-sentences were left hanging in mid-air, arms waved in awkward angular movements, eyes avoided his. They could not find words adequate to express what they felt, but they felt it all the same. Hell, he was as awkward as they were. You don't talk about dying. When the time comes you just do it. And do it quietly.

Hugh sought refuge in his own small office. An old

photograph of his mother in her debutante days stood on the mahogany desk, but apart from one of Zola, the others were all of planes. There were models of the planes, too, lining the mantelpiece and windowsill.

He slumped into the leather chair, finished a cup of coffee, then pressed the buzzer on the intercom. 'Angela, ask Saunders, Bishop and Slipper to come to my office, if you please.'

Hugh had always assumed that his father would hand over the control of the company to him one day. He had envisaged, though, a period of transition in which his father would gradually have transferred more and more of the day to day responsibility to him — but that was clearly impossible now.

Even so, his credentials for the number one position were quite respectable. He was thirty-five and had served in the RAF for seven years, retiring with the rank of squadron leader. He had worked in each of the company departments in turn and now divided his time between Ken Slipper's department, marketing, and acting as his father's general *aide-de-camp*, which had given him a pretty good overview of the whole business. He had energy and, he hoped, some flair.

And who else was there? Ken Slipper had spent all his life in marketing. He was not managing director material. Neither, Hugh suspected, was Don Bishop who was in charge of research and development and an engineer through and through. The only serious contender among the senior staff was Phil Saunders, the financial director, but although highly competent in his field, he knew next to nothing about aircraft.

No, unless someone was brought in from outside, he, Hugh, was the natural choice. A Rudlow had always been in charge. Fifty-five percent of the shares were held by the various Rudlow family trusts. They would be calling the tune.

In the early days, of course, his brother Anthony had still been a contender. He had joined the firm with a degree in aeronautical engineering, had even been his father's *aide-de-camp* for a while. Anthony, however, had never had the same rapport with his father as Hugh had and gradually, subtly, he had implanted in his father's brain the idea that such a general position as assistant to the managing director was an inordinate waste of Anthony's specialist training. Within six months of resigning his commission, Hugh had supplanted Anthony as his father's *aide* and under the guise of receiving a promotion, his brother had been given a backroom rôle, supervising production and assisting on research and development.

He might, however, still have been a contender if the revelations of the last six months had not been made. Once their father had fully appreciated the seriousness of the situation, there had been really no alternative: Anthony had been forced to leave on an indefinite sabbatical.

The intercom buzzed. 'They're waiting outside, Mr Rudlow.' His secretary's voice was only just recognisable in the treble twang of the machine. 'Shall I show them in?'

'Yes, please.'

Hugh took a deep breath to calm the beating of his heart. It was important that he should seize the initiative, that his every action should carry the stamp of natural authority, the easy self-confidence of a born leader.

Hugh remained seated as the three men trooped in.

Saunders was first, a tall willowy man with thick black spectacles. He was followed by the portly shape of Slipper, his belly straining the shirt buttons above his belt. Finally came Don Bishop, diminutive and balding, staring rigidly ahead through thick metal-rimmed glasses.

'I'm sorry to say that it does not look good,' Hugh said in a dry controlled monotone. 'Even if Father does recover, I don't think he'll ever be able to take up active duties again.'

'Not even in some kind of advisory capacity?' pleaded Saunders. Even his clipped pattern of speech had an accountant's precise measured air.

'Not in any capacity, I'm afraid, Saunders.'

The three men exchanged glances. 'We had hoped . . .' began Slipper. He pulled at the cuffs of his neatly pressed blazer.

'I know. Thank you all for your flowers. They were much appreciated. This is a great shock to us all, but nothing is going to change. We will continue to run the business with the same verve and energy for which my father was famous. We owe it to him. We owe it to the workforce.'

'If only . . . ' Bishop gulped and started again. 'If only we hadn't had those problems with the ailerons, he'd have seen her fly. Three years' work, and . . .' He shook his balding head and blinked through his thick metal-rimmed glasses, close to tears.

'I know, Don.' Hugh nodded slowly. 'I know.'

He knew that Don Bishop would be hit as hard by the news as anyone. Forty years ago, then a young mechanic, he had hitched his star to that of the dashing young aviator with grand ideas and hugely ambitious plans. He had shared the young Lord Rudlow's triumph when the prototype of the Rudlow Scimitar had won the King's Cup. He had been there when the company had received its first order.

'We go on exactly as before,' added Hugh. 'Father might still see her fly. Only we'll show him the completed production aircraft not the prototype, won't we, Don? It's still a great day for us, and a great day for Father. Is she ready to go?'

Bishop wiped his spectacles with his handkerchief and nodded.

Hugh turned towards the others. 'Anything else we should deal with immediately?'

'Nothing that can't wait until after the flight,' replied Saunders. 'You might be interested to know, though, that Art Laithwaite from AIP called. He has asked for a meeting when he comes over in a month's time. Eight-thirty breakfast at the Connaught on the twentieth.'

'Hmm.' Hugh leaned back in his chair. 'What did he want?'

'Wouldn't say.'

'Think he's got wind of the Condor?'

Saunders shrugged. 'You know how it is. However hard we may try to keep a project under wraps, word gets out. Too many people are involved: suppliers, subcontractors . . .'

'But we've been very careful. Maybe it's something quite different. I don't know — maybe he just wants to convey condolences from all at AIP.' But even as he spoke the words sounded hollow in his ears. Laithwaite was not a sentimentalist and the Condor would be in direct competition with Aeronautical Industries of Philadelphia's now ageing 386. Still, there was little that they could do about it if their secret was out.

82

Hugh glanced at his watch and rose to his feet. 'OK, gentlemen, let's go and see what she can do.'

Down in the No. 3 hangar, the plane was waiting for them. The yellow-green epoxy primer that covered her gleamed dully in the light of the arc lamps above. She was seventy feet long with a seventy-four feet wingspan. She had high lift flaps, narrow wings, leading edge slats and wing tip sails. There were no markings anywhere, nothing to detract from the sleek lines that flowed from her stubby nose to her fin.

Hugh stared up at the plane and shuddered. By his side, Bishop gazed up at his creation with something akin to adoration. Except for one man adjusting something under the Condor's belly, all work had stopped: tools lay idle on benches; compressed air hoses were rolled and hooked in place on the wall.

A lean man in dark blue flying overalls nodded and walked casually towards them. He had long side-burns which sported more hair than the crown of his head.

'Nervous, Archie?' asked Hugh.

The man shrugged. 'Well, the first time you take anything up, it always gets the adrenalin going. But nervous, no. Come on, Mr Rudlow, tell me? Have you ever seen old Archie nervous?'

Hugh smiled. 'Never.'

'So long as Don's done his job, there's nothing to worry about. Nothing.' Archie leaned across and playfully nudged him in the ribs. 'And you're the best, aren't you Don?'

Bishop backed away. He mustered a smile. 'Think I'd let you anywhere near her unless we were sure —

absolutely sure — she could take your rough treatment? For once in your life, Archie, *please*, try and be gentle.'

'I'll treat her like a baby.'

The man standing on a dock underneath the aircraft fastened the flap. He nodded to Archie. 'All yours. Ready to go.'

The dock was pulled away. The hangar doors opened. Light flooded in. A tug slowly backed through the entrance. The hydraulic system hissed as the nosewheel of the plane was lifted on to the ramp and again as it was clamped into place. At a signal, the tug moved forward. Slowly the plane crawled out of the hangar.

Archie zipped up his overall and donned his headgear. The corners of his mouth twitched. 'Well, here we go.'

Hugh squeezed his shoulder. 'Good luck.' He walked out of the hangar into the sunshine and took up position on the edge of the runway. He watched as Archie and his co-pilot gave one last wave and climbed up the steps into the aircraft. Seconds later, their shadows filled the cockpit window.

Men in overalls, still wiping the grease from their hands, poured out of the hangars. Some stood behind Hugh on the edge of the runway, while others climbed up on to the flat roof of the administration building. Some brave girls were up there too, holding down their skirts in the wind.

The engines started, sending a shimmering heat haze out through the back of the exhaust pipes. The sound throbbed in Hugh's ears and made the tarmac hum. The draught froze his cheeks and tugged at his hair.

The body of the aircraft was trembling now. She was ready to surge forward.

Archie gave a signal. The chocks were away. The plane

started gathering speed up and along the runway. Sixty
. . . seventy . . . eighty . . . eighty-five knots.

Hugh clenched his fist and stabbed at the air. 'Go for
it!'

If the crowd made any noise, it was inaudible. The only
sounds were the tattoo of the propellers, the roar of the
engines. He saw Don bite his lip as the plane raced across
the field.

The nose lifted, at first just slightly, then up it turned.
The nosewheel was in the air, then the undercarriage. The
plane was airborne.

Don whistled, wiped his brow.

'The first hurdle passed.' Slipper smiled. 'Looking
good. That's one great lady up there. We've built a world
beater.'

A great yell went up from the men outside the hangar.
A forest of hands waved from the rooftop.

'Congratulations, Don,' said Hugh, shaking his hand
and slapping him heartily about the shoulders. 'Top of
her class.'

Already Slipper was rehearsing press releases. 'The first
of a new generation of short-haul STOL aircraft to reach
the market-place.'

Hugh craned his neck and watched as the plane crossed
overhead. For a moment it obscured the sun, then it shot
past them with a sudden roar. Slowly, he smiled. Go on,
my beauty, he prayed. Do it right. For God's sake, do
it right . . .

# Chapter 7

The gates of Conningsby Park were before them now. The headlamp beam fell on a network of concentric wrought-iron spirals and speared finials that dissolved into the night. On either side, greyhounds of pitted stone gazed contemptuously down their long noses.

So this was it. Wide-eyed, Loretta stared up at the gates, and shuddered. She already knew that this was going to be no ordinary party. For once André had not been exaggerating.

Just as they were about to drive through, a man in a fluorescent yellow tunic stepped out of the shadows and flagged them down. The car stopped. A torch beam flicked over each face in turn. 'Your invitations, if you please.'

Loretta turned sideways and glanced at André who was seated next to her in the back of the car. She felt very ill at ease in the costume he had hired for her from Berman and Nathan's. It was a Cinderella ballgown of rose pink silk taffeta embroidered with small dusty pink rosebuds around the hem. It was slightly tight under the arms. Around her neck she wore a very fine ruby and diamond necklace that André had lent her for the evening. Her hair was piled high and a silk rosebud was pinned to one side of her chignon.

To her embarrassment, André had insisted on going as her Fairy Godmother. Once he had seen the costume in the showroom, there had been no stopping him. He wore a lime green tutu with matching sequined top. His wig was lime green too and crowned by an emerald and diamond tiara of fabulous proportions. She hoped that the Rudlows had a sense of humour.

'Now, young man, let me see,' replied the woman in the front seat, reaching for her petit-point evening bag. 'I'm sure I must have put the invitation somewhere safe.' She was dressed as Marie-Antoinette, in a lavishly embroidered heavy satin dress. Her face, smothered in white powder, was almost the same shade as her powdered pompadour. 'Ah, there.' She flourished a very stiff, gold-rimmed card.

The man lowered the beam on to the card. 'Thank you . . . er, Lady Wellingham.' The light flashed again. On Loretta this time. She shielded her eyes. 'And the ladies in the back, if you please.'

'They are with me,' Lady Wellingham replied with an imperious flick of her fan, 'I can vouch for them.'

The man shook his head. ''Fraid, Your Ladyship, we've got our instructions. Names, please.'

Loretta swallowed. 'Loretta Lorenz and André Swert.'

'That's right.' André bent forward. He affected a deep gravelly voice. '*The* Mr André Swert.'

The man clearly did not know who was who in the world of international jewellery. All he said was, 'How do you spell it?' Then, when told, pulled out a crumpled typewritten list and scanned the names with slow deliberation. 'S-W-E-R-T, you say?' His tunic crackled as his arms moved. He shook his head. 'I'm sorry. I can't find a Swert on the list, male or female. And no Lorenz.'

Loretta bit her lip. She glanced again at André who looked equally bewildered.

'I ask you . . . Secretaries these days,' tutted Lady Wellingham without a moment's hesitation. 'Well, we can't stay here all night. And neither should you, young man. You'll catch your death of cold.' She struck the dashboard with her fan. 'Driver, on!'

The chauffeur nodded. The car jerked forward, wallowing through the thick gravel.

André turned around and stared out of the back windscreen until the man in the tunic was only a yellow dot, then he blew a silent whistle. 'Veronica darling, I'm just the teensiest little bit confused. You did clear all this yesterday with Lady Rudlow, didn't you?'

Lady Wellingham sighed. 'I tried, my dear, I really did try. But you know how it is with poor George in hospital. I could only get that butler of theirs. And he's a stone wall.'

'So,' André took a deep breath and nodded, showering the back seat with glitter, 'let me get this straight – you have *not* spoken to Lady Rudlow. She does *not* know we are coming. Right?'

Lady Wellingham fanned herself hard. So hard, in fact, that a stiff breeze was felt in the back of the car. She gave no answer.

'Veronica? In other words, technically . . . officially . . . we are gatecrashers. My dear, you do realise what this means? We could be *forcibly* ejected.' André patted his brow with a white lace handkerchief. 'Can you imagine the humiliation? The publicity? I'd be a laughing stock. It could *ruin* me.'

Lady Wellingham snapped her fan shut and wagged it inches from his nose. 'André, you disappoint me. What

89

has happened to your spirit of adventure? Keep your wig on and your mouth shut and we'll sail through.'

'You'd better be right, Veronica.' André bit his lip. 'You'd better be right.'

Specimen trees saddled the drive like a monumental archway: oaks; weeping beeches; sequoias; maidenhairs; white and blue cedars. After a mile or so, the surroundings gave way to open parkland. Here the car's headlamp beam fell on a herd of roe deer. The sudden drumming of their running hooves drowned the rumble of the engine.

Further on, they crossed a stone bridge. It was not until they were halfway over that Loretta turned and saw the lake. A ruined Grecian-style temple stood on a small island, its reflection shimmering in the water below.

Then the drive veered to the left and she saw the house with its cupola, parapets, and columned portico. It was even more magnificent than she had imagined, larger than a whole block of flats. She suppressed a gasp. 'You mean to tell me that only *one* family lives in all that space?' she said, then immediately regretted the remark.

'That's right,' said Lady Wellingham with a condescending smile on her lips. 'I can't see the Rudlows relishing the idea of a commune, my dear.'

Loretta felt a blush bloom on her cheeks.

André leant forward anxiously. 'Veronica — *darling* — as I see it, we've got one big problem right here. That guy at the gate is bound to have a walkie-talkie, right? Now just supposing he passed the word to the guys down here, what will they be doing but getting together a nice warm reception committee for us? They've probably tipped off Dempster for a photo-exclusive — '

'Relax, André,' Lady Wellingham replied with growing impatience. 'Just leave it to me.'

They were approaching the main sweep of the drive now. The windows of the orangery hummed to a disco-beat, flashing magenta, yellow, orange. The car slowed.

'No, Stevens, not the front porch,' Lady Wellingham signalled to the chauffeur. 'I don't like the look of those men with bulging pockets and ill-fitting dinner jackets. Ridiculous! There wasn't any nonsense like this in my day.'

They drove on at a snail's pace for thirty yards or so, then the driver stopped the car and let Lady Wellingham out. 'Stay where you are, boys and girls,' she said as one leg landed on the gravel. 'I'm going to take a look.'

'Not deserting us, Veronica, are you?' crooned André.

Her voice had the texture of honey. 'Would I do that, darling?'

'To think I trusted her,' he whispered immediately the door clicked shut. 'Just one tiny favour and she screws up. And after all I've done for her . . .'

'I'm sure it will be all right,' soothed Loretta, and patted his knee.

André was only slightly calmer by the time that Lady Wellingham returned. Her embroidered silk dress filled the passenger window. A jewelled finger tapped on the glass. 'It's as I suspected,' she told them, 'Elizabeth and her daughter are greeting guests in the hall. If you like we could run the gauntlet down the line-up − stylish but fraught with danger − or we could play safe? Which is it to be?'

'What about my grand entrance?' wailed André.

'Save it for later. I'll lead the way.'

Loretta smiled, plucked up her hem and followed Lady

Wellingham. She shivered at the cold but the thrill of the party was getting to her now: the lights, the throb of the music, the grandeur of the setting.

She scampered over the gravel and on to the grass behind the orangery. There stacks of dirty plates and unwashed glasses lay outside an undecorated marquee. Rows of champagne bottles stood in an ice-filled metal bath. Dead ones littered the ground everywhere. Waiters in white coats bustled back and forth.

She tried to appear relaxed and at her ease, as if she were a guest who was just taking a stroll, but at her third step she felt the heel of her shoe sink into the soft earth. The ground squelched back at her. 'Oh, God!' She tottered forward. She flailed her arms to keep her balance. Once . . . twice . . . 'Hah!' She was steady now. She sighed, relieved, then looked down at her once perfect satin shoe. The heel would not budge.

'Don't just stand there like a wax dummy,' hissed André from behind. 'This isn't a fashion show.'

'I'm stuck,' she whispered.

He shook his head and unexpectedly smiled. 'Hey, don't you know anything? Cinderella doesn't lose her slipper until the end of the ball. Oh dear, Fairy Godmother to the rescue, I suppose.' A bejewelled hand grasped her heel and tugged her free.

'Why thank you, sir,' she gushed à la Scarlett O'Hara.

'Don't mention it. Just another service from the Godmother Corporation. Now where has Veronica got to?'

They spied Lady Wellingham standing outside a side door. 'Oh, there you are,' she called. Two passing waiters followed her gaze and glared at them suspiciously. 'I do feel better,' she continued, presumably for the benefit of the waiters. 'So unbearably stuffy inside, wasn't it? But we ought to go back now. I did promise Hugh a dance.' She flicked her fan in the direction of the door.

They followed her in. The side door led to the scullery, a tiled room with sinks the size of baths. Beyond was the kitchen with two coal-stoked ranges, three Agas and six buzzing refrigerators. Huge copper pans lined the walls. A bewigged and liveried footman eyed Lady Wellingham and quickly hid a cigarette between thumb and forefinger.

Further along the serpentine passageways the doors changed from white-painted wood to polished mahogany. The hubbub of conversation grew louder. Lady Wellingham walked straight on to the door at the end which was larger and more imposing than the others. She pushed it open . . .

Loretta tried not to gasp or gape. She almost succeeded. Goose pimples broke out on her skin. The scale and the elegance of the scene amazed her. A carved mahogany staircase wide enough for a busy department store rose to a gallery forty feet above her. A dozen gilt candelabras each with a dozen candles rose above the banisters and lit the room with a soft shimmering light. Portraits of rather bosomy ladies were stacked three high on the walls. She looked up. There was a mural on the ceiling too — Venus or Aphrodite or someone, surrounded by handmaidens, cupids, and some very old, lecherous-looking men.

All her life, Loretta had been used to living in undersized rooms. To her, a hall — if this were a hall — meant an entryphone and a hook for a coat. Here, four or five hundred guests could circulate at their ease without so much as ruffling their clothes. Yes, she decided with a shiver, this was style.

André had lent her a ransom in rubies and diamonds, yet still she felt underdressed. A fleet of tiaras sparkled around her on waves of lacquered hair. The guests were all so elegant, so poised, they made her feel awkward and stiff. Most were in eighteenth-century costume, but she also spotted Captain Hook, Humpty Dumpty, Boadicea, and a rather dykey Joan of Arc. Marie-Antoinette was definitely the flavour of the month. Loretta had counted fifteen so far.

Lady Wellingham's face fell. 'So much for Marie-Antoinette. If anyone asks, I'm the Comtesse du Barry.'

André grimaced. 'Barry who?'

Loretta picked a glass of champagne off a nearby tray and took two lengthy sips. The bubbles went up her nose and made her splutter. She scanned the room for a friendly face. There was not a soul she recognised. Everyone seemed to know everyone else; everyone but her. She watched as they sipped their champagne, as they flirted and talked, as they patted their hair and fingered their jewels, as they appraised the new arrivals.

Panic-stricken, she looked around for André or Lady Wellingham. They had vanished. She was alone. The occasional enquiring gaze flicked over her, making her feel desperately self-conscious. She felt the blush on her cheeks deepen. It was great to be here and to see this wonderful spectacle, but for all her beautiful accessories, for all the hours she had spent at the hairdresser, she felt like a creature from another planet. She wished she were invisible so that her embarrassment and awkwardness would not show.

She must have been standing there by herself for some time now because already her glass was empty. She plunged forward into the throng in search of André. She circled the room twice. Christ, she wasn't normally this shy. At home, she would have gone up to someone by now and introduced herself, but here something held her back.

At last a face she thought she recognised. From the shop, maybe? A middle-aged woman with wide dimples on each cheek. From her neck hung a rock the size of an ice cube. One of the Marie-Antoinettes. She really had to talk to someone. Loretta dodged through the crowd until she was close to the woman.

Well, here goes . . . 'Hello. Didn't we meet in New York? Loretta Lorenz.'

The woman's eyes looked straight through her, as expressionless as marbles. 'I think not,' she growled. 'I haven't been to New York in an age. Now if you'll excuse me . . .?'

'Yes, of course.' And then she remembered. Newspapers. Television. That woman had received the biggest divorce settlement ever in Britain. Something about moral turpitude . . .

Loretta swallowed hard and turned away. As she raised her eyes, she saw a tall, thin man in a kilt staring straight at her from only a foot away. He smiled.

She quickly lowered her eyes again. She wished she could relax, act natural, but the stare of strange men always made her shudder. It made her feel so vulnerable. Of course a part of her was flattered by the attention, but always it carried an implicit threat.

The man walked up to her. 'How do you do? I saw you standing over there and I thought maybe . . .'

A toothy redhead appeared from nowhere. She too was in Scottish dress. She slipped a thin freckled arm into the man's. 'Darling, the music's terrif.' She turned towards

Loretta and smiled. Loretta had met that particular smile before. It meant, hands off or I'll smash your teeth in. 'Now, if you'll excuse us . . .?'

The man grinned a weak apology as Loretta watched them go.

'Oh, there you are.' It was Lady Wellingham. One of her beauty patches had fallen off, leaving a slight red mark on an otherwise white face. 'Having fun? I'm sure you are. You look a picture. So fresh, so very beautiful. I do so envy youth . . .

'Silly of me — I forgot to point out your hostess. Always useful to know if you're a guest. We don't want to risk an unnecessary *faux pas*, now do we? My dear, what has happened to your shoes? Covered in mud. That's the trouble with satin, it gets ruined so easily.'

Loretta was about to reply but Lady Wellingham cut her short with a flick of her fan.

'Over there. By the main entrance, facing us. Can you see the short grey-haired woman dressed as the Queen of Sheba? That's Elizabeth Rudlow. It's really such a pity George can't be here. He loved a good party.

'On her left is her daughter, Camilla . . . God, what is she wearing? She looks like the Bride of Dracula. Not suitable at all, and hideous to boot. Elizabeth must be losing her marbles. As soon as I have a chance, I really must have a word with her about parental guidance.

'And on the far left is her son, Hugh . . . Oh there you are, André! Have you seen the mural?' She flicked her fan towards the ceiling. 'It's by Matthew Cotes Wyatt. Venus at her toilet.'

'Really, Veronica,' André grinned, 'isn't the poor girl allowed privacy *anywhere*?'

Loretta's gaze was fixed on Hugh Rudlow. He was dressed as an eighteenth-century buck with breeches and a lace ruffle, just like a character out of the romantic novels which she had read in her teens. Very fitting, she thought, for the future owner of an eighteenth-century palace. Curious, she moved closer. The slightly effeminate costume did not make him look any the less dangerous. He was powerfully built if a shade under six feet. He had a strong jaw and deep-set hazel eyes.

His eyes scanned the room. For a moment, she thought that they caught hers. She turned quickly away and resumed her study of Venus.

She smiled at her own idiocy.

André was up to his tricks again. He skipped around the room, pirouetting in his tutu, his silver wand high above his head. 'Lords, Ladies and Gentlemen,' he announced in a high-pitched whine, 'your own real life Fairy Godmother is gonna cast a spell. Are the children all ready now?'

No one seemed to be paying much attention to him but André was in one of his hyperactive moods and too drunk to care.

'Zap! Ptazz!' He shook his arm. In a cloud of glitter, a rubber spider slid out of his sleeve and splashed into Napoleon's champagne glass.

André laughed out loud. Lady Wellingham looked the other way, quickly distancing herself from the scene. One of the Marie-Antoinettes said, 'Oh dear.' The Emperor deposited the glass with the spider on a nearby tray and picked up a fresh one without a word. He was distinctly unamused.

Loretta winced. She stepped forward and gave André

her arm to lean on. Immediately she felt his whole weight.

'Oh,' he crooned as she led him away, 'it's so tiring spreading light and happiness around the world. So tiring. But do not despair, my fair Cinderella, I have saved a little magic for you.' He flourished the wand wildly, narrowly missing a very punk Struwwelpeter. 'To you I grant the pleasure of escorting your dear old Fairy Godmother for a dance,' his voice lowered to a growl, 'that is, unless you wanna turn into pumpkin pie.'

'No, no, no,' Loretta answered in mock horror. 'I am a good girl, I am. But . . . don't you think you might like to sit quietly for a while? We could have a dance later.'

'No.' He shook his head vehemently. 'This is a dance, so dance we will. And though I say so myself, you're just about the prettiest girl here.'

'Oh, no, André, there are dozens – '

'No. No one to touch you. If only . . . if only you'd let yourself loosen up just a little bit.'

'André! I am what I am.' She lowered her voice. 'And it's not easy when you don't know a soul here.'

'Forget it.' He smiled. 'Lead me to where the wise fools play.'

The ballroom throbbed to the sound of bass guitar and drums. Spinning searchlights traversed and scoured the room, splashing ever-changing colours over the elaborate plasterwork ceiling, the pink silk walls and the strutting harlequins on the parquet floor.

Loretta weaved between the dancers, through the smoke and sudden flashes of light. Velvet-clad arms, bejewelled hands and silk-stockinged legs flashed in and out of the darkness. Here, Humpty Dumpty's tiny buckled feet hoofed beneath his painted smile. There, a gorilla tap-danced. She smiled at André, let the music take her and flicked her feet to the beat.

On the small stage, the lead guitarist, a man with a wide mouth and twinkling green eyes, grabbed the microphone. He nestled the stand between his legs and spat out the words. His voice was hard and strong and sensual. Lady Rudlow's daughter, the Bride of Dracula, was up there too. She had a streak of white in her otherwise jet black hair. Her green-fingernailed hand rested on the guitarist's shoulder. She boogied to the beat, then leaned over towards the microphone, sang 'Yeah', and giggled. The guitarist smiled and blew her a kiss.

André's face was set in stone. Poor dear, that was the third time she had seen him hitch up his tutu. André did have beautiful ankles, but, if she were being brutally honest, he did not really have the knees for a tutu.

André was a follower of the minimalist school of dancing where anything other than a slight shuffle of the feet was thought of as an immoderate waste of energy.

She leaned towards him and shouted above the music, 'Anything wrong?'

'I don't know how you girls do it,' he groaned. 'These shoes are killing me. When the music stops, that's it. *Finito.*'

Lights flashed in her eyes, the tempo was faster now. For the first time that evening she felt the tension leaving her body as her limbs slowly curled and swayed to the music. She gazed at the other dancers, their smiles, their hoofing, their display. There was a ripping sound as a flailing pirate's hook caught in the flounces of a dress; then, later, a yell as Boadicea's trident impaled soft flesh.

The music stopped too soon. André sighed with relief. He was visibly wilting; even his wig had lost its curls.

Loretta glanced towards the door. Hugh leaned against a marble pillar, casually surveying the dancers. A sleek, dark-haired girl stood by his side. She was dressed as some temptress or other – Cleopatra, Salome, Mata Hari. Anyone who might have worn a figure-hugging, gleaming black, serpentine Azzedine Alaia and long black gloves.

Loretta squinted through the haze of smoke as the lights flashed over them. That girl looked familiar: the brown eyes; the thin, slightly pinched face; the sultry turn of the lips. Where had she seen her before? Of course, New York. The shop. Marie-Louise . . . Marie-Louise Vosse. A go-getting, diamond-snatching, grab-it-quick trollop. The kind of woman mamas' nightmares are made of.

So how had she wormed her way in here? And not only in here, but centre-stage next to . . . wait, she was tilting her head, saying something into Hugh's ear. He was stooping slightly, his cheek level with one ruffed wrist. He smiled. His eyes glinted. Yes, there did seem to be some sort of understanding between them, even intimacy – but she must be mistaken, she had to be. A man like Hugh would be able to see through Marie-Louise. Her ambition was utterly naked.

His arm was around Marie-Louise now and he was looking at her questioningly. She was grinning at him and shaking her head as if fielding an improper suggestion. Major eye contact. The bitch!

Loretta turned. André's lime green wig with its emerald and diamond tiara was bobbing towards the bar. 'André, *please*,' she called, 'you can't leave now. It's my favourite song.' She'd felt the tension return at the thought of yet another circuit of the Great Hall. 'Please, please!' She reached out for his arm.

'OK,' he sighed. 'Just one more.'

The moment she was back on the dance floor, she closed her eyes, took two deep breaths and listened intently to the music. She felt the beat surge through her body, let the rhythm become part of her. Slowly, her feet began to move.

Ever since childhood, she had loved to dance. Whenever she had wanted to relax, whenever she had wanted to forget, she had locked the door of her room, turned the music up loud and danced and danced.

She remembered a great routine she had learnt in the dance studio which fitted this music perfectly. Left foot over, cross your legs, sharp turn, swivel your hips, shoulders back, head up, pout. Her fingers ran down her body. Her dress swirled and swooshed. She flung her head back, twirled herself around.

A group of three men, standing by the bar, burst into shouts of encouragement. One of them gave her a catcall: 'Yahoo!'

She shuddered for a moment, her arms fell to her sides, then the music took hold again and her smile returned. She lost herself in the throbbing beat that pulsated in her skull, flowed effortlessly through her limbs. There was more room for her to work out now. Couples were leaving the floor, standing and watching her. Some were chuckling, some egging her on.

She gasped for breath. The heat in the room was getting to her. A cold band of sweat trickled down her spine. André had gone and the gorilla had taken his place. She put her arms around his hairy body, wriggled her hips, then spun around again and again. Feet stamped. Hands clapped. Whistles and shouts rose above the drum of the music.

On and on she went, basking in the applause until finally the footsore gorilla too slowed. His paws fell to his side. He bowed and stumbled off the floor.

She had only taken one pace towards the bar when a group of men encircled her, gesticulating, blathering nonsense at her. Then she saw Hugh's burgundy tail coat, the glint of his gold buttons. The others separated to let him pass. He fixed his deep-set hazel eyes on her, and for a second she feared that he knew that she was a gatecrasher and was going to throw her out, then he smiled and said, 'I've brought you a drink.' He handed her first a tumbler of water, then a glass of champagne. 'Where did you learn to dance like that?' he asked. His voice was low and soft.

Beads of sweat pearled her breasts. 'Oh,' she said lightly, 'High school.'

He grinned. 'Seriously? Dancing like that, you could have been a professional.' His eyes flicked up and down her. He smiled.

Marie-Louise appeared from nowhere. She slipped her hand through Hugh's arm. 'Oh, but she *is* a professional,' she sang sweetly. 'A professional sales girl, aren't you, my dear? She works in a jewellery store in New York. She's always very helpful to the customers.'

Loretta took a deep breath and forced her best smile. Hugh ignored the remark.

Loretta tried not to feel self-conscious as his eyes swept over her tangle of chestnut curls, her wide sapphire eyes, flushed cheeks and low neckline. 'Once you're recovered,' he asked, 'may I have the next dance?'

'Oh, I don't know,' she teased.

'In England it is considered very impolite not to dance with the host,' he said in formal tones, but his eyes were laughing. He turned to Marie-Louise, 'Now if you'll excuse us . . . ?' and moved off before she had time to reply.

Loretta put down her glass and followed Hugh on to the floor. The other dancers separated as they passed. The music was slow and soulful now. She shuddered as his arm encircled her. It had been a long time since she had danced with a total stranger. Of course, she had been approached often enough in bars, on the disco floor, at the dances to which André had taken her, but almost always she had refused. She did not want to feel the touch of alien skin, to feel their bodies next to her, to hear their sweet talk.

Here, though, in this cultivated, sophisticated world, she felt deeply flattered that the man who could have his pick of the girls had chosen her. Her replies to his simple questions sounded tongue-tied and awkward but he did not seem to mind. There was power and a quiet confidence in each of his movements. He definitely knew how to dance.

The music changed and still they danced on. Somehow he must have sensed her nervousness, because he was very gentle, very correct. His warm hazel eyes assured her, flattered her, egged her on, told her that nobody mattered in the room but her.

She hardly noticed the approach of the man in the butler's coat. She still swayed to the music as he whispered in Hugh's ear.

His arms fell to his side. 'I'm sorry,' he said, 'I must go. Where can I reach you?' He quickly scribbled Loretta's address and telephone number on the back of an envelope and slipped it inside his pocket. Then he kissed her on the cheek, bowed low, and was gone.

# Chapter 8

'OK, girls. Chop, chop!' Chatter stopped instantly. André was in one of his hyperactive moods despite the hour: 8.55 on a drizzly Monday morning. All the staff had been there since seven o'clock preparing for the first day of business.

He strutted around the showroom with a proprietorial air: nodding approvingly there; rearranging a show case there. Some he had already rearranged three times that morning. Wherever he went a cloud of eau-de-cologne followed in his wake.

The walls were pale sapphire blue, the curtains of matching embroidered silk. Small circular showcases shaped like portholes studded the walls. Long cases with even thicker brass frames formed an octagon in the centre of the room. Diamonds, sapphires, rubies and emeralds blazed and sparkled everywhere.

André straightened the diamond tie-pin on his silver tie and tugged at his white cuffs with their matching diamond and platinum links. He raised his arms and waited until there was complete silence before he began.

'Girls. Girls. Girls. Welcome to the first day of business. I want you to know that I love you all. And, darlings, have we got a thrilling time ahead of us! This showroom – it's *not* a showroom, it's a palace, for a palace is the only setting possible for the most exciting collection of jewellery ever devised.' He cupped an ear with one hand. 'The jewels positively whisper "buy me". Can you hear them? Now, now, no tittering. I'm being quite serious.'

Still the girls giggled. Whatever else might be said about André, he was a great showman.

He moved over to the centre showcase, his expression changing as the businessman in him took over. 'All you have to concentrate on, my darlings, is the small matter of clinching the deal. It might be with a crown prince, or someone you read about in the papers every day, or even a cocaine smuggler – who cares? The technique is the same. Don't be bashful. Don't be fazed. Put on gentle pressure that does not seem like pressure, understand? Flatter them, cajole them, make them feel good. Make them feel important. Let them know – whoever they are – that in an André Swert creation they are announcing to the world that they have arrived, and arrived in style.'

A finger pointed towards each girl in turn. 'I want you all to make a resolution, darlings, it's quite simple. Anyone who comes in here with so much as a credit card in his pocket will never, never, go out empty-handed. Got it? OK, we open in three minutes. To your stations, girls!'

André beckoned to Loretta. She walked over. Like all the other girls, she was wearing the André Swert regulation uniform: a sapphire blue silk blouse with a matching bow and a dark blue skirt.

'Well,' he sighed, 'here we are. We've done it. All we need now are the embarrassingly, self-consciously rich.' He edged towards a chair. 'And in my particular case, the name of a first class chiropodist. After that dance my feet are marshmallows.' He flicked back his white bouffant curls. 'What sacrifices we make in the name of glamour, my dear. The discomfort!' He looked beyond her. His mouth twitched. 'Shona dear, re-tie the bow on your blouse. It should be soft and flowing, not like something off a package in the mail.'

'Yes, Mr Swert.'

André glanced at his watch. One minute to go.

'Thank you so much for taking me to the party,' said Loretta once she had regained his attention.

'Don't mention it.' He smiled. 'It was my privilege. You were the belle of the ball.'

'It's very nice of you to say so, but — '

'Me, exaggerate?' André's hands clasped his chest. 'Do the lame walk, the blind see? And anyway, my dear, it wasn't entirely altruistic. The more you get known, the more friends you make in the right circles, the more useful you'll be to me.'

The security buzzer sounded. André turned, galvanised. The commissionaire touched his cap. The first potential customer entered the shop: a small man with hair like sealskin and a lopsided grin. André ran over to greet him and shook him enthusiastically by the hand. It soon became apparent, however, that the man was a jeweller weighing up the competition. No sale.

Apart from a candy-floss blonde with legs a lot longer than her charge account, and a gaggle of journalists from the glossier magazines, the shop was relatively quiet until lunchtime. Then the men arrived: first, a guilt-ridden husband in search of a peace offering for his wife; then another, no less worried, with an acquisitive mistress; then a man alone who bought two identical bracelets, one for the wife and one — allegedly — for his daughter.

Loretta had just finished serving him when the telephone rang.

Shona, her new flatmate, picked up the receiver. 'André Swert, jeweller extraordinaire, how can we help you? . . . Just a moment, sir.' She put her hand over the mouthpiece. 'Loretta,' she called, 'it's for you. A personal call.' A grin puckered her plump cheeks.

Loretta strode towards the telephone. She grabbed the receiver. 'Yes?'

It was Bob.

She flicked back her hair with a sigh and pulled up a chair. 'Yes, how good of you to call . . . I'm fine . . . Settling in OK . . . Sharing a flat with one of the girls who works here . . . Yes, Bob . . .'

The buzzer sounded. She glanced towards the door and felt the warmth rising in her cheeks. Bob kept talking but she no longer heard him. Despite the sober pin-striped suit he wore today, Hugh Rudlow still had something of the look of a Regency buck in that arrogant stance, that self-confident curl of the lip. 'Sorry, yes, what was that, Bob? . . . Yes, I do hope you'll be able to come over soon . . . Yes, it's work, work, work.'

A couple leant over the central display cabinet, blocking Hugh from her sight. She saw André cross the room towards him, wringing his hands, salivating like a wolf at the sight of a juicy, young chicken. Then she heard André's high-pitched laugh. 'I'm sorry. I'm so sorry,' he exclaimed. 'I just did not recognise you without your gorgeous costume on and those divine buckskin breeches.' He laughed again. 'I suppose you didn't recognise me in mufti either.' He was beckoning Loretta with a frantic movement of his arm.

She nodded. 'I'm afraid I've got to go now, Bob.

André needs me. Thanks again for calling. Talk to you soon.' She put down the receiver, collected herself and slowly walked over to them.

'Hello.' She gave Hugh a quick smile, just warm enough.

He smiled back, tilting his head slightly to one side.

'Mr Rudlow would like to see around the showroom.' Though the tone of his voice was measured, André's eyes rolled mischievously. 'Will you take care of him?'

'Of course, André.' She turned to Hugh. Her eyes sparkled but her demeanour was that of the perfect salesgirl. 'Now, what would sir particularly like to see?'

'Er . . .' Hugh's eyes flicked over her. 'What have you got? Maybe some emeralds?'

'Certainly, sir.' She walked across to the central display cabinet. Her finger swept along the glass top. 'There are, of course, emeralds in these front showcases.' She pointed to a small emerald and diamond bracelet, a pair of matching earrings.

He glanced down at them casually, then back at her. The corner of his mouth curled again. One eyebrow lifted. 'Yes, they're nice enough, very pretty in fact, but not what you'd call serious pieces.'

'No.' Her shoulders rose a fraction. 'The stones are hardly noteworthy. They're just sorry-I-was-kept-late-at-the-office baubles.'

She had never expected to see Hugh again. Sure they had danced at the ball, but his world, the world of Conningsby Park, seemed only tangentially connected with her reality. 'We have others, of course. The real goodies are out the back.'

'Well . . . that is, if it wouldn't be too much trouble?'

She swallowed. 'Of course not. If sir would care to follow me?'

She led the way through the silk curtain to the rear of the shop. She did not turn but at each step was conscious of Hugh's presence close behind. 'If sir would take a seat.' She gestured towards a gilt armchair, in size and style more like a throne than an ordinary chair.

Loretta quickly killed the overhead light, leaving nothing but spots carefully placed to show the gems to their best advantage. They would do no harm to her own appearance either. 'I did enjoy our dance,' she said, almost involuntarily.

He crossed his legs and sat back like a pasha. 'So did I.'

'Yes, well . . .' She was brisk again. 'If sir would excuse me a moment?'

'Yes, but not for long.'

As soon as Loretta was out of sight, she took the opportunity to comb her hair and make a few temporary repairs to her make-up, then let herself into the walk-in safe. She returned with a tray covered with a black satin cloth. 'Now what would sir like to see first?' she asked half-mockingly. 'This, perhaps?'

She held before him a flashing tiara whose central stone was as big as a child's fist. Diamonds in gradually diminishing sizes spread from the central flower motif of emeralds, like rays from a sea-green sun.

'Very well,' he nodded. 'Put it on.'

'Oh, no,' she said. Then, 'We really aren't supposed . . .'

'Put it on, damn it, Loretta.'

She smiled. 'If I must.' She swivelled the mirror on the gilt commode towards her, and looked into it as she placed the glittering jewel on her head. She scooped up her hair in her hands. 'There!' Feeling very regal, she turned towards him.

'Come here,' he ordered.

She did not move. 'Sir will appreciate the overall effect better from a reasonable distance,' she replied lightly. 'As you see, there's a matching necklace.' She turned away from him. Her hand trembled as she plucked the river of diamonds from its cushioned bed. She held it up to her throat. 'Of course,' she said, and her voice was suddenly high-pitched, 'this should be worn over a low-cut dress. Décolletage is infinitely more flattering to fine jewels, as I am sure sir is aware.'

'I can imagine,' he grinned, enjoying the game.

'Yes, I'm sure you can.'

'Put it on,' he said again.

She rolled her eyes heavenward and sighed. Again she turned to the mirror. Her fingers fumbled at the necklace's catch. The chair creaked. Suddenly she felt the warmth of his fingers on hers. She stiffened. His breath touched the nape of her neck. Her hands flew away. Very gently, he fastened the clasp. 'There,' he said softly in her ear, and she swallowed nervously.

She heard him return to his seat. 'Turn around,' he said.

Loretta took a deep breath. She knew that her cheeks were red. She turned.

'Perfection,' he announced.

She looked at the ceiling, at the floor, anywhere but straight at him.

'Thank you,' she murmured. 'Of course, I don't always wear quite so much jewellery during the day, except on my birthday.'

He grinned. 'And when is your birthday, Loretta?'

'Um,' she reached up and removed the tiara, 'if sir has seen enough . . .'

'No,' his voice was low, 'nothing like enough. Sir would like, for example, to see you for dinner this evening — if, that is, the perfect salesgirl is not otherwise engaged.'

Loretta sighed, closed her eyes and counted to ten. She was about to make some excuse, but then she thought of the alternative — a movie with Shona, television? The words came out all in a rush. 'April the fourth and that will be great,' she said, then, as an afterthought and with a wicked half-grin, 'Sir.'

# Chapter 9

Hugh double parked behind two Rolls-Royces and a Daimler. He tossed the keys to the liveried doorman with the dead-mouse moustache.

'If this is Berkeley Square,' remarked Loretta, 'who shot the nightingales?'

He shrugged and ushered her under the green awning down the steep, narrow basement steps, past the whir of the news teleprinter in the gents' loo and the reception desk where he signed his name, through into the bar with its country house chic.

Twenty pairs of eyes stared at Hugh, then at her. He returned the occasional slight smile or nod, barely detectable sign of acknowledgements like a secretive bidder at an auction.

One girl was staring at him intently from her seat in a high-backed chair on the far side of the room. She had a full mane of swept back blonde hair and very clear blue eyes. If looks could kill, hers would have given him a spontaneous coronary arrest.

Hugh merely smiled at her with a slight shrug of the shoulders and walked on.

Loretta thought the most tactful thing to do would be to pretend not to notice, but curiosity got the better of her. 'Who's that?'

'Who?'

'The girl staring at you.'

'Oh, her. Her name's Fiona Cummings,' he replied without further elucidation, pushing open the swing doors and ushering Loretta through into the black twinkling night of Annabel's dining room. Mirrored columns reflected silver. The sounds of the discotheque rose and fell above the murmur of discreet voices, the ring of laughter.

A man with silver-grey hair stood in front of the leatherbound reservations book at a desk just inside the entrance.

'Any chance of a table, Louis?' asked Hugh.

'For two, Mr Rudlow? I'll see what I can do.' He nodded to one of the waiters. 'Number seven.'

Loretta was placed at a banquette against the wall. She breathed in deeply and smiled. 'They seem to know you here, Hugh.'

'I have been here, from time to time.'

Close to, Hugh was not conventionally good-looking, but that did not concern her. She had met enough wet, pretty men in her time to fill a laundry. She was impressed by the way he seemed so at ease in the place, but then she remembered — it would be as natural for him to be at ease here as for her in the pizzeria a block from her old New York apartment.

The man at the next table looked vaguely familiar, but Loretta couldn't place him. He was dark and fat and swarthy, altogether one of the ugliest men she had ever seen. Beneath his thick black glasses, his jowls seemed to move with a life of their own. His knuckles were pudgy and hairy and covered with rings.

His companion must have been at most half his age.

She had a kind of dreamlike beauty about her with her long, perfectly coiffeured golden hair and pale skin. There was not a line on her face. Only a slightly distant look in the eyes marred the effect. His secretary perhaps? Then Loretta saw the ring. His wife.

A menu flashed open before her. She could hardly stop herself from grinning like a fool. Yes, this was happening to her. In less than a fortnight little Loretta Lorenz had rocketed from the wrong side of the tracks to the high ground of British society.

'What would you like? I'm going to start with the *gnocchi verde*,' announced Hugh, 'then the sea bass.'

'What a good idea,' replied Loretta. She did not have any clear idea of what *gnocchi verde* was, but did not think this was the time to reveal her ignorance. A lady would know, wouldn't she? She had heard that English young ladies were sent to finishing school where they were taught such things, together with how to balance books on your head (deportment); how to get out of a sports car without showing too much leg (disembarkment); and how to deal with men who were not safe in taxis (disembowelment). Loretta's finishing school had been the school of experience. The certificates weren't printed on vellum but you could learn a lot at a drive-in movie house when the boys in the audience had some beer inside them. 'I'll have some *gnocchi verde* too,' she said. It sounded sophisticated.

Apart from a quick glance at the menu, Hugh's eyes had not left her since they sat down. They were softening by the moment. He was gazing at her now as they sat quite silent but strangely at ease. Even the sounds of the discotheque, the prattle from neighbouring tables, the chink of glasses, did not encroach on them.

Finally he said: 'Loretta, I want to know all about you. Everything.'

To her astonishment, she found herself talking fluently and easily. She told him all about her step-father and his chain of laundromats; about her step-brother, the scholar; about her year at New York College of Art and Design, where she majored in fashion design . . . By the time the *gnocchi* arrived — little green sausages of spinach and cheese — they had reached her first job as a junior designer at Sazzy Furst. What a disaster that had been! She could still mimic her first boss real well: ' "See what they are buying at Macy's, at Bloomingdales and on Fifth. Check the prices and feel the cloth. We will do it cheaper, cheaper, and cheaper, and *still* we make a profit." Six months ripping off other people's stuff. Not one original design. "Why take risks, when you can have dresses that sell already?" So frustrating!'

The sea bass was cold by the time she got round to it, but it was delicious anyway. The white wine had a very fancy label. Premier cru.

Hugh seemed so much more human and natural than she had imagined possible. Not stuck up at all. He seemed really interested in her life, and in what had happened to her. He talked to her as an equal, he sought her views — all with the same easy, natural charm.

Momentarily his eyes held a distant look. She guessed that he must be thinking about his father. 'How is he?' she asked.

'My father?' He took a deep breath. 'So, so.'

She felt like telling him about her own father, about the way she had borne that loss, found strength within herself to cope, but that was something she had never discussed with a man before. Maybe some other time. She laid her hand lightly on his sleeve. 'I feel for you,' she said softly. 'I really do. I wish I could do something to help.'

'But you are.' He mustered a broad smile. 'In good company, nothing seems quite so terrible.'

Later, they laughed as they danced. He pressed her to him, and though she was always on guard, somehow she felt that it was all right. The power which she sensed within him frightened her a little, but she did not want him to stop. It was a long time before she noticed how empty the place had become, the way the waiters were standing around, watching and waiting.

Outside in the cold still air, she thought she heard a nightingale at last. Hugh pointed out that the brakes in London taxis just happened to squeak that way. She laughed and squeezed his hand.

He escorted her to the door of her flat and kissed her softly on the lips. He did not ask to come in. 'Thank you,' she sighed contentedly, 'it's been a wonderful evening.'

Already, despite herself, Loretta was powerfully drawn towards Hugh. That frightened her. In a way she hoped he would not ring her again, that she would not be drawn deeper into something over which she did not have complete control.

In the flat she switched on the light, walked over to the fridge and took a long drink of iced water. As the liquid cooled her dry throat, she assured herself repeatedly that her mind must have been temporarily unhinged by the extravagance of Conningsby and of Annabel's, by being away from home, by the wine and the dancing and the suddenness of it all.

She glanced up at the clock. Four thirty-five. She hurried into her bedroom. She had to get up in precisely three hours. She would land back with a thump in the real world then, that was for sure.

# Chapter 10

The nurse on duty turned around and gave a quick, harassed smile. It was more a nervous reflex than a gesture of welcome. 'Yes, I think it's all right to go in, dear.'

Camilla nodded. Her pale face, devoid of make-up, rose like a flower on its stem from the thin black woollen tube she wore. She curled her fingers into a fist and hesitantly raised her hand towards the door. She knocked twice and slowly twisted the handle. The door opened a fraction. The pumping and puffing sound of each mechanical breath filled her ears. She saw the corner of the small white windowless room; the bank of machinery on the aluminium trolley, flashing lights at her like a hi-fi amplifier; the curved iron footboard; the bulge of feet and legs under the candlewick bedspread. She froze.

'Well, are we going in or aren't we?' called a voice from within.

'Yes.' She took a deep breath. 'Yes.'

She stepped forward and saw him. A maze of plastic worms stretched from his body. One from his wrist was connected to a bag of fluid hanging on the wall, another to a bag beside the bed, a third led into his mouth, secured with sticking plaster. His usually florid complexion was now a translucent baby-pink. His face had narrowed into a grotesque parody of the man she once knew.

Her lower lip trembled. Despite the weeks that had elapsed since his fall, despite her daily visits, she still felt revulsion at her first sight of him, a kind of horror.

'Is he quite comfortable, nurse?' she asked, not taking her eyes off her father.

'Yes,' came the reply, 'quite comfortable.'

Camilla waited for the first wave of nausea to pass, then very slowly took a step forward. She stood staring for a while, then finally stretched a single cautious finger towards him. It twitched. She lowered it very gently, very lightly, on to his forehead. The skin was smooth and warm and slightly moist.

Hesitantly, she leaned forward and pursed her lips. She kissed him just above the eyebrow. 'Daddy,' she sighed, 'though you couldn't . . . be there, I just want to say thank you for the party anyway.'

She pulled up a wooden chair and sat down beside the bed. 'Daddy?' she called softly.

'It's no use, love,' announced the nurse behind her. 'He can't hear you.'

Camilla turned. 'How . . . how can you be sure?'

The nurse looked small and squat and very white in the harsh fluorescent lighting. 'Sometimes they can be "locked in" — as we professionals call it. You've got to be careful then.' She held her hand to her mouth and yawned behind it. 'Sorry, love. Lady Rudlow asked the very same question. They all do. Mr Robinson said it was highly improbable in this case. State of the brain, you see.'

Camilla turned back to her father. 'They don't know everything.' Her nostrils flared at the sharp antiseptic edge to the warm musty air. 'Daddy?' she repeated, 'can you hear me? Can you hear me now? It's Camilla. Camilla!'

She stared at his unblinking eyes, at the long tube that separated his pale lips, the plasters that puckered the baby-pink skin.

'We never really did get to know one another, did we?' she mouthed to herself. 'We never did . . .'

All she heard in reply was the continual blowing and sucking of the machine, the amplified sigh.

'Just, I don't know − a chat, a few words of interest, of encouragement − I would have sacrificed everything for that.'

Her fingers pulled at the wool of her dress. 'If we had had five minutes a day − the time it took you to shave and brush your teeth − I would at least have . . . but we were like the dwarfs in the palace at Mantua. Little things locked away.'

She sniffed and fought back the tears, but still they came, tumbling down her cheeks, varnishing her eyes. 'Were we not good enough for you, or did we just bore you? We tried, Daddy. Good God, we tried!'

A hand lightly brushed her shoulder. She started.

'Would you like a cup of tea, love, and a nice biscuit?'

She nodded and blinked up at the nurse's face.

'I couldn't help overhearing.'

'God, was I . . .?' Camilla blushed. 'I'm sorry.'

'Don't take it so badly. I'm sure he loved you. There now, don't upset yourself so. Take my advice, that's quite enough for today.'

'Maybe you're right.' She searched in her bag for a handkerchief. 'Tell me one thing, though. There's absolutely no hope, is there? None at all?'

The nurse shook her head. 'Brain has gone. I'm sorry.'

Camilla gazed at the nurse through wet eyes. 'Why . . . why all this, then?' she pleaded. 'Why can't . . .?'

'Ooh, that's not up to me, love. I only do what I'm told. You must ask Mr Robinson.'

'I know what they said . . . it's just so . . .' Camilla wiped her eyes and blew her nose. 'Has Mummy been in today?'

'Yes, this morning.' The nurse pressed a buzzer hanging from a length of flex. 'But I haven't seen the foreign lady yet.'

'Who?'

'The foreign lady. Can't say I know her name.' The nurse glanced at her watch. 'I would have expected her to have been here by now. If she was coming, that is.'

Camilla checked her reflection in the back of a surgical metal dish and smoothed back her hair. 'I thought visiting was restricted to family.'

'It's none of my business, but she said she *was* family.'

'Oh? Well, thank you very much.' Camilla took one last look at Lord Rudlow and walked out into the corridor.

A white-coated orderly was swabbing down the floor outside the lift. Two nurses were chatting behind a glass partition. The smell of cabbage and fried fish came from behind a closed door.

She was just about to take the lift when the tea trolley rattled around the corner.

'Tea?'

'Yes, please,' Camilla replied.

The trolley stopped. The woman gave her a warm smile. 'Sugar? No, you don't, do you?'

'Clever of you to remember.' Camilla rubbed her swollen eyes with the back of her hand and smiled back.

'Oh, I know them all.' The tea lady twisted the tap on

the tea urn. 'They only have to ask once and I lodge it in my little computer here.' The finger of her free hand touched her very blonde permed hair.

'Perhaps . . . perhaps you could help me?' Camilla began hesitantly. 'I was going to ask Sister. It's probably nothing but the nurse said something about a foreign woman coming to visit my father . . .'

'Oh, yes,' the tea lady nodded. 'I know who you mean. I'm afraid we're right out of shortbread, dear. But I've got some Rich Tea, and somewhere there should be one packet left of ginger − '

'The Rich Tea will be fine, thank you. What's this woman like?'

'Most unusual.' Her lip curled. 'Takes it black. Watered down. The first time she came, she asked for lemon. Now where did she imagine I was going to find a lemon?'

'Yes, yes,' Camilla said impatiently. 'But what does she look like?'

'Look like? Can't recall exactly. There are so many people always popping in and out here, you can't remember them all − though she's always nicely turned out, I do recall that. Foreign, you say?' She nodded. 'I guessed as much. Maybe you should ask Sister.' She was about to hand Camilla the cup of tea when she stared behind her along the corridor. 'Talk of the devil,' she said, 'there she is.'

A tall, elegant woman in an immaculate black velvet suit had just turned into the corridor.

Camilla tilted her head slightly and watched the woman as she walked towards them. A black pill box hat perched on shoulder-length auburn hair. A spotted veil half concealed an olive-skinned face to just above a pair of shiny red lips. A black Chanel bag swung from her shoulder. There was something familiar about the slightly pinched face, about the casual yet purposeful stride, but Camilla could not place her.

Then the woman's pace slowed. She turned her head this way and that, as if she had suddenly remembered something. Her eyes were indistinct white ovals underneath the veil. One hand closed around the gold chain of her bag. She spun on her heel and began retracing her steps.

Camilla ran towards her. 'Excuse me? Were you by any chance looking for Lord Rudlow's room?'

The woman ignored her. She walked on, quickening her pace.

Camilla skidded along the floor behind her. 'Excuse me? Excuse me! Can I help you?'

She was almost parallel with the woman now. Still she could not place her. Then she smelt the heavy scent the woman was wearing and she remembered . . . The Italian woman. The Italian woman with the fantastic clothes.

'Hello,' she paused for breath, 'I'm Camilla Rudlow. I think we've met?'

The woman stopped. 'Camilla? Yes, of course, at Conningsby. Little Camilla.' Her voice was surprisingly deep. 'What a good memory you have. You could not have been more than ten or eleven . . .' the red lips smiled ' . . . and now quite a beauty.'

That's right. It was coming back to her. The Italian woman and her husband − a short, dark man − had been frequent weekend guests at Conningsby at one time. One visit she had worn a different, fantastic outfit every day. Once, she had given Camilla a model gondola that lit up with fairy lights.

'Thank you. Have you come here to see Daddy?'

The woman's lips quivered for a moment before she replied: 'Yes . . . yes, I had. But I don't want to intrude. It's not important.' Her head rose slightly. 'I'll come back some other time . . . *Ciao*.' Already she was moving away.

'No, I've already been in,' Camilla called after her.

The woman gave no reply but kept on walking.

Once more, Camilla ran after her. 'You've been here every day, haven't you? Why?'

'Not every day.'

'Well, most days then.'

The woman's mouth made a nervous little movement. 'What is this? An inquisition?' she snapped. 'Isn't losing a loved one enough?'

The veil was drawn tightly over her handsome features but even through the mesh Camilla could see the running mascara, the pain in her eyes. Suddenly she felt extraordinarily possessive of her father. She resented this woman's proprietorial tone.

She reached out and grabbed her arm. Through the velvet, it was trembling.

The woman's eyes blazed with indignation. Her lip curled. 'Leave me alone!' she said sharply. 'Please.'

Camilla relaxed her grip a little.

The woman tugged herself free. Her features crumpled behind the veil. She wavered a moment on her high heels, then walked on.

'Oh, Christ!' shrieked Camilla. 'So that's it. That's it! Daddy . . . *Daddy* . . . how could you?' Slowly she slumped down on to the floor and covered her face with her hands.

# Chapter 11

Every morning now after Loretta had had a date with Hugh, the girls in the shop would ask her where she had gone, what she had eaten, who had been there. She had always been led to believe that the English were a reserved race, but that did not seem to stop them asking what were really rather personal questions.

Zoe, the slim brunette, seemed to have a particular knack for guessing when Loretta had been out with Hugh the previous evening. The first time it had happened Loretta had suspected Shona of betraying her confidence and had asked indignantly: 'How do you know?'

Zoe had grinned. She had gently squeezed Loretta's arm and cooed very softly. 'It's written all over your face, dear.'

That had shocked her. She had always thought of herself as an intensely private person. It had surprised her, frightened her a little, that her inner emotions were so visible.

Reluctantly, she had also to admit that her work was suffering just a little bit. On a couple of occasions she had forgotten to return a ring or bracelet to the locked cabinet immediately after the customer had finished with it. Once she had lost the tag with the coded price attached to a ring, and André had been forced to search through the ledger. That certainly had never happened before. She had always prided herself on her professionalism.

It was not as if she were excessively tired, because as often as not, Hugh had an early morning meeting to attend and did not want a late night. It was more that, despite herself, she could not stop her mind wandering back to him and their last date, to something he had said or their parting kiss, especially if business in the shop was slow.

She had asked herself a thousand times: 'Why me?' Surely there must be hundreds, if not thousands, of girls Hugh could have chosen who were as pretty as her, English and of his own class.

Two nights ago she had asked Shona the very same question. Her flatmate had hugged her, and grinned as if in some way it had been a stupid question. She had made Loretta a mug of Horlicks and then answered, 'Why not? I mean, he has to choose *somebody*, and why the hell shouldn't that somebody be you?'

'Yes,' Loretta had replied, 'but that doesn't answer the question, does it? I mean – why he chose me rather than somebody else.'

Shona shrugged dismissively. 'Look, if I knew what made the perfect match, I'd be making a fortune running a dating agency, now wouldn't I? I don't know. I simply do not know. But nobody could deny that you're pretty – beautiful, even – provided you don't count first thing in the morning! And opposites attract. From my in-depth reading of the *Daily Mail*, I'd say that the English aristocracy has a definite *penchant* for foreign girls. You're always reading about some Earl or Marquis marrying a Swede or German or American. Don't ask me why.'

'Oh, not that I was thinking of marriage,' Loretta said hurriedly. 'We're only dating, that's all. But I hope that it's not just . . . not just that he finds me physically attractive.' She shuddered then.

'I am sure there's more to it, much more,' Shona replied consolingly. 'It's just that — hell, how do I say this? — you should be careful, that's all. Try and keep your feet on the ground, hmm? I am not saying that everything isn't going to work out in the most wonderful way possible . . . but I would hate to see you hurt. Tread carefully, OK?'

Loretta bit her lip and nodded. Of course there had been a small voice inside her which had told her to expect the worst, to run for cover while she still had time, but after every date the voice had become a little less insistent. It had been very loud and clear when on their third date Hugh had kissed her on the lips for the first time, but now, when he kissed her, it barely bothered to make even a token protest.

Sometimes she had to pinch herself for reassurance that what had happened to her over the last month had not been just some kind of protracted day dream from which she would awake suddenly, alone and afraid.

Hugh had rung her the very next morning after their evening at Annabel's and asked her out later that week. They had gone to Tramp and had a great time. Since then, he had seen her on average twice a week. She knew, though, that on many evenings he had to work late at the plant, especially now that the board of the company had confirmed his appointment as acting managing director.

Sometimes he took her to a fancy restaurant like San Lorenzo or L'Arlequin, and whenever they could they went dancing. Sometimes they dined alone, sometimes in a group. He took her on a yacht off the Isle of Wight, to the races and to weekend parties in two other houses – neither of which had been a match for Conningsby.

In comparison, the other men she met seemed like poor carbon copies of the quintessential Englishman that she saw in Hugh. Some lacked his charm, others his power of command.

Although she could feel the tension rising between them, in all that time he had never laid a finger on her. And she had found the strangest thing happening to her: for the first time in her life, when she thought of men her mind had not been sent reeling back to her father's betrayal or that awful time in the elevator. Instead she had thought of her dance with Hugh at Conningsby, of their quiet suppers together, of the good times – dancing, sailing, partying – when they laughed and had fun.

An even greater surprise had been the dream she had had the previous night. In it, Hugh had come to her in her sleep and very gently, very slowly, made love to her. She had never, ever had a dream like that before. She had woken up with her hair and forehead damp with sweat. She had felt deeply embarrassed, ashamed even, as she had pulled down her nightdress and scurried off to the bathroom.

This was not like her. It was not the way Loretta Lorenz behaved.

She had gazed at her reflection in the bathroom mirror in disbelief, trying to come to terms with this unfamiliar creature who now inhabited her body. Then the realisation had struck her that for the first time in her life she was living. Really living.

She had held on to the hand basin with trembling hands, thrown back her head and laughed.

Loretta was sitting at her desk putting the coded price tags on a new consignment of rings when the shop door swung open. She glanced up and her face fell. 'Uh, oh. Trouble.'

Marie-Louise was wearing a fitted red suit with large black buttons, gold medallion earrings, black tights and black suede shoes. She glanced only cursorily at the jewellery in the cabinet before her. Plainly she was not here for the trinkets. She peeled off her gloves with much the same look in her eye as a boxer when pulling on his.

'Loretta,' Shona walked over to her, 'a lady at the front counter is asking for you. Says she knows you.'

'I guessed as much.' Loretta nodded and stood up. 'I can handle it.'

Marie-Louise did not take her eyes off Loretta as she approached. Her mouth was set in a rigid, unconvincing smile. 'Hello, Loretta,' she said sweetly. 'So this is where you work. Charming.' She glanced about her. 'What a dreamy job for you. All day, every day, playing with other people's property.'

Loretta smiled back at Marie-Louise, as she would at any prospective customer. 'We sell and buy jewellery, Marie-Louise, if that is what you mean. What can we do for you?' she added in her most businesslike voice. 'Are you looking for something to buy or do you have something to sell? If you are in need of money fast, we can pay cash.'

'No, no, dear.' Marie-Louise shook her head forcefully. 'That's not why I'm here.' She fixed her gaze on Loretta. 'I came about a rather pathetic attempt at theft.'

131

Loretta smiled again. 'Oh, I'm sorry,' she said lightly. 'I guess you'd better visit the police station down the road. The British police, I'm told, are really great.'

'You know very well what I mean.' Marie-Louise leaned forward and glanced down at the glass cabinet in front of them. 'That little ruby and diamond bracelet is quite pretty. Take it out for me, will you?'

'Sure.' Loretta bent down. She unlocked the side of the cabinet and slid her hand inside. She could smell the heavy, musky scent Marie-Louise was wearing — too heavy, she thought, for mid-morning.

'Leave Hugh alone, there's a dear,' said Marie-Louise quietly. 'You run the risk of making yourself look the teensiest bit foolish.'

Loretta picked up the bracelet and relocked the cabinet. 'Oh, I don't think so,' she said, enunciating every word carefully. Suddenly she was angry, and very, very cool. 'Same with zircons, you know. Strictly party wear. They just don't keep their sparkle. We find that our more sophisticated clients prefer the real thing.' She smiled. 'The bracelet.'

'Thank you.' Marie-Louise held it up to the light. 'Do you really know the difference, my dear?'

'Ah, that's what comes of earning one's living. Let me help you with the clasp.' Marie-Louise held out her wrist. 'We don't all have the good fortune of having someone kind and considerate to look after us,' Loretta continued. The clasp clicked shut. 'How is that sweet, white-haired old man in New York, by the way? Your friend, the retired banker. In good health, I trust?'

'Don't be ridiculous! He was like a father to me.'

'Of course he was. A very rich and generous father, who never wanted a thing in return.'

Marie-Louise unfastened the bracelet. 'Ah, well,' she sighed, '*you* would not understand such things.'

'Wouldn't I?' Loretta asked softly. 'All that malicious and misinformed gossip going around New York. I should have covered my ears when they told me that he threw you out a year ago. Poor dear, how could people say such things? No, I mustn't go on . . . but it must be terrible to be so misjudged. How they could even imagine that you might have popped a single one of his extraordinarily generous presents! You would have been far too attached to them, far too sentimental . . . the bracelet not quite you? Is there anything else that I can show you, "my dear"?'

Marie-Louise laid the bracelet down on top of the cabinet. 'None of that has anything to do with Hugh,' she growled.

'You're so right. No one in London need know of it. I'm certainly not going to tell them, unless . . .' Loretta picked up the diamond and ruby strand. 'But it won't be necessary, will it?'

Marie-Louise struggled for self-control. Her lips worked furiously, then she gave way. 'You little bitch,' she hissed. She snatched her gloves and turned towards the door.

Loretta grinned as she watched her go, then turned the key and put the bracelet back into the cabinet.

'No sale?' asked Shona from the desk behind her.

''Fraid not,' hummed Loretta with a smile on her lips. 'Just another timewasting browser who I don't think we'll be seeing again for quite a while.'

# Chapter 12

'Mr Laithwaite's table?'

'Certainly, sir.' The black-suited waiter lowered bleary eyes and nodded. He ushered Hugh and Philip Saunders into the Connaught's sedate panelled dining room.

Since Laithwaite had rung up over a month ago, they had received no further word from him except a fax from his secretary confirming the meeting. They still did not know whether somehow word had got out and he knew of the Condor.

Morning light streamed through the large Victorian plate-glass windows and made the china and cutlery sparkle, the starched table cloths shine.

Instead of heads and torsos, most of the breakfasters had newspapers sprouting from their napkined laps. The angostura-pink *Financial Times* Tribe predominated, but the black and white Wall Street Journalists came a close second, followed by the diminutive Tabloid Boys.

The waiter led them over to a table by the far wall. Sandwiched between two keen-eyed, dark-suited acolytes sat an enormous man in a multi-coloured, wide-checked sports coat. He had a purple-tinged face, blubbery lips and wiry grey hair. 'Welcome,' he bellowed as they approached, in a voice as loud as his jacket. 'I am so pleased that you could make it.' Broad fingers pressed against the edge of the table and his balloon stomach rose a few inches. Under the pressure of his hands, the starched linen table cloth moved too. The cutlery skidded. The tulips wobbled. The pepper mill overturned.

The waiter moved forward to repair the damage. He stopped suddenly as Laithwaite's hand rose and slowly stretched across the table.

Hugh shook the meatplate hand. 'Good to see you, Mr Laithwaite. You remember Philip Saunders, our financial director.'

'Call me Art. Yes, of course. Nice meeting you, Phil.' Laithwaite clasped his hand, then pointed to the two skinny men who flanked him. 'My aides, Pete Isaacs and Mitch Napetino.'

Once more the waiter was caught in the cross-fire of hands. He had no alternative but to duck out of range.

Laithwaite winked at Hugh. 'Now let's move swiftly forward to the most important item on our agenda — breakfast. I am on a diet, alas. My wife insists just coffee and orange juice. But don't let that stop you.'

Hugh smelt kidneys, sausages, kippers . . . but he had been out with Loretta until three that morning and was not feeling hungry. 'No, just a continental breakfast for me.'

'Are you sure?' There was genuine surprise in Laithwaite's voice. 'And Phil?'

Saunders showed no such restraint. He had had a lean and pasty look ever since his wife had discovered the convenience of a microwave.

'It's a great pleasure to me that you're here,' Laithwaite continued as soon as they had placed their orders, 'but first I must . . . I really want to . . . express my deep felt sense of loss at your father's accident.' He raised one hand. 'I know that we were on different sides of the pond,

136

and I know that our interests were often diametrically opposed, but that doesn't stop one having the deepest admiration and respect for a competitor — someone who did a great deal for the industry.' A solicitous tone entered his voice. 'Did you get my flowers?'

'Yes, thank you,' said Hugh. 'They were magnificent.'

'I told my secretary to send something special, something unseasonal. "Spare no expense," I said. Good.' He nodded. 'I'm glad they were noticed.'

Laithwaite wiped his forehead with the napkin and sighed. 'And I gather that you, Hugh, are now acting managing director of the company? Am I right?'

Hugh nodded.

'Well, congratulations. I'm sure that you will do an excellent job.' He ran a finger across the prongs of a fork. 'I know it's early days and you haven't had much time to think about it, but what I would like to know is what you guys plan for Rudlow Aircraft now that Georgie Rudlow will no longer be able to take an active part in the business. I take it I'm right? Even if he recovers somewhat, he won't be able to take on, shall we say, ordinary duties.'

'Even if my father can no longer take an active role in the company, we shall continue as before.'

'Hmm.' Laithwaite was just about to say something when his attention was diverted by the arrival of the waiter, bringing coffee and croissants for Hugh and a full cooked breakfast for Saunders. He eyed Saunders' plate and swallowed hard. 'Hey, Phil, just taste one of those kidneys, will you?' He waved a hand. 'Tell me if they're good or just middling, will you?'

Saunders obliged. 'Yes, very good.'

'Oh, what the hell! Won't make much difference.'

Laithwaite reached out and grabbed the tail of the waiter's coat just as the man was leaving. 'Hold it! A side order of kidneys, if you please, maestro.'

Still hanging on to the coat, he turned back to Saunders. 'The sausages good, too, eh?' At Saunders' nod, he turned back to the waiter. 'And one of sausages, please, just to taste.'

Laithwaite watched the waiter go and then turned back to Hugh. 'So you plan to run the business as before, hmm? Well, let me just put a little thought in your mind. As you know, we at Aeronautical Industries of Philadelphia already have a twenty-four percent share of the world short haul aircraft market. Now, we're looking to increase our European market penetration. We see growth potential there. Of course, a company our size could do it alone, but one of the options available is to carry out this expansion in conjunction with a European partner.' He paused and looked quizzically at Hugh.

'And ours was one of the names that came forward?'

'Well, obviously — especially bearing in mind recent events. It's early days yet. I'm just here to sound out your initial reaction, but I think we could put together something attractive. Very attractive.'

Hugh slowly buttered a croissant. 'What exactly do you have in mind? Collaboration?'

'Initially, yes . . . or maybe — if we liked one another enough — something more permanent. Either way we would be looking to pool our joint expertise in our respective fields and develop a market leader.'

Hugh reached for the marmalade. 'Your company is ten times our size. Say, just say, we liked this idea of collaboration, what part of the manufacture would be carried out at our plant?'

'As I said, it's early days, too early for any detailed proposals . . . but as we all know, important economies of scale would only be achievable if there was one central manufacturing plant – '.

'And that would be in the States?'

'Well, thinking this thing through logically, I don't see that there's any real alternative . . . but there would be plenty of assembly work, and some of that could be done in Europe.'

He pointed to his empty coffee cup. One of his aides immediately picked up the pot and poured him another cup. 'Hell, provided we can maintain volume, you shouldn't have to shed significant labour on your short haul side, if that's what you're worried about. Labour would merely be freed for alternative projects. And if the thing really takes off – who knows? – you might be hiring more. It's a possibility. Anyhow, we'd make the deal sufficiently attractive to cover any redundancy payments. And, I can assure you, the package for management and shareholders can be made highly persuasive.'

'So you would use our technology but not our manufacturing base?' Hugh held out his cup and Laithwaite's aide re-filled it. 'Thank you. We would also lose our independence.'

Laithwaite shrugged. 'As in any marriage, depends how you look at it. I'd like you to think instead that you were gaining a partner, and a world-beating partner at that.'

On the outside Hugh was calm and collected, but his brain was reeling. Laithwaite's proposal would in effect amount to Rudlow Aircraft becoming, in time, a subsidiary of AIP. Hugh would be reluctant to give up control of the company, but he too had his price. If he were to play his cards right, he could leave a very rich man.

The problem, though, would be the board who would be extremely apprehensive about the level of redundancies which the amalgamation would cause. Unless they supported the proposal, Hugh knew he would be unlikely to gain the support of Sir Arthur, who as trustee of the Rudlow Estate voted the majority of the shares. This was going to require some very careful handling.

The best policy for now was to stonewall. 'Well, of course, I'll put it to the board but my initial feeling is that they would be reluctant to support any scheme that would erode our manufacturing base.' He turned towards Saunders. 'What do you think, Phil?'

Saunders had a kidney in his mouth. He chewed hard and swallowed. 'I agree wholeheartedly.' He swallowed again. 'Absolutely.'

'That's brave talk.' Laithwaite folded his napkin in three separate places. He pressed each crease in place with his meaty fist. 'How old are you, Mr Rudlow? A note of condescension had entered his voice. 'No, let me guess. Thirty-four?'

'No, thirty-five. But I don't see what possible relevance that has.'

Laithwaite smiled. His napkin was now shaped something like a plane. 'Look, I've been in this business longer than you've been alive. Now I don't say that age is everything – in any innovative business there's a lot of scope for a young man with fresh ideas – but in those forty odd years I've seen so many companies come and go, many much larger than Rudlow. One duff machine and it's curtains.'

He crumpled the napkin plane in his fist. 'I'd hate to see Rudlow go the same way. You know and I know that nowadays there isn't much place in the market for a company your size. It just doesn't have the muscle and development costs are just too high. You can't afford to make a single mistake – and yet as inevitably as night follows day, mistakes will be made. Even if you've got a good product, your competitor might have a better one, or be able to market his better, or you could be plain unlucky. With us, you'd have security. Rudlow Aircraft would have a future.'

Hugh smiled back at him. 'We reckon we have a future anyway.'

Laithwaite raised the palms of his hands in a conciliatory gesture, narrowly missing the plate of kidneys and sausages which the waiter now placed before him.

'Look, this is the way we'd like to do it, all friendly-like and with mutual co-operation.' He speared the sausage. 'That way everyone wins. But there are other ways.' He waved the pronged sausage in the air as if to emphasise his point, then leant forward and bit it in half.

'A little birdy tells me that you are about to launch a rival to our 386. Not such a clever move, trying to take us on. Mustard, please.'

As Hugh had suspected, news of the Condor had leaked out. That was a great pity. It would, however, he knew, be a positive factor in persuading the board to back amalgamation with AIP.

Laithwaite spooned mustard on to the side of his plate. 'You don't think we're going to stand around and watch our market share go up in smoke, do you? We're offering you the chance of co-operation. Failing that, we'll be just as tough as it takes. You know that, don't you? Mmm

141

. . . these sausages are out of this world. If it comes to it – hell, let's not pussyfoot around – we *could* destroy you.'

He forked a kidney into his mouth and chewed slowly for a while. 'We'd prefer, of course, to work with you, but that's up to you. It's our livelihood, too, you know . . . do you get my drift?'

'Yes, indeed.' Hugh nodded. 'Thank you, Mr Laithwaite, you've made your position very plain.'

'Well, no point in leaving room for misinterpretation, is there?' He leaned back in his chair. 'I'm sure on mature reflection you'll see it our way. It makes sense, you know it does. And I can assure you that AIP are very warm, considerate partners. You couldn't find anyone better to jump into bed with.' He smiled. 'Businesswise, that is.'

'Thank you for the breakfast.' Hugh rose and shook Laithwaite by the hand. 'We'll let you know once we've discussed your proposals with the board.' He nodded to the aides.

'Yes, you do that. And, once again, my condolences. I hope your poor father recovers.'

Immediately he was in the passage outside, Hugh took a long, deep breath. His heart was racing. If he played it right, this could be the deal of a lifetime. It could make him personally a great deal of money and would secure the continued existence of Rudlow Aircraft, albeit in a slightly different form.

He would comb the data bases and do some initial research on AIP tonight in good time before the board meeting. He was meant to be going out to dinner – a little party that Marie-Louise had arranged weeks ago in honour of some visiting Venezuelans. He would cancel. He was sure she would understand.

# Chapter 13

The sun was low on the horizon when they finally arrived at Conningsby. The air was still but for the crunch of the tyres on gravel and the distant neigh of horses. The magnolias were just coming into bud. Great clouds of apple blossom surrounded them everywhere.

Loretta looked up through the car window at the massive Palladian portico, at the intricately chiselled capitals with interlocking acanthus leaves, at the majestic sweep of the steps, at the rustic stonework gilded by the evening light. She tried not to show how overawed she felt.

Hugh opened the car for her with a low bow. 'Now, wait here,' he said. He strode up to the house and vanished through a side entrance.

She stood, confused and very exposed, on the sun-dappled gravel. The upstairs windows were all shuttered. The portico painted strange ghostly shadows across the façade. No sound came from within. In the vibrant bustle of the party a month ago, the very stonework had seemed alive. Now the house seemed more imposing, more monumental, even threatening. In the stillness, it was a sleeping giant, waiting for the flick of a switch to bring it to life.

She heard the ringing echoes of footfalls on the stone

floor of the Great Hall. She sighed and wished that Hugh had warned her that they would be driving to Conningsby for dinner. For a formal introduction to Mama, the Versace copy with the slit up the side was, to put it mildly, inappropriate.

The bolts were shot. The large oak doors swung inwards. Hugh stood framed in the doorway. 'Welcome home.' He put his arm around her as she snuggled up to him. He kissed her very lightly on the lips and led her through into the hall.

Loretta's thoughts went back for a moment to the small house in Queens. She called that 'home'. Three such homes would have fitted into this hall alone.

The only houses of this size which she had visited in the States had all been museums of some sort and not so old. She had dutifully gone around them, catalogue in hand, admiring their treasures and wondering why all that grandeur, all that fine workmanship, somehow failed to stir her. They had been great show pieces of a bygone era for sure, but now they were fossilised, institutionalised. That was the difference. Their nurseries would never again sound with a baby's cry, their dining rooms would never again echo with drunken laughter. Their soul had been ripped out.

Conningsby, by contrast, was a real home. Generations of children had been raised here. The trappings of everyday life were everywhere to be seen. The kitchens still carried the smell of the last meal, not just antiseptic and polish. The chimneys still smelt of real log fires. Conningsby was alive and embodied so much of what was special to her about England. And now, in some small way, she was part of it.

The Great Hall seemed even larger now that it was

deserted. She noticed the detailed carving on the banisters, the exquisitely painted portraits on the wall: men in red coats, in powdered wigs; women with laced bodices and long flowing dresses. Their faces, though, seemed to sneer at her with aristocratic contempt, as if somehow she did not belong here.

Hmm, she thought, I'd like to see how all of *you* would make out, stripped of your finery and having to make your own living in New York. Then, on reflection, she decided that some of them would have done rather well. They had managed to keep the estate in the family for all those years without its falling into the hands of the moneylenders or being confiscated by avaricious Royalty.

The last portrait on the wall was a modern one: the present Lady Rudlow. At least, she assumed it was the present Lady Rudlow. The small, practical woman that she had seen at the Ball had been depicted as a statuesque goddess silhouetted against a stormy sky.

Loretta pointed. 'Is that of your mother?'

'The Annigoni? Oh, yes. Rather good, don't you think?'

'Er, yes. I look forward to meeting her.'

'You will, but not tonight. She had to go to London,' he replied casually, and tightened his grip on her.

She gently removed his hand. 'It's just that I naturally assumed . . . as we were coming here . . .'

He shrugged. 'A drink?'

She nodded and followed him through into the Yellow Drawing Room. By the time she caught up with him, he had already switched on the lights.

Frayed yellow silk curtains hung at the huge casement windows. The swags, she guessed, had more than enough material for a dozen ball gowns while the yards of heavy gold braid that trimmed them would have kept the entire British Army in epaulettes. The furniture was heavily adorned with ormolu and very French. Again she had to remind herself that this was not a museum; that real people, that Hugh, actually lived here amid all this luxury.

A bottle of Bollinger RD 1982 stood waiting for them in the silver ice bucket. Hugh opened it with no more than a discreet hiss as the cork left the bottle. He held out a glass for her.

'Thank you. Have . . . have the other guests not arrived yet?' she asked.

'I thought,' he replied smoothly, 'it would be nicer to have the place to ourselves.'

She sipped the champagne. 'Oh, Hugh, how very thoughtful of you,' she said in a mocking tone, fingering her glass. 'No doubt so that you can show me its treasures?'

She knew that even a fortnight ago his words would have sent her into panicky confusion as she mapped out possible escape routes. Now she was genuinely pleased. Other guests would have been intrusive. She would have had to share Hugh.

She turned away, surveying the room. 'I can't help thinking about your poor father,' she said softly, over her shoulder. 'He must have loved this place so much.'

'He did. When he inherited Conningsby, it was riddled with dry rot. It was entirely due to him that it was not pulled down after the war – that and the success he made of Rudlow Aircraft.'

'Good for him.' She ran her hand over the fine rosewood and walnut inlay of the French commode in the centre of the right-hand wall. A strand of tapestry wool – Lady Rudlow's no doubt – drooped from the top left-hand drawer. The piece was somehow familiar. She wished that she had paid more attention during the decorative arts lectures at college. Then she remembered – the dentist's waiting room. Sotheby Park Bernett's Preview of Forthcoming Sales. A piece just like it had been on the cover: the star lot. 'This beautiful commode . . . is it *Louis Quatorze*?' she ventured.

Hugh shrugged. 'Don't ask me.'

She shrugged back dismissively and grinned. She admired scholarship but it pleased her more to know that to him the piece was just something of beauty. He did not need to know its value, and that was very refreshing.

She changed the subject. 'You must have had such fun being brought up here. It's like a wonderland. With so many rooms, it must have been an amazing place for Catch as Catch Can.'

'What? Oh, hide and seek? Yes.' He smiled. 'Strange that you should say that. We used to play it whenever it was too wet to go outside, then when we were older it was badminton in the hall, then billiard fives and freda.'

Her hand brushed against the tapestry at the far end of the room. It was in petit-point throughout. Two oriental potentates in ridiculous hats were issuing instructions to a row of simpering minions. Gobelin, she guessed.

'Such a wonderful house,' she sighed. 'So much must have happened here. It must have heard so many secrets.'

'It was a royalist stronghold during the Civil War. Peel planned the repeal of the Corn Laws here. Kings and Queens have stayed here throughout the generations. King Edward VIII was here three weeks before the abdication, Chamberlain just before Munich. But so much for history.' He put his arm lightly around her waist. 'You must be hungry?'

She smiled back at him and nodded, suddenly tongue-tied. She was not sure what to do with her glass. It was still half full. 'Take it through with you,' Hugh said, as if anticipating her question.

He ushered her into the dining room. She walked through very slowly. She was conscious at each step of the great men of history who had trodden that same path before her. She could almost sense their presence. It made her skin prickle.

A long mahogany table with a skating rink shine ran the length of the room. Two vast silver candelabra and a huge ornate silver bowl stood along its centre. At the very far end, underneath the red velvet curtains, two places were set.

'And where are the footmen?' she asked jokingly. 'I understood that a lady of quality expects at least two behind her chair.'

'Thursday is their evening off,' Hugh replied quite casually.

'Oh,' she stiffened in mock dismay, 'then remind me never to accept your invitations again . . . if they are for a Thursday.'

He grinned. He struck a match and lit the first of the candles in the first candelabra. 'Can you eat lobster?'

'Mmm,' she cooed. 'Never more than three.' She moved over to the mahogany side board where the lobsters were set out in a regimental line on a blue and gold Spode dish. She lifted one on to her plate. 'Have you ever been to Florida?' she asked.

'Unfortunately not.'

The home-made mayonnaise was so fresh and creamy

it stuck to the silver spoon. 'They have the most fantastic soft-shell crabs there. Out of this world.'

She pulled back a slightly rickety Chippendale chair and sat down at the table. A linen napkin was set out in a fan on the Brussels lace mat.

Steady, thought Loretta. In some wild untamed corner of her imagination she had already moved in as the chatelaine of Conningsby. Chairs needed mending, reupholstering. Those curtains needed replacing and the walls repainting. Why did the English have such an affinity with beige? A terracotta shade would show off those horsey pictures to perfection.

'I never asked you,' he said immediately he had joined her, 'do you ride?'

'Not since I was a girl,' she replied.

She tried not to stare into his deep-set hazel eyes. She did not trust herself not to sit mesmerised with the silly grin of a schoolgirl at a movie idol. After all, she was a mature woman now. Her head should not be set spinning by his tiniest pleasantry. She should not subject each of his remarks to exhaustive analysis for some clue to his inner feelings. She should conduct this whole affair in a thoroughly adult manner.

She could not deny, though, that she found Hugh's company thrilling. At work, she thought of him. On her evenings at home with Shona, she thought of him. In fact, whenever they were apart, something as stupid as a chance reference to someone else's boyfriend or a smell akin to the aftershave which Hugh sometimes wore made her sigh wistfully. Then, embarrassed, she had to do her best to disguise her feelings, to prevent unwelcome comments from the other girls.

Despite the grandeur of the setting, despite the

differences in their upbringing, Loretta felt totally at ease sitting here next to Hugh in the candlelight as she entertained him with quirky stories of New York life. He laughed a lot as she told him about the bizarre characters she had met, about some narrow escapes in very *outré* nightclubs.

Whatever he was saying, his voice had that particularly English rounded tone which could make even the weather report sound seductive. Hugh, she knew, was a very physical animal. Every gesture he made seemed to carry some veiled sexual undertone. His manners, though, had always been impeccable. Only once during dinner had he been close to overstepping the mark. When she had questioned him as to why he had left half his lobster untouched, he had replied lightly, 'How the hell am I meant to concentrate on crustaceans with you here next to me?' And, rather than simpering coyly, she had had the presence of mind to counter with: 'So, my darling, douse yourself in some very cold wet wine before I have to do it for you.'

They drank a bottle and a half of Chablis with the lobster, Beaumes de Venise with the fruit salad, and Graham's '48 with the Stilton. The coffee in the thermos was still hot.

'Would you like to see around the house?' Hugh suggested after the second cup.

'I would love to,' she enthused. It would be safer than the sofa.

He rose. They left the dining room through a side door and passed down a long dark corridor. They turned right into some sort of annexe to the main house.

Hold it, thought Loretta, checking her bearings. But she was right first time. It *was* an annexe. She marvelled at the sheer crazy *folie de grandeur* of the enterprise. Who but a Ludwig of Bavaria would even think of building still more rooms on to Conningsby?

Hugh pushed open the door. A layer of dust fell from the architrave. He switched on the lights. 'The games room,' he said casually.

They were in a huge Moorish pavilion. In the centre of the room was a full-sized billiard table. The green baize glowed under the dusty light from the low fringed, fretwork lamps. Racks held rows of slightly bent cues. The table was surrounded by a dozen black and white fretwork arches traced in gold. In each alcove there were red divans with padded tasselled bolsters.

'What an extraordinary room!' exclaimed Loretta.

'It is rather unusual. We owe it to Edward VII — he used to come to shoot here when he was Prince of Wales. Once he casually mentioned to my great-grandfather that he thought it rather a pity that Conningsby did not have a room where the men could smoke and relax in some sort of comfort.' He shrugged. 'This was the result.'

He walked across the room towards a far door. 'And not to be outdone he also built an extra wing on to the house to accommodate his guests' entourages — they were always having fifty to stay in those days. Building, entertaining and gambling nearly bankrupted him.'

Loretta tried to imagine the scene: the shielded lights thick with smoke; the frogged velvet smoking jackets; the smell of port; the laughter at the naughty stories; the ricochets of the billiard balls. What were those divans really for?

'Hugh?' she called. He was opening the far door. A cold draught of musty air swept into the room.

'Come and see what else he built.'

'Hang on,' she said, 'I don't want to miss anything . . .' She shuddered, hugged her shoulders and ran to his side. She followed Hugh through the door, feeling her way in the unlit room. Bare wooden floorboards creaked at each step.

A skylight in the pitched roof high above them shed a faint, diffuse light over a hall the size of a school gymnasium. She could just make out the outline of rows of chair backs dissecting the room. There were ornate ormolu sconces on the walls and some kind of mural there too. The desperate fluttering sound of a trapped bird filled the air above her.

Hugh flicked a switch. Thirty yards ahead of her a worn red velvet curtain shone in the footlights.

'Oh,' she gasped, and pressed her hands together. 'I don't believe it! I really don't believe it! It's too much. Your own private theatre . . . when was it last used?'

'Not for years, except for the annual hunt dinners. The last performance was *Ruddigore* in 1938, just before the war.'

'Promise me, promise me that you'll open it up. *Please*. You could have visiting troupes here, fringe theatre, happenings, anything. What are the acoustics like? Hugh, why don't you go up on the stage and say something . . . sing a song?'

'If you had ever heard me sing,' he said rather sheepishly, 'I don't think you'd ask that.'

'It doesn't matter. Give it a try, please!' she begged. 'For *me*.'

He raised his hands in surrender. 'All right. I'll do it. But I'm not musical, OK?'

As he walked up the central aisle through the rows of dusty armchairs, Loretta found a cord attached to the skylight. She cranked it, the skylight opened — but the bird failed to find the opening. Still it kept flapping and swooping, flying into walls.

Hugh mounted the stage. The footlights caught his blue city suit, made his broad forehead and well-groomed brown hair shine. He adopted the wide, toothy grin of a variety show compère.

Loretta clapped, then moved along the chairs and chose a seat in the centre of the third row. She dusted it down and made herself comfortable.

He squinted into the footlights. 'Thank you very much, ladies and gentlemen, for that overwhelming round of applause,' he mimicked. 'You are a great audience. The best since the matinee. Now, for the particular pleasure and delight of our distinguished American guest, I would like to give you my personal rendition of that great Southern classic "Ol' Man River". Thank you very much.' He gave a quick bow.

'Bravo! Bravo!' she yelled. After the echoes of her cries had died down, it was suddenly silent above her. Loretta smiled. The bird had escaped.

Hugh was down on one knee, his arms splayed, fingers waving. He cleared his throat three, four times . . .

'Get on with the show!' she called, taunting him. 'Money back!'

'I am just warming up,' he shouted back. 'Clearing the tubes. *Laaaa. Laaaa.*' Whatever sound he thought he was making, it certainly was not in the musical register. 'I've got it now,' he said earnestly. 'Ready?' He held out his arms again in a wide embrace.

> Ol' man river,
> It just keeps rolling . . .

Loretta held on to the armrests and giggled helplessly. Hugh's voice was just as flat as her step-brother Matt's. Up there, alone under the arc lights, he could have been a small boy at the Fairview Elementary Christmas Concert, desperately seeking his parents' approval.

Hugh's hands had dropped to his sides. 'How does it go after that?' he called. 'Prompt! Loretta, I need some help!' He shielded his eyes with his hand and squinted over the footlights to the empty chairs beyond.

As she stared at him playing the fool, a mischievous childlike grin crossed Loretta's face. Her eyes gleamed. She knew exactly what she wanted to do next. She stood up very quietly, cushioning the return of the spring seat with her hand. She tiptoed towards the door.

'Loretta?' he called. 'Loretta? Where the hell are you? Surely it wasn't that bad . . .'

She flicked the switch. The theatre was plunged into darkness. 'Catch as catch can!' she shouted in a high-pitched childish voice. 'Catch as catch can!'

A crash like falling tin cans came from the stage. 'Damn! Blast! Loretta?'

She giggled and ran out of the door. She skirted around the billiard table and ran back through the black and white Moorish billiard room; back along the dark winding corridor; back through the beige and red of the dining room; back through the Yellow Drawing Room into the blue and white Great Hall. The echoes of her clicking heels bounced off the walls around her.

Where to hide? She paused for breath. In the house in Queens, there had really only been three viable options: the cupboard under the stairs behind the squeezy mop and Hoover; the walk-in larder; or one of the bedroom cupboards. The games had never lasted more than five minutes. Unless, of course, she had been playing with Ma. Games with Ma hardly counted. As often as not, she had kept on ironing for a full ten minutes before so much as opening a single cupboard.

This place was a kid's wonderland. You could rot before anyone found you here.

She ran the length of the Great Hall and slid through the mahogany door at the far end. She fumbled for a switch.

A thousand crystal prisms sparkled from the chandeliers, slicing the light into rainbows, dappling and painting the pink silk walls. She looked up at the elaborate Rococo plasterwork, down at the smooth expanse of the parquet floor. It still bore heel marks from the ball. Some, maybe, were hers. She hugged herself and pirouetted and thought that again she could hear the group play . . .

'*Loretta*?'

She snapped out of her reverie. Escape. The door on her left . . .

An overwhelming sweet smell filled her nostrils. Everywhere she looked there were jungle ferns, exotic plants, orchids.

The full moon above her seemed so close that it could have been painted on the panes of the curved glass roof. It washed the plants with silver and made the little droplets of water on the leaves shine like jewels. The floor was patterned with black and white marble squares. The heat was intense. Moisture trickled from her brow.

'*Loretta*?'

She heard a rapid scramble of footsteps outside, and suddenly she froze. 'No,' she gasped. Her heart thudded against the walls of her chest. Her fingers clenched. She struggled for breath, trying to steady her brain . . .

Suddenly the two black men were scrambling down her apartment block stairwell again. Their dilated pupils, like black-centred stars, were winking at her out of the darkness. The steel of the swaying elevator floor was cold on her back. The sweet, sickly taste of bile was in her mouth, stale sweat in her nostrils.

I'm here. In Conningsby. I'm safe. This is only a stupid children's game, she told herself. But the feeling of panic that had seized hold of her was real enough. The old scar on her cheek was red and pulsating.

The pursuing footsteps had reached the ballroom now. She shuddered at each fresh step. Her teeth chattered. Her wide staring eyes darted this way and that, desperately searching for an escape route. She must get away. She must . . .

She swung blindly to her left, into an unlit passageway. She skidded into a wall, pushed herself away. It was so dark, but she could not risk turning on the light and the air was so thin . . .

'*Loretta*?'

The cry grated on her nerves, made her shudder.

Around the corner, she saw a dim orange light. A narrow winding flight of stairs led off to the right. She launched herself at them, stumbled and picked herself up. Then she climbed the first step, thankful that an old piece of haircord deadened her tread.

At the top of the stairs, a long straight corridor stretched ahead of her. She hesitated for a moment, then ran to the left. A yellowing floral paper decorated the walls. Identical white bedroom doors marked each eighth stride.

Towards the end of the corridor, the paper changed to a frieze of blue and pink ducks with ribbons around their necks. A huge Pooh Bear was painted on the door ahead of her. Perched on his head was a coronet.

She could not stop herself from smiling. She felt the frenzied pace of her heartbeat slow. She crept forward. Carefully, silently, she turned the handle . . .

She sighed and blinked.

The nursery looked as if nothing in it had been changed for twenty years. A frieze of bunnies ran around the top of the pink and blue striped walls. A Victorian rocking horse, a dappled grey with a worn and chewed tail, stood in the centre of the room. There was a toy E-Type Jaguar, big enough for a boy to ride in. A vast dolls' house — it looked just like . . . it was Conningsby in miniature. The tiny dining room looked the same as it had tonight. The same beige walls, the same pictures. She could even identify the chair on which she had sat.

She slumped down on the floor, fascinated. She opened and shut the curtains in the theatre. She rearranged the furniture in the Yellow Drawing Room. All the time, she felt the tension being gradually drawn out of her body as if by some strange magnetic field.

Then, on the painted dresser nearby, she saw a doll with a porcelain head and fine chestnut hair. She recognised the cream dress covered in gold lace, the burgundy velvet cloak trimmed with speckled fur. She smiled and reached out for it with trembling hands. Yes, the Lady of the Court, the same type of doll as the one her father had brought her from England, but here it was one of many among Kings and Queens, pages, courtiers and jesters.

She remembered how she had treasured that doll, how it had been her passport to dreams. She hugged it to her as she had done as a child and rocked it in her arms.

It was some time later before she noticed the low, rhythmical sound of breathing filling the room. She stood, put the doll back and listened again.

The far door was slightly ajar. She walked over quietly and peered around the jamb. A grey-haired old woman lay asleep in a high-backed armchair. Her mottled hands were cupped in her lap, still half clutching a pair of knitting needles and a baby's bootie. She had a kindly, contented expression on her sleeping face.

Loretta took a deep breath, carefully closed the door and, calm now, left the nursery and retraced her steps towards the centre of the house.

As she walked silently on, the ceilings gained in height, the doors began to sport pediments. She reached the gallery overlooking the Great Hall and stared up at the mural of Venus surrounded by clouds of billowing toile, then down at the marble floor forty feet below. The light from the sole lit candelabra cast giant shadows on the wall. She listened. All was still.

She tiptoed along the gallery, listening intently to the tiny clicking sound her heels made at each step. The brass plaque on the first mahogany door was inscribed 'The Chinese Bedroom'; the second 'The Venetian Bedroom'; the third 'The State Bedroom'.

She stopped. The State Bedroom . . . so this must be the room where Edward VII and later Edward VIII had stayed; where the present Queen would stay if ever she came here. Her heart fluttered at the romance of it all. Curious, she twisted the heavy gilt knob.

The shutters were drawn. In the narrow wedge of light from the gallery, she could see no more than the outline of a huge four-poster bed. She pushed the heavy door shut behind her and switched on the lights.

Huge sweeps of faded pale pink damask hung from each corner of the great bed. Above, the material rose in an elaborate puffed canopy to a coronet of floppy, grey ostrich feathers. The posts of the bed were exquisitely carved with an elaborate pattern of clinging vines. On the cornice above, two fat cherubs were plucking at wooden grapes.

Wow! thought Loretta. Some bed.

Old embroidery was everywhere in the room: petit-point on the walnut armchair; lace on the dressing table; an Aubusson on the floor. Even the walls were covered in an embroidered fabric in the same soft pink.

On the dressing table lay a carved ivory box. Loretta opened it. Inside were four exquisite silver and cut glass scent bottles, a mother of pearl button hook, an ivory fan.

A door banged. She heard heavy footsteps outside. She started, suppressed a cry. Again, for a split second, panic clutched at her heart.

The footsteps grew louder. The door opened.

Hugh.

He moved swiftly towards her. 'Got you!' he said. Before she could reply his arms were around her, his mouth on hers. She felt the slight roughness of his chin, the warmth of his breath, the light touch of his lips.

Her body was so tense, she grabbed at his sleeve to stop her hand from trembling.

His mouth retreated, then returned. This time he pulled her forcefully against the contours of his body and kissed her hard. 'And I have got you, haven't I, Loretta?' His voice sounded deeper than usual. 'I have got you. Body and soul.'

'No,' she said firmly, and pushed him away. 'No one

gets me. No one. I'm my own woman. No, Hugh, no . . .' And to her astonishment, tears burned in her eyes.

'But I love you,' he murmured.

'And I you, but that doesn't mean . . .' She shuddered and quickly turned away. Her eyes strayed to the mahogany door, to freedom. 'Look, why don't we just go downstairs, discuss it all . . .'

'For Christ's sake, my darling.' His eyes were soft and beseeching, but an instant later the pupils narrowed, his jaw hardened. 'You don't doubt me, do you?' he said accusingly. 'I'd do anything for you.'

'Anything?'

'That's what I said.'

*Anything*. The word echoed in her brain, what did he mean, then she shuddered and dismissed the thought. She strained to compose her face, her eyes fixed on the dull gilt handle of the door. Blinking away the tears, she strode towards it. 'No, Hugh. No.'

He side-stepped too swiftly for her and barred her way.

'Now, come on,' she said, 'we're both adults here. Let me pass. I order you to let me pass.' But she knew that her voice was trembling. She knew that if she looked at him all would be lost.

'For a kiss,' he pleaded. 'A single kiss.'

And then suddenly his arms were around her, his mouth on hers, and this time she felt her body tingle. She felt her body go limp in his arms. She felt the ache in her. She closed her eyes, struggling for breath, trying to regain control, but her traitor mouth was pleading for more, betraying her with each slow twist of her tongue.

It's all right, said a little voice inside her, it's all right.

His urgent hands were moving over her body, stroking,

cupping, feeling. She felt the worsted weave of his jacket rough against her. 'No, no,' she said weakly, then sighed as she felt the warmth of his hands on her, and sighed again as her nipples hardened to his touch. She gazed into his eyes. 'Oh God . . . oh God, I adore you.'

' "License my wand'ring hands," ' he murmured against her lips ' "and let them roam, Above, behind and . . . in between," ' suiting his actions to the words. She offered no resistance.

The fabric at her shoulders twisted. Her dress slid to her ankles. Loretta stood naked but for her panties, tights and shoes as he kissed her. Her full breasts, nipples erect, cast shadows on her smooth white skin. Another shudder shook her shoulders.

He picked her up gently and laid her down on the bed. The soft mattress dipped. The embroidery lightly scratched her back.

In the half shadow, she watched as he stripped off his jacket and ripped off his shirt. Hunting had kept him fit. There was not an ounce of spare flesh on his body.

The four-poster squeaked as he joined her. His lips brushed her ear, her throat, her nipples. She closed her eyes waiting for the sorcery of his fingers to take hold once more. One wrong move, she knew, would turn her again into a frightened animal. She tried desperately to block out the images which flashed before her — the staring eyes in the darkness; her father's shrug and mumble as he left her and her mother forever. She tried to quell the shaking of her limbs.

He was very slow, very gentle. His hands were like velvet as they stroked and teased her body. They played for a long time, tickling and caressing her. His lips were working too, on the nape of her neck, behind her ears, along her shoulders.

Her body throbbed to his touch. It seemed to shrug off the burden of her thoughts. It told her everything was all right.

As his hands finally moved down to her thighs, she felt the burning inside her intensify. She wanted him now, despite her fear, but still he waited. His hands kept working, demanding of her that she should want him more.

When finally he came to her, the slight initial pain passed quickly. She felt the power and the strength of him separating her, cleaving her until he was deep inside her, occupying every part of her. She closed her eyes and bit her lip. She had to stop herself from crying out.

The rhythm of his movements grew faster and faster. His shoulder muscles gleamed above her half open mouth. His breath was warm on her ears, her lips. His chest was hot and damp against hers.

When she opened her eyes again the urbane businessman had gone. Only the hunter who had searched out and captured his quarry remained. There was a distant look in his wide unfocused eyes. His mouth was tight and hard, cruel even. It seemed to her almost as if he was no longer aware that she was there, as if he were communing only with her body in an act of subjugation, of conquest. Crazily, for a second she saw herself as a fox at the moment of kill.

Suddenly he thrust deeper than ever, and the pulsing heat of him suffused her stomach, her thighs. Through teeth clenched, he cried 'Oh, God!' and fell forward into her arms.

She swallowed back the silent sobs that threatened. She

clutched him to her still, gripping the muscles of his back with her outstretched fingers. Her body was still shaking, but now with pride. Somehow she had held the old ghosts at bay. She had shown them that she was no longer frightened of their taunts. She was a woman now. She let out a long soft sigh. 'Good, good, good.'

'You too,' Hugh grunted.

Loretta stared up at the rosette of rose silk in the centre of the canopy. She remembered what Julie had told her about her first time: 'Just forget it. I tell you, it gets better and better.' She rubbed her cheek against his coarse brown hair. Her legs languidly straightened. 'So who, lover, has slept in this bed before?' she said lightly. 'Anyone I might know?'

'Oh, Elizabeth I,' he said lazily, 'though that doesn't really count as that was before the fire, the house has been rebuilt since then. Queen Victoria, Edward VII . . .'

She stroked his back, running her fingers down his spine. 'You have a lot to live up to, Hugh Rudlow.'

'Just there,' he said. 'That's the spot.'

'Hunting? We'll have to get your back straight if you're going to cope with all your newfound responsibilities.' She pressed down gently on the muscle with her forefinger.

He gasped. 'At least I don't have to worry about the house, thank God.'

Her body stiffened slightly. 'What . . . what do you mean? Your mother can't be expected – '

'The house is Anthony's problem.'

'An-thony?'

He grinned. 'My brother. My elder brother. Poor sod. You've never met him, have you?'

'No.' Loretta's hand froze.

'He's been away for the last three months for what my

mother would term "a little rest cure".' Suddenly Hugh laughed. 'You didn't think that all this was going to be mine, did you?' He was still laughing as he clambered out of bed.

Loretta bit her lip. Feeling dazed and confused, she watched Hugh silently as he smoothed back his hair and slipped on his trousers, then padded across the carpet. He opened the door. 'Where are you going?' she asked.

'I've got to put a call through to the States. Philadelphia. Just make yourself comfortable. You'll find a toothbrush and everything that you need in the bathroom.'

Alone now, she blinked and sighed. Her body was heavy and listless. It also felt a little sore. Using her arms to support her weight, she dragged herself off the bed. She looked around her for the bathroom. She tried a small panelled door cut into the fabric on the wall but found only an empty cupboard. Her nose twitched at the smell of mothballs. A second door revealed only a wash basin.

She slipped on her dress and shoes, pulled open the door and padded along the corridor. Hugh's laugh echoed up from below. She stopped. A light was on in the Yellow Drawing Room. His voice was quite distinct. 'No, I promise you . . . of course, I haven't just rolled out of bed with some stupid bitch.' That laugh again. 'It was the Japanese delegation from Mitsatchi . . . and, yes, of course they left their geishas behind. Look, I've only just this minute got your message off the answering machine. Tomorrow evening will be fine. Pick you up at eight, OK? Yes, and a big kiss to you too.'

Her knees went weak. Her fingers tightened about the hand rail of the banisters.

She stood there, staring down at the narrow wedge of light between the drawing-room door and the jamb. The wedge broadened as the door opened again and Hugh walked back into the Great Hall.

She shivered. Anger made her skin prickle.

'Hugh?' she called.

His running footsteps thudded up the stairs and he was before her, advancing on her in the half-light. 'What's the matter?' He laid a hand on her forearm.

'The acoustics in the Hall are great, you know? Quite good enough for a concert.'

His eyes flashed at her. 'What the hell does that mean?'

'Who were you speaking to just now?' She strained to keep her voice on an even keel.

'What's it to you?'

'I just want to know.'

'Oh, for Christ's sake.' He clenched his fist. 'Look, Loretta, you know the score. We've had a good time, a great time. We could go on having a good time. That doesn't mean that you own me. That does not justify — I don't know — all this . . . emotion!' He spat out the last word as if it were an obscenity.

'Absolutely, Hugh,' she said softly on a monotone. She straightened her back. 'So order me a cab. No emotion. Quite right. Just order me a cab, will you?'

# Chapter 14

A bunch of four dozen red roses was waiting for her on the lobby table when she returned from work the next day. She picked up the cellophane package at arm's length, just as she would any piece of garbage. Slowly she climbed the stairs, breathless by the time she reached the top. After the long taxi ride, she had not got to bed until four that morning and now had little energy left.

Immediately she entered the flat, she walked straight over to the flip-top bin by the sink and pressed the pedal with her foot. Without even reading the accompanying note, she dropped the flowers inside.

Even from the bin, though, the heavy, sickly scent wafted up into the room. She unrolled a black plastic rubbish sack and threw the flowers inside, along with two empty sardine tins and the kitchen waste. She fastened the sack with a knot and took it back down the stairs to the bins below.

The telephone rang half a dozen times during the first hour, but fearing it was Hugh, she let it ring. She did not know whether she would be able to handle hearing his voice on the telephone. All the time that she had felt that there was some understanding between them — love even — he had merely been playing a game of make believe, filling her heart with what he thought she wanted to hear, playing with her, waiting for the brief moment of physical gratification, the pay-off. Her hand rose to her face and softly stroked her scar.

He would never know how much that fleeting moment of gratification had cost her. Even the birds fluttering and singing in the trees outside seemed to be laughing at her, taunting her for her misplaced trust, her naivety and hollow dreams.

There were no tears in her eyes, though. She was beyond tears. She just felt sad and sorry for all womankind. They were always the ones who had to pay the price for the shallow temporary boosts to the fragile male ego of men like Hugh. She had been a fool to believe in her own dreams. She would not make the same mistake again.

She had planned not to tell Shona about it, but when the moment came, when she saw the concern in her flatmate's eyes, it all spilled out in a rush. Shona told her in turn about her own sad love life, about the men that she had loved and lost. 'Hugh's no different from the others,' she said as she warmed the milk on the cooker to make a second mug of Horlicks, 'you give them everything — every last inch of yourself — and all they do in return is kick you in the teeth.'

Loretta swallowed. She brushed the hair from her face. 'But I really loved him.'

'Come on! You only thought you did . . . and that was before you found out he had the emotional maturity of an amoeba.'

Shona handed Loretta the refilled mug. She slumped down on the sofa beside her. 'From what you've told me,' she continued, 'I'd say that Hugh was one of those men who only get their kicks from conquest. They're not interested in a *real* relationship. It's always got to be someone new, someone different, as if – I don't know – they're continually having to prove something to themselves. A tortured soul, if you ask me. Simply not worth bothering about. Good riddance.'

Loretta smiled and slowly sipped her drink.

Shona lay back on the sofa, sending a little wave through the foam cushions. 'You know, Loretta, I think the ideal husband for me would be an octogenarian billionaire on a drip feed with two months left to live.'

Loretta laughed. 'No, seriously. What about Brian? What's happened to your sense of romance?'

'Safely locked away in my top drawer for whenever it's needed.' Two dimples appeared in Shona's cheeks. 'Brian's just for fun. Nothing serious. Wise up, Loretta. There are other men out there. Rich men. Titled men. Handsome men. And you – it makes me green with envy every time I think about it – you, Loretta, could have virtually any one of them. Just one of those understanding, disarming smiles of yours – '

'Yeah, but looks . . .'

'Get you a long way down the track. Now no moping. Get straight back into the swim of things, that's my advice. Kiss a lot of toads and eventually you'll find your prince.'

'Thanks, Shona,' Loretta replied quietly, 'but that's just not me. I don't really need anybody. I'm happy the way I am.'

'Come on! As they say, everybody needs someone.'

'Uh, uh. Not me!'

The shop closed promptly at five-thirty. As the weeks went by, Loretta began to dread the lonely tramp home and the empty routine of supper in front of the television and a book at bedtime.

Shona was out most evenings with Brian and rarely spent the night in the flat. Loretta had dined with them a few times. He was nice enough, but she always felt guilty and awkward playing the gooseberry. The more relaxed Shona and Brian were together, the more awkward and excluded she felt.

London had lost its attraction and her thoughts went back to Bob. She missed their brother and sister camaraderie, their innocent evenings together. There, at least, she had always remained in control.

She had little appetite for parties, but occasionally the excuses ran out and she was obliged to go. It was as much as she could do to change her clothes of an evening and smile as the taxi drew up to take her somewhere she did not want to go with someone for whom she did not care. All the houses she visited she compared, almost unconsciously, to Conningsby and they seemed like insubstantial shells next to the great house. With none could she begin to feel that same sensation of walking into a magical world, or the sense of belonging which she had felt there — fool that she was.

The moment she walked into a room she could sense the men eyeing her up like a business proposition and it made her shudder. Every remark, however outwardly matter-of-fact, seemed to be sexually laden. It made her hate them. She told herself again and again that not all men were like her father, or like the men in the elevator, or like Hugh . . . but still she could not bring herself to trust any of them. She wished that she was back in her baby bed in Queens again playing with her toys, or stooped in front of the dolls' house in the nursery at

Conningsby, and then she had to kick herself mentally and tell herself not to be such a timorous darned fool.

Yet despite Hugh, the magic and timeless solidity of Conningsby still haunted her. She longed to go back and see it again, look once more into the nursery. She wanted to dance in the ballroom again, see the giant shadows cast by the candelabra across the Great Hall, smell the sweetness of the jasmine that had filled the dining room throughout dinner. Once through the wrought iron gates of Conningsby, the ordinary world ceased to exist.

Her opportunity came a week later. At a dinner party in London, someone called Simpson, a small persistent man with spectacles, said that he had been asked to a homecoming party for Anthony Rudlow and if perhaps she was not doing anything, might she like to accompany him?

At first she shook her head, but then, out of devilment, she said OK, why not? It would be amusing, after all, to see Hugh's face as she came through the door. It would be good to see him watching her as she skirted the room, outshining all the other girls there. She'd love to see the pain of longing on his face. It would be some sort of revenge at least.

# Chapter 15

'Honestly, I'm not at all sure that I'm up to this,' said the tall, thin man sitting perched on the edge of the sofa. 'It's been a long day.' In the light reflected off the yellow silk walls, his skin had a healthy country glow. He tapped his glass nervously with long fine-fingered hands. 'If you don't mind, I might just go to bed.'

Lady Rudlow stopped plumping the cushions on the sofa opposite and turned to him. She wore a black satin calf-length dress trimmed with brown mink at collar and cuffs. 'Darling, you simply can't! They'll be here any minute now.' She moved towards him. 'I thought it would be a nice surprise for you. You're going to have to start circulating again sometime and surely the best way is to plunge in right away?'

Above the commode hung a Lawrence portrait of Cecilia, the fifth Lady Rudlow, and her two King Charles spaniels. The thin man shared the same fine bone structure as Cecilia, the same worried-looking grey eyes, the same golden hair.

'But not the day I come home, surely?' He tugged at the cuffs of his cream silk shirt. 'I've got the estate accounts to look through, and then tomorrow I want to see Father and go to the plant. The last thing I feel like

now is several hours of pointless small talk . . . I'd just
rather not.'

'Only because you're a little bit out of practice.' His
mother sat down next to him and put her hand on the
sleeve of his dinner jacket. 'And, darling, is it wise to
do so much so quickly? I'm sure Hugh can keep
everything ticking over for you.'

'That's not the point, Mother.' He tapped his glass
again.

'Oh, darling,' Lady Rudlow soothed, 'I know just how
you must feel – '

'You don't, Mother, or else you wouldn't be forcing
this on me now. For me it's like stepping on to another
planet. Work I can cope with . . . socialising for the sake
of it, no. I don't want it. I don't need it.'

'Think of it, if you must, as part of your therapy,
darling. Part of your rehabilitation . . . it's family, apart
from a few people whom I thought you might be
interested to meet.'

'You mean Suitable Young Ladies,' he said
sardonically. 'Mother, although I appreciate that you are
doing this with the best of intentions, at thirty-six I really
think I'm old enough to make my own friends.'

'Look,' Lady Rudlow started, then, seeming to change
tack, 'Anthony, could you get me a drink? A very small
gin and . . .' Her mouth puckered, her hand touched his
sleeve. 'On second thoughts, darling, just stay where you
are. I'll get it myself.'

'Mother,' he sighed, 'I might be off the booze myself,
but I'm quite capable of pouring you a gin and tonic
without making a feverish lurch for the bottle.' He gently
prised her hand off his sleeve and stood up.

'If you're quite sure, darling?'

'Yes, Mother, quite sure.' He strode towards the black lacquer chest by the door. 'Anyway, as you know, drink was never my problem.'

'Just a very small, weak one, darling,' she called after him. 'Look, I thought it might amuse you to meet some fresh faces. After all, you've been out of the swing for some time now.'

'Only four months.'

'Yes, four months away, but before that you weren't exactly – how can I put this? – active socially?'

He poured out a gin and tonic for his mother and refilled his own glass with soda. 'I was seeing my friends,' he answered tetchily. 'I'd call that "active socially".'

Lady Rudlow sighed. 'Yes, darling, and I'm sure that your "friends" were all very charming. But you are different from them now. You are cured, and from what you tell me, they are not. You have to make a clean break.' Her voice carried easily across the length of the drawing room. 'Anyway, I do hope you'll at least make an effort to make the party go.'

'Yes, Mother.'

'I've tried to weed out the plain and dull ones but, you know, some of the young people coming I haven't seen for years – not since they were quite small, actually. I did get a little stuck on the girls. So many of the nice – and yes, suitable ones – are already married, sadly. So two of the men coming down from London are bringing someone, just to even up the numbers. It's not easy organising a party for another generation.'

He picked up their glasses. 'Not that I give a damn, Mother, but who out of this select gathering has been given the doubtful privilege of sitting next to me?'

'I've put Jane Chalmers on your right. Now she's a pretty thing.'

'Is Philip Eynsham coming too? I gather they're inseparable.'

'Not any longer. According to her mother, that broke up a month ago. So difficult to keep track of these things.' She sighed and took the glass from him. 'Thank you, darling. And on your left I've put Louise Sprigget. Her mother is a great friend of mine and a tower of strength in the Red Cross.'

A discreet and much practised cough came from the door. 'Miss Louise Sprigget,' announced Gander, the butler.

A small blonde dumpling in a bright turquoise dress stood awkwardly by the door. She stared ahead of her with a panic-stricken expression at the near-empty room.

Anthony raised his eyes heavenward. 'Mother . . .?'

'Well, she was very pretty as a child,' Lady Rudlow whispered, 'and I have heard that she has a very sweet nature. Looks aren't everything, darling.' She stood and said in a loud voice, 'Louise, how nice of you to come. And at such short notice too. So kind.'

'No, thank you for asking me, Lady Rudlow.' The girl swallowed. 'I'm sorry if I'm early.'

'Not at all. Not at all.' She rapidly traversed the distance between them. 'It's the others who are late. We were always brought up to be punctual. Champagne?'

'Yes, please. Rather.' Gander coughed again, this time to draw attention to a silver tray held perilously close to the girl's elbow. 'Oh.' She picked up a glass.

'And how is your dear mother? Well, I hope.'

'Yes, fine. Absolutely fine.'

A short silence ensued.

'I hope you didn't have any difficulty finding us here?' Lady Rudlow said finally.

'No. Not a bad journey, actually. I took the A4 as far as Bampton, then the A374, and the ring road around Little Sandby.'

'Oh, how clever of you! That ring road does make a difference, doesn't it?' Lady Rudlow turned. 'Now, have you met my son Anthony?'

The girl's cheeks reddened. She extended a damp pudgy hand. 'How do you do? I've heard about you, of course.'

'A pleasure.' Anthony shook her hand and returned it swiftly.

The girl bit her lip. She continued to stare at him as if waiting for him to make some profound pronouncement.

He blinked twice, raised thumb and forefinger to his nostrils and sniffed. 'Er − nice dress,' he said.

It was obviously the right conversational gambit. She smiled and gave a sort of wriggle. 'Oh, this old thing. I'm so glad you like it . . .'

Gander's cough was only just audible above the whine of Miss Sprigget's voice, but to Anthony it resounded like a bugle call. He smiled. Relief was at hand.

' . . . they're so expensive now − dresses, I mean. You men are so lucky not having to bother. Unfair, really . . .'

'Anthony, darling?' Lady Rudlow came forward, brandishing a brunette with knowing little eyes. 'I'd like you to meet Perdita Malmsbury. Her father is one of the best shots in England . . .'

Other guests began to arrive steadily as eight-thirty approached: a girl with a fresh uncomplicated country face; a thin angular sylph with a pink punk hair-do; two men with stiff military gait talking hunting. Only fitful bursts of strained small-talk punctuated the long silences as they all sipped champagne and chewed on stale peanuts.

Lady Rudlow dashed between the new arrivals effecting introductions. She corralled them into a group and primed their flagging conversations with little snippets of useful chit-chat.

It was only later that she noticed that the sylph with the punk hair-do was nowhere to be seen. She found her in the hall looking at the pictures and smartly brought her back into the fold.

In Lady Rudlow's book, an interest in art at parties was an unequivocal sign of desperation.

'Hello, Mummy,' called a familiar voice from behind her. She turned.

Camilla was wearing a simple black cotton dress and no make-up. Her long black hair was tousled and unkempt. By her side was a man with dark curly hair, a wide mouth, big hands and green-brown eyes. He was not in black tie, but tight blue jeans and a battered leather jacket. His shoes were brown suede.

Lady Rudlow's smile faltered only for an instant.

'You remember Steve, don't you, Mummy?' Camilla said jauntily. 'He played at my ball.'

Lady Rudlow nodded and shook his hand. 'Yes, of course. The young . . .' She started again, 'We *all* enjoyed your performance enormously. So pleased that you could come.'

She put her hand on Camilla's shoulder, kissed her and whispered: 'Hair, darling . . . and didn't you know it was black tie?'

'The wind, Mummy,' Camilla whispered back. 'I promise you that when we set off from London my hair was perfect. Steve's got a convertible, you see.'

'Very well, I believe you, but you can do something about it now, can't you? And the dinner jacket?'

'I know. But he doesn't have one and I didn't think it was that important.'

'But he's the only man without. I'm only thinking of him — he may not feel very comfortable. Maybe one of the boys has one that he could borrow.'

Camilla shook her head. 'No, Mummy. I'm sure he's fine.' She straightened and turned to him. 'Steve, are you feeling comfortable?'

He flexed his shoulder blades and gave a slow, toothy smile. 'Yeah? I'm comfortable, Lady Rudlow. Really comfortable. Honest.'

Once again Her Ladyship's smile dimmed momentarily then returned. 'Well, if you're *quite* sure. Camilla will introduce you around . . . Champagne?'

Loretta stood in the doorway, surveying the room. During the long drive to Conningsby, tongue-tied with nerves, she had hardly spoken. Twice she had thought of asking Simpson to drop her off and go on alone.

Her plan of sweeping into the party, cool, elegant and relaxed, inciting envious glances while gently snubbing Hugh, seemed very foolish now. The lump in her throat remained stubbornly there, however hard she swallowed. She had to stop her nervous fingers from plucking at the side of her best black lace dress. Her cheeks were hot and flushed.

This room had been the first chamber in the labyrinth which had drawn her inextricably towards the State Bedroom. The totems were all the same: the frayed yellow silk curtains; the rosewood commode; the Gobelin tapestry. Tonight, though, the room was very different.

In the bray and chatter of the unseeing guests, it had lost its intimacy and its power. It had been sanitised. It had been made safe.

She was relieved too that she couldn't see Hugh there. She recognised the thin redheaded man chewing peanuts − Henry someone-or-other, a friend of his − but she did not know any of the other guests. A couple of them turned stiffly as the butler showed her and Simpson in, then returned to their own conversations. It threatened to be a long evening.

Simpson ushered her forward and introduced her to Lady Rudlow. Loretta breathed in, smiled, held out her hand. 'Loretta Lorenz . . . it's a great pleasure − '

Lady Rudlow smiled back and took her hand. 'Your accent − American?'

'Yes.'

'Visiting over here, are you?'

'No, working.'

'Oh, really.' Her Ladyship continued without waiting for Loretta to explain further. 'I do so love travelling myself, but George, dear George, had to travel so much on business, we never went further than Scotland for our holidays . . . Anthony,' called Lady Rudlow above the subdued chatter, 'Come and meet Miss − it is Miss, isn't it? − Loretta Lorenz who is visiting from the States.'

Anthony stepped forward with a small smile of welcome.

So this was the brother. Loretta was immediately struck by the contrast between the two men. Where outwardly Hugh was suave and relaxed, Anthony seemed full of nervous energy. Every muscle was tensed. Some part of him − his mouth, his hand, his foot − was always moving. His eyes ranged around the room without focusing distinctly, like a fish in a bowl, before finally coming to rest on her. He had a charming smile. 'Er, visiting, you say?'

She flashed a warm and only slightly flirtatious smile back at the future master of Conningsby. 'No, working. In the jewellery business.'

'In the jewellery business? How very interesting. Um, you don't deal in jewelled embroidery work, by any chance?' Loretta shook her head. 'No? Pity. Some years back I found an extraordinary collection of liturgical vestments in the attic here – really beautiful things, some of them.'

'Yes?' Over Anthony's shoulder, suddenly she caught sight of Hugh across the room. He was handing a glass of champagne to a new arrival. He turned and saw her. She could see the surprise, the anger even, in his eyes.

She had expected to feel fazed, to find something of her old feelings for him stirring inside her, but bitterness was a better anaesthetic than she had believed possible. She felt precisely nothing.

'It is rather a neglected area,' Anthony continued. 'I've added one or two pieces myself. I bought my first set on impulse at auction. It was wrongly catalogued and ridiculously cheap. Got about thirty pieces now.'

Loretta tried to concentrate on what he was saying. 'Er . . . fascinating.' She warmed to the enthusiasm in his voice. 'Certainly bucking the trend of fashion – the only way to build up a collection. I'd love to see them.'

Hugh was making his way through the guests towards them now. Loretta slowed her breathing. She must stay very calm. She must stay in control.

'I'll show them to you sometime, if you really mean it. I store them in London.' Anthony's hand fluttered nervously at the silk facings of his dinner jacket. It froze as Hugh approached. He nodded, acknowledging his brother, then turned back to Loretta. 'Have you met my brother Hugh?'

'Yes,' Hugh replied for her. 'We're old friends. I must say you're looking very beautiful this evening,' he added smoothly, 'but I didn't realise that you were coming.'

His voice had that same resonance that had so moved her before. She tried to free her mind of the empty promises that had been delivered in the same rich tones.

'Oh, didn't you? I very nearly couldn't. London is so busy at the moment,' she replied lightly. 'So glad I did, though, otherwise I wouldn't have met your charming brother. He's very kindly going to show me his collection of rare liturgical vestments.'

She turned back to Anthony and put her hand lightly on his arm. 'Yes, really I would like to see your collection some time.'

She saw the anger flare in Hugh's eyes. It made her smile.

'Dinner is served,' announced Gander, after a double ration of his now familiar cough.

Slowly the guests began to file through into the dining room. Loretta held back to let them pass. They did not know that this was the second chamber in the labyrinth. She would wait until they had deadened its power.

Only after ten guests had entered and she could hear their small-talk coming from the room was she sure that it was safe to go through the double mahogany doors.

Four vast silver candelabra cast a soft, flickering light over the long mahogany table. Between them, buffed and polished silver game birds crouched and strutted beneath silver bowls filled with orchids. Five different crystal wine glasses sparkled at each of the fourteen places. Loretta noted that four footmen were on duty.

'Anthony, darling,' called Lady Rudlow, 'take your father's place at the head of the table . . . Jane, you're next to him . . . Hugh – oh dear, on the right somewhere, I think . . .'

Loretta swept around the table, squinting at the italicised name cards held by little silver shells. She found her name spelt 'Lawrence' three places along from where Anthony sat. She glanced up casually and noticed Hugh watching her every move from the other side of the table. She did not let him see her smile.

The man in the battered leather jacket came and looked at the name cards on either side of her. He shook his head. ' 'Fraid not.' The men who finally took the places both had the type of ruddy complexion which, she guessed, owed as much to port as to fresh air.

A footman helped her into her chair. For a split second, she wondered whether he had believed her to be pregnant or – heaven forbid – arthritic; then, as she leaned back and he splayed out her napkin for her, she grinned. She thought how nice it would be if she never had to do such deeply tiring things as unfolding a napkin ever again.

'The name's Baxendale. Philip Baxendale,' said the man on her left as soon as he sat down. He had a thin mouth, and short brown hair that stopped parallel with the tips of his ears. 'Not local, are you?'

'No,' she replied. 'American.'

'Guessed as much. Nothing wrong with that though. Nothing wrong at all. Known Anthony long?'

A steady hand placed before her a gold-rimmed porcelain plate half-filled with a dark brown soup. 'As

183

it happens, I only met him for the first time this evening. William Simpson invited me along.'

'Hmm, yes, I see.' He looked over to where Simpson sat, and nodded.

She was not at all sure that being associated with Simpson had done much for her social standing, but she let it pass. She picked up her spoon. 'Are you an old friend of Anthony's?'

The man sprinkled his soup with liberal quantities of salt. 'Yes and no. Known him since we were both at Eton − almost grew up together − but sort of lost touch. Silly, really, as we're almost neighbours. But for the last few years, I've hardly seen him down here.'

She took a mouthful of soup. It tasted of flour and gravy. 'Yet he asked you here this evening?'

'No, Elizabeth Rudlow asked me.' He gave her a thin smile. 'I think she asked everybody present except for a few of the girls and Camilla's − er − friend.'

Spoons clattered against the sides of soup plates. There were sudden bursts of conversation around the table and equally sudden lulls, like someone tuning a radio.

'Are all Anthony's friends abroad then?' she ventured.

'No, but . . .' he glanced quickly over each shoulder then lowered his voice to a conspiratorial whisper '. . . they're a pretty rum bunch − know what I mean?'

Loretta's mind was suddenly filled with surmises. She forced down a second spoonful of the soup. 'You mean they aren't quite proper?' she asked with light mockery.

'Far from it,' the man said knowingly. 'Oh dear, oh dear. Far from it.' He shielded his mouth with his napkin. 'Do the terms "Speed King", "Acid Head" and "Coke Freak" mean anything to you?'

'I didn't know.'

He nodded gravely. 'Oh, yes. 'Fraid so. All over now, though. Been drying out. Looks well, I must say. Not really his fault. Some devilish car crash. Quacks pumped him full of all sorts of painkillers. Body couldn't cope. Then he just got into a bad crowd, you know? Dreadful girlfriend called Corinna someone or other. Could happen to the best of us. All over now. And well done him, I reckon.'

'Very well done.' She looked at the girls to Anthony's left and right. Neither looked as if she had ever partaken of anything stronger than smelling salts. 'And is Corinna here?'

'Of course she's not here!' her neighbour fumed, sprinkling yet more salt on his soup. 'You don't break bread with a Jezebel.'

Loretta glanced along the table at Anthony, the cured junkie, the collector of vestments, the heir to Conningsby. She had come across drugs problems before, of course, at high school and at college.

'. . . *you can tell she doesn't have any friends. If she had, one of them would have told her not to wear that ghastly blue eye-shadow . . .*'

'. . . *don't you realise what irreparable damage you personally are doing to the ozone layer . . .*'

'. . . *I think the Pope was very badly briefed . . .*'

Snippets of conversation caught but rarely held her attention.

The beef was tough and swimming in a thick brown sauce which was almost indistinguishable from the soup. Loretta forked a squidgy carrot into her mouth and chatted to the man at her other side. He had curly brown hair, plump cheeks and an engaging smile, and turned out to be the son of a neighbouring farmer. She talked to him about New York and jewellery, and he in turn told her all she ever wanted to know about fertilisers.

For twenty minutes now, Anthony had been locked in conversation with a pretty round-faced girl wearing a green-spotted Laura Ashley evening dress. She had shoulder-length blonde hair which had been teased and backcombed for the evening.

'I hardly know anybody here,' Loretta remarked, interrupting her debate with the farmer's son on the present size of the EEC butter mountain. 'Could you tell me, for instance, who's that girl Anthony is talking to now?'

'Oh, her,' he said, slightly petulant. 'That's Jane Chalmers. Now, as I was saying, the present system of milk quotas and subsidies means . . .'

'Yes, yes, I am sure you are right. Jane Chalmers, you say?'

'Yes. Lady Jane Chalmers. Her family own the neighbouring estate.' He smiled mischievously and leaned closer to Loretta. 'An only daughter too. If Anthony has half a mind left after this drugs business, he'll marry her — if she'll have him, that is.'

'Oh!' Loretta exclaimed, and quickly lifted her napkin to her face. 'You mean . . . you mean that they're in love?'

He sipped his claret and smacked his lips. 'Didn't say that. If joined, their estates would make a marvellous unit, and I don't see why they shouldn't, too.'

As the farmer's son carried on expounding the virtues of a landowner's ideal marriage, Loretta's mind wandered.

' . . . *the tropical rain forests are the world's oxygen bank and if . . .*'

' . . . *it works well enough with cows. I don't see why it shouldn't work with humans . . .*'

' . . . *they'll never get planning permission . . .*'

' . . . *I have simply no idea what she thought she was doing in the Royal Enclosure . . .*'

The beef was followed by a crème brulée that had not set, and an excellent Sauterne. The footmen were busily clearing the plates under the watchful eye of Gander.

Throughout dinner, Loretta had deliberately prevented herself from looking across at Hugh. At times, though, she'd thought that she'd sensed his eyes on her. She had been sure to appear very animated then, interested in her neighbour's conversation and slightly flirtatious.

She glanced quickly across at him now under the pretence of scanning the length of the table towards where Camilla had risen to her feet. Their eyes met for an instant, then broke away.

Camilla tapped her spoon on the table top for the second time. 'Please, everyone, silence a minute.' Lady Rudlow looked around her quizzically. Conversation stopped. 'I'd . . . I'd just like to say first, Welcome home, Anthony. Good to have you back.'

'Hear! Hear!'

'Yes, indeed.'

Anthony flinched, then blushed. 'Thank you,' he said quietly.

'And, secondly, after much arm-twisting and persuasion down this end of the table, we have a surprise for you.' She grinned. 'Steve has very kindly agreed to play something for us after dinner.'

A chair squeaked. Someone coughed.

'Darling,' Lady Rudlow leaned across the table, 'do you think this is quite the moment?'

'But Mummy, he's terrific. You'll love it.'

'Yes, er, darling, but . . .'

'*Please.*'

Lady Rudlow folded her napkin. 'Very well then. Thank you, Camilla.' She stood. 'Girls,' she called imperiously like a schoolma'am before her class, 'time to powder our noses and leave the men to their port.' She wagged a finger at Hugh. 'Now, don't be too long.'

At her nod, all the women present at once rose to their feet. Loretta quickly folded her napkin and rose too.

She followed the crocodile of girls back through the Yellow Drawing Room, across the Great Hall, up the staircase on to the gallery above. There, rather than turning left to where the grand guest bedrooms were, Lady Rudlow wheeled right. This was a part of the house that Loretta had never seen before. Her Ladyship passed through three double doors, each surmounted with pediments, then turned sharp left.

Loretta sighed. The State Bedroom was merely a blind chamber. This, she mused, was the real centre of Conningsby. It was very tranquil here, bright and airy, homely even.

Lady Rudlow's bedroom was framed by the sweep of a huge bay window. The sun had faded the heavy folds of crimped and gathered flowery chintz into soft pink and blue pastels. The same chintz, covered by a gauze of yellowing lace, rose to a half-tester above the large bed. The pale blue silk moiré walls were studded with collections of eighteenth-century pastels in gold frames. The furniture was delicate, French and feminine.

There were flowers by the bed and on the dressing room table, but what scent they had was masked by the all pervading smell of wet dog. The room suddenly filled with girlish giggles.

Loretta disengaged herself from the other girls. She walked across to Lady Rudlow who was seated at her dressing table teasing her hair with a kirby-grip and comb. Silver photograph frames were everywhere: Anthony and Hugh by the rocking horse; Camilla in her christening robes or on her first pony; Lord Rudlow on a dappled grey; the Meet. 'What a lovely room, Lady Rudlow.'

'Yes. I'm pleased you like it,' replied Her Ladyship with a hint of sadness. 'So blissfully peaceful — George loved it. Such a pity you can't see the view over the park. First thing in the morning the light is quite wonderful, sort of yellow and milky.' She sighed, still working on an obstinate curl with the kirby-grip. 'Nothing like it. This and the State Bedroom are my favourite rooms.'

'Mine too,' Loretta nearly said, but instead she swallowed and took one step back in case Lady Rudlow were to notice the bloom on her cheeks.

She walked through into the adjoining room, which she took to be Lord Rudlow's dressing room. Mahogany cupboards, slightly ajar, were full of tweed, hunting clothes and velvet smoking jackets. Hunting trophies and paintings of dogs and horses covered green baize walls.

Loretta guessed that nothing had been changed since the day of the fall. Two matted ivory hair brushes and a riding crop lay askew on the chest of drawers alongside two bottles of Trumper's hair oil. The corner of a pair of neatly folded flannelette pyjamas peeped out from under the counterpane of the small single bed.

Two girls were chatting by the far wall. The one on the right was the blonde round-faced girl in the Laura

Ashley dress who had sat next to Anthony; the one on the left, the brunette with the knowing eyes.

Loretta called, 'Hi,' and moved forward to join them.

The blonde girl swivelled half-round. She glanced quickly at Loretta in a bored, pre-occupied way, then turned her bare back to her.

Loretta stopped. Whistling silently to herself, she continued her study of the objects on Lord Rudlow's chest of drawers. None of the girls who she had spoken to so far that evening had been particularly friendly. It was almost as if they thought of Conningsby as their private sanctum and her as an interloper, trespassing on their personal property. Yet it was they who seemed to pass through Conningsby blinkered, unseeing, blind to the magic of the place.

They might not welcome female competition from someone outside their charmed circle, she supposed. Well, gone were the days when slights and snubs would send her to cower in the shadows. She might not have the benefit of their fine breeding but she was a woman now, a survivor. A match for any of them.

'Hello.'

Loretta turned, saw Camilla and smiled.

Camilla's wide kohl-rimmed eyes flicked over her from head to toe, then she returned the smile. 'You're the American William Simpson brought, aren't you?'

'Yeah, that's me.'

Camilla pushed her long black hair off her face. 'Well I hope you weren't too bored at dinner. You were between Philip Baxendale and John Crop, right?'

Loretta nodded.

'Nothing to do with me, I promise. Talk about plunging you into the deep end.'

'No, honestly, it was fun. It's fun just being here.'

A short girl in a turquoise dress barged past them. 'Gangway! Gangway! Laura's dog's been naughty. I told her she shouldn't have brought it up here.'

'Oh dear,' said Camilla wryly, 'Mummy's not really interested in the problems of global pollution but she does care passionately about her bedroom carpet.'

Loretta grinned. 'Yes, William told me that you work for Friends of the Earth. That's really great. In New York last year, I took part in a demo against air pollution. A friend took me along. Over a thousand of us, all in makeshift gas masks, stormed City Hall.'

Camilla's eyes lit up. 'I read about it in the papers. So you were there? Keep up the good work, girl. Come and see us at the office sometime, hmm? I'll fill you in on what we're doing over here.'

'Yeah, I'd like that,' Loretta replied enthusiastically.

'Good.' Camilla leaned against the door jamb. She tilted her head to one side and her wide eyes ranged over Loretta again. 'You know, maybe I'm very wrong but you don't strike me as the type who would be going out with Simpson. He's, well – how can I say this? – just very, very straight.'

'Oh, no! You didn't think . . .? We're only friends. Hardly that even. I've met him a couple of times at parties, that's all.' She moved a little closer to Camilla. 'And you? The musician?'

Camilla smiled coyly and nodded. 'Yup. Dishy, isn't he?'

'Definitely edible. There's something about musicians.' She squeezed Camilla's arm. 'What's he play? I bet it's rhythm.'

191

'Right. Though this evening he's brought his classical.' She sighed. 'Steve's so versatile.'

'I bet.'

'I just hope it's going to be OK with this crowd. I had to do something to liven up the evening. I mean immediately Mummy told me about this party, I said I thought it was a mistake. It's just too soon. Anthony needs time.' She pushed back her hair again. 'Did you meet him?'

'Anthony? Well, only briefly.'

'He's great. I think you'd really like him.' She shrugged and smiled. 'But as his sister, I suppose I'm just ever so slightly biased.'

'Camilla, darling!' Lady Rudlow's voice carried easily from the bedroom.

She turned, sighing. 'Yes, Mummy.' She apologised to Loretta and walked through the door, smoothing her dress as she went. Loretta followed her into the bedroom.

Two girls lay together on the bed, their white legs hanging like clappers from their bell-shaped party frocks. They were giggling and chatting. On the floor beneath them, two other girls were down on their knees, sponging the carpet. A little Highland terrier with hair like twisted hemp yapped at their side. 'I'm really sorry, Lady Rudlow. I'm really sorry,' the girl in the red dress repeated with each stroke of the sponge. The sounds of Steve tuning and strumming his guitar rose from the stairwell, counterpointing her chant.

Lady Rudlow sat facing them at her dressing table stool, framed in the light from the two tall, thin candlestick lamps on either side. Her spine was very straight. She held a hairbrush in one hand and gently tapped its silver back against the palm of her other hand.

'Camilla, come over here this instant. I want to get to grips with that hair.'

'Right, everybody ready?' asked Steve. He sat cross-legged on a spindly *Louis Quinze* chair in the corner of the Ballroom.

'Has everybody got everything they need?' Lady Rudlow called. 'Drinks? Ashtrays? Everyone comfortable? Good. Steve, you may proceed.'

He struck the first few chords. To everyone's surprise it was a classical piece. A sigh came from one of the girls. A dress rustled.

On the far side of the room, Hugh crossed his arms and lay back, clutching his whisky with the look of martyrdom on his face. He had already been seated when the girls had returned and had smiled pointedly at Loretta, patting the chair next to him, summoning her like an obedient terrier. The gall of it!

Loretta had Simpson on one side, Baxendale on the other. She really did not mind who her companions were provided they did not fidget. She wanted to listen to Steve.

She glanced across at Anthony. He was seated next to Jane Chalmers, and while she was slightly restless, he was staring ahead, absorbed in the music. He appeared at ease with Jane though. They seemed to share the relaxed familiarity of a long-established couple. Jane's eyes swivelled towards him periodically but there was no passion in them, no enquiry.

Loretta did not know much about classical music, but even she could tell that this was no amateur performance. Steve's long fingers skidded over the strings, contort-ing, twisting, plucking, somehow squeezing the most perfect, clear, precise notes out of stretched wire.

Apart from the music the room was entirely silent. All the coughing and fidgeting had stopped. The girls in particular were very still. For many, Loretta guessed, it was not so much the music as Steve himself. There was a look of intense concentration on his face, ecstasy even. Each movement seemed to carry with it an immense emotional burden. As the intensity of the music deepened so too did the lines that creased the skin around his eyes and the veins that swelled on his neck.

Camilla was smiling softly, her face flushed with pride. Lady Rudlow had relaxed. Her folded arms now hung loosely in her lap, and she was nodding and smiling. Only Hugh sat with the glum forbearance of an airline passenger waiting for a delayed connection. The music rose and swelled one last time and then Steve strummed frantically into the finale. Beads of sweat fell from his brow.

'Bravo! Bravo!'

'That was wonderful, Steve,' exclaimed Lady Rudlow with emotion in her voice. She stopped clapping for a moment and reached in her bag for a handkerchief.

'Great. Really great.'

'Really good,' called Anthony. 'Rodriguez, wasn't it?'

'Thank you,' Steve said quietly. He stood up and nodded an acknowledgment of their applause. Immediately Camilla came up and hugged him.

'You were . . . amazing. Amazing.'

'More! More! More!' called Anthony. For the first time this evening, he seemed genuinely to be enjoying himself.

Loretta nodded to Simpson and got to her feet. She walked across to Lady Rudlow. 'Thank you so much.

I have enjoyed myself.' Then she said goodbye to Camilla. 'Lunch some time?' She told Steve, 'I love the way you play. So much feeling,' then smiled again at Camilla.

She allowed Hugh to kiss her on the cheek. 'Let me give you a lift back,' he said quietly. His car keys jangled in his pocket. 'I really don't like the idea of your entrusting your life to Simpson's driving.'

She was calm, even matter-of-fact. 'No, Hugh, I can assure you, he is quite safe.'

Last, she went up to Anthony. 'So pleased to meet you, and I really would like to see your collection sometime. I mean it. Here's my card. You will call, won't you? Promise?'

A shy half smile was his only reply. He shook her hand very formally.

# Chapter 16

'I'm sorry, Steve,' said Camilla, gazing out of the plate-glass window at the corkscrew lights from the barges. The dawn was coming. A diffuse yellow mist rose over the far bank of the Thames. 'It's not always that deadly, but what with Daddy and Anthony and all that . . .'

Behind her the kettle hissed. 'No I really enjoyed myself. A long drive back to London, though. It's good to be home.' Steve sighed. 'I like your brother.'

'Who, Hugh?'

'Nah. I mean, I'm sure he's all right, but I don't get the feeling we'd have much to say to one another. No, Anthony. Nice guy. A sensitive sort. An old soul.'

'Yes,' she mused, 'he's very sweet.'

'Wish you hadn't forced me and my guitar on the assembled populace.'

She turned. Steve lay propped on his elbow on the shiny red counterpane of his giant bed. Everything in the sparsely decorated room was ultra-modern and brilliantly coloured, from the crane-like swivelling standard lights to the bright green perspex and lacquer bedside tables. 'That,' she said firmly, 'was the only real success of the evening. Even Mummy had tears in her eyes at the end of it.'

'Yeah, well, all the same.' He pulled himself up from the bed and walked through into the kitchen.

Camilla glanced across at the large modern painting of two entwined figures hanging on the unplastered brick wall. She unbuttoned her jacket and threw it on a chair by the bed. 'God, I'm tired,' she yawned. 'Nerves as much as anything, I suppose.'

She slipped out of her dress and sat on the bed. 'Thanks, darling.' She smiled as Steve handed her a steaming mug of coffee. She sipped once, shuddered, and put the mug on the shiny top of the bedside table. She unclipped her bra and quickly climbed into bed.

Steve, on the other side of the bed now, pulled off his shoes which clattered noisily on the floor. 'No, I was expecting a really heavy scene, but it worked out OK. I felt, you know, easy there.' He pulled off his shirt and her hand came up to stroke the rope-like contours of his spine. He turned to her then, dressed only in his jeans. He kissed her very gently and her hands ran lightly over his shoulders and chest. 'I thought you were tired,' he murmured.

'I am. Come to bed.' She rolled over, turning her back to him.

A moment later, she felt the warmth of his naked body pressed close against hers. There was a click, and when she opened her drowsy eyes the room was in darkness save for the rippling reflections of the Thames on the loft ceiling. Steve's hand stroked her side, her thighs. He nuzzled at the nape of her neck.

'Mmm,' she sighed and rolled over once more on to her back. He kissed her throat, teased each nipple into life while all the time his right hand kept working gently.

'Cammy,' he croaked softly.

'Hmm?'

'Stay.'

'I am staying.' Her voice was very small.

'No. I mean for good. Stay with me. Move in. Make it official.'

'Is this some sort of proposal?' she murmured, then, 'Oh, do that again.'

He lifted his head from her breasts. In the dim light she saw his tousled hair and broad grin just inches away from her lips. 'Live together, get hitched – all the same to me. Whatever you want.' He lowered his head again. His tongue flicked each corner of her mouth, then her ear.

'Oh, don't do that,' she moaned. 'Romantic tonight, aren't you? Oh, yes.' She sighed. 'I do love you, Steve. Oh, I do love you. More. But let's leave it for now, huh? I've seen what – Oh God – I've seen what marriage can do to people. Makes them liars, cheats. I'm just – I'm just – oh, *Christ*!' she shrieked. 'I love you, love you, love you . . .'

# Chapter 17

With the afternoon sun streaming into the room, the figure behind the desk was cast into sharp relief. For a second Anthony thought it was his father there still. But the hair was wrong. His father's scalp was almost smooth, the thin white hair brushed with all the care properly bestowed on an endangered species. Hugh's hair was thick and slightly unkempt.

He glanced upwards then returned to his papers. 'With you in a minute, Ant. Take a pew.'

Anthony sat down in the familiar leather chair, positioned as always about a yard from the desk. Nothing much had changed. The old photograph of his mother in her debutante days was still on the desk. His father's old models of the Rudlow fleet still lined the mantelpiece and windowsill. They still needed a good dust.

Hugh was a study in concentration, his head slightly bowed over the papers in front of him, his mouth set in a rigid line. Anthony suspected though that this was no more than power play: Hugh's way of reminding him who was boss.

It had been in that office, in that chair even, that his father had first told him Hugh was resigning his commission and joining the firm. Since then, however hard Anthony had tried, his father's continual comparisons – 'Look at Hugh', 'Do it like Hugh', 'Take a tip from Hugh' – had rung in his ears like a monotonous plain chant. Despite the fact that the physiognomy was all wrong, Hugh was his father's blue-eyed boy.

It was not a question of intelligence. It was not a question of ability. It was a question of style.

Sure, he should have controlled his liking for the glistening white powder, but that had not become a serious problem until later – a symptom of his frustration and stress as much as anything – and if sniffing coke were deemed a disqualification for high office, well, stubby-nosed Porsches would be snorting from the forecourts of every second-hand car dealer in the land.

But what was done was done. That old confidence had been punched out of him now.

'Seen Father?' Hugh stopped scribbling. He leaned back in the chair, his legs crossed.

'Yes. On . . . on my way here.' Anthony bowed his head and swallowed. 'Very sad. Very sad . . . to see him like that. Mother broke the news to me when she picked me up from the centre.' He swallowed again. 'I wish you hadn't kept it from me. Damn it, I'm not a child. I had a right to know!'

'And ruin all their good work? Didn't want to compound the tragedy, old boy.' Hugh shrugged. 'Nothing that could be done anyway.'

'Yes well, thank God – at least – *that* is all over now.' Anthony's fingers tapped against the chair's arm rest. 'I'm back in good shape and keen to get into the swim once more. Would you believe it, I even missed the old place? My congratulations, by the way, on your elevation to Chairman.'

Hugh's chair squeaked. 'No resentment, then, seeing I'm a mere second son? Think we can work together?' The tip of his pen touched the desk. 'You needn't, you know. What with the − er − change of circumstances, I mean, *I* certainly am not going to strap you to your desk. There's a lot that needs doing at Conningsby, and if you wanted, you'd be free to indulge your whims. Find something − I don't know − more to your taste. Dealing in vestments and rare tapestry, perhaps? It's an idea.'

'Don't be a damn fool, Hugh. Those are only hobbies, you know that. My place is here − in the family business.'

Hugh circled his pen. His lips tightened. 'Fully recovered, you say?'

'Yes. Fully recovered.' Anthony tried to keep a note of petulance out of his voice. He sprang to his feet. 'Look, Hugh, I don't say that if I'd been brought up differently, it would've even entered my head to become an aeronautical engineer, but I've done it now all my adult life . . . and I enjoy it. I enjoy the intellectual challenge.' He stopped pacing. His voice softened suddenly. 'What's happened to the Condor by the way? Have I missed the maiden flight?'

Hugh looked up at him. 'You have, I'm afraid. It was three days after Father's accident. But there are problems. She's back in the workshop.'

'Oh. Serious?'

'Could be. Don will fill you in.'

Anthony frowned. He moved back to his chair and sat down. 'Anyway, this place is our bread and butter. Without it Conningsby would become an uninhabitable

203

shell or a school, maybe. Nobody is ever going to accuse me of being someone who sits at the table without getting his hands dirty in the kitchen.'

'Well, that's just it.' The corners of Hugh's mouth curled. He sat back in his chair and twisted the pen between his fingers. 'I mentioned the alternatives for a good reason. It's quite possible that we won't be in need of so many cooks in the kitchen from now on.'

Anthony leaned forward. 'I don't follow?'

'AIP.'

'Pain in the butt, I know, but I don't see —'

'They're seriously interested in the company.'

'Not thinking of selling, are you? It would be —'

Hugh made a calming gesture with the flat of his hand. 'Let me finish. At first I dismissed it as mere opportunism, but they're talking real money now. Forty-two times earnings. Twenty times asset value or thereabouts.' He whistled. 'Tempting?'

'But when the Condor is launched . . .'

'Yes, I know. The Condor could be a very profitable aircraft, but everything — the whole future of the company — hinges on its success, and that depends on stealing a march on AIP. That's like playing poker blindfold. If the full deal materialises, what AIP is offering us would be very, very tempting. And risk free.'

'But this company meant more to Father than anything. More than Conningsby, even.'

'Yes.' Hugh mimicked the low growl of his father's voice: 'Rudlow Aircraft Company . . . the independent force in the industry.' He shrugged dismissively.

'Father wouldn't have sold, whatever they offered him.'

'Sadly, it's a different world now, Ant, from when

Father started. You know that. The days of the independent are numbered. You've seen the way in which the development costs of the Condor have spiralled. Our capital base is just too small to compete on proper terms with the Cessnas, the Gates and the Grummans.'

Anthony shook his head. 'OK, but that doesn't mean that we've got to pull the plug just when we're breaking through. And what about the workforce? Father wasn't the easiest man to work for – never bothered much with the velvet glove – but they knew he would never, ever let them down.'

'Yeah.' Hugh shrugged. 'Jobs for life. A fine noble concept but out of touch with the real world. Like Conningsby really.'

'And there will be job losses?'

'Some wastage, naturally, but we can afford to be generous.' Hugh was suddenly brisk. 'Look, Ant, forget what Father might or might not have done. This deal will secure you and yours and Conningsby well into the next millennium.'

'And you are doing all this for me and Conningsby, eh? What will you get out of it?' Anthony added almost casually.

Hugh shrugged. He rolled the pen on the desk. 'I'll do very nicely too, of course. They will compensate me for my loss of office as managing director, give me a new role in the organisation, fully in keeping with my status . . . oh, all the usual. I'm not trying to pull the wool over your eyes. I'll come out of the deal a very rich man.'

'Hmm.' Anthony brushed an imaginary piece of fluff off his trouser leg. 'I thought that just might be tucked away in the small print somewhere.'

Suddenly Hugh's eyes flashed with anger. 'You don't resent that, do you? You have no right . . .' His fingers tightened around the pen, then dropped it.

He stood. Anthony's eyes followed him as he paced back and forth in front of the window.

'Look,' Hugh explained, 'the lion's share goes, of course, to the majority shareholders who − I need hardly remind you − are the Rudlow family Trustees. Sir Arthur has been his usual discreet self and so I have got no official information on how the spoils will be divided, but I suspect that Father with his old-fashioned ideas of primogeniture and preserving the estate and that great white elephant of a house, whatever the cost, will leave the lot to *you*.' Suddenly he tilted his head to one side and with an air of light mockery recited the Second Son's Grace: ' "For what we might have received; May *they* be truly thankful." '

Hugh stopped. He turned and faced his brother. 'Look,' he said quietly, 'let's get one thing absolutely clear. I don't resent you your inheritance. It's just − as they say − the accident of birth. I don't see why you should resent it if I make a little money out of a deal that I have worked hard to set up to benefit us all.'

'No. It's not the money,' Anthony replied in a soft reflective voice. 'We're not just talking money here, we're talking people's lives.'

He tilted back his head and stared out through the window, lost in thought. The flags in the forecourt still hung at half-mast as a sign of respect. There was no wind to unfurl them. Slowly his hand clenched and unclenched. 'I don't like it. I don't like it at all. I'm going to fight you on this.'

Hugh merely smiled. 'Well, just think about it,' he said

smoothly. 'I'm sure that, on reflection, you will see that it's for the best.'

'Of course I'll study the terms in detail, but I don't think that I'll change my mind. It's the principle of the thing.'

Hugh shrugged, the smile never leaving his lips. 'Well, you'll have an opportunity to air your views at the board meeting when the whole thing is discussed. Of course,' he waved a hand, 'I'd much prefer it if you went along with me, but, with respect, it doesn't make a whole lot of difference. It's up to the board in the first instance − and I think that they'll find the terms very attractive, as indeed will the shareholders.'

'You mean Sir Arthur and the Trustees?'

'Yes. In an uncertain world, there's never anything wrong with a mountain of cash.'

Anthony moved uneasily in his chair. 'We should at least wait − out of respect, I mean − until Father's condition is settled one way or the other.'

Hugh shook his head. 'Uh huh. The doctors say that he could be like that for years, but he won't be coming round, if that's what you mean. And this can't wait. On Tuesday I'll be going over with the lawyers to Philadelphia for a further meeting. Should imagine that I'll be shuttling back and forth for most of next month. But five weeks from now we should have a deal on the table.'

'Does the workforce know?'

'No. I've kept Sir Arthur abreast with developments, of course. The board know, but only in the most general terms.' He smiled. 'I presented it to them in terms of a collaborative relationship. Meanwhile, not a word. I can trust you for that, can't I?'

Anthony nodded.

'Good. So as far as everyone else is concerned, it's business as usual. Keep Don up to scratch. That's if you feel up to it after your ordeal?'

'Yes, Hugh,' Anthony replied sharply. 'I thought I made it clear that I am absolutely fit now and ready to return to work.'

'Don't be so tetchy, Ant,' Hugh soothed. 'It was a perfectly reasonable question. I'm running a business here, after all. I'm sure that you will be a great help. You know I'm no good at the technical stuff. Your brief is to make damn' certain that there are no avoidable delays and that the Condor is ready on time.'

Anthony nodded. 'For the Paris launch?'

'Right.'

Anthony smiled wistfully. 'The Rudlow Condor, the star of the Paris Airshow.'

'The AIP Condor,' Hugh corrected. 'AIP.'


The meeting over, Anthony closed the door behind him and made his way along the pale beige corridor.

At the centre they had told him that the only cure for addicts was radical personality displacement. They had told him that when he left he would feel as if he had been reborn.

He had scoffed at the time, but it was true. He did feel like a new man. No longer did he wake up each morning with cramps in his gut, his head aching, his body limp. No longer was his day made up of highs which just weren't highs anymore, downers which would never end, desperate panic as the stash got low, hours of anxious waiting for the man to show.

He was free now, free to be himself — whoever that

was. It would take time, he knew, to get used to this new persona who now inhabited his body, but so far he was pleasantly surprised by what he had found. Gone was much of the self-loathing, the hot-headed attention seeking. The new Anthony, he thought, was more reflective, more tolerant. Altogether a nicer person.

He had walked down that pale beige corridor every day of his working life, but he noticed for the first time since his addiction the singing of the birds and the way the sunlight came through the window and washed the far wall with an orange glow. He smiled. There was so much to rediscover.

He turned right into the design studio. The hum of the computer and the staccato tapping of the matrix printer drowned out the birdsong. Don was in his usual place by the far window, working on a drawing. He was perched on a high stool like a gnome on a mushroom, short legs swinging.

Anthony walked over to him. 'Hello,' he said softly.

Don started as if suddenly waking from a dream. His back straightened. His head turned. Then the muscles around his tired eyes slowly focused on Anthony and he gave a grin so wide and open that his crooked yellow teeth showed. His eyes smiled too. Magnified through his thick spectacles, they were like ping-pong balls.

Even in Anthony's darkest moments when the history of his addiction had come out, Don had been a true friend. Now, tactfully, he did not even mention the clinic. 'Anthony!' He nodded vigorously. 'Good. Good. Good. I just knew you wouldn't be able to keep away for long. Not from the Condor. Great to have you back on board. We missed you, you know? And you're just in time.

We've got some very interesting problems for you.' He pointed to the plan before him. 'The aerofoil section.'

He stabbed at the drawing with his pencil as he explained the suspected points of weakness in the existing design, then gestured across to where a very thin man with a head of wiry hair was scanning figures as they scrolled upwards on a computer display screen. 'Jonathan is going through all the figures from point one. Something's wrong somewhere. It's just . . . we can't put our finger on it.'

'Do you think we might have to redesign the whole section?' Anthony asked. He already had his jacket off and was keen to get down to work.

'I don't think so. But we won't really know until we are into it a little further. Oh,' he turned back to Anthony and beamed at him, 'but you haven't seen her yet, have you? Not the completed Mark 1 prototype?'

Anthony shook his head and grinned.

'You must. You must.' Don jumped off his stool and hurried him through the door.

They walked down the passage, past the secretaries' pool and the paintings of the Rudlow fleet. Everywhere the red and white of the Rudlow insignia was blazoned on the walls. The people that they met in the passage, all people he knew, smiled or nodded at him, welcoming him back.

When they crossed the tarmaced forecourt and stopped momentarily at hangar number one, it was the same story. Mike Cutter, the engine fitter, gave him a wave of welcome. 'Good on you,' called someone from behind. There must have been ninety to a hundred people working there. Men in overalls tapping, pushing, probing, fixing.

They trusted him because he was a Rudlow. They

trusted him because his father had never let any of them down. His managerial style might have been blunt and autocratic, but if they ever had a problem, he always had the time for them. He would solve it with sound advice, a kind word or a thick envelope. They had loved him for that, and had given him their loyalty. They had loved him too for the passion with which he had talked about his planes. His eyes would light up like a small boy's, his voice would soften, become almost whimsical, and they too would be drawn into his dream. They were not just making aircraft to ferry harassed executives around the world. They were part of man's struggle to reach beyond himself, to conquer the skies, to pit his wits against nature.

If AIP ever took over, the hangars would be closed. They would be left to the wind and rain.

Anthony hurried past the second hangar. He did not want to see any more friendly faces. Not now. They made his skin prickle. They made him feel like a traitor.

Don strained against the dull metal door of the third hangar. He pushed it open with shaking fingers. He straightened, stuck out his chest like a turkey cock, then flourished an arm proudly. 'There,' he said, 'there.'

He led the way, entering the hangar almost with reverence, head slightly bowed. Anthony followed and could not stop himself from shuddering.

An aluminium access dock surrounded her but to his eyes did nothing to detract from her sleek lines and daringly narrow wings, the sheer beauty of her.

'What do you think, eh?' asked Don. 'She's so nearly perfect. We've just got to get these last few problems sorted out.' He shook his head, his eyes almost misty for a moment. 'If only your father could see her fly. He would be so proud. Whatever happens to him, he lives on in this plane. He lives on so long as his planes . . . so long as the Rudlow Condor is burnishing the sky.'

Anthony turned away. He looked down at his shoes and swallowed hard.

# Chapter 18

Shona chewed loudly. She swallowed, licked her lips and sighed. 'Aren't you going to eat your breakfast, Loretta? There's nothing worse than cold fried egg.'

They were seated on either side of the small check-clothed table next to the kitchen units. The window was wide open but still the smell of frying clogged the air. Loretta felt the grease clinging to her white towelling dressing gown and filling her nostrils and throat. She averted her eyes from the thin crisp strands of dead pig. 'Really kind of you, but just coffee and a piece of toast will do me fine.'

'You sure?' Shona's eyes opened wide. 'A cooked breakfast is one of the things Brian and I really look forward to about Saturday.' She speared another piece of bacon with her fork. 'I think it's only right, though, that he goes and visits his family once in a while. They're in Cardiff, you know? His mum's probably making some for him right now. He wouldn't miss his cooked Saturday breakfast. Not Brian.'

Loretta's thoughts were far away. She poured herself a cup of coffee and sipped at it until her flatmate had finished talking, then said casually: 'Shona, I wonder whether you could do me a big favour?'

She grunted through a mouthful of breakfast, 'Sure. What?'

'Call the Rudlows' London number for me after breakfast?'

'Uh, why?' Shona put down her knife and fork and sighed. 'Not still moping after Hugh, are you, dearest? What's done is done. Over. *Finito*. I've told you a thousand times, he's just not worth it. There's absolutely no point —'

'Hugh should be away,' announced Loretta firmly. 'He told me at the dinner party he was about to go off to the States. That was ten days ago now.'

'So we rave and rant at his answering machine. Great.'

'No.' Loretta glanced towards the open window, hearing the low rumble of traffic outside. 'I just want you to check whether Anthony's in town.'

'And why me?'

'Just in case Hugh's still there, of course.'

'Silly of me.' Shona's mouth twitched. She gave Loretta a long quizzical look then picked up her knife and fork again and returned to her breakfast. There was only half a slice of bacon and the yolk of one egg left on her plate now. She cut the bacon into four small pieces, speared one, then plunged the fork into the yolk, letting the yellow juices run.

Loretta waited patiently until Shona had scraped her plate clean before she asked her again: 'Will you make the call?'

Shona sucked in air through her teeth. She pushed her plate away and put her arms on the table. 'Look, dearest, I'm really not at all sure that this is a good idea. I know what you've been through,' she soothed, 'but this obsession of yours with the Rudlows and Conningsby is beginning to get just a little bit unhealthy. Why not just forget about it, hmm? There are other men — houses other than Conningsby.'

'You haven't been there so you don't know what it's like,' Loretta answered defensively. 'I don't know how to describe it — it's so special, magical in a way. It sort of wraps around you in a protective cocoon. The world outside — the cruelty, the muggings, the sordid business of it all — it just stops dead at the gates.'

'Go there in the winter. Probably damn' cold and draughty to boot. A house, Loretta, is only bricks and mortar, however grand it might be. And nowadays it's bound to be a liability, too.'

'Oh, this has nothing to do with the house or with Hugh,' Loretta said lightly. 'Anthony is lonely and afraid. He's just been through the most traumatic experience of his life. He needs help.'

'From you?' Shona's eyes stared at her disbelievingly over the rim of her coffee cup. 'Look, you told me all about the dinner party and the way that Hugh got hot under the collar when you were flirting with Anthony —'

'I wasn't flirting, only chatting. We were discussing art.'

Shona waved her hand dismissively and sighed. 'OK, discussing art. It's just — oh, how to say this?' She frowned, took another sip of coffee and started again. 'Look, if I didn't know you better, I might just think that the only reason you want to get to know this Anthony is to get back at Hugh. Now is that really fair? You said yourself Anthony's just been through one of the most traumatic experiences of his life. I know that you're bitter about Hugh, and with good reason, but is it really fair to involve his poor brother in your little games of revenge?'

Loretta's mouth moved but for a time no sound came out. When finally she spoke, it was briskly and fluently. 'As I told you, Anthony needs help, and he won't get it from his family, that's for sure. With a father like I had, there's hardly anything I don't know about addiction. Drink, drugs . . . it doesn't make any difference.'

'But, Christ, this is crazy. You barely know him.'

'Well enough to know that he won't be able to stay off drugs without a helping hand. No one can. He's also an aesthete. He collects ecclesiastical vestments, would you believe?'

'Yeah. I wondered why the usual reading matter on the coffee table − viz, *Vogue and Great Country Houses* − had been replaced by a book called *Ecclesiastical Vestments Then and Now*.'

'A girl's got to improve her mind.'

'More coffee?' Shona nodded. Loretta poured her another cup.

'He promised to show me his collection, and that was ten days ago now. I really would like to see them. There can't be any harm in that, can there? Hugh will never even know. Is that agreed, then? We'll make the call after I've had my shower.'

She did not wait for Shona's reply but rose from the breakfast table. She sauntered across the room, humming softly to herself, and nudged the bathroom door open with her big toe.

When some forty minutes later Loretta emerged from the bathroom, she was smelling of Stephanotis bath oil and fully made-up. She walked across to the sofa where

Shona sat leafing through the *Daily Mail*. 'How do I look now?'

Shona glanced up briefly, then returned to the paper. 'Great. Going some place?'

Loretta shook her head and smiled. 'No, of course not. It's just, for anything important, I don't feel comfortable unless I'm looking my best. Strange, really. I feel sort of naked.' She smoothed back her freshly washed hair. 'Ready?'

Shona turned a page without looking up. 'Ready for what?'

Loretta leaned forward and whipped away the paper. 'The call, honey. The call.'

'Hey, I was reading that! Really interesting too. All about the trials of being married to a pop star.'

'Well, you can go on reading it to your heart's content just as soon as you've made this call.'

Shona frowned and sighed. 'Look, I still don't think this is a good idea.'

The paper fell to the floor. Loretta's eyes momentarily flashed with anger. 'Shona, are you seriously telling me that you are not going to do this one small favour for me? And after all I've done for you. Who does the shopping around here, hmm? Who lends you their earrings? Who does the hoovering after they return home tired after work?'

'OK, OK.' Shona's hands rose in surrender. 'I'll do it . . . but as I said, I still don't like it.'

'Right.' Loretta picked up the telephone and carried it over to the sofa. She sat down and perched it on her lap. All the time, she was explaining to Shona exactly what she wanted her to do. She lifted the receiver and pressed out the sequence of numbers in rapid succession.

She heard the ringing tone. It rang eight times. She swallowed.

'So?' asked Shona.

'No answer.'

'Huh! Fate, you see. It just wasn't meant.'

'Hello?' said a deep male voice.

Loretta nodded her head wildly and held out the receiver.

Shona took it. She breathed in. 'Er . . . could I speak to Mr Hugh Rudlow, please?' she asked in a borrowed flowery accent.

'He's away, I'm afraid. Won't be back for ten days or so,' replied the bored voice. 'Who's calling?'

'Er . . . Lady . . . Lady Wellingham's secretary. Ringing about a charity dance . . . no, no message. I'll write. Thank you ever so much, byeee.' She quickly dropped the receiver.

'You were magnificent,' cried Loretta, and hugged her. She jumped up; 'Just time for another cup of coffee, then it's my turn.'

She walked back to the machine, and poured out two more cups of coffee, then retraced her steps to the sofa. 'Are you *sure* I look all right?'

'Yeah. Like I said, you look great – but anything's good enough. You're only making a phone call.'

'I know, I know.' She put the telephone on her lap and picked up the receiver with trembling hands. 'Well, here goes. Wish me luck.'

Shona sighed too. 'Oh, Loretta, just get on with it, will you?'

She dialled.

'Hello.'

'Er . . . hello. Yes . . . I was wondering . . .' her

fingers tapped nervously against the side of the machine. 'Could I speak to – er – Hugh, please?'

Shona looked up from *Harpers and Queen*. 'Chicken!'

'Afraid not,' said the voice. 'He's away.'

'Away?' Loretta said in a surprised tone. 'Sorry, who am I talking to?'

'His answering service.'

'His answering service? Um . . . yes . . . I see. Does his answering service by any chance know whether Anthony Rudlow is in residence?'

'This is Anthony,' replied the voice.

'Oh, Anthony.' She smiled into the telephone, speaking confidently now, all nervousness gone. 'You had me fooled for a minute. It's Loretta Lorenz here.' She paused for a moment, but as no reply was forthcoming continued: 'I don't know whether you remember me, we met ten days ago? That dinner party your mother gave?'

'Ah, yes, how rude of me. I'm very bad at names. Of course, I remember now.'

'Yes, that's right. The American,' she prompted. 'The awful thing is that I think I left a bag of mine in the house in Wilton Crescent when . . . er . . . a group of us went round for a drink – let me see, it must have been almost a month ago now. Like a damn' fool, I didn't even notice it was missing until I was looking for it last night – and I do need it rather urgently. I just wondered whether I might come round one evening and pick it up?'

'Can't say I've seen it. I'll ask the butler, of course, but he's off duty right now.'

'Oh, I'm sure *I'll* be able to find it. And I'd love to see your collection of vestments if that were at all possible? Would this evening be OK, or tomorrow maybe?'

'I'm going out later, but early Monday evening? About seven?'

'Yes, perfect. Very kind of you. I am sorry to be such a nuisance. 'Bye.' Loretta lowered the receiver, her face glowing with triumph. She blew Shona a kiss. 'Thanks a million,' she said. 'I won't bother you any more and I'll do all the washing up for a week, OK?' She put the telephone down on the coffee table and picked up the copy of *Ecclesiastical Vestments Then and Now*. She balanced the heavy tome on her lap. 'Time,' she said with a mischievous smile, 'for some serious study.'

The taxi drew up outside the elegant sweep of grey Georgian buildings at 7.05 sharp. Loretta climbed out and paid the driver. The houses faced on to a central crescent-shaped garden with a long herbaceous border filled with pale pink roses, iris and delphiniums. Above her the evening light filtered through the stone balustrade perched high above the semicircle of Ionic pediments. She smiled. Wilton Crescent was quiet, grand and suitable. It was also highly convenient for shopping.

She had thought long and hard about what to wear and had settled on a simple low-cut black silk jersey cocktail dress. Not too flashy, but stylish. It also showed her figure to best advantage. Her jewellery was low key too – just a simple diamond brooch and matching bracelet, both borrowed from André. She breathed in three lungfuls of the cool night air, stepped up on to the portico and pressed the doorbell.

A white-haired man in a black jacket and striped trousers came to the door. 'Yes?'

'Mr Anthony Rudlow?'

'Is he expecting you, madam?'

'Yes. Most definitely.'

She found herself in a hallway: the floor was of black and white marble; the walls stippled French grey. On the only occasion when she had been to the house with Hugh, they had used another entrance which led up a winding staircase to his rooms on the top floor.

'This way, madam. Mr Anthony is in the library on the first floor.'

'Thank you.' The main staircase had sweeping wrought iron banisters, dimly lit by ormolu sconces with opaline glass shades. She climbed the carpeted stairs following the butler, tottering slightly on her very high heels, her body erect, fingers lightly brushing the wooden hand rail. She paused for a moment on the first-floor landing and glanced in the gilt mirror. The glass was so mottled by age, and the light so dim, it told her nothing. 'Miss Lorenz, sir,' announced the butler.

'Thank you. That will be all.

'Come in. Come in,' said the same voice in a slightly distracted tone.

The spines of old leatherbound books covered each of the dark green walls. Busts of Roman Emperors on porphyry columns stood at regular intervals like sentries guarding the trove. The evening light cast a yellow beam down the centre of the room, illuminating the figure at the leather-topped library table at the far end.

Anthony rose and walked quickly towards her. He was wearing narrow tapered jeans and a blue blazer. 'Loretta, hi. We meet again.' His eyes were on her now. He smoothed back his hair and smiled awkwardly.

'I'm so sorry to disturb you,' she said.

He moved forward. The smile broadened, then faded as suddenly. 'No, no. You're not disturbing me at all.

The pleasure . . . the pleasure is mine. Have you time for a drink?'

She could see him clearly now. He was taller and finer boned than she remembered, his skin very pale, cheeks slightly sunken. 'I don't want to put you to any trouble,' she said, 'but that would be kind. Something soft, if you have it.'

'Will bitter lemon do?'

'Yes. Fine.' She noticed the stack of thick embossed invitation cards on the mantelpiece. All were marked 'refused'.

Ice rattled in a tumbler. There was a slight fizzing sound as he unscrewed the bottle top.

'These books . . .' she asked for want of something to say '. . . have you read them all?'

'Good God, no.' He grinned and shook his head. He seemed to find her remark amusing. 'At least half of them no one will ever read.'

'Are they all that boring?' She made herself comfortable on the scuffed leather sofa by the fireplace.

'Oh, no.' He grinned again. 'But the pages are still uncut. If anyone were to cut them now to do something as silly as actually read the book, they would lose much of their value. Ridiculous, isn't it?' He shrugged and handed her the drink.

'Thank you.' Towards the far end of the room, she saw something glimmer behind a glass frame. 'May I?' She smiled, got to her feet and walked past him.

The frame contained a richly embroidered fragment of three raised work figures, worked in coloured silks and gold and silver-gilt thread.

'Hmm,' she said, racking her brains. 'Extraordinarily

delicate . . . er . . . split stitch work. A truly wonderful piece. Let me see now?' She turned to him and smiled. 'From the Opus Anglicum period, I would guess.'

His face beamed a surprised smile back at her. 'Opus Anglicanum,' he corrected. 'But very good.'

She strode on to the next. 'This one, I think, is later. Sixteenth-century. German, perhaps?'

'Very nearly. Sixteenth-century Spanish. I'm very impressed. How did you know?'

'Oh, one picks up these things,' she replied casually. 'But I would never trust my judgement in an auction. As they say, a little learning . . .' She smiled.

'Another bitter lemon?'

She handed him the glass. 'Yes, please. I was very thirsty.' She moved back to the sofa, tugged at the hem of her dress and sat down.

As she had guessed, the interest that she had shown in the embroidery had put him at his ease quicker than any amount of small talk. 'So you're a friend of Hugh's?' he asked quizzically.

'Only an acquaintance,' she replied, taking the glass. 'Thank you.' At the dinner party she had sensed the tension between the two brothers. Now, she thought, was not the time to admit to any closer relationship with Hugh.

He sipped his soda water. 'Oh? I thought he said that you were old friends.'

'Did he?' she replied dismissively. Her fingers tightened about the glass. She was skating on very thin ice. 'He was probably − er − just trying to make me feel welcome. I did so enjoy going to Conningsby,' she added quickly, changing the subject. Pausing only for rapid intakes of breath, she then went on to explain how much she enjoyed working over here and how different and refreshing she found England after the States.

He sat on the matching sofa opposite her, his legs crossed, hand occasionally running through his blond hair. Every now and again he nodded, showing a polite interest in what she had just said. She feared, though, that his mind was elsewhere.

In an effort to entertain him, she moved on quickly and related some of her wacky stories on the quirks of New York life.

She knew that she looked good in that dress, but just to make sure she rearranged it again, tugging gently at the hem so that the full lines of her breasts were not marred by even the lightest crease of loose fabric. Her legs, too — always so important — were in full view. Men had often remarked on her legs.

After her third story — the one about her time as a designer at Sazzy Furst — Anthony rose once more to replenish her glass. She was just wondering what to tell him next when, suddenly reflective, she asked herself what on earth she was doing here?

She had been brazen enough to get herself invited under a false pretext to the house of someone she hardly knew, with the express purpose of trying to persuade him to ask her out to dinner. She was sitting here now flirting — yes, flirting, there was no other word for it. She was wriggling her body like a whore, giving him a teasing display of ass, tits and leg. *Her* ass, tits and leg.

Previously, she knew, Loretta Lorenz would rather have risked travelling all night alone on the New York subway than have degraded herself this way. It just was not her.

She was even drinking bitter lemon. She loathed bitter

lemon. And to make matters worse, she had already drunk three tumblerfuls. One more sip and she would be in urgent need of the bathroom.

Anthony returned now and with a slightly weary sigh set her glass on the table.

The truth of the matter was it just was not working. She was coming over too strong. She was doing it all wrong.

She had been so blind. Instead of loudmouthing relentlessly with her best party chatter, she should have tried to put herself in his shoes, think about what he had just been through, try to understand the delicate balance of an ex-addict's mind.

The only time that his eyes had bothered to run up and down her, she had not felt the threatening sexual vibrations which men usually sent out in her presence. She guessed that the hangover from the drugs must have stifled his normal healthy instincts, at least for the time being.

All he would be looking for now, she thought, was a friend, a companion, someone who would not pressure him, someone who could amuse him and take him out of himself, someone who would understand.

She feared, though, she had already outstayed her welcome and that only good manners had prevented him from throwing out this loud and overbearing American. She feared that if she rose, he would take it as the cue to show her the door. But needs must . . . She would have to risk it.

Very pointedly she left her small clutch bag on the sofa, smiled at him and said, 'Is there a bathroom in the house?'

He nodded, rose, followed her to the door and issued

her with a full set of directions in a brisk formal tone.

When she returned, she was relieved to find him still sitting in the same position on the sofa. She tried to think herself into a different frame of mind, away from the desperate, nervous assertiveness of before. She tried to think herself out of her formal cocktail dress and act as if she was wearing jeans. She felt faintly ridiculous now, tottering in on the stilts of her high heels.

She began again. She talked to him some more about the vestments, only to find that they were a collection formed principally for investment and that dealing in them had partially financed his habit. He had been astute enough, too, to suspect that her knowledge of them had been acquired only very recently. He said with a laugh that he was flattered. No one else had ever taken the trouble.

He spoke in a soft clear voice about his love of Conningsby, about his time at the centre, about the problems of readjustment, every now and again punctuating his speech with the question: 'Not boring you, am I?'

He was not. After the fourth time of asking, she smiled and said, 'Look, Anthony, if you're boring me, I'll tell you right away, OK? Otherwise, just keep on talking.'

He said 'Right' and laughed at that, then explained shyly that the problem of trying to make conversation with recently reformed 'users' was that the cure was always uppermost in their minds. Once they got on to the subject, they could bore for Britain.

She told him about her alcoholic father, and from then on he spoke with greater confidence. He seemed more relaxed, too. It was almost as if something had clicked in his brain. She sensed he was treating her as an ally now.

He was still, she could tell, deeply vulnerable. A sparrow with one wing in a splint.

They talked on for another half-hour before he glanced at his watch. 'I'm sorry.' He sprang to his feet. 'I mustn't keep you. I see you're all dressed up?'

She fingered her glass. She had planned to spin him a tall story about the dinner party that she was going to being cancelled at the last minute. She had rehearsed it in the taxi on the way over here.

She had had enough of artifice now. 'No. I only put this thing on to come here,' she replied with an embarrassed shrug. 'I am going home for a TV supper and Humphrey Bogart.' She rose too and held out her hand. 'But thank you. It was very kind of you to put up with this totally unwarranted invasion.'

'Hmm.' His eyes swivelled around the room before coming back to rest on her. 'I'm sure that you'd much rather see the film —'

'I've seen it before,' she said quickly.

'I would ask you to come too, but it's going to be —'

'Anthony,' her eyes flashed at him, 'I'm used to more things than you can imagine. I wasn't born to dinner parties at Conningsby, you know. If you mean it . . . if you really mean it . . . I'd love to come whatever it is.'

'If you're sure . . . great. Um, you haven't got anything — well, less formal?'

'Nope. They can take me as they find me.'

'And consider themselves lucky.' He grinned. 'Oh, by the way,' he added as an afterthought, 'we never did find that bag. . .'

For her sake, Loretta suspected, Anthony made a detour.

The car stopped outside a stucco-fronted house in the middle of Belgravia.

He was tense even before he entered the L-shaped drawing room. His eyes moved nervously, restlessly, as he saw the wall to wall pin-striped suits and little black dresses: all black, white and grey with only occasional flashes of colour. He winced at the blanket of sound – the braying, the chatter. He swallowed and fingered his lapels as he refused the proffered champagne. He shuddered as knowing, quizzical eyes swivelled in his direction. He never ventured into the centre of the room at all, preferring the small space that he had made for himself close to the wall by the door. He answered the questions of those who invaded it briefly, dutifully, monosyllabically, more often than not only with a shrug, a nod or a strained grin. The tension never left him for a moment. 'Yes, I have been away . . . Yes, all in the past now . . .' Gamely, he tried to make a joke of it all.

Loretta spotted Lady Wellingham there, Louise Sprigget, the girl with the pink punk hair-do and a number of men whom she had met with Hugh, but she did not leave Anthony's side. After less than ten minutes he turned to her and said, 'To hell with it, let's go.'

They moved on to a basement flat somewhere off Bayswater. The air was already so thick with smoke that the far side of the room was lost in a shifting diaphanous haze of soft light. Everyone except for her and Anthony wore jeans and jumpers or leather jackets. Everyone seemed to move either very fast or very slowly. Guests slouched against every available inch of wall, enclosing the room in a surrealist skirting.

Those still perpendicular huddled at the centre. Everything was 'OK' or 'fine' or a 'drag'.

The only thing there to eat was a chocolate cake and a large bowl of spaghetti Bolognese. Discarded paper plates lay everywhere. The stubs of hand-rolled cigarettes nestled among the pasta worms.

At first Anthony seemed to relax at the sight of the familiar territory, but soon his air of tension returned. He said hello to a few people, then helped Loretta and himself to some of the spaghetti. It was cold. He stood for a moment surveying the scene and trying to smile.

She knew he should not be spending time in this sort of company if he were to stay off drugs. 'Careful,' she whispered to him, 'it's a little early for you to be playing St Anthony, isn't it?' but he just put his arm lightly around her and smiled.

At one point his eyes lit up. Loretta followed his gaze. A girl stood in the corner. She was talking to a burly man with two-day designer stubble, but her eyes kept swivelling towards Anthony. She was skeletally thin. Pelvic bones protruded from her narrow jeans like anchor points. She had very long ash-blonde hair and must once have been strikingly beautiful, but now the pulled, pinched skin gave her face the look of a varnished skull.

At last she broke away from her companion and crossed the room. She put her arm on Anthony's shoulders, more for support than as a gesture of welcome. 'So how are you doing, darling? Back from the rest home?'

'Yup. Back to the real world.'

'Three cheers!' She chewed noisily on something, 'Bravo! No more nasty little toxins dancing about in *your* body. A Clean Machine, right?' She used his shoulder to steady herself. 'This calls for a celebration. A drink?'

'Yes, please.' His smile was strained. 'Something non-alcoholic?'

'Oh, of course, I forgot. Silly me. Coffee, tea? No, more stimulants. Water then? A nice glass of pure spring water to get you in the party mood.' She grinned, taunting him. Then, just as suddenly, her jaw slackened. She put her face close to his and, serious now, stared at him from glazed blue eyes. 'Think it's going to work?' she asked in a voice that Loretta could only just hear.

He put down his half eaten plate of spaghetti. 'Yes, Corinna, I do.' He tried to sound casual but his voice trembled. 'Why weren't you there? You *promised*.'

She half turned away. Her hand fell languidly from his shoulder. 'Something came up, darling. Couldn't spare the time.'

'Damn it, I told you that I'd help you.' He spoke more with pity than with anger. 'I told you I'd pay, get the money for you somehow. Excuses, excuses. You know what's going to happen to you if you don't go?'

'Oh, yeah, I've heard it all before,' she droned. 'Three months in Alcatraz and you're on to your soapbox, preaching redemption. Just let me see you in six months' time!'

'No.' Anthony's voice wavered just once. 'I'm – I'm not giving in. I'm back on course. Honestly, just tell me, do you even get a kick out of the highs any more? Corinna, you must get help. Corinna . . .'

Her long bony hand rose to smother her giggles.

'What's so funny?' he snapped.

She was giggling convulsively now. The corners of her eyes moistened. 'You, of course. You have no idea how pompous you sound.' Her body swivelled around and in one quick movement she planted a hand on each of his shoulders. 'Hey,' she sighed, craning towards him, 'what's happened to the old Anthony? The one who was fun?' Her lips pouted. 'Puff! Puff! Puff! Blown away with the toxic waste.'

'Corinna . . .'

Her mouth hardened. Her hands dropped away. '*Ciao*,' she mumbled. Already her back was turned and she was walking away.

Anthony sidestepped closer to Loretta, still watching the girl as she returned to her previous companion. 'I'm sorry. I shouldn't have brought you here. It was a mistake.' He shook his head as though to rid himself of tormenting thoughts. 'Come on,' he said with one last disgusted look around. 'Let's get out of here.'

After the closeness of the room, the night air was harsh and cold. Loretta put her arm lightly around his waist as they reached the top of the basement steps. She felt him shaking slightly through the cloth of his jacket. 'I thought that was very courageous of you,' she said softly.

He shook his head. 'Ridiculous, more like, but I had to try. She could be . . . worth so much, you know?'

'I don't doubt it. But it's not easy playing the priest in a Dracula movie.'

He grinned at that.

On the way home, he apologised twice for giving her such a miserable evening. As he lightly kissed her goodnight and walked away, she feared that left to his own devices, he might never call. Then, just as she was about to shut the door, he turned back and said: 'Would the girl who mugged up so expertly on vestments like to try music next? Covent Garden. Tuesday. Pick you up at six-thirty, OK?'

'Yes, sir,' she called back. 'I'll be down at the library first thing tomorrow.'

He nodded. His lips curved in an uncertain grin which trembled slightly at the corners. Then, with a shrug of his shoulders, he stepped out of the circle of light which filled the porch and disappeared into the darkness below.

# Chapter 19

'Mummy, I've got some news,' announced Camilla as soon as she entered the Yellow Drawing Room.

'Good or bad?'

'Good, I think.'

'Splendid. We could do with some of that variety. Darling, come and sit down and tell me all about it.'

The overblown purple roses that peppered Lady Rudlow's cotton dress were almost identical to those on the chintz sofa-covers. Camilla knew that dress of old; amongst the family it was known as 'the herbaceous border'.

The light streamed in through the wide French windows at the far end of the room. A slight breeze sent the wistaria, now in full bloom, tapping gently against the panes.

Camilla strode quickly across the room and perched on the sofa next to her mother. Her back was perfectly straight. She swallowed and flicked back her long black hair. 'Mummy, Steve's proposed.'

A lawnmower rumbled outside. 'Steve?' Lady Rudlow lowered her eyes and pursed her lips. 'Ah, yes, Steve. Now let me get this right. Steve is the fellow who gave us that wonderful rendition with his banjo, right?'

'Guitar, Mummy.' Camilla sighed. She recognised this

exasperating game. 'He's a very talented rhythm player. Yes, that Steve.'

'How touching, darling. How very touching.' Lady Rudlow smiled vaguely. 'Were you touched?'

'Touched? I'm more than touched, Mummy. In fact . . . in fact,' she swallowed, 'I'm planning to move in with him.'

Lady Rudlow frowned. 'Move in? Don't be silly, darling. You can't just go moving in with people, however talented they are at rhythm.'

'Mummy, I'm serious. We love each other.'

Her mother turned weary but clear grey eyes on her. 'My God, you are serious,' she breathed. 'Oh dear. What's the time, darling?'

'Mummy! This is important.'

'The time, darling?'

'Ten to six.'

'Near enough. Get me a gin and tonic, will you? I think I need it.'

Camilla nodded and rose silently. She strode over towards the drinks tray.

Lady Rudlow sprang up too. She stood facing the marble Adam mantelpiece, and sighed. 'Temporarily infatuated, that I can believe. But love? God's great gift of love? No, I can't believe that. Love is sharing, darling. It's companionship.'

She took hold of a bronze figurine from the mantelpiece and moved it an inch to the left. 'Now how on earth can you share everything with someone like — Steve?' She pronounced the name as though she would now have to brush her teeth. 'It's like saying that a racehorse loves a pit pony. Both excellent things in their way, but hardly suitable as lifelong companions.'

Ice clinked in the tumbler. 'I think I am the best judge of that.' Camilla crossed the room again and handed the glass to her mother.

'Thank you, darling.' Lady Rudlow sat. She patted the cushion by her side again. Dust rose through the chintz. 'Sit down. We must talk.' She sipped her drink. 'That's better. Wasn't there any lemon, darling? You see, marriage — how can I put this? — is about much more than sex . . . I won't presume to ask you about that as nowadays standards are so different from in my youth . . . but when you marry, you are marrying a way of life. You have been brought up in one particular way, Steve another. I just don't know how well you'd cope — whether his way is really you.' Her eyes narrowed. 'Have you met his family?'

'No. They're up North somewhere.'

'I would.' Lady Rudlow nodded slowly. 'When you marry someone, you marry their family as well. Does Steve do anything else but play the guitar?'

'He's good on the harmonica too.'

'Oh dear, oh dear. The banjo and the mouth organ. What about a job?'

'That's his job,' Camilla explained indulgently. 'He's had three hit singles, Mummy. He's a star.'

'Oh, yes, I'm sure he is, and very nice too, but for how long is he likely to remain one? Stars fall, and then all they have left are wishes. He would be offering you no security. To put it in vulgar terms, in a few years' time he will probably be living off you. The well isn't bottomless, you know, Camilla. Your way of life would change.'

She tugged with nervous fingers at the hem of her brown woollen dress. 'I'd survive, Mummy.'

'Survival is not everything,' proclaimed Lady Rudlow. 'Newts *survive*.'

The door swung back. In the light, the butler's black coat looked distinctly grubby. He coughed.

'Yes, what is it?' Lady Rudlow asked impatiently.

'Your Ladyship, Mr Biggins would like a word. It's about the greenfly.'

'Oh dear, not now, Gander. Tell him I'll see him later.' She turned back to Camilla. 'I'm sorry, darling,' she trilled. 'Now where was I? Yes. Now, I think the best thing would be for you to forget all about this for the time being. If it hadn't been for Daddy's accident, I am sure, darling, that you wouldn't even be thinking of such a thing. You are feeling vulnerable − we're all feeling vulnerable, shattered and vulnerable − but that doesn't mean you've got to cling like glue to the first man who will give you a glass for your toothbrush. I can understand, darling, how you feel. Really I can. But I'm sure if you were to make a hasty decision now, you'd regret it later.'

Camilla leaned forward and laid a hand on her mother's sleeve. 'But Steve is a genuinely good person, Mummy. He's so kind, so considerate −'

'I don't doubt it for a moment. So are some corgis, but you don't live with them. Well, you do, but you know what I mean? You don't *live* with them.' She patted Camilla's hand. 'Darling, you're pretty, well connected, have independent means, and *can* be good company. You could have the pick of the bunch. It would break my heart to see you throw yourself away on some banjo player.'

Camilla shook her head. The tiny muscles around her eyes tensed. 'But I love him.'

'Yes, yes, of course you do. Or at least, you think you do.' Her hand left Camilla's and reached across for her glass on the skirted and fringed table beside the mantelpiece. She sipped her drink and sighed. 'I have never told you this before, but there were many men I took a shine to before I met George. At least three I could have married, and I think I could truly say, hand on my heart, that I loved each one of them. I was about your age then, Camilla, and frankly I was falling in and out of love quicker than I changed ball gowns. All the men seemed so dashing and glamorous, but then of course it was just after the war. There was an altogether better class of man about then. They had come straight from the front. There was an infectious enthusiasm about them, a longing to forget. By a strange coincidence, one of them, Matthew Petershot, used to play the trumpet, so you see there's nothing new under the sun . . . he's dead now, of course.'

Lady Rudlow nodded. She ran her finger around the rim of her glass. 'Yes, they were all very charming, and with women always so courteous. Apart from the few — the very few — who were known to be "Not Safe In Taxis", they treated you with so much respect. I pity your generation, Camilla, so much of the romance has gone out of courtship.'

'So . . . so why didn't you marry any of the three?' she asked softly. 'Didn't they ask you?'

'Each of them did, and five more besides.' Lady Rudlow smiled, wistfully but proudly. 'But, you see, I was saving myself. None of them could offer me the way of life I wanted, and I knew without it I would never be wholly content.'

Camilla laughed in disbelief. 'You mean they weren't

rich enough? You turned them down because they weren't rich enough.'

'Oh, don't start that nonsense, darling,' her mother chided. 'It's so simply said. Money isn't everything. Of course a life-style isn't exclusively dictated by money, but I knew the type of life I wanted to lead and the sort of man that I wanted to lead it with. I knew what I would like to come to expect, and I knew that none of those three, dearly as I loved them, would be able to provide it. Of course it was a risk,' she said, expansively now, as if marvelling at her own daring. 'In those days one tended to marry younger. A girl had a very definite shelf-life. If at the end of one season, or maybe two, someone suitable had not come along, my dear mother would probably have sent me off on the fishing fleet to India to be a tea planter's memsahib . . . but I felt I could trust to my charms.'

Lady Rudlow glanced down at her polished fingernails. 'Anyway,' she shrugged, 'George came along and I knew at once he was right for me. He was very good-looking in his youth, you know, with a jaw as strong as an ox. You've seen that photograph of him on my dressing table, haven't you?'

Camilla nodded and blinked.

'But what really struck me,' continued Lady Rudlow gazing into the empty fireplace, 'was the air of authority which seemed to emanate from him. He made the others seem like . . . I don't know . . . boys dressed up for a school outing. Strangely enough, he hardly noticed me at first, but that didn't worry me.' Her voice was suddenly stronger. 'I made him fall in love with me.'

Camilla's head shot forward. 'You did what?'

'I made him love me. Everyone seems to live in a dream

world now,' she added briskly. 'They expect love to come and hit them like a bolt from the blue. Like anything else, it requires work, hard work. I charmed him, I flirted with him, I gave little dinner parties, I contrived to arrange that at least occasionally we were alone together. Men are such children! You can flatter them outrageously and they believe every word. I affected an interest in fly fishing — even, I remember, bought a book on the subject.' She grinned. 'I stood by him like a well-trained labrador at shooting weekends, tried to make myself indispensable and never dull or heavy. And of course we had hunting in common. Men tire easily if they are not continually amused.'

She chuckled silently. 'At that time, it did not become a girl to appear too bright or too opinionated or try to steal the limelight from the men . . . she just had to be fun, decorative and loving.'

Camilla's hands twisted together. 'Like a dog!'

'No, no.' Lady Rudlow glanced at her wearily. 'Like a man dreams his wife will be. Of course you can upstage them if you like, tell them a few home truths, make them feel small, but then don't expect them to queue up to put the ring on your finger. No, take my advice, try to see it from the man's point of view. Be clever, try to be everything a man wants you to be. Then,' she gestured again, 'provided you pick right, in time he will be everything you want him to be.' She sipped her drink. 'After three months, George was eating out of my hand, and was wildly, uncontrollably in love with me.'

'But . . . but,' Camilla drummed her fists against the sofa, 'that was dishonest, Mummy.' Her manner was suddenly haughty. 'You were pretending to be something you were not.'

Lady Rudlow turned suddenly and looked her straight in the eye. 'I resent that, Camilla. I just used a little feminine guile, put my best front forward. There's nothing wrong in that. You powder over your imperfections in public, don't you? You wear your best frock? Or rather, that's one of the things *you* don't do, darling. You seem to lack instinctive feminine guile. You wear your heart on your sleeve.'

'I believe in honesty in a relationship, Mummy,' Camilla persisted. 'It makes me wonder if you really did love him. Daddy, I mean. Really love him?'

'Don't be silly, darling, of course I did. You romantics don't have a monopoly on the thing, you know.' She sipped the last of her drink. 'Though, to be fair, what I thought of as love when I was your age is very different from how I would view it now. Then I suppose,' she shuddered, 'ninety percent of it was animal attraction, goose pimples, hot flushes, jelly legs, that kind of thing, though of course we didn't think about it like that – didn't analyse it at all. But then, later on, it matures into something almost spiritual – a bond between two people, an instinctive awareness, an indescribable closeness. George and I were so happy together,' she ruminated wistfully, 'so very happy . . .'

Camilla sniffed. Her chin rose an inch. 'How can you say that?'

'Say what?'

'About being happy?'

'But we were. Honestly, darling, we were.'

Camilla's tone hardened. 'Don't pretend, Mummy. You know very well what I mean.'

'Of course we had our ups and downs. Any marriage does.'

'I am not referring to your ups and downs, but . . .
but to Daddy and Silvana Luzzi.'

Lady Rudlow clicked her tongue and nodded slowly.
'So you know?'

'Damn' right I know — I saw her at the hospital! And
you . . . you knew too?'

'Oh, of course I did. Poor dear Silvana, she loved
George so. You really are terribly unsophisticated these
days, aren't you, darling? All high principles and no
humanity. I suppose you're deeply shocked?'

'Sad, Mummy. Sad and disappointed. You mean you
put up with it?'

'Why shouldn't I? I'm not saying that I was exactly
overjoyed, but George needed the glamour and
excitement of a mistress, and she took nothing from me.
On the contrary, she did me a favour.'

'I don't believe this.' Camilla sprang to her feet. She
walked over to the mantelpiece, then turned and fixed
blazing eyes on her mother. 'When did you first know
about this — this woman.' Her hand flapped. 'When,
Mummy, when?'

'Oh, almost from the beginning. Nearly fifteen years
ago now,' she replied without evident emotion. 'Look,
since you are up, darling, will you get me another small
gin and tonic? I sensed that something was a little odd
the second time she came to stay. That ghastly little man
who posed as her husband just didn't ring true — he was
just like an Italian waiter from Soho, probably was —
and how he used to sweat! Don't forget the lemon,
darling. At first it used to give me pleasure winning off
him at bridge, until it dawned on me George would be
picking up the tab anyway.'

Camilla sliced a slither of rind off the lemon and

dropped it in the glass. 'And what did Daddy say when you confronted him with it?'

Lady Rudlow shook her head sadly. 'Why on earth should I do such a thing?'

'Mummy, how could you? I mean — some nights he must have climbed straight out of her bed into yours.'

Her mother stiffened. 'I imagine he washed.'

Camilla handed her the glass and remained standing. 'Didn't it worry you?'

'Thank you, darling. Not particularly. George was always a gentleman. I don't think he would ever have left me, even if I had had it out with him. But I don't think my making a thing of it would have stopped him and it would have put our relationship under strain, destroyed the trust. And, anyway, I had the lion's share. I was Lady Rudlow, I lived at Conningsby, I bore his children.'

'But you were sharing him with another woman —'

'You shouldn't be so selfish, darling. Can't think where you get it from. George, you see . . . George wasn't a domesticated animal. I knew from the beginning that if I were to tame him, he would have to be allowed a long leash. And, if one looks on the positive side of things, the occasional twinge of guilt did keep him pliant, amenable, and generous to a fault.'

'And now,' Camilla shuddered, 'he's kept like a vegetable plugged to that machine. Is that your revenge?'

'Good God, no. That's Sir Arthur's doing. He says it's legally imperative.'

'But —'

Lady Rudlow raised her hand. 'It has nothing to do with me.'

'Mummy, I don't think we have anything more to talk

about.' Camilla's hand fastened about the cold marble of the mantelpiece. 'Frankly, your generation disgusts me. God protect me from a marriage like yours. All I want is a good-looking, straightforward, sexy bloke who loves me. That's all that matters. I don't need things!'

A cough came from behind them.

Lady Rudlow started. They both turned. 'Gander, please don't creep up on us like that.'

The butler nodded. 'I'm sorry, my Lady,' he replied in a flat, unapologetic voice, 'but a number of persons from the Red Cross arrived some ten minutes ago. They are under the impression that there is going to be some form of meeting on the premises.'

'Oh Lord! Give them some sherry. I'll be with them in a moment.'

'Very well, Your Ladyship.'

Lady Rudlow turned back to Camilla, still clutching her glass in her lap. 'You are young, so young,' she announced wearily as soon as Gander had closed the door behind him. ' "Things" are very helpful to a marriage. Now, please, Camilla, if you do decide to marry or, as you say, move in with Steve, I think you will be making a monumental mistake. I am convinced it will all end in unpleasantness and an acrimonious divorce. For your own good, I want you to have a trial separation for three months.'

'Mummy, how could I?'

'If you really love him, your love will stand the passage of time. You'll have a lifetime together afterwards. I can assure you that you will find that quite long enough.'

'But Mummy . . .?'

'Hear me out, darling. If at the end of that time, you decide you still want to move in with Steve – though it is very much against my instincts − you can do so with my blessing. Understood?'

'But three months, Mummy,' she pleaded, 'I don't think −'

'Well,' Lady Rudlow sighed, 'Maybe you would like to think it over while I go and talk to these people?' She smiled lamely, rose and took one last sip of her drink.

Camilla shook her head. She looked across at her mother with sad eyes. 'Not necessary, Mummy. My mind is already made up. I only came here to let you know. I thought you'd understand.'

Lady Rudlow swallowed. 'Darling, please, please, *please* don't do anything rash. For your own sake, I beg you!'

Gander was hovering outside the door. He coughed again.

'Look, darling, I've really got to go now. I can't keep these people waiting any longer. It's the last meeting before the annual fête.' She smoothed down the creases in her floral cotton dress. 'Yes, Gander, I'm coming . . .'

Camilla slipped quietly into the studio. She had been thinking long and hard over what her mother had said throughout the train journey back to London. She smiled at Doug, the producer, who greeted her with a quick nod of his prematurely balding head. His hands were too busy pushing and pulling knobs on the console to remove the roll-up which dangled from his lower lip.

Beyond the glass, Steve sat on a high stool. He had not looked up. He did not know that she was there. He frowned intently, nodding in time with the music. It sounded faint to Camilla. She could just discern the fizzing bass, the croaking voice, the shriek of the saxophone. To Steve and Doug, she knew, with the headphones on, it would be an all absorbing, overwhelming sound.

And, suddenly, smoothly, Steve started to play. The clear voice of his old Fender seemed incredibly loud and cool and sharp after the fuzzy sounds before. He was laying down a solo on a blues number. There were no fancy riffs, no virtuoso arpeggios. He just let the guitar speak for itself with slow, rhythmical rest strokes.

The tempo of the drumbeats increased. He was playing dead, staccato notes and then, as the drums purled downward and the strings seeped back in, his nimble, strong fingers darted this way and that up the frets, creating a tortuous argument which ended on a long high fading note which, to Camilla, recalled the singing of the stars.

The backing music continued. Steve relaxed. He laid the guitar on his thighs.

Doug leaned forward and spoke into the mike. 'Great Steve, that's super.'

Steve pulled off the cans and looked up, tousled-haired. He saw Camilla, narrowed his eyes against the light then gave a big, broad, boyish grin of undisguised happiness.

'Cammy!' He laid down his guitar and ran for the door.

She, too, was running. Tears stung her eyes and misted her vision. The door swung inward. She took one look at him, then flung herself into his arms.

His kisses were on her brow, her hair, her cheeks. 'You've told your ma? Everything OK?' he whispered urgently.

'Well, yes, I've told her. Didn't take it too well.' She bit her lip, laid her head against him and listened to his rapid heartbeat. 'I need you, Steve.'

'I need you, too.' She felt the words vibrating in his breastbone.

She looked up at him through wet eyes. 'Think Mummy will come round to the idea eventually?'

'Yeah, I'm sure she will,' he soothed. 'Whyn't I get one of the roadies to go round to your place right now, pick everything up?'

'Yup,' she answered finally. 'You do that.' He bent to kiss her. She reached up and pulled herself hard against him, and for a minute or more there was only darkness and warmth and the rustling of his leather jacket, his crisp cotton shirt, and the moisture of her tears on his hair.

# Chapter 20

A bedraggled but orderly queue of music-lovers ran from beside the white stucco columns of the façade of the Opera House, along the wet pavement and around a corner, out of sight. The chances of return tickets must be low now, thought Loretta, marvelling at their dedication and her own good fortune.

The commissionaire in a braided burgundy frock coat opened the taxi door. Anthony smiled at her, took her by the arm and swept her through the crowded foyer, up the stairs and into their box.

The auditorium was all glittering gold and white, the seats and curtain red plush. The discordant sound of tuning strings cut the air. Loretta gazed down at the stalls beneath, at the coiffeured heads and shiny bald pates. Heads and buttocks bobbed up and down in a game of musical chairs as late arrivals squeezed along the rows.

High above her was the dome, like the lid of a huge Fabergé pill box. The rich blue ground decorated with cross-bands of gold shimmered like enamel.

Anthony stood stiffly beside her. 'First time?'

She smiled and nodded.

'Great, isn't it? And, in the nicest possible way, rather addictive.'

'You bet! So what's playing tonight?'

He handed her the programme. She had hoped for ballet. It turned out to be opera. Wagner. *Der Ring des Nibelungen.*

'Tonight, we're just going to see the prologue.'

'What?' she answered indignantly. 'The orchestra on strike or something? The leading singer got tonsillitis?'

'Oh, no.' He smiled, amused. 'You see, the whole thing, with intervals, lasts about nineteen hours. It's usually performed over four days.'

'Nineteen hours! I see . . . a sort of operatic mini-series.' She sat down on the red plush chair. She was pleased to see that although the box was for four, they had it all to themselves. She opened the programme, found the synopsis and began reading:

Long ago Wotan, one of the noblest beings, set out to find what caused discord in the world. He came upon the tree of the universe whose roots were fed by the spring of eternal knowledge. He asked the three Norns who guarded the spring if he might drink from its waters and in return gave one of his eyes . . .

She was lost already. And it got worse. There were some characters called the Rhinemaidens, with the unusual names Woglinde, Wellgunde and Flosshilde — poor girls! How could their mother do it to them? — who as far as she could make out were some sort of swimming security guards. There was a midget called Alberich, who renounced love to gain dominion over all the world after the Rhinemaidens gave him the cold shoulder. He changed himself into a snake and then a toad. Dumb. Very dumb. There were some giants in the construction business. A Mr Fixit and God of Fire called Loge . . .

The lights dimmed. The conductor mounted the podium. He bowed to the applause, tapped his baton.

Loretta closed the programme. Forget the plot. She would just sit back and enjoy the music.

Immediately it started, Anthony's mouth curved in a contented smile. He rested one elbow firmly on the edge of the box and tilted his head towards the orchestra pit. He stayed like that without moving a muscle, without even an involuntary twitch, for the entire performance.

Even when she turned towards him, he seemed hardly to notice her, save once when she was sifting through the box of chocolates in search of the last violet cream. She was doing this as quietly as she could, but nonetheless a flicker of annoyance passed over his face. Wagnerites, it seemed, took their pleasure sombrely.

Anthony took her out to dinner afterwards at a small Italian restaurant of the old school – tortured ironwork, raffia Chianti bottles crowned with yellow candle wax and a hand-coloured photomontage of the Colosseum on the wall. One glance at the other diners told her that society had yet to discover this place.

Anthony summoned the waiter with a slight movement of his head and ordered the house wine for her, mineral water for himself, and pasta for the main course.

He had that strange ability some Englishmen had of making anything he wore look as if it doubled as pyjamas, and had cast its particular spell on the black worsted suit he now wore. Nothing about him would have suggested that he was heir to a great fortune. He spoke rather fast, rather impersonally, in a soft, clear voice about the performance while he broke a bread stick into regular inch-long pieces and popped them into his mouth one by one.

Though still edgy, he seemed more relaxed than on the previous occasions they had met. Loretta did not know whether to take the credit for this herself or whether it was merely exhaustion from the barrage of sound that had battered their senses for the last two and three-quarter hours.

She kicked herself for not having done her homework properly. She nodded a lot. Exactly what was a *leitmotif*? Yes, she answered. Yes, she had enjoyed it . . . Yes, it *was* the first time she had heard any Wagner . . . Unusual, she would have said. Yes. Definitely unusual. Majestic . . .? Intense . . .?

As if dredging his memory for long ago events, he began to tell her about his days at Oxford. Although he did not say so in so many words, she formed the picture of a one time blue-eyed boy, a natural sportsman, an academic, burning for new challenges, new experiences, to whom everything had come just too easily.

He talked about the freedom he felt when he had left the cloistered world of Eton behind him, about the parties, the balls, the long drunken evenings that flowed into the mornings. He spoke with enthusiasm about the mad exploits of the Oxford Dangerous Sports' Club, about the time he'd thrown himself off the Clifton Suspension Bridge for a dare, harnessed only to a length of heavy duty elastic, and the extraordinary sensation of well-being he had felt when the elastic had held and he had bounced up and down above the gorge like a yo-yo.

The life that he described was so different from her own where necessity had governed all her actions, where opportunities had been few. As he spoke, only occasionally did she detect flashes of the old arrogance that must have driven him before. Although he still paid lip service to his old youthful enthusiasms, the pain and suffering of the addiction, she knew, had changed all that. The gilded youth had soared to the heavens and been burned.

He would not be drawn on the subject of women, but from the slight halting of his breath and the tensing of his hand, she guessed that there was some sadness there, a love even before Corinna that had been lost or gone tragically wrong.

She changed tack. 'So it was there that it started. The drugs, I mean?'

He dabbed *pesto Genovese* from his lips and answered without hesitation. 'I experimented a bit, but nothing that I couldn't control. At least, that was what I thought. Then came the car crash —'

'A bad one?' She swallowed a mouthful of *tagliatelle*. 'You Rudlows are very accident prone.'

He nodded and sipped his water. 'Bad enough to be prescribed a pretty exotic collection of pain killers. On them for nine months. My back, you see. By then, they were part of my life. When the supply from the doctor finally dried up, I just picked up what I needed on the black market.'

'Did anyone else know?'

'Hugh. He guessed early on.'

'And didn't he do anything?'

'Oh I spun him the usual line. It was easy enough to justify. I was still in pain. Without drugs I couldn't sleep, and without sleep I couldn't work.'

She lowered her fork and stared across at him. 'And he bought that?'

Anthony smiled. 'Hook, line and sinker. He even loaned me money. And, bless him, picked up supplies for me once or twice. I think he honestly believed that it was only a temporary thing. And of course he was worried about the scandal breaking in the family.'

He shrugged and stabbed a lettuce leaf. 'It's the old, old story. Soon I was taking something to get up in the morning, something to help me get into the office, something to pep me up in times of stress, something to counteract the uppers and let me sleep. It just got worse and worse.'

'But that's all history now.'

'Yup,' he nodded. 'After my time at the centre, I'm so full of fresh country air and organic foods that I feel like a prize vegetable at a horticultural show . . . utterly transformed into some kind of back to nature freak.'

'Good food and sleep are the best cures that there are.'

'Great if you happen to like people like that. I, for one, do not . . . but,' he raised a finger, 'they do have the resounding merit of being alive.'

His time at the centre might have freed his body of physical dependence on drugs, but she could tell from his nervousness, from the dull lifelessness of his pale grey eyes, that he still was not free of mental dependency. He was dry but not sober.

For all his talk of being cured, he clearly was no longer at ease in what should have been familiar territory. He was like a baby, reborn, blinking out at the light for the first time, curious to discover things anew.

He was struggling to walk now without crutches. He would need an abundance of willpower, she knew. He would also need a helping hand when times were tough. Someone whom he could trust. Someone who would not patronise. Someone who would share the daily mental torture which she knew he would be going through for a while yet.

She would spar with him, make him laugh, take him out of himself, slowly build up his confidence again.

'A back to nature freak? Oh, come on,' she said. 'Stop teasing. You're not like that. Otherwise, I for one, would not be sitting here. You might not know it, but I'm totally ruthless about how I spend my time.'

An eyebrow twitched. 'That,' he said, 'is a very backhanded compliment.'

She leant across the table towards him. She stared into those dull grey eyes, trying to kindle life in them by the power of her thoughts. 'Anthony,' she ventured, 'you know what you're suffering from, don't you? You're *sensitive*, that's all.'

He looked at her with wry amusement. 'In England that's a term of derision.'

'Well, it isn't where I come from,' she said firmly. 'All I mean – and I don't want your head to swell, when I tell you this – is that sensitive types – and I would include myself in that category – have a greater capacity for feeling. What counts as a scrape of a briar to some people might be an open gash to us. We just feel more. Live more intensely. It's a burden and a joy. It's just the way some people are made. It means, though, that you've got to be extra careful before you lower your defences and take a walk in a dangerous neighbourhood.'

He nodded. He understood.

She twisted the last strand of *tagliatelle* around her fork. 'You know what I reckon?'

'Hmm?'

'In a few months, you'll be back to your old self . . . and I, for one, am going to find that extremely

253

interesting. Think I'm going to like you?' she teased. She had finished her *tagliatelle*. He was still toying with a charged plate. She eyed the sweet trolley as it rattled past.

He grinned. 'We'll just have to wait and see.'

'Yup.'

He pushed his almost untouched bowl of pasta away. 'You don't want pudding, do you?'

Loretta shook her head and hoped that her tummy wouldn't start rumbling. 'So tell me . . . in the old days, if you were so very kind as to take a girl out to the opera and dinner, where would be your next port of call? If you did not know her all that well, that is.'

'Well, I would normally have a glass of Armagnac, then take you off to the Clermont to play blackjack. Both, alas, are now strictly *verboten*.' He leant back in his chair and drummed those long fingers on the red-checked table cloth.

She still could not be sure if he thought of her as anything more than an amusing dinner date, a decorative companion. Over the coming weeks she would show him, though. She would be his confessor whenever times got tough. She would show him her strength, her dependability. 'If you felt like it,' she ventured, 'we could go dancing? Not Annabel's, of course, or anywhere we are likely to see anyone we might know. Just somewhere quietish and deeply unfashionable.'

With the triumphant air of a conjurer, Anthony raised a hand to summon the bill. He grinned and nodded. 'Why not?'

# Chapter 21

The Turf Club is situated in one of the large imposing neo-classical buildings on the Mall between Buckingham Palace and Trafalgar Square. After a long leisurely bath to recover from the cross-Atlantic flight, Hugh arrived there at about four-thirty.

The main reception rooms and the library were deserted apart from one man snoring softly in a leather armchair. The newspaper lying loosely on his stomach rose slightly at each breath. Hugh smiled. He would thankfully have joined him, but he knew that, much as he wanted to, he would not be able to sleep. His mind still raced from the negotiations with AIP, from the flight, from the figures that kept on flashing before his eyes.

The final negotiations had gone well. If AIP had planned this initially as a bargain hunting exercise, they certainly would not be thinking along those lines now. He had been as tough as them and very thorough. He had a deal now which he thought had every chance of going through. The executive directors on the board would all receive sizeable sweeteners, the shareholders would be bought out at a very attractive premium, and he would receive the kind of package which would mean, if he so chose, that he need never work again. All the main players would win.

He blinked away the tiredness that pressed down on his eyelids and strode into the billiard room.

Henry Brooksbank was standing at the bar, swapping racing tips with the barman. Henry, as always, with his pale almost sallow skin looked as if he had not seen the light of day for a month. He turned and nodded to Hugh. 'Ah, the Chairman. Back again from God's own country, eh? Good trip?'

Two men playing backgammon at a nearby table looked up.

'Yes, thanks,' replied Hugh. 'Quite satisfactory.'

Henry carefully folded his copy of the *Sporting Life*. 'Coming from you that means bloody fantastic. I bet you've got some poor blighter so stitched up in small print he doesn't know his. . . What would you like?'

Hugh smiled. 'Oh, I don't know. I'm still a bit jet-lagged. Getting used to it, though. Sixth time I've been over this month. Maybe just a whisky with lots of water.'

The barman nodded.

'Heart bleeds, old boy. Not too jet-lagged for a game of snooker, I hope?'

'Why not?' Hugh took one small sip of his drink, thanked the barman, then strolled towards the mahogany cue-stand by the door. Paintings of race horses and hunters covered the red-striped walls. A collection of well-polished silver cups stood on the mantelpiece framed by two marble caryatids. He selected a cue and held it up to his eye like a telescope to check that it was true.

A full-sized billiard table filled the centre of the room. Under the low-slung lights, the green baize looked very bright. The light caught Henry's closely cropped mop of carrot-red hair as he racked up the balls in the triangular frame and slid them into position on the table.

Hugh chalked the end of the cue. 'You break.'

Henry took off his jacket. He wore red felt braces over his pink shirt. He lined up, running the cue through the hollow between the thumb and the forefinger of his pale freckled hand. He clipped the pack. The ball bounced off the bottom cushion, touched the side and returned to a safe position in baulk close to where it had started. 'There,' he said smugly, 'see what you can do with that.'

Hugh sipped his drink and studied the position. There was just one loose red which might – just might – go into the corner pocket. He decided to risk it.

He struck the ball a little light. The red slowed down just before the pocket, then stopped and teetered on the edge. 'Come on. Come on,' urged Hugh.

'No blowing or puffing now,' quipped Henry. 'Against the rules.'

The ball dropped.

'Lucky,' sang Henry.

'Skill.' Hugh grinned. He lined up for the next shot: pink to the centre pocket. 'Hmm,' he said lightly, 'shouldn't be a problem. Just needs a bit of side.'

Henry stopped studying the top of his cue. 'Talking about a bit of side, seen anything more of that American girl? The Martha Graham acolyte?'

'No. Been far too busy. Anyway, we had a little disagreement. The silly bitch saw herself as the prima ballerina in a pas de deux.' He grinned. 'Didn't take it kindly when she realised that she was only a member of the corps de ballet.'

Henry chuckled. 'Pity. Quite a little mover.'

'Yeah, but, what the hell? Girls like that are so demanding. Who needs the complications?' He shrugged.

He lined up the cue for the next ball. He struck it clean. The pink slid into the pocket. 'How's that?'

Henry nodded. 'Lucky sod.'

'Good shot,' a thin wiry black-suited man called from the backgammon table. His spectacles glinted in the light. 'Didn't realise, Hugh, that you didn't know?'

'Know what?'

'*La danseuse* has a *penchant* for Rudlows . . . which, of course, I'm sure, has absolutely nothing at all to do with titles or Conningsby or anything quite so vulgar.'

Hugh lined up for the next shot. 'What are you jabbering about now, Simpson?'

'I'd've thought it was patently obvious.' Simpson threw the dice. 'Sticking the claws into your dear, much maligned elder brother . . . and – as far as I can gather – doing a thoroughly professional job. They've been seen together on at least six occasions over the last three weeks.'

Hugh's jaw clenched. He felt the sudden race of his blood as he struck at the ball.

Henry gasped. 'Steady on, old chap. That's a new baize.'

'I'm sorry,' said Hugh, collecting his breath. 'Damn jet-lag.' He wiped the beads of sweat from his brow. He turned towards Simpson. His hand was tightly wrapped around the cue, showing the whites of his knuckles. 'Let me get this absolutely straight. You were saying. . .?'

Hugh drove slowly. The sun shining through the trees sent little patches of light scurrying over the windscreen. Each tree, each lamp post, each litter bin in the street was familiar. Hell, he had picked Loretta up from here often enough. He noted that the overhanging branch of the silver birch had now been lopped, the For Sale sign outside number seventeen had gone and two privet pyramids now stood outside in shiny white tubs.

He checked his mirror and double-parked outside number twenty-six. He glanced across at the bottle-green door with its large, lacquered brass knob; at the centre step that had been patched with the new piece of stone that did not quite match; at the entryphone with the little scraps of paper sellotaped over the illuminated panel.

He leaned forward and squinted up towards the third floor where Loretta and Shona had their flat. He could see the grey net curtains through the film of dirt on the windows. No lights shone inside, but it was still early for electric light.

He glanced at the digital clock on the wooden fascia. 6.20. She should be back from work any minute now.

A horn tooted behind him. He drove on.

Cars lined the street in one continuous row of shining metal. The nearest empty parking slot was just visible twelve, fifteen houses along. If Loretta took a taxi, she would be dropped right outside number twenty-six. If she took the tube, she would walk down the street past his parking place. It was a fine evening. He would take a gamble on the tube.

He manoeuvred the car into the space, pulled on the hand brake. He tapped the steering wheel, then his hand tightened around it. He sighed. He stabbed at the buttons on the radio and switched mindlessly through the channels . . . music . . . recipes . . . traffic news.

He stared out at the narrow strip of pavement, checking every person who passed: the fat woman in a jogging suit slowly wheeling her shopping in an aluminium trolley; the man with razor-sharp permanent creases in his trousers, glancing at his watch at every fourth stride; the tramp with the paper bag under his arm, asking for money for 'tea'.

There was, he knew, a small but distinct breed of women who were very sure and very confident about what they wanted out of life. They were as ruthless as any male. The ones who made the grade were, like Loretta, good company. They were fun to be with, clever and attractive, beautiful even. They added zest to life. They knew how to please men. Hugh could not but have a sneaking admiration for the best of them. They had earned their place.

If they let him, he flirted with them, slept with them, took what they had to offer. He revelled in every moment of the giddy dance, but always, he stayed on guard. Before the trap could be sprung, he quietly walked away. Just as he had done with Loretta. Just as, soon, he would have to do with Marie-Louise.

These girls had DANGER writ large over every inch of their soft, lissom bodies. Maybe they had been starved of affection when young. Maybe they had hugely ambitious mothers. Maybe they just had a very exaggerated idea of what money and position could buy. While other young girls had been tucked up in bed reading *Jackie* and *True Romance*, they had been the ones reading *Debrett's Peerage* or quietly sifting through the *Forbes Four Hundred*.

They were, he had observed, extremely good at their job. It was so instinctive, their guile did not show. When the right man came along, it was almost as if a trigger clicked somewhere deep in their subconscious. They acted for all the world to see as if they had fallen genuinely in love. Maybe they even believed it themselves.

Loretta, he knew, was capable of a very convincing and expert performance. Good enough, he feared, to fool someone as deeply vulnerable as Anthony.

Hugh's eyelids were heavy. The faces that passed were blurred now. Only the colour of their clothes distinguished them. He shook himself, blinked and looked down again at the clock on the fascia. 6.48.

Then he saw her. . .

All the tiredness left him. His brain was suddenly clear and sharp.

A shapeless red jacket hung loosely from her shoulders. It moved as she walked revealing the sapphire blue of the Swert uniform underneath. She clutched an Armani carrier bag in one hand, balanced a carton of milk in the other. Her chestnut hair blew about her face framing her clear features, her full lips. Hell! Despite his mission, he could not help feeling again the twisting in the gut he had felt the first time he had danced with her.

She was only fifteen yards away now. She flicked back her hair and looked sadly down at the poor lame terrier that an old woman was coaxing step by step along the pavement. She passed some remark or other with the woman and smiled at her in that disarming, winning way of hers. He knew that under the influence of that smile, the woman would have done almost anything for her. The old woman beamed back. Loretta nodded and walked on.

Her eyes fell on the silver BMW. She glanced down at the number plate just to make sure, then slowly up at Hugh. . .

He flung open the car door and swung out on to the pavement. The air outside seemed cold after the fug of the car.

'Hugh!' Her voice quavered. She swallowed.

'Loretta, I . . . I was just dropping by. Let's go up to your flat.'

'Why?'

'Old times.' He tried a warm smile, a casual shrug. 'And, anyway, I think we should have a talk.'

'Hugh, honestly,' her grip tightened about the carrier bag, 'I don't think that we've got much to say to one another.'

'You're not still angry with me, are you? I'm sorry about what happened.'

She flicked back her hair and stared at him with steady unblinking eyes. ' "Sorry"? Well, I suppose that makes it all right, then.' There was a sharp note of irony in her voice. 'One short word and everything's undone. Eh? As simple as that. Now,' she made to move off, 'if you'll excuse me? I've had a long day.'

Hugh sidestepped and barred her way. He nearly barged into a man passing him on the pavement.

'Hugh, you are making something of an exhibition of yourself,' she replied imperiously, 'and you're blocking a public right of way. This — I might remind you — is Kensington not Conningsby.'

Hugh held his ground. He was very conscious of the closeness of her. His eyes narrowed. He asked almost casually, 'Is it true that you're seeing my brother?'

'And what if it is?' she snapped.

He could hear the triumph in her voice and it grated. 'Of course, my darling, you told him that we just so happened to be lovers, hmm?'

She breathed in deeply. 'You and I — well, it didn't exactly turn out like Romeo and Juliet, did it?'

'And of course you're only going out with him because he is a warm, sensitive human being.' He stared at her accusingly with hard, cold eyes. 'Bullshit!' His hand rose suddenly and grabbed her roughly by the chin. His other hand made for her back.

For a moment, she was off-balance. The milk carton fell to the ground and splattered their shoes. She toppled backwards against the iron railings. The cold blunt points of the iron finials were hard against her back.

'Don't think I don't know, Loretta,' he breathed.

His fingers bruised her skin. 'Take your hands. . .' she hissed. 'You're hurting me. . .'

He held her hard, pressing his body against her. Anger, he thought, brought out a different beauty in her. There was a flush to her cheeks, an earthiness about her that was usually submerged beneath cosmetics, fine grooming and artifice. His lips were only inches from hers. 'I know your game,' he breathed. 'I know you. You stay away from him, you hear? I'm warning you – stay away.'

He felt the quivering of her spine. 'Do you know what you are, Loretta? Do you? You're a whore. A beautiful, goddamned whore.' He strained forward. His lips came down on hers. He kissed her hard.

Though he knew that she was fighting it, her mouth finally yielded. He felt the warm, nervous wetness of it, then the shudder that traversed her whole body.

Immediately his lips and his hand relaxed, she twisted her mouth away from him. She shuddered again. She dodged beneath his outstretched arm and spat at him angrily, 'If that's what you think I am, and I most certainly am not, it's you – you and men like you – who made me one!'

She turned and strode along the pavement towards her flat. It was as much as Hugh could do to keep up with her. 'So that's settled then,' he said. 'You won't be seeing any more of Anthony.'

She stared ahead and did not relax her pace. 'You're not going to stop me seeing him. Not you. Not anyone. You've got it all wrong. Jumping to conclusions like all self-centred men. I just so happen to be in a position to help him.'

'*You* help *him*!'

'Yes.' He could tell that she was still very shaken, but her voice was firm. 'Do you know the first place he took me to? A dealer's party. A *dealer's* party. Everyone was on it. Yes, everyone. If it wasn't for me . . . Christ! Do you want him back on the stuff?'

'Of course not but – '

She stopped. She was on the porch now outside her flat. She slung the carrier bag over her arm and searched her handbag for her keys. 'Look, Hugh, you breathe one word about our relationship to Anthony, and you'll destroy him, you hear?'

Hugh threw back his head and barked out a humourless laugh.

'I mean it,' she snapped. 'Emotionally he is very fragile. He has had next to no help from his family. Like it or not, he has come to trust me. He has come to depend on me. He needs me. He can't do it on his own. No one can. Destroy that fragile trust and you'll be saying goodbye to his chances of recovery, understand?' She flourished her keys.

'You bitch!' he breathed. He grabbed her arm just as she was about to put the key in the lock. 'That's a risk we'll just have to take.'

'But you can't! Think what you'd be doing to him.'

He looked deep into her startled eyes. 'Yes. But then,

of course, it won't be necessary for me to do anything, will it! *You* are going to stop seeing *him*. Because unless you do, I'll tell him everything. We'll see what he thinks of his avaricious Mother Teresa then.'

Hugh let go of her arm. He wiped his mouth with the back of his hand, breathing hard. 'I'm warning you, Loretta, stay away from him. You hear? I mean it.' Then he turned, stepped off the porch and strolled back towards the car.

# Chapter 22

Loretta glanced at the deserted red brick pavilion on the other side of the green railings, then gazed out at the murky green lake beyond. She checked the sign on the gate: 'The Serpentine Swimming Club. Members Only'.

The early morning light had a steel edge to it which she knew would vanish as soon as the rush hour exhaust fumes wafted into the park. She zipped up her track-suit against the cold, then bent her knees and flexed her arms. She shuddered at the thought of jogging.

She watched the other joggers as they puffed and panted by, the grey squirrels sporting in the plane trees, two boys squabbling over a football. Then, dead on time, she saw Camilla coming towards her along the track in a CONQUER HEART DISEASE sweat shirt, long black hair flapping behind her.

'Hi. I hope you haven't been waiting too long?'

Loretta smiled back at her. 'Oh, no.'

Camilla slowed down and ran on the spot. 'Good. Sorry about lunch, but we're so hectic in the office at the moment. First thing in the morning is about my only free time.'

'It really doesn't matter. This will do me much more good.'

'Shall we go then?'

'Right.'

Already Camilla was bounding along the path. Loretta had to sprint to keep up with her. When at last she was level with her again, she asked: 'So, how's Steve?'

'Oh, fine. Cutting an album at the moment. I've moved in with him, did you know? Everything's great . . . except with my mother, of course. It's a shock, I suppose, when the baby of the family finally grows up.' She slowed down until Loretta had caught up again. 'Have you ever lived – I mean, *lived* – with anyone?'

'Oh, no. Never got that far. That takes courage. Speaking personally, I think I like the idea of a ring on the finger first. Reassuring. Kind of means he's serious, you know?'

'All the legal shit!' Camilla shuddered. 'Have you ever watched two people forced to live together once love had died? Marriage is a killer.'

They turned the corner and Camilla led the way over a stone bridge. A fisherman in a battered green oilskin jacket was trying his luck in the stagnant green water. Fat overfed ducks were waddling up the embankment and snapping at the crumbs of stale bread which an old man scattered around his feet.

Loretta was sweating already. She wondered how much longer she would be able to keep this up. Camilla's pace had not slowed at all.

When they were level again, Camilla turned to her. 'Anthony tells me you're seeing quite a bit of each other?'

'Yup,' Loretta replied. 'I admire the way he is being so resolute about the treatment – that takes guts.'

'You know, before he went to the clinic, he was so closed up that I couldn't get through to him at all and stupidly I didn't have the faintest idea why. They always say the family are the last to know.' Camilla looked straight at her and grinned. 'A romance is just what he needs to take him out of himself. I thoroughly approve.'

'Hold it.' Loretta stopped, straightened. 'Nobody said anything about a *romance*.'

Camilla stopped too. 'I was only talking hypothetically. Future tense.'

'Of course.'

'Oh, don't listen to a stupid word I say. When you're in love yourself, you just want everyone else to be happy too.' She shrugged and grinned. 'Shall we go on? You really think the treatment is working?'

'Yeah, but it's tough.' Loretta felt her heart pounding as soon as she started running again. 'I think Anthony's got what it takes to see the thing through, though.'

'That's the best news ever. If at any time there's anything I can do to help, just ring, OK?'

'Thanks.' A sharp stabbing pain crossed Loretta's chest. She nearly kicked over a sign which once had read UNEVEN FOOTPATH, before the graffiti artists had modified it to UNEVENTFUL FOOTPATH. 'You think we could stop for a moment? I'm pooped.' She bent double trying to recover her breath. 'And I thought I was fit!'

Camilla stopped and turned. 'Oh it's just practice.'

Loretta glanced up at her. Camilla looked just as fresh as when she had started. 'Do you really torture yourself this way every morning?'

'I used to, but now I'm with Steve it's only once a week. Got to keep in touch with your body, girl.'

'Is there anywhere you can get a drink around here?'

'Sure.' Camilla led the way back along the side of the lake.

On their right, a line of rowing boats rocked gently in

the water. On their left, two small boys rode by behind a tall, stiff-backed man on a dappled grey.

Loretta wiped the sweat off her forehead. 'You know, there's one thing that I can't make out. In all the time that I've been dating Anthony, he's hardly ever mentioned Hugh, except in connection with the business.'

'Sad, really. If either was in serious trouble, I'm sure the other would be the first to race to the rescue,' Camilla said defensively, 'but there is a lot of rivalry between them. They've been sparring for at least as long as I've been around, and no doubt before.'

'Strange, seeing that they're brothers.'

'Not really. My father, like most of his contemporaries, had an abomination of "soft" men. Stiff upper lip and all that. The boys were brought up to be extremely competitive, just as he had before them. They had to prove themselves worthy. They had to compete against each other academically as well as at sports, they even had to compete for his affection.'

'So – er – Doctor Spock was not exactly his bedside reading.'

'Good God, no.'

'And who won?'

'Well, Anthony was certainly the cleverest. He was also the better at sports. But our father discounted natural ability. That wasn't the name of the game. It was the old military qualities of grim determination and leadership that he was looking for. Hugh was undoubtedly my father's favourite.

'I, of course, being in my father's eyes a "mere" girl for whom education was very much secondary to learning "how to be a lady", escaped all that. I was also much younger, of course.' She shuddered. 'Poor, poor Daddy.

To think of him now on that machine. It just can't go on. It's not right.'

They had reached the café now. The chairs were upturned over the tables. A lone woman in a dirty white apron was swabbing the floor. A sign hung on the inside of the glass door: CLOSED.

'I'm sorry,' said Camilla. 'I should have realised. It's still very early. How about an icecream?' she asked, suddenly pointing to the van parked further along the road.

'Anything,' replied Loretta, already walking towards it. 'And you?'

Camilla shook her head. 'I only eat fruit until midday, but go ahead.'

The man in the van was just pulling back the shutters. Loretta scanned the chart and ordered a soft icecream.

She shuddered at the first lick. 'Hmm, just what I need.' She threw back her head to catch the warmth of the rays of the early morning sun, then they wandered back along the lakeside. 'So tell me. . .' she tried to sound casual as if the thought had only just struck her, '. . . before Anthony's problems, both brothers must have moved in the same social circles. I mean, the choice couldn't have been that wide. Did they ever, by any chance, both go out with the same girl?'

'Christ, no.' Camilla shuddered. 'I don't think either of them would relish the idea of sharing each other's toothbrush, far less each other's women. I mean . . . brothers wouldn't, would they? Who'd want to walk around with the knowledge that his own brother had been there before — yuk! Does that kind of thing go on a lot in the States?'

'Oh, no.'

'Thank God. I mean, the idea of a loving, sharing family can be taken too far.'

Loretta took another lick of the icecream and tried to hide her embarrassment behind the cone.

Camilla was restless. She was running on the spot again. She glanced at her watch. 'Ready to go on?'

'Er . . . well, I do have to shower and change before getting to the shop, and frankly I'm pooped.'

Camilla grinned. 'You're excused. Are you seeing Anthony again tonight?'

Loretta nodded.

'Good. Give him my love. Have you anything planned for this Saturday?'

'No, nothing special. Anthony is going to be away.'

'Fine. We're holding a Day of Action. We plan to hit all the garden centres in the South East. Are you on?'

'Sure. And what would I have to do?'

'Nothing to it. You just stand outside the shops with a load of leaflets and try to get as many people as possible to sign the pledge.'

'Oh,' she exclaimed, confused. 'In England, are garden centres full of drunks, then?'

'Oh, no,' Camilla smiled, 'the *Peat* Pledge, silly. Digging up peat is destroying unique wildlife habitats. We've got to "Keep The Peat In The Bogs". Assemble outside the office at eight-thirty, OK?'

'Right on!'

'Attagirl. See you on Saturday then. Keep up the good work with Anthony.' She smiled and trotted on. Soon she was only one among the many white legged tracksuits that bobbed up and down at the water's edge.

# Chapter 23

'Yes, yes. Come in, come in.' Sir Arthur ushered him through the door into the spacious office overlooking Gray's Inn.

Every wall was lined with books. The smell of leather polish and old cigars filled the air. Anthony glanced at some of the titles as he walked towards the armchair opposite the desk: *Archbold's Criminal Pleading, Evidence and Practice; Smith and Hogan's Criminal Law.* He swallowed.

As an addict, he had always lived in fear of the law. Information from a policeman's nark, a sting, the chance discovery of his contact number in a pusher's address book and he would have been before the beak, his name all over the tabloids. Once a party that he had been at had been busted and in the confusion he had been able to escape through a basement window. Others had not been so lucky.

'Keeping well, I hope?' asked Sir Arthur as soon as he had returned to his chair behind the desk. 'All this — er — unfortunate business behind you now?'

'Oh, yes. Fully recovered.'

'Good, good.' He leaned back in his chair, drew on his large cigar and exhaled. 'Hugh tells me that your nose is back to the grindstone, what? Very well done.'

'Yes. It's about the company that I've come to see you. Have you read Hugh's report on the negotiations with AIP?'

'Naturally. I'm no expert myself, of course, but I have taken soundings and it seems that Hugh has managed to winkle a very good price out of them.'

Anthony's fingers clenched and unclenched. 'Yes, but that's not really the issue, is it?'

'Hmm?' Sir Arthur took another pull at his cigar. 'How so?'

'My time at the centre gave me ample opportunity to reflect on life. I see things a lot clearer now. I think I understand what's important . . . to me, anyway. The company was Father's dream — the dream of creating an independent force in the industry. And that dream was realised. The company now employs over four hundred people. What about our duty to them? All this is going on behind their backs. If we sell, less than a quarter will remain. They will wake up one morning to find a redundancy notice in the mail. Is that their reward for all the years of dedication and hard work?'

Sir Arthur flicked the long ash of his cigar into the silver ashtray on his desk. 'Very noble sentiments, I agree. Glad they teach that sort of thing at the centre. But, my dear boy, business is business. The redundancies would be highly regrettable, but — as I understand it — an inevitable consequence of the . . . er . . . restructuring of the company.'

'But it's absolutely unnecessary, don't you see?' Anthony jumped up from his seat. 'In the Condor, we have a world beater. It's got a proven market, it's revolutionary in design, and it will be cheaper than all its competitors. No wonder AIP are worried! It's a risk,

I know, but now is not the time to sell. Father would never have done so.'

Sir Arthur waved his hand in a calming gesture. 'Look, I understand your concern, but you're talking to the wrong person. The relative merits, or otherwise, of the Condor is a question for the board. It's up to them to make the commercial decisions. They understand the aircraft business. I – emphatically – do not. I'm only the trustee. My business is to give legal advice, not pronounce on the commercial potential of aircraft.'

Anthony took a step closer to Sir Arthur's desk. 'And if the board recommend the offer?'

'Then we as trustees will consider it very carefully. Very carefully indeed. Of course, in the old days,' he nodded, 'we would have taken your father's advice . . . and in all likelihood followed his suggestion, but the circumstances are very different now. I think, provided the price was right, we would follow the recommendations of the board.'

Anthony swallowed. 'And betray Father's dream? Betray the workforce?'

'Protect the interests of the Trust for the good of the beneficiaries. That, Anthony, I might remind you, is what I am paid to do . . . and if we consider that selling the shares at – I might remind you – a substantial premium is a beneficial move, then that is what we are bound to do.' He leaned forward and rested his arm on the desk. 'Anthony, my dear boy, you've been out of it for quite a few months now. Your father, sadly, is no longer in – I suppose you would say – the cockpit. You must understand what might have been the right decision when he was in command, might not be the right decision now.'

Anthony could see the likely sequence of events all too clearly. The board would endorse Hugh's recommendations and Sir Arthur, the professional trustee, would feel bound to follow.

'Will you at least come as an observer to the board meeting when the whole thing is discussed?'

'It's not exactly the usual procedure. But, if I'm asked and if I'm available . . . yes.'

'It's next Thursday. Ten o'clock.'

Sir Arthur pressed the button on the intercom on his desk. 'Eileen, what am I doing next Thursday morning?'

'Sir Arthur,' the voice crackled back, 'you've asked for the morning to be kept clear.'

'Oh, yes, that's right. The dentist. Cancel him, will you, and make another appointment.'

'Very well, Sir Arthur.'

The trustee rose. He put his arm around Anthony as he led him towards the door. 'I'll read the report again, my dear boy, and I'll be there if you think that it will serve any useful purpose. But as I said, the decision is up to the board. It's them you'll have to convince.'

He shook Anthony's hand. 'So very pleased you're feeling better. It was all such a worry to your dear father. You know your way out, don't you? My love to your mother.'

Anthony nodded. He said goodbye to Sir Arthur, then as soon as the door closed, he glanced at his watch. He quickly made his way through the reception area and down the flight of stairs to the courtyard below. He ran across to the street and searched for a cab.

That evening he was 'doing a chair' at Narcotics Anonymous in Chelsea. He could not be late.

\* \* \*

The church hall had been used an hour before by the Women's Institute, but a very different group were gathering now. The room was already thick with cigarette smoke. The familiar NA slogans hung from pegs on the wall: 'A Day At A Time'; 'One Is Too Many And A Thousand Not Enough'.

Anthony made a special effort to make any newcomers feel welcome. He knew how difficult it was to accept that you had a problem that you could no longer deal with on your own. Coming here could be the first step on the road to recovery.

There were girls so young, fresh and beautiful that you could be forgiven for thinking that they had wandered into the room by accident in search of an aerobics class; but something − a nervous twitch, a blank stare, a small repetitive mannerism − always gave them away and showed that there was no mistake. Among the crowd, too, were faces which Anthony recognised from his schooldays. Drugs and alcohol were great levellers; there were no social distinctions here.

All these people had one thing in common: they could never be social drinkers again or − even if the law were to permit it − take the occasional puff of an exotic cheroot. It was not just a question of willpower. Drug addicts and drunks had a different physio-chemical make-up to other people. One sip, one puff, and they might not be able to stop. They would be back again on the helter-skelter ride to black-out and oblivion.

That's why these meetings were so important. Everyone here could take some small comfort in the fact that they were not alone, that they were all struggling to keep away from their particular addiction every hour, every minute, every second of the day.

There was a bond between them. They shared a sense of a new beginning, of hope. Anthony felt it strongly now amid the smiling, harassed faces all around him.

As he walked across to the chair on the small raised podium, his thoughts went back to the speech which he had given at Eton all those years ago. Hell, a few of the people listening now had been there then. At Eton, he had been a school boy, showing off with a carefully rehearsed Latin text. Now, he spoke from the heart.

'It began,' he announced in a soft clear voice, 'with a car crash. When my supplier could no longer get the pain killers I was on, I turned to coke. At first, I thought I had found the answer. I felt terrific. I did not need much sleep. I had an enormous capacity for work. I was able to concentrate for extraordinarily long periods. . . Everything was rosy, except of course after the first two months, the occasional snort was not enough any more . . . I upped it to a gram a day.

'I did not realise it, then, but my judgement had been blown away. I had the moral sense of a hungry rat. I saw no kindness or beauty in anything around me. I would take even the smallest critical remark as a slight. There was a time,' he grinned, 'when I even thought that the pictures on the walls and the furniture in the room hated me − such was my paranoia.

'Within less than a year, I was on four grams a day. I needed a hit now every three-quarters of an hour . . . I spent a lot of time in the lavatory. My nose continually running, I was very thin, yet still I would not admit to myself that I had a problem that I could not cope with − the only problem, as I saw it, was getting and paying for the supplies.

'I was so sure that I was being so discreet, that nobody was any the wiser. Then one day when I arrived at the office, I found my father and brother standing by my desk. The locked drawer where I kept my stash had been prised open. I had expected my father to be white with rage, but he was very controlled, sad, and matter-of-fact. He said quite bluntly that he was calling the police and to hell with the scandal unless I went to a treatment centre. Only when he had already dialled 999 on the telephone and I could hear the ringing tone did I finally give in.

'I still have the occasional panic attack, of course. I still crave for a snort every second of the day . . . but I feel confident that I have thrown the hog off my back now. I am free, and with God's help will never, ever touch drugs or alcohol again.'

Loretta sat alone at a small table in a crowded Chinese restaurant off the Kings Road. The waiter had come up to her twice already and asked her whether she was ready to order. Each time she had explained patiently that she was waiting for somebody. Each time the waiter had grimaced and sighed.

Loretta, too, had been to a meeting run by NA. She had been to Families Anonymous, as she did twice a week now.

She had learnt that addicts soon became experts in manipulation and emotional blackmail: to get what they wanted, nothing was beneath them. They would promise the sky. They would bully. They would lie.

Family and friends bore the brunt of this deception. Often, through guilt, through a forlorn hope that the problem was containable, or simply to hide the truth, they would 'buy into the addict's line'. They became his 'enablers'.

Soon they were showing similar psychological symptoms to the addicts themselves. *They* were supplying the money. *They* were hiding the visible signs of addiction. *They* were explaining away the addict's behaviour with quiet convincing lies.

Loretta had been close to tears the first time that all this had been explained to her. She had shuddered as she had realised that her mother, despite her best intentions, had shown the classic symptoms of an 'enabler'. Ma had gone out night after night to the late-night liquor store to buy whiskey for Pa rather than risk the neighbours laughing at him as he lurched in, barely able to stand. Ma had regularly collected all the empty liquor bottles, packed them in the boot of the car and driven them off to the city tip, rather than let gossip spread about the glass army in the Lorenz garbage. She remembered, too, Ma's anxious late night searches for Pa when he had failed to return of an evening. She had lived in fear of him being picked up by the law as a vagrant.

Loretta knew that Ma had taken Pa off to AA meetings. With Pa, the treatment had not worked. This time, she was prepared. This time, for so long as she had anything to do with it, the cure would be complete and lasting.

There might be times when Anthony would be prepared to swap his soul for an ounce of white powder. She could expect blackmail then. She could expect him to try to persuade her that this was only a temporary lapse, like a smoker taking a quick farewell puff at a cigarette for old times' sake. At the meeting they had taught her the principle of 'tough love'. She would give him her love, she would comfort him, but she would be totally ruthless. Already she had told him that she would never see him again if he weakened just once. And he knew that she meant it.

'Hi.' Anthony beamed a warm smile at her. He leaned over the table, squeezed her arm, then kissed her softly on the cheek. 'Great to see you. Sorry I'm a bit late.'

'The "chair" went well?'

'Yup. Great. Tired, though.' He summoned the waiter. 'While we're making up our minds what to order, could we have two plates of "seaweed", please, some sparkling water, and – er – half a bottle of white wine?'

Loretta shook her head. 'No wine for me.'

'Are you sure?' he asked, surprised.

'I think it's unfair on you to watch me pouring it back when you're not having any. I'm going to give up until you're completely better.'

'That's a very sweet thought but honestly, darling, it's not necessary.'

'No. Don't try to talk me out of it. I really won't miss it much.'

'OK. Just for this evening, if you really insist.' He turned back to the waiter. 'You'd better make that a large bottle of mineral water. Thank you.' He picked up the menu.

'And how did your meeting go with Sir Arthur?'

He lowered the card. 'That,' he sighed, 'did not go so well.'

'You mean the trustees are going to approve Hugh's plan?'

'It's possible, probable even. I get the feeling the trustees will follow the line of least resistance.' His eyes flashed angrily. 'Hugh stands to make a small fortune dismembering all that Father built. How could he? At times like this, I feel ashamed that he's my brother.'

Loretta raised the menu card to hide her face, and swallowed hard.

# Chapter 24

Hugh looked up at Anthony from behind heavy lids, and drummed the desk rhythmically with his fingers. 'Take a seat, Ant. I just thought it would be a good idea if we had a talk before we went into the boardroom.'

Anthony nodded and eased himself into the chair opposite his father's old desk.

'I want to know whether you are still set on opposing my plans for reorganising the company . . . It won't make one jot of difference to the final decision, but it would look better if the family were seen to be united. Better for you too, old boy. Wouldn't look good if you were out on a limb.'

'I thought I'd made my position very plain,' Anthony replied defiantly. 'I would, of course, have been delighted if we could have put forward a common front on this one, but unless you are prepared to modify your position—'

'*Me* modify *my* position.' Hugh stared at him with incredulity, and shook his head. Anger suddenly flashed in his eyes. 'You, not me, are the odd one out here. I'll be surprised if there is a single dissenting voice on the Board apart from you. Just don't want you to look too isolated, too out of touch—'

'Then,' Anthony interrupted, 'I don't think there is

anything which we have got to discuss.' He rose and turned. 'See you in the boardroom.'

'Ant,' Hugh called, 'there's just one other thing. Nothing to do with business.'

'Oh, what?' Anthony swivelled round.

'When I was at the Club the other day, someone mentioned that you've been seeing something of Loretta Lorenz?'

Anthony stiffened. 'And what if I have?'

'Well,' Hugh paused as if searching for the right words, 'it's not for me to interfere in your private life, but I thought you ought to know that she hasn't got an exactly enviable reputation. Been round a bit, if you know what I mean, out for the main chance.'

'Locker-room tittle-tattle.'

'Look, Ant,' Hugh rose, and walked around to the other side of the desk. 'I am only mentioning this because I don't want to see you mucked about. She's a looker all right, but — you know the score — there are fifty like her in Tramp every night of the week.'

'You mean she's "not quite our class",' Anthony replied sardonically. 'That's a bit rich coming from you, Hugh. What about that black model from Sierra Leone, or the Eurasian who hardly spoke a word of English?'

'Yes. But I didn't bring them home, did I?' He sat down on the edge of the desk facing his brother. 'Look old boy, I'd be the last one to voice a word of criticism if you just wanted to have a bit of fun, but I'd hate to see you getting all dewy-eyed and emotional about someone like Loretta. She's just not worth it.'

'That's something for me to decide,' Anthony replied firmly. 'I happen to be very fond of Loretta.'

'Yes, but surely you must see that you would be quite

a catch for a girl like her. Do you honestly think that she'd be taking so much interest in you if you were a clerk living in a semi on the North Circular Road?'

'I really don't know. I am who I am.'

Hugh's tongue clicked. 'Wise up, Ant. It's a dangerous game and right now, after all you've been through, you're just too damn susceptible to be playing war games with mercenaries. From what I've heard, the standard advice to anyone who has been through that kind of treatment is to avoid emotional entanglements for at least two years.'

'Look, Hugh,' Anthony's hand stabbed in the air, 'Loretta's been a great support to me. In fact, without her this whole damn' drugs thing would have been much more of a trial. And if you really want to know – though it's no damn' business of yours – my relationship with her to date has been entirely platonic – a word which doesn't feature in your vocabulary.'

Hugh nodded thoughtfully. 'Pleased to hear it. I'd keep it that way if I were you. Hate to see you getting hurt.'

'Is that all?' Anthony asked, and turned to leave. He was just opening the door when Hugh called to him from his desk.

'By the way, Ant. You do me an injustice.'

'How?'

'I did have a platonic relationship with a girlfriend once, but it didn't work out.'

'Why not?'

He grinned mischievously. 'Why do you think?'

The boardroom hummed with the sounds of the works floor below, the click of ball-point pens, the shuffle of feet. The only light came from the recessed spotlights in the ceiling. It shone down on the oval boardroom table, on the hands and bald pates of the board members, and obliquely on the portrait of Lord Rudlow hanging at the centre of the hessian-covered wall.

The board members turned and mumbled some acknowledgement as Anthony entered. 'Good to have you back, old boy.' 'Right as rain now, bet you are.'

He had taken extra special care with his dress. His cuffs, his shoes, the knot on his tie, the press of his trousers, were all immaculate — just like the model business executive of Sunday paper advertisements. But he knew what the board were really thinking. Behind the pleasantries, they would be sighing with forbearance, and this evening would be telling their wives the next instalment of a cautionary tale. 'Anthony Rudlow had so much,' he could almost hear them say, 'too much. Threw himself away. Pity. Great pity.' And their wives would shake their heads and suck in air through the sides of their complacent mouths and think how lucky it was that their little Johnny or Freddie was such a sensible chap.

Only reliable old Don Bishop stood and pressed his hand in Anthony's. It felt good.

Anthony took his place next to Hugh who was at the head of the table. Hugh was too preoccupied to give him more than a cursory nod. One of the non-executive directors, Sir Leonard Semple, the banker, sat on Anthony's right. Saunders sat opposite.

Sir Arthur was the last to arrive. 'Ah, Hugh,' he called. 'Most kind of you to let me attend as an observer. It will be of great assistance to the trustees when they come to make their decision. Now, where would you like me to sit?'

Hugh indicated a place at the far end of the table. 'Right, gentlemen, if we are ready to proceed?' He removed the paper clip at the corner of the sheaf of papers before him and cleared his throat. 'If we can take the minutes of the last meeting as read?' He tugged at his cuffs. 'Gentlemen, I believe that you have all now seen the memorandum that followed my series of meetings with AIP . . . and, as you have seen, their proposals are much more wide-reaching than we had initially envisaged.'

Anthony shuddered. Today was the day when the fate of the Rudlow empire would be sealed. It was just bad luck that it was also one of the bad days when the power play of his treatment was just not getting through. He had been fighting the addiction all last night. He was rubber-brained, rubber-bodied and seriously disorientated: in fact, just as he imagined a snail might feel, squatting in a pool of hot garlic butter. An army of pygmy warriors were doing a rain dance on his skull. They were beating their drums too. He feared that they were about to launch a guerrilla attack on his jaw. And he had so much to say . . .

Being here in the holy of holies of his father's empire did not exactly help either. He glanced up at the portrait of the old man on the wall before him. Although it was not of the first rank, the eyes had the unnerving, annoying habit of following you wherever you moved in the room; ever vigilant, ever watchful. He could almost hear the familiar growl: 'Look at Hugh' . . . 'Do it like Hugh, my boy' . . . 'Take a tip from Hugh'.

' . . .so that,' continued Hugh smoothly, 'summarises in broad terms the main points of AIP's approach. For all its fancy phrasing about 'synergy', and 'respective mutual partners', Anthony knew that the proposal amounted to nothing more than selling the company lock, stock and barrel to the Americans.

Now he was getting nicely into his stride with his apologia: 'The Condor is the most ambitious project ever launched by the company. A fifty-seater with STOL capability, built using a state-of-the-art integrated engineering systems approach.

'We knew . . . we always knew . . . that we would be in direct competition with AIP but that was the gamble we took. We were relying partially, as you know, upon surprise. Our product development was top secret. With luck we reckoned that AIP would not learn about it until the project was well advanced.

'Of course, we could expect price cutting on their 386. Of course, in time, they would come up with something to rival our Condor. But by then we would have hoped to have broken through and sliced out a large chunk of the market for ourselves.

'A risk — of course it was a big risk for a company our size — but one worth taking, one we all made the decision to take.

'Now AIP have somehow got wind of our plans — how I don't know — and have made what on the face of it seems a very interesting offer. We have two options.

'First, we could go on as before. If we do that now, we can expect a much more rapid response from them. We do not know how much they know about Condor but the very fact that they want to jump into bed with us implies that they know we have something special. The possibility cannot be ruled out that somehow they have even gained access to our technology . . .'

Anthony suspected that the two bankers representing the institutional shareholders would be in favour of the deal. The decision would hinge on the vote of the executive directors. Anthony knew that Don Bishop was against it, but he would need Saunders' and Slipper's votes too if he was to stop the deal, and they were both playing their cards very close to their chests.

Here he was in the centre of his father's empire, the exclusion zone, where a strange movie was running: The Fall of the Rudlow Empire . . .The Conjuring Trick of How To Pack Three Hangars, A Staff of Four Hundred and a Fleet of Planes and Human Aspirations Into a Briefcase.

Easy.

The actors' lines had all been scripted and rehearsed. Just before the final credits rolled, the script read: ' . . .well, I think that our acceptance of AIP's offer is the only realistic course.'

There would be a lot of nodding, smiles and back slapping, then a girl would come round with coffee and biscuits.

One man's dream of a great independent force in the aircraft industry would be reduced to a pile of paper tokens. A dream realised. A dream destroyed.

Hugh had finished with the niceties now, turning over the alternatives only to shoot them down. He was moving in for the kill.

'The other alternative would be to respond to their offer. We would lose our independence, but we would guarantee the future of the company. That would be the safest option, and if AIP are preparing a counter to our Condor, to my mind by far the best option. I need hardly remind you what would happen to the company if the

Condor failed in the market place. We haven't the capital base to survive failure.'

'Quite so.' A couple of the board members nodded. 'What do you think, Saunders?'

Anthony looked up expectantly.

The financial director straightened his glasses. 'A company our size lives precariously. We can't afford to take production risks, but unless we do, we die a slow death from antiquated products losing their competitiveness. At the moment, our future lies entirely with the Condor, and the success of the Condor depends solely on our stealing a march on AIP.'

Anthony drummed his fingers on the baize table top but they did not seem to make any sound. He could understand the banks and the institutional shareholders wanting to convert the Rudlow Aircraft Company into nice manageable pieces of paper. But a paid employee with no interest in the equity? Some mistake here surely, Mr Scriptwriter?

He felt a tightening in his gut. His vision blurred. His heart raced. The pygmies had digested their dinner and were back on the warpath again.

Saunders was drawing his remarks to a close: '. . . so in conclusion, I fully support the proposed deal.'

Saunders reached for the glass of water in front of him. To clean the taste of betrayal from his mouth, no doubt.

Across the table Slipper nodded too. 'I agree.'

He must get a hold of himself. Reach out into that space beyond. Come through. 'Mr Chairman?' called Anthony.

He heard the words echo in his skull. He looked across quizzically at Hugh, who did not turn to face him. He glanced the length of the table. No one met his eyes. It was as if he had not spoken.

'Mr Chairman?' he called again. This time Hugh did turn towards him. 'From my study of the file, I find it difficult to ascertain the level of payments being made to senior management to compensate for loss of office. Are these fully documented?'

'Anthony,' Hugh replied smoothly, patronisingly, 'those are small details. If you don't mind I'd like to keep the discussion on the substantive points of the deal.'

'I consider this to be entirely substantive.' Anthony's voice was firm now. 'I find it very strange indeed that both Saunders and Slipper have come down in support of a deal that is clearly contrary to the interests of the workforce.'

There was a complete hush in the room now. Saunders and Slipper exchanged glances, but it was Hugh who spoke. 'It would hardly be in the interests of the workforce if the company went under and that is the risk we run if the Condor is not the success we all hope for. I'm sure that both Saunders and Slipper appreciate that point.'

'The level of payments?' asked Anthony again.

Hugh sighed. He spoke as if trying to explain something to a petulant child. 'You will, I think, find a full note on them on page eighteen of appendix four in the report before you. As you can see, they are nothing out of the ordinary. They follow exactly the formula set out in their respective contracts of employment. Now if we could move on . . .?'

Someone coughed. A pen clicked. Paper crackled. Anthony was sure this was not the whole story. 'I have, of course, read the appendix. It was not those payments which concern me. What I want to know is whether AIP has made any promises of further payments should the deal go through?'

For a second Hugh stiffened like a terrier sensing danger, but his words were calm and measured. 'Really, Anthony, that is an entirely private matter between the individual employee and AIP. After making a substantial investment, it would be reckless indeed if AIP did not take steps to keep key staff. That is their concern, their money, and I don't think we should waste any more of the board's time on such a small point.'

The room was silent again. Anthony nodded slowly. 'Even so, Saunders might wish to make a statement?'

The corner of Hugh's mouth twitched. 'I really don't see that it is relevant,' he barked.

'I am sure the board would feel reassured to hear that key employees will be properly looked after. Well?'

Saunders shifted uneasily in his chair. He removed and replaced his spectacles. He cleared his throat. 'Mr Laithwaite has − er − given certain guarantees to the executive directors that they will be given contracts which recognise their present positions in the company.

'He indicated that we could all expect a significant increase in our present levels of remuneration. These, he said, would correspond with the package offered to our American counterparts. These indications were only preliminary and informal, and therefore I. . .we didn't think it appropriate to raise them with the board at this stage.'

Anthony nodded. 'And were there to be any other payments made to the executive directors should the deal go through?'

Saunders tugged at his cuffs. He looked suddenly

worried. He glanced quickly at Hugh. 'We will also receive what is termed a "golden hello" when AIP gain control. It is, I believe, usual practice in the States.'

'And how large is this "golden hello"?' Anthony enquired.

'Approximately five times annual salary.' He swallowed. 'But that would not, of course, in any way influence my decision – or any of our decisions – on the merits of AIP's approach, which I firmly believe to be in the best interests of the company.'

'Satisfied?' said Hugh, turning to Anthony. 'It is clearly in all our interests that key staff are properly remunerated if this deal goes through.'

So that was it. Hugh had the wheels well greased. Investors happy, executive directors laughing, employees not represented. Smooth passage home.

'If he was here today, our father would never have agreed to the sale,' Anthony announced in a cool collected voice. 'He wanted to build the Rudlow Aircraft Company into an independent force in the industry.'

Don Bishop nodded vehemently, but the rest of the board avoided his gaze.

Hugh's fingers and thumb tightened on the edge of the table. 'Really, Anthony, I know that you have been out of touch for some time but you must see that the climate is against the small independent producer. AIP can afford to take losses if the need arises. We can't. They could put us out of business by price-cutting and then pick up the company for peanuts from the liquidator. Probably get a fat government grant into the bargain. I don't believe that is a risk which the Company should take when there is such an attractive deal on the table.'

Anthony refused to give in. 'By all accounts we've still

got a world beater on our hands. We are way ahead of the competition. What other fifty-seater aircraft has the same low operating costs? And it's to be priced at two and a half million less than its nearest competitor. Mr Chairman, are you seriously arguing that this is the moment for us to sell out to the competition?'

Sir Leonard, the florid and almost completely round man next to him spoke now for the first time. 'Anthony, aren't you in danger of becoming a little over-sentimental about this?'

'What, Sir Leonard?'

'I'm a banker rather than an aviator so I must bow to your judgement on the significance of the technical advances which have been made. The projections on market share against the 386 are certainly impressive, but I would sound a note of caution. Already your development costs are seventy-five percent above budget . . .'

Don shook his head. 'Those ailerons.'

'Yes, yes, I'm sure there are excellent reasons, but there is still some way to go on development, is there not? And,' he gestured with pudgy red hands,' the company's borrowings are already close to their sustainable limit and eroding profitability, are they not? An agreement with AIP would bring in the necessary capital. Collaboration and consortium are the trends business is following these days.'

'Co-operation's one thing,' Anthony retorted, 'a take-over's quite another. This agreement would reduce the company to a minor subsidiary of an American conglomerate. I know we're highly geared, but we have never encountered any difficulty before raising the necessary finance. If the banks require further collateral,

I'm sure that the family would be able to find a way.

'We're so close now. The remaining problems — and there are bound to be some with any revolutionary design — should not take long to iron out, isn't that right, Don?'

Don Bishop beamed at him, and nodded. 'Provided we don't hit any more problems — and I don't think that's likely — the revised prototype should be ready in time for the launch at the Paris Airshow next year. I think if the deal goes ahead, we as a company will be throwing away a great opportunity.'

Someone sighed. Someone else coughed. Anthony could tell that the mood of the board was still against him.

'Thank you very much for your contribution, Bishop,' said Hugh. 'We can of course understand the strength of your feelings for your creation as a technical man.' He looked down the table and smiled confidently. 'Now, unless anyone else has anything to add to the debate, I suggest that we put it to the vote?'

Heads nodded.

Anthony saw their smiles of anticipation. Saunders and Slipper were already banking their 'golden hellos'. 'I tried Father,' he muttered silently to himself.

Then suddenly, at the far end of the room, he saw the flourish of a red polka-dot handkerchief. Sir Arthur coughed. Heads turned.

'Mr Chairman, I know that I am here only as an observer, so it would be quite improper for me to comment on the discussion. I just wondered whether it might be of assistance to the board if I gave some indication of the way the trustees view the matter? I am right, aren't I, in thinking that unless the trustees as majority shareholders are prepared to sell, then effectively there will be no deal?'

Hugh swallowed. 'Er, yes, Sir Arthur. That is quite right.'

'Good. Well, I think that you should know that, bearing in mind the strong feelings and arguments expressed on the matter by one of the main beneficiaries of the trust, I feel that the trustees would be very reluctant to sell. For the time being, at least, they will not be parting with shares.'

Hugh's cold eyes dwelt first on Sir Arthur, then on Anthony. 'Is that final?' he asked in a stony voice.

'Yes.'

All around pens clicked, board members sighed, fingers drummed in annoyance.

Anthony's eyes drifted up to the portrait of his father. He wished that the old patriarch could see him now. He had paid his dues. He had saved the dream. He hoped that when Father finally reached the Great Boardroom in the Sky, he would look down and smile benignly.

Maybe, even, forgive.

# Chapter 25

The small sixteen-seater plane stood on the grass landing strip before them. Its stubby fuselage glinted in the morning sun.

Loretta's hair curled and twisted in the gentle breeze. She glanced back at the grey corrugated hangars, across at the plane, then up at Anthony.

He was casually dressed in jeans and a blazer. His right hand held one of hers; his left, a scuffed black briefcase.

'Is she ready to go?' he called to the lean man in an orange overall.

He smiled and nodded. 'All yours.'

Anthony nodded back. He squeezed Loretta's hand, then led her up the small flight of steps into the cabin.

The inside was surprisingly spacious. There were only four seats in the cabin and these were wide, contoured, and grouped around a removable table. Between the windows were framed photographs of the Rudlow fleet. At the back there was a sofa, a bar and a small kitchen.

'Sit up in the front with me, if you like,' said Anthony casually. He led her through to the cockpit and pointed to the co-pilot's seat.

'Er, thank you,' Loretta replied. 'This was not really what I was expecting when I asked whether I could go with you to the next auction. Where did you say we were going?'

'Tours,' he repeated, and lowered himself into the seat next to hers. He donned a pair of headphones. He glanced at the flight plan. He flicked switch after switch. First the panel in front of them lit up, then the twin turbo-props began to turn. It was surprisingly quiet in the cockpit though. The sound was all behind them. All Loretta felt was a slight vibration.

Anthony gave a thumb's up sign to the man in the orange overall, muttered something into the microphone. He took his foot off the brake pedal. The plane surged forward then slowed and taxied down the runway.

He glanced across at her. 'Ready?' he said with a grin.

'Yes. All ready. This sure beats public transport.'

He smiled, reached up and pulled a lever. The throttle opened. The plane surged forward. The runway sped past beneath them, leaving trees and the hangar far behind. It seemed to be only seconds before Anthony gently touched the joy-stick and the bumping stopped. Effortlessly, easily, the plane swept upwards.

Loretta relaxed. She reached across and put her hand lightly on his sleeve. 'You're good,' she said. 'Maybe, one day, you could teach me to fly?'

The auction house was a large nineteenth-century building in the centre of town. The once white paint had long since turned a deep tobacco yellow. The strip lights hanging from the ceiling gave out a misty green glow.

Already it was hot and crowded. Grey-suited men lined the edges of the long trestle tables where the artefacts were displayed. They pawed the fine old silks and embroideries, they sifted through large plastic bags, occasionally stopping to make notes in their catalogues or to wipe the dust and dirt from their fingers.

'Sorry, Loretta,' Anthony said, 'but I think it would be better if we pretended not to be together.'

'What on earth for?'

'Because some of the dealers here know me. I'll explain later.'

Anthony walked up to a table and started sifting through some old needlework. Only later did he move across to the vestment. He glanced at it only casually, as if uninterested, then turned it over and examined the back.

'Mr Rudlow, *bonjour*.' A small lean man with round wire glasses approached and extended a bony hand. His black hair was cut short and greased to his scalp.

'Monsieur Pontelle, a pleasure.'

'And what brings such a distinguished collector to a little provincial sale? I would not be here myself if I weren't taking my family to my mother's birthday. Ninety-eight, you know. Ninety-eight tomorrow.'

'Many congratulations.'

'It is not me you should congratulate. You will come and see me when you are next in Paris, won't you?' He gave a little bow. '*Bonne chance*.'

Anthony walked out of the hall, beckoning surreptitiously to Loretta as he went.

She followed. It was only when they were some way down the street that he turned. 'Loretta,' he said urgently, 'that man I was talking to is one of the top dealers in Paris. He doesn't specialise in ecclesiastical vestments but he knows a good thing when he sees it, and he knows that I'm interested in it. Will you bid for me?'

'But I never have before . . .'

'Oh, it's easy,' he said glibly. 'You just stick your finger in the air. Like that,' he gestured. 'Nothing to it.'

Loretta stood at the back. It was hot and airless now. In front of her was a sea of bobbing heads.

Beyond stood the auctioneer on his raised podium. He had small piggy eyes that flicked ceaselessly about the room and a thin wet smile that never left his lips. Already he had pointed in Loretta's direction twice and claimed bids, though to her knowledge no one around her had moved a muscle. His hammer fell on the desk with such rapid regularity he might almost have been trying to squash a recusant fly.

At last, a porter in a dirty white apron walked forward holding the vestment. He turned it slowly in an arc.

'*Numero cent dix. . .un vêtement ecclesiastique du seizième siècle. Exceptionnel. Je commence à vingt mille. S'il vous plaît? S'il vous plaît?*' His eyes skipped once more around the room. '*Bien. Le Monsieur dans le deuxième rang . . .*'

'*Vingt-deux. . .vingt-quatre. . .vingt-six. . .trente.*'

The auctioneer flicked his finger from side to side. Loretta could not be sure who was bidding, but it wasn't Anthony. He was in the middle of the third row and the auctioneer had not looked in his direction once.

'*Trente.*' That bid came from the small lean man whom Anthony had spoken to earlier.

'*Trente-deux? Trente-quatre, quelqu'un? Trente-quatre?. . .Monsieur?*' He looked down almost directly in front of him. That must be Anthony.

The bidding rose rapidly to *quarante-six* and the auctioneer looked at Anthony again. '*Monsieur. . .quarante-huit?*' Anthony hesitated. The auctioneer asked again. '*Quarante-huit*?' Anthony nodded. Pontelle countered with '*Cinquante mille.*' This time Anthony shook his head.

Loretta raised her hand in the air. She flapped her catalogue. The auctioneer's eyes were on Pontelle. He seemed to have assumed all the bidding had stopped. He raised his hammer.

'*Monsieur*!' shouted Loretta.

He turned. '*Voulez-vous* —'

'*Cinquante-deux,*' she shouted.

'*Bien. Cinquante-deux, dernier rang.*'

Pontelle looked up angrily to see who he was bidding against, then the bidding moved quickly forward.

'*Soixante-douze. . .quatre-vingt-quatre. . .cent mille.*' At *cent vingt*, Pontelle wavered. At *cent quarante*, he shook his head.

'*Plus d'enchères à gauche ou au fond*?' The auctioneer's smile widened, then he rapped down the hammer. '*Adjugé à la dame du dernier rang. Cent quarante mille.*'

Loretta sighed. Anthony rose and with only the slightest nod in her direction, left the hall.

They dined that evening in an eighteenth-century château set in the hills above the Loire valley. As it was October now, it was too cold to linger on the terrace overlooking the moated garden, so they retreated to the warmth of the panelled dining room where a huge log fire blazed on an open hearth.

This restaurant, Anthony explained, was one of the great temples of French gastronomy. For the French, it seemed, a great chef was as much of a celebrity as a movie star. Already in the foyer, Loretta had seen on sale recipe books written by the chef, videos of his television programmes, jams made in the kitchen, wine glasses, cutlery, even bathrobes, bath salts, soaps and sun-glasses bearing his name. It was probably only a matter of time, she thought, before he had a scent too – but then again, maybe *parfum du chef de cuisine* was not such a great idea!

'Hungry?' asked Anthony as soon as they sat down.

'Famished,' she answered. A waiter in a crisp white tunic came forward, flourishing heavily tassled menu cards. Immediately she had opened hers, she wished that she had brought her dictionary. 'Anthony, you choose,' she sighed.

He glanced at his card only quickly. '*Deux menus gastronomiques, s'il vous plaît, et une grande bouteille de l'eau gazeuse.*' Then he turned back to Loretta. 'Are you sure that you don't want any wine?'

She shook her head. 'Absolutely.' With a little bow, the waiter took away the menu.

There was a hushed atmosphere about the room, with no laughter at all. The other diners talked in subdued whispers, rather as if they were in church.

She watched the expression on the face of the diner opposite who was just savouring the first mouthful of the dish before him. It reminded her of a statue she had once seen of St Teresa in ecstasy.

The first plate that arrived before her contained a terrine of *foie gras de canard* shaped like an egg. It was cradled in a perfect bird's nest woven from thin strands of fried potato. Loretta marvelled at the hours of work which must have gone into its preparation. She could hardly bring herself to cut it open. When finally she did, she, too, was grinning like a fool.

Course followed course. Each one was a still life which, she thought, should have been in a museum somewhere rather than on a plate which would soon be scraped clean. Each dish was more delicious than the last.

After the third — sole with a little crayfish soufflé rising from its centre — Loretta really had had enough to eat; but somehow she found room for the three further courses and even for the *petits fours* which accompanied the strong black coffee.

After dinner, they climbed the cherry-wood staircase to the first floor. Anthony had booked two rooms. Hers was the best room in the hotel; his a small adjoining single. When they reached her bedroom door, he did not say goodnight but turned the key to let her in, then silently followed.

The moonlight filtered in through the shutters that covered the high, arched windows. The crisp cotton sheets on the bed had been turned down. A little bag of chocolates lay on the pillow. The flowers on the table filled the room with their scent.

'Loretta,' he breathed from behind her, and already she could feel the gentle touch of his hands about her waist.

She turned slowly and looked up into his grey eyes. She saw love there. She saw respect. She saw understanding.

He leaned forward and kissed her, at first very softly, then harder. 'I love you,' he whispered, 'I love you.'

His arms enclosed her and she felt warm and safe in his embrace. 'And I you,' she sighed, nestling closer, steadying herself, listening to the rapid beating of his heart.

She thought how very different she felt now from when she had been with Hugh. She had never really even begun to penetrate the front which he had put out to the world. Foolishly, she had fallen for what in truth had been no more than her own idea of what he was like. She had fallen for her own make-believe creation.

She knew Anthony. She knew his fears. She felt somehow in touch with his soul. The wayward angel had fallen down to hell and was now slowly climbing the ladder back to the stars.

His hand ran playfully through the long, velvet strands of her hair. Gently, he raised her chin and kissed her again. His lips were eager, intense, hungry.

She felt the warmth of his hands through the silk of her dress. Smoothly, they caressed her waist, her sides, then very slowly, very gently, cupped her breasts. She felt the heat of them burning through her body.

'Loretta,' he breathed again, 'Loretta.' Even the way he spoke her name had more poetry about it, more intensity of feeling, than a thousand words of love.

She felt the coldness of the metal fastening sliding down her back, the warmth of his hands. She closed her eyes and held him tight.

Her dress fell from her shoulders, and like Hugh before him, Anthony gently picked her up and carried her over to the bed.

She slipped between the cold cotton sheets while he quickly undressed. In the moonlight she watched him. He was of finer build than Hugh. His body was that of an athlete, strong, supple and wiry.

Still it frightened her.

As he moved past the window towards her, she saw the dark outline of his maleness erect before him.

She shuddered and swallowed, the old anxiety returning. 'Anthony . . .?' she began.

'Hmm?'

'Er. . .N-nothing, darling.'

The bedsheets stirred as he climbed in beside her. She felt the heat of his body next to her. His arms went round her soothingly. He kissed her again, warm and wet. His hands worked slowly over her neck, her breasts.

She told herself that this was not like before. She could trust Anthony. He cared for her. He loved her.

She thought that maybe if she could make herself reach out and touch him, he would not seem so alien, so threatening.

He was lying on his side now. His warm breath was in her ear. His hand was moving down across her stomach.

Tentatively, her hand reached out. She felt the taut muscles in his leg. Trembling, she moved higher. Her fingers slid along his leg. They touched the soft loose flesh of his scrotum and for a second she felt herself lose control of her own hand, the fingers tightening into a claw . . .

Her body jackknifed. Cold beads of sweat coursed down her back. Wave after wave of spasms shook her. She was gasping for breath. Her mouth was very dry.

She turned wild eyes towards him. 'I'm sorry,' she sobbed, 'I'm sorry. You must *hate* me!'

'It doesn't matter. It really doesn't matter,' he soothed. 'My mistake. Selfish of me. Too soon.'

She turned her back on him and slipped into the foetal position. She was still shaking. After her encounter with Hugh, it seemed she would never be comfortable in bed with a man no matter how secure she felt. 'You mean it?' she pleaded. 'You really mean it? It's not you. Not you, I promise.'

'Of course I mean it. It's unimportant. We've got time enough.'

She had never told anybody except Julie about the attack in the elevator. Anthony, though, she thought would understand. Slowly, tearfully, she began to explain. She related every move the two men had made, remembering as clearly as if it had happened yesterday. But she wouldn't tell him about Hugh.

Anthony moved across to her and hugged her back, then remained very still. As she relived every moment, as the pain that she had experienced then once more shook her body, she felt him somehow drawing it into himself.

Three times she faltered, unable to continue, but each time she felt his understanding, his strength, feeding her with the power to go on.

When at last she finished, the dawn was already turning the trees outside a misty grey. She had no tears left to cry. She turned to Anthony with wet, red eyes. He clutched her to him, and all she could remember was the slow throb of his chest and warm reassurance of his arms, holding her safe, before she fell asleep.

# Chapter 26

'Mother, I'd like you to meet a friend of mine,' called Anthony from the doorway of the Yellow Drawing Room. He winked at Loretta and smiled reassuringly. He ushered her forward. 'Loretta Lorenz.'

A fire was burning in the cast iron grate. Lady Rudlow put down her tapestry and rose slowly from the sofa. The bright morning light from the French windows made her look older than Loretta remembered. The black labrador jumped off the sofa too and bounded towards her. It jumped up, pawing her skirt.

'Down, boy, down. I am sorry,' said Lady Rudlow. 'Delighted to meet you.' She smiled and shook Loretta's hand warmly. Her searching eyes, though, ranged over her guest like X-rays.

Loretta had bought especially for the occasion an Edina Ronay hound's-tooth check suit with green velvet collar and cuffs. She had thought it very 'country' at the time, but now she feared that she was a little overdressed. Lady Rudlow was wearing a green wool pleated skirt and matching cashmere twinset. Both showed signs of repair.

'Of course, we've met before,' said Her Ladyship. 'That little dinner I gave for Anthony. You're the American?'

'Yes.'

'From New York, I suppose? Everyone seems to come from there.'

'Yes.'

'How interesting. Come and sit down, my dear.' She indicated the cushion on the sofa which the labrador had only recently vacated. As Loretta sat, the dog gave a low growl of annoyance. 'Anthony darling,' Lady Rudlow called, 'you will look after the drinks, won't you? A small gin and tonic for me and —'

'Something soft for me,' added Loretta.

'Good.' Lady Rudlow's eyes still had the same searching look. 'I have a great friend in New York. Lives on Park Avenue. Nancy Richmond?'

Loretta swallowed. Even André had not been able to worm his way into her parties. 'Well, I've heard of her, of course, but I don't know her exactly.'

'Pity. She's such a dear. Funny, I thought everyone knew everyone in New York.'

'Well, it is quite a large place.'

'Yes, but — socially, I mean, the whole world is a village,' Her Ladyship announced vaguely. She picked up her tapestry again, and pulled a thread through the design which Loretta recognised as the Rudlow coat of arms. 'Do your parents live on Park Avenue too?'

'No. Queens.'

'It's just outside Manhattan, Mother,' explained Anthony as he handed Lady Rudlow her drink.

'Thank you, darling. Oh, I'm sure it's charming. It must be so much nicer in the countryside. Manhattan can be such a *trial*.' She sipped her drink. 'And what does your father do?'

'My parents are divorced. My father was in the airforce. My step-father is in business.'

'Oh, fascinating. What business exactly?'

'He owns a chain of laundromats.'

'Mother,' Anthony began to explain, 'that's a — '

'Darling. . .' Lady Rudlow's lips pursed '. . . I know perfectly well what a laundromat is. It's a place where people go to get their clothes washed — and a very commendable idea too.' She turned back to Loretta. 'Very commendable. I suppose he has one in every high street now, just like those beef patty people?'

Anthony winked at Loretta as he handed her a drink. 'Anyone else coming this weekend, Mother?' he asked, changing the subject.

'Only us for lunch, darling, but we're twenty for dinner. Philippe and Dauphine Lepré — you know, the French Ambassador and his wife — will be staying. They've both been so kind to me since George's accident, I really thought that I ought to do something. Otherwise it's just locals — oh, yes, apart from Gerald Wishton, poor dear. Do make a special effort with him, darling. He's still most frightfully upset that he wasn't made Foreign Secretary in the last reshuffle. Loretta, I do hope you've brought a nice frock?'

A shrunken grey-haired woman dressed in a grey uniform had just entered the room.

Anthony leapt to his feet. 'Nanny!' He bounded the distance between them and hugged her. 'Looking younger and younger! How are you?'

'Don't think you can get round me with your nonsense, Master Anthony,' she trilled, on regaining her breath from his bear-hug. She smoothed her tunic with mottled hands, suddenly stern. 'How are *you*, Master Anthony? That's more to the point.'

'All the better for seeing you. A drink?' he asked.

'A small sherry, if that's all right, M'lady?'

'Of course it's all right, Nanny.'

Anthony had already poured the drink. He put it carefully into her left hand; her right hand he took in his own and escorted her across the room to where Loretta sat. 'Nanny, I want you to meet a very special friend of mine.'

Loretta stood. 'Hello.' The pale mottled hand which she clasped seemed to have no substance to it.

Almost at once the smile on the woman's face faded. 'We've met before. Not to talk to, but we've met.' She withdrew her hand rather suddenly.

Loretta smiled and shook her head. 'No. . .no, I don't think so.'

'I never forget a face. You came up late one evening to the nursery.'

'No. I'm sure you're mistaken.' Surely the old lady hadn't seen her that night at Conningsby, Loretta thought anxiously. What if she were to insist on it − it didn't bear contemplating.

'Oh, Nanny,' called Lady Rudlow from behind her, 'Miss Lorenz is American. Probably someone you saw on television.'

The old woman's lips pursed. Her eyes were cold. 'If you say so, M'lady. If you say so.' She turned away.

Just then the door opened and Gander, the butler, announced lunch in his best operatic bass.

'Oh, good.' Lady Rudlow sighed and stood. 'Come along, Loretta.'

She was about to make her way towards the double mahogany doors that led through into the dining room when Lady Rudlow corrected her. 'No, not that way, my dear, we're having lunch in the Small Dining Room. It's on the other side of the Great Hall.'

She turned. By the doorway where Gander had been standing, now stood Hugh.

She swallowed and felt the blood drain from her face.

'Oh, there you are, Hugh!' called Lady Rudlow. 'We're just going through. Have you met Miss Loretta Lorenz, a friend of Anthony's?'

'Yes,' he said almost casually. There was no hint of emotion in his voice. 'Yes. We know one another – very well.'

He remained in the doorway as Lady Rudlow and then Nanny filed past. For Loretta, even with Anthony beside her, the distance between her and the door was like a force field which somehow had to be crossed. Her legs felt weak, her breathing unsteady. She looked away. She tried to ignore him, but wherever she looked she still felt the power of his gaze on her, his cold silent anger.

It was the same during lunch.

Loretta was seated at the small round table between Lady Rudlow and Anthony, but she was forever conscious of Hugh's steely eyes on her from across the table.

She picked at leek flan, steak and kidney pie – 'snake and pygmy', as the boys and Nanny gleefully referred to it – bread and butter pudding, and Stilton. All the time, Lady Rudlow continued with her gentle but persistent questions about Loretta's parents, her background, schooling, job, hobbies and friends.

Loretta did her very best to charm her. She spoke with knowledge and wit about the arts, jewellery, the London scene, the quirks of New York life, but she knew that when Lady Rudlow laughed, she was only preserving the front of good manners. She was a mother hen protecting her brood, and in her eyes Loretta was the fox.

Anthony beamed with pleasure whenever Loretta made a witty remark or said something which drew Lady Rudlow's approbation; but as lunch progressed, the signs of tension in his face and gestures became more pronounced.

Twice, Lady Rudlow gave him a look as if to say 'You're not serious about this girl, are you?' Later, she let slip that Jane Chalmers was among the 'locals' coming to dinner that evening, then suddenly she switched the subject to racehorses. 'You know,' she announced vaguely, 'it's so strange but I always find pedigree a far more reliable guide than conformation when it comes to choosing yearlings . . .'

Immediately after lunch, Anthony took Loretta for a walk in the grounds.

The park looked magnificent in the steely November light with its grazing herds of deer and great oaks, now devoid of leaf, like giants' gnarled hands. Anthony pointed out the hole in one of the tree trunks where a family of tawny owls had their nest.

Later, they boarded the small boat and rowed across the lake to the island where the ruined Temple of Music stood. They spent an hour there, maybe more, talking, laughing, watching out for the sleek backs of huge trout, or just gazing out at the parkland beyond.

Then they went back to the House, to the library — another room Loretta had never seen before. It was a perfect circle of brown and gold beneath a pale blue plasterwork dome.

Anthony had just pulled out a book of Audubon engravings when Hugh entered.

'Oh, there you are, Ant,' he said casually. 'Mother was asking for you.'

'Think it will wait until tea?'

'Dunno.' He shrugged. 'Something's ruffled her feathers.'

Anthony sighed. 'Oh, very well.' He turned to Loretta. 'I'm sorry. I'll be back just as soon as I can.'

She smiled at him, nodded, then opened the book of engravings he had handed to her.

Immediately the door closed, she heard Hugh's footsteps behind her. 'My dear Loretta,' he said in the same casual tone, 'you are even more naive than I thought. I did make the position very plain.'

She turned another page. 'I don't know what you mean.'

'Come, come now,' he chided. 'You know very well. I think we ought to go somewhere we can talk quietly.'

She turned and faced him. 'If you have anything to say to me, you can say it here. Your threats aren't going to stop me seeing Anthony, if that's what you mean. We have every right to go on seeing one another, when and how we wish.'

'Look,' said Hugh, 'there's an echo in this room. Every sound carries through to the Hall. If you don't mind, that's fine by me. Do carry on.'

'OK.' Loretta stiffened. 'Let's get this over with as quickly as possible. Where do you suggest we go?'

'Come on,' Hugh beckoned. 'Follow me.'

He led the way through into the Great Hall, up the staircase, and along the gallery. He stopped outside the State Bedroom and beckoned towards the door.

'Oh, very funny, Hugh,' she jeered. 'Grow up.'

Suddenly his eyes were like marble. He turned quickly and leaned over the railing. 'Ant!' he called. 'Ant! Could you come up here for a moment?'

'For Chrissakes!' She grabbed his shoulder. 'What the hell do you think you're doing?'

'What do you think?' he snapped.

She shivered and tugged at his shoulder. 'Couldn't we at least discuss it first?'

He shrugged and straightened up. 'As you wish.' Without looking at her, he opened the door opposite them and walked through into the State Bedroom.

Loretta bit her lip. She followed.

'Remember this room?' Hugh asked mockingly as soon as he had closed the door. 'There's no echo here. In a State Bedroom, it would be considered lacking in decorum.'

'That's enough schoolboy humour, Hugh.' Her voice was firm, but her hands were trembling. 'Look, I haven't told Anthony about us — that was just a sad, sorry episode, a mistake for both of us — and if you were half the man you pretend to be, you wouldn't tell him either. What on earth's the point of dredging up the past?

'Later, maybe, he could handle it, but not now. Emotionally, he's still very fragile. He needs me. Destroy his trust in me — the one dependable anchor in his life — and you'll have a junkie back on your hands, I swear it. Is that what you want? You couldn't do that to him. You wouldn't!'

'Try me,' Hugh sneered.

'But he's your brother!'

'Better a temporary relapse than a mistake he'll be paying for the rest of his life.' He walked slowly towards her, his eyes hard and cold.

'Hugh, if you dare . . .'

'Yes, Loretta, I'm going to tell him everything.'

He made a sudden lunge at her. His hand clamped about her wrist. He pulled her to him with jarring force.

'No, please.'

'Yes. Every little detail. How much you told me you loved me . . .'

His eyes were unfocused, the veins in his neck swollen. His hands went around her buttocks and pulled her to him, hard against the contours of his body.

'No!'

He mimicked her voice. ' "Oh God. . .oh God, I adore you." '

She trembled. She gasped for breath. She reached up with both hands and made to grab his face. No sooner were her hands on his cheeks than she felt her body twisting around, her legs swinging and kicking in the air.

He let go then and she felt herself falling, winded, into something very soft. The embroidered bedspread was all around her, the rosette of rose silk above.

'How wet and inviting you were . . .'

And suddenly Hugh was there too, the full weight of him bearing down on her. His fingers tightened about her wrists.

'Just like old times, isn't it, Loretta?' he barked. 'Shall we call Ant up now, hmm? Ask him to join in the fun with the family whore?'

'You bastard!' she spat. '*You bastard*! Get off me!'

She swallowed. She closed her eyes, then snapped them open again to try and clear her vision. She strained against his hands, she wriggled. And all the time Hugh's gloating laughter cut her to the quick.

'You stupid little bitch! Don't you see? The second Ant

315

knows about us, he'll ditch you. Occasionally Ant and I might choose to slum it for a change. But, Christ,' he shuddered, 'we don't share the same sewer!'

He rose from the bed, brushed down his jacket. 'You're a beauty, Loretta, I only wish you weren't so fucking stupid. I ask you,' he sighed, shaking as if to free himself from something unclean, 'two tricks on the same patch.'

She watched him as he moved towards the door. She stiffened, fearful now. 'Where are you going?'

'To get Ant, of course.'

'You can't!'

He stopped, turned. 'Look, you give me no alternative. You won't listen to reason. You're too fucking obstinate to take the elegant way out. You're too blind to see that you've blown it. Christ. . .don't you understand? Once all this is over, Ant and I will both be laughing about it. The family whore from the jewellery store!'

He shrugged. 'So you take down Ant with you. Great. He gets hurt unnecessarily — maybe has a relapse — and it will be entirely *your* doing!'

'But the last thing in the world I want is for Anthony to be hurt,' she stammered.

'Then fucking well take the elegant way out!' He walked back towards her. 'Loretta, haven't you got any self-respect? Don't you see, it won't make the slightest difference? Ant would never in a thousand years marry one of my cast-offs. People in our position just don't marry your kind.

'Look,' his hand stabbed the air, 'you can walk away from here and nobody need know anything. . .or you can make a fucking exhibition of yourself, hurt Anthony, and be the laughing stock of London. It's your choice.'

She took a deep breath. 'What if I were to agree. . .what would you want me to do?'

'Just *go*!' he breathed. 'Forget your hopeless crazy plans for Ant. Go, and never come back.'

She shuddered. 'And if I go, will you promise never to tell him about us?'

'Everything will be forgotten. He need never know.'

'But . . .'

'No buts, Loretta. Either you agree to go, or I call Ant in here, now.'

She gulped back the tears filling her throat. Suddenly she felt very cold. 'All right,' she nodded. 'I'll do it.'

'Good.' He sighed. 'This way nobody gets hurt. Nobody will ever know.'

Loretta moved over to the far side of the bed. She wanted to stand, but did not have the strength. She stared out through the window across to the deer park beyond. She held her hands tightly together to stop them from trembling. 'I can't just walk out. It would look strange when I've been asked down for the weekend.'

The floorboards creaked behind her. 'During tea, the telephone will ring.' Hugh was brisk and businesslike now. 'You'll take the call. You'll make out that there's some sort of emergency. I don't know — Mother ill, business, something like that. You will make your apologies and take the next train. I want you out of here before dinner, understand?'

Loretta nodded. 'I love Anthony,' she said stiltedly. 'I'm only doing this for him. To stop him from being hurt.'

She heard Hugh's footsteps cross the room. 'Sure,' he said sardonically. 'Sure.' The door closed behind him.

\* \* \*

'Ah, Loretta, there you are,' called Lady Rudlow from her usual seat on the sofa in the Yellow Drawing Room. Two silver teapots were set before her on a low table. They glistened in the flickering firelight. On a second table there were plates of sandwiches, crumpets, and small diamond-shaped biscuits. 'May I introduce the French Ambassador, Philippe Lepré, and Madame Lepré.'

A tall, balding man in a pinstriped suit rose to his feet and offered his hand. *'Enchanté, Mademoiselle.'*

'Mr Ambassador.' Loretta shook his hand dutifully, then turned and shook the hand of his wife, a very thin and elegant woman with a cool, fixed smile.

'Miss Lorenz is an American friend of my son Anthony,' Lady Rudlow explained. 'China or Indian?'

Anthony was standing in front of a chair that had been pulled up by the side of the sofa. Loretta moved towards him, smiled, and sat down on the sofa between him and Madame Lepré.

'Loretta, would you like China or Indian tea?' Lady Rudlow repeated.

'Oh, I'm sorry, Lady Rudlow. Er. . .whichever is the least trouble.'

'Well, they are both here, my child. You can have whichever one you want.'

'Er. . .Indian, please.'

Anthony looked to her. 'I was searching everywhere for you.'

'Yes, well, I went up to my room for a rest.' She wore heavy make-up now to disguise the tell-tale signs of weeping.

'Your tea, Loretta.'

Anthony rose and picked up the cup. He carried it across to her.

'The country air is rather tiring if you are not used to it,' remarked Lady Rudlow. 'Would you like a crumpet or one of Mrs Grundy's special ginger nuts? The Women's Institute have been trying to lure the recipe out of her for years.' She turned to the Ambassador. 'You know, Philippe, I am sure that the *entente cordiale* would be much more *cordiale* if only your great nation understood the civilising influence of afternoon tea. The gap between lunch and dinner is really much too long. Men, I assure you, are not good on an empty stomach.'

'Civilising, yes,' the Ambassador replied, 'but also, alas, fattening.'

'But you are a beanpole, Philippe! A veritable beanpole.'

The telephone rang. . .five, six times. . .then it fell silent.

Loretta could hear Gander's footsteps behind her. He coughed, and bent down beside her. 'Excuse me, Miss Lorenz, but a Mr André Swert wishes to speak to you on the telephone. Would you like to take the call or shall I tell him to ring back at a more convenient time?'

'Thank you, no.' Loretta swallowed. 'I'll take it.' She rose and followed Gander out of the room.

He led her through into the library, then left her. There was a long wait before the call was connected. Finally she heard Hugh's voice down the line. 'Everything ready?'

'Yes,' she replied.

She walked back through the Hall, back into the Yellow Drawing Room. She was very pale.

Anthony stood up at her approach. 'Anything wrong?'

'Oh,' she tried to make light of it, 'only a teensy-weensy

319

crisis, that's all. André wants me to take the next flight back to the States.'

'Christ! Not until after the weekend, surely?'

'No. I'm afraid he wants me back there now.'

Anthony's hands clenched and unclenched. 'And how long. . .how long will you be away?'

She looked up at him with soft, hurt eyes. 'I don't know exactly but it could be a while.'

She turned and made her apologies to Lady Rudlow. 'I'm so sorry,' she said, 'it comes from being a career girl.'

'What a shame,' replied Her Ladyship, 'but of course we quite understand. If you like, I'll ask Mrs Grundy whether she can rustle up some chicken sandwiches or something for you. George and I, you know, once had the most appalling attack of food poisoning on a flight to the States.' Then she turned back to the Ambassador. 'Now tell me, Philippe, I bet you always travel with something quite delicious tucked away in your diplomatic bag . . .'

Anthony offered to drive her to the station. As the car made its way down the drive, Loretta turned and gazed out of the back window for the last time at the great expanse of the House. She sighed and tried to fix the image forever in her memory. She did the same as they passed the Temple of Music on the island in the lake, with the deer grazing on the high ground in the park, with the huge specimen trees along the drive.

'Have you no idea how long you'll be away?' asked Anthony again as they reached the open road.

'No,' she sighed. 'Just however long André needs me over there. He kind of hinted, though, that it could be a long haul.' A long trip had struck her as by far the kindest excuse for their separation. She would just have to lie low in London for a while.

His fingers drummed against the steering wheel. 'God, I'm going to miss you.'

'And I you. . .but the only thing that's really important is that you stay strong. Keep up the good work. Don't weaken even for a moment. You'll do that for me, won't you?'

He nodded silently and drove on.

When they reached the station, the train was already standing at the platform. She just had time to kiss Anthony one last time. She felt the warmth of his mouth, the gentleness of his touch. She hugged him with trembling hands. 'Take care, my darling. Take care,' she whispered.

She clambered on board just as the whistle blew. She opened the window and leaned out, but already the train was clattering down the track away from him.

She waved at the distant figure until he was out of sight, then closed her eyes. She sat down on her suitcase and buried her head in her hands.

# Chapter 27

'Come in,' called Sir Arthur.

Camilla entered and closed the door behind her.

Every wall of the spacious room was lined with books. The smell of leather polish and old cigars filled the air. The only concession to modernity was the green computer monitor on the leather-topped desk.

'Damn' thing,' muttered Sir Arthur. He stabbed a button on the computer keyboard and stood up. 'My dear Camilla, such a pleasure to see you — and looking so pretty too.' He towered above her as he shook her hand. 'Keeping well, I hope?'

She nodded. 'Yes. Extremely well. . .under the circumstances.'

Sir Arthur ushered her towards a leather armchair. 'Hmm, yes. Your mother mentioned that there had been — er — a slight change in your personal arrangements.' He drew on his large cigar and exhaled. A column of smoke rose from his mouth. 'Leaving that aside, remind me what you're doing now? As a job, that is.'

'I work for Friends of the Earth.'

'Quite right. Excellent.' He cut through the smoke with his hand. 'The Earth needs friends. Rain forests. Pollution. Thoroughly for these pressure groups myself.'

He returned to his seat behind the desk. 'So what can I do for you? You said it was important.'

'It's about Daddy,' she replied in a small voice.

Sir Arthur sighed deeply. 'My dear girl, what else can we do? He is in the hands of the best doctors — and very competent they are too.'

'Mummy told me that the charade at the hospital was your doing.'

Sir Arthur's brow furrowed. His jowls shook. 'I'm sorry, I don't follow?'

'I want to know *why*?' An urgent note entered her voice. 'Why, for God's sake, are the doctors being forced to keep Daddy alive in this. . .this terrible way?'

'Where there is life — '

'There *isn't* any life,' she sighed. 'It's no use pretending to me. He's brain dead. The doctors told me. It's unnatural. It's wrong. Christ, he's been on that machine for over eight months now!'

'Please, Camilla.' He made a soothing gesture. 'I understand perfectly what you're saying, but I assure you that it is imperative that your father is kept alive for as long as possible. I think I know what he would have wished.'

'Huh! He was a proud man. He would not have wanted his family to remember him like this.'

'True,' Sir Arthur conceded. 'But, as I said, it is imperative. Much depends on it, not least a great deal of money.' He leaned forward and pressed his hands flat on the desk. 'Your father, Camilla, was fully conversant with the tax implications of his death. He knew that without proper planning, his demise would be a financial catastrophe for the family. Much of the land, and maybe even Conningsby Park itself, would have to be sold.

324

'I therefore suggested a scheme which in the ordinary course of events would have cut the tax payable to a small — very small — fraction of what it would otherwise have been. The bulk of your father's property was transferred into trust — I have your mother's approval to tell you this — and all that was required for the scheme to be fully effective was that your father should survive for seven years from the date of the grant.'

'But — '

'Let me finish, Camilla. Of course, there is a snag: when we set up the scheme four years ago, we never envisaged that your father would not survive for the full seven years. After all, he was only fifty-seven and in excellent health. Am I making myself plain?'

Camilla nodded.

'So, you see, the longer he can be kept alive now, the more we save. If we can keep him technically and legally alive for another year, or even two, it will save the family a fortune.'

Camilla's cheeks darkened. The veins in her neck swelled. 'Has it occurred to you that there are things more important than money? Like a man's dignity, for instance? Like the feelings of those who loved him? Like a man's peace and tranquillity before he faces God?'

'True, true, my dear.' Sir Arthur's voice struck a formal tone. 'But I am only doing what I must as trustee and executor of your father's estate. It is my duty . . .'

The hidden valve clicked open with a small sharp sound. The pumping started. First, there was a hiss like gas escaping through a pin-hole; then, an amplified mechanical sigh. The black rubber sack ballooned. Lord

Rudlow's chest swelled. Involuntarily, unknowing, he breathed one more breath.

Two bags of fluid – one clear, one yellow – hung from hooks on the wall. A pillow bulged under his bent knees. Another lay flat against his back. Worm-like plastic tubes and black wires extended from his body like guys staking him to the hospital bed.

He lay there as he had lain every day for the last eight months. His pale open eyelids never blinked. His taped and tubed mouth never made a sound.

The machines, though, had changed. More fairy lights came on now. There was the new one on the left with its columns of red and green and yellow that constantly fluctuated as if transcribing some secret melody. There was the black puffing sack, of course, and the green monitor which coughed little pyramids. Camilla ran her finger along the green cathode-ray screen. It crackled back at her.

She glanced down very casually at the pair of thirteen amp sockets in the wall that were feeding the machines with power. They were plastic. Three pin.

She sighed and turned away.

The nurse sat in the corner of the white windowless room. She was small and squat and had straight, cropped, mousy hair.

'Nurse, I'm sorry to trouble you,' called Camilla, pressing the back of her hand to her brow, 'but I'm feeling a little faint.'

The nurse rose to her feet. 'Well, at least you are in the right place. Let me take your pulse.'

'No, I'm sure it's nothing,' she shrugged. 'Just so airless in here. Do you think there's any chance of a cup of tea or something?'

'Afraid Daphne won't be round with her trolley for half an hour or so. Will the machine do? Not that I'd call that tea . . .'

'Fine. That would be very kind.'

'Now you sit down, you hear? Look after yourself.'

Camilla nodded and smiled. She sat down on the wooden chair by the bed. She looked across at her father with cool, determined eyes.

Immediately the door closed, she knelt by the side of the bed. For a second, she closed her eyes in prayer, then, as quickly, she rose. She leaned across and planted a kiss on her father's smooth, warm brow. She pressed her cheek next to his. 'Nothing to fear, Daddy,' she murmured. 'If I wasn't a good daughter in your terms, at least . . .'

She shuddered. Without turning back to look at him, she bent down in front of the bank of switches by the wall. Her finger stroked the first switch once, then jabbed.

And that's it, she thought, startled, a human life extinguished, a once powerful, complex force annihilated by the flick of a switch. That's it.

She hardly noticed the jangling bells that echoed the noises inside her head, the wail of the siren, the hurried footfalls from the corridor . . .

She waited until the door was just opening, then jabbed at the switch once more.

A sudden seething mass of nurses and doctors came from everywhere then. She watched as they thumped her father's sagging body, as they pounded and prodded, as they listened and pressed, as they pranced and twirled about his naked white chest to the deafening sound of the siren's wail.

327

Then suddenly the siren stopped. The black nurse twiddling the knobs of the ventilator sighed deeply.

'I think it's getting through,' said one of the white-coated doctors.

Another nodded.

Wide-eyed, unbelieving, Camilla stared across at the circle of nodding heads around her father. She saw his chest swell. The first breath.

'Seems to be stabilising,' said someone.

She bit her lip. All she saw now was the flickering lights of the machines on the trolley before her. All she heard was the puffing and wheezing as the black rubber sack filled, then emptied once more.

A nurse pushed by her, lightly nudging her.

This was her chance. This was her excuse. Camilla threw her weight forward as though caught off-balance. Her arms went out. They fastened around the rail of the trolley as she fell. They twisted, spun around. The trolley jolted forward with a clank and skidded a few feet.

At first all that happened was that the leads and wires tightened around Lord Rudlow's body, but then as the trolley skidded further across the floor, the thin black wires started pinging off his body, followed by the tubes. They strained at first and it looked for a moment as if they were going to stop the trolley's advance, then the plaster attached to Lord Rudlow's mouth gave way and the clear plastic tubes began to spring back on themselves, curling and sprinkling fluid.

There was nothing to stop the trolley now except the leads attached to the plugs in the wall. A male voice shouted. A nurse rushed forward and tried to intercept it, but as she grabbed the rail, the trolley pulled against the leads. It tilted. It toppled forward. It fell.

There was a flash. An intensely bright blue spark crackled. A puff of noxious black smoke mushroomed from the floor. Splinters of glass tinkled as they hit the walls.

Camilla picked herself up off the floor. A trickle of blood came from a finger of her right hand. She sucked at it like a little girl and looked up at the bewildered, shocked faces staring at her in disbelief. There was complete silence in the room. For a second everything had stopped.

'I – I tripped,' she said in a small high-pitched voice. 'I'm really sorry.'

She straightened, pulled down her skirt and walked stiffly through the door. She stared rigidly ahead, eyes wide and unfocused. 'Really very sorry,' she mumbled, and a small smile touched her lips although her eyes were full of tears. 'So very sorry . . .'

# Chapter 28

They collected in the graveyard in the shadow of the church's heavy Victorian masonry. Outside the freshly mown circle, the grass was long and unkempt. It danced in the breeze, swathing the old broken gravestones with a heavy green collar. Lichen and moss obscured the inscriptions, claiming for their own the once fulsome epitaphs to the now nameless dead.

The sky was uniform steel grey. The fine drizzling rain blew in their faces, pattered on their hats, dampened their clothes.

Camilla stood perfectly still, wide-eyed and blank-faced, staring ahead of her. Against her black coat, her skin looked very white, almost opalescent. The rainwater which snagged her lashes made her only tears, she could not weep.

She nodded blindly at the estate workers, farm labourers, kennel-huntsmen, grooms, footmen, kitchen staff, gardeners, gamekeepers and maids as they slowly filtered out of the church in their Sunday best and stood a discreet distance away from the red soil void before her. There was Mrs Grundy, the cook for the last twenty years, portly and sobbing beside her crippled daughter; there Davies, the head keeper, his Edwardian moustache flapping as he puffed down his long hooked nose; there

331

Gander, the butler, his broken-veined face washed with rain, offering a steadying hand to the worthy Mrs Dauney, the housekeeper.

The vicar opened the *Book of Sacraments* with stubby fingers. The hem of his vestments billowed and flapped like sodden flags over a mud-caked cassock. ' "Man that is born of a woman hath but a short time to live and is full of misery," ' he intoned. ' "He cometh up, and is cut down, like a flower . . .He fleeth as it were a shadow . . ." '

A tall woman stood alone a few yards to the right of the servants, dabbing the tears from beneath her veil with a thin voile handkerchief. She looked incongruous next to the staff in a black velvet suit worn with a flowing matching cape. Strands of auburn hair were just visible between the felt Homburg and the veil.

Camilla glanced quickly at her mother, wondering whether she too had noticed Silvana Luzzi standing there. Her mother's stoic face was expressionless except for a slight quiver of her red-painted lips.

As the pall-bearers approached, Lady Rudlow's gloved hand gripped Camilla's clenched fist and squeezed it tight. For a fleeting moment, she turned hard quizzical eyes on her daughter, as if she had guessed, then she squeezed the fist again in a gesture of support. 'Be strong, dear,' she whispered, 'be strong.'

Grim-faced, they came with a steady measured tread. Anthony and Hugh were first. Anthony's shoulder was wedged under the corner of the black mahogany coffin, his body taut, blond hair flapping. Hugh stared ahead with sad, angry eyes. The undertakers were next: burly thick-set men with professional solemn expressions. Behind was Cecil, Lord Rudlow's younger brother, a thin grey-faced man with a pronounced jaw and a cold look in his eye; then, last, the puffing, diminutive figure of Don Bishop, his thick metal-rimmed glasses so misted with rain and tears that he felt his way forward with the tentative steps of a blind man. His shoulder barely touched the edge of the coffin.

The coat of arms – the greyhound supporters, the Griffon rampant, the fusils of ermine – was visible now as the coffin was laid on the turf by the side of the grave. Rain-water trickled from the cups of the giant lilies on the surmounting wreaths and spilled down its sides.

' "Thou knowest, Lord, the secrets of our hearts . . ." '

Camilla thought she saw Sir Arthur's keen glance directed at her. She turned away.

The pall-bearers took their final positions around the grave. They held the thick woven straps in both hands and heaved the coffin off the bank. Slowly it rose, then swung forward over the grave. For a second it hung there, the men straining under its weight, then it dipped and rasped on the red soil sides of the grave. Camilla involuntarily reached out to support it.

The black box steadied. Slowly it descended deeper and deeper into the shadows, until it landed with a soft thud on the red mud below.

' " . . .earth to earth. . .ashes to ashes. . .dust to dust . . ." '

Lady Rudlow threw in a posy of wild violets. Anthony and Hugh threw in handfuls of earth. Camilla stepped forward, eyes dry. She knelt down and picked up a clod of earth. She threw it in and watched as it fell on top of the coffin and broke into three pieces. She wiped her wet hand on her black woollen coat, leaving a broad pink streak.

' " . . .through the Lord Jesus Christ; who shall change our vile bodies, that it may be like unto his glorious body . . ." '

She heard, she was sure she heard, the hounds howling in the distance. She nodded. For the first time she smiled.

' " . . .We give thee hearty thanks, for that it hath pleased thee to deliver this our brother out of the miseries of this sinful world . . ." '

Silvana Luzzi moved closer to the graveside, gave one last bow of respect, then turned and walked quickly along the gravel path towards the wooden gate.

Camilla watched her for an instant, blinking, picking at the stitching on her coat with earth-stained hands. She snapped her prayer book shut, pushed past Anthony and Hugh and raced down the path.

'Wait!' she cried. She tugged at the passenger door handle of the red Mercedes convertible.

Signora Luzzi turned. She slowly lifted her veil.

'I'm sorry,' said Camilla. 'May I. . .can I ask you something?' She scrambled inside.

'Here? Now? You think I feel like chatting?'

'I'm sorry,' Camilla blinked through the rain-blurred windows, 'but I've got to know − it's just − I don't know − what was it? That held him to you, you know? Was it sex?'

Signora Luzzi chuckled and slowly shook her head. 'Oh, Camilla, how sweet you are!' She brushed the girl's cheek with her gloved hand. 'You haven't changed, have you? Sex − after thirteen years? You credit me − and sex − with too much. It takes more than that to keep a man − much more. It takes love, understanding, never taking anything for granted − I don't know − knowing how to make things exciting.'

Camilla bit her lip. 'So it was a proper relationship?'

'Well,' Silvana smiled, 'a proper improper relationship.'

Others were coming out through the gate now, approaching the parked car.

'Can you give me a lift?' asked Camilla.

Signora Luzzi nodded. 'If you like.' She put the car into gear.

'It must be strange — to share the man you love with someone else, I mean. I don't think I could ever handle that.'

'It isn't always easy, of course, but there are compensations.' Signora Luzzi smiled nostalgically as she steered the car out on to the narrow road. 'If I can be frank with you — it's very difficult to live with anyone full-time. I tried once, so I know. You will find the same when you marry, *cara*, whatever they tell you. All those silly, petty unimportant things. . .and so without mystery.'

She shrugged, turned the wheel sharply and they sped around a blind corner. 'You see, I only saw George when he was at his very best, when he wanted love — and by that I don't just mean sex — and wanted to make it thrilling. We had nothing but the good times together — the trips abroad, the clandestine dinners. Every second we were together we lived, really lived.'

Camilla gripped the sides of the seat. 'Yes,' she said vaguely, 'I can see that. It's marriage that's wrong. It — it raises unrealistic expectations, smothers freedom. I don't think I'll ever marry, no matter how much in love I am. I couldn't face watching it slowly turn sour.'

'No, never anticipate failure, *cara*. I'm not condemning marriage. All I'm really saying is that there are some small

335

compensations to being alone. When my one short marriage went wrong, I never had the heart to try again. Somehow . . . somehow I lost confidence − not in marriage but in myself. I need my face on . . . my nails . . . my hair. Then I can face the world.' She smiled sadly. 'George only ever saw me like that. Painted. Perfect.'

'You're kidding?'

'No, I promise. But that is me, not you, *cara*. My advice to you is simple: if a man is right, marry him. Bear his children. That's what I miss most. Giving pleasure is such a transitory thing.' She turned towards the girl. 'Is there someone, *cara*?'

'There is.' Camilla nodded slowly. 'But right now I can't relate to him. . .to anything, really. Shock, I suppose.'

'Give it time, *cara*. Give it time.' Silvana pressed her foot on the brake. 'There,' she said, 'your front door. Conningsby. The other world.' She glanced up at the portico and sighed.

Camilla shook herself as if waking from a dream. 'Please, you will join us, won't you?'

'And embarrass your mother?' Silvana shook her head. 'Never. But if sometime you would like to come and have tea with me in my flat in Mount Street . . .?'

'Yes, I'd like that,' answered Camilla. 'Really.' She smiled and swung open the car door. 'And thanks for the lift.'

The drinks had been drunk; condolences given. The last of the guests had finally woven an unsteady passage to the door. The caterers were now clearing away the empty glasses, sliding in and out through the pantry like shadows under Gander's watchful eye.

Anthony was just tipping the head waitress when Sir Arthur drew him to one side. 'If you could join us in the library?' said the trustee, looking down at his shoes. 'It's best to do these things while the family are still together.'

Anthony nodded. He followed Sir Arthur through into the library, then closed the double doors behind him.

His mother was already seated on the scuffed leather sofa to the left of the fireplace. She sat in the same way as he had seen her so often since the accident: hands folded in her lap; eyes rigidly ahead. Throughout the service, the drinks and the condolences, she had conducted herself with quiet, controlled dignity. Now the strain was beginning to show in the quivering lines on her face.

Hugh sat next to her, his legs crossed, one hand lightly on the arm rest. Camilla sat hunched in the sofa opposite, staring down at the Turkey rug.

Anthony sighed as he walked around the large partner's desk in the centre of the room. It had been at that desk — one of the few remaining pieces made by Chippendale especially for the house — that his father had always sat when dealing with the estate accounts. He felt his father's presence there still. He lowered himself onto the sofa next to Camilla and squeezed her hand.

Sir Arthur stood by the mantlepiece. Above him, rain still pattered on the central glass panel of the pale blue plasterwork dome, sending little dappled shadows down on to the room.

'Good.' Sir Arthur's chest puffed out and his thumb slipped into his waist-coat pocket in one smooth movement.

'I would just like to say first — on a personal note —

how much I will miss George. He was a good friend and a man of extraordinary talent and vision. He was driven by two great passions – aviation and Conningsby.

'As we all know, he built the Rudlow Aircraft Company from scratch into a business which could compete with any in the world; and Conningsby he restored to its former glory after the many years of neglect. This was no mean achievement for one lifetime so tragically cut short.

'Quite naturally, he was desperately anxious that all this work should not go to waste.'

Anthony glanced across at his mother. She was still staring rigidly before her, still in control.

Sir Arthur tapped a sheaf of papers with his forefinger. 'To this end, and under my guidance, George made a number of dispositions during his lifetime. Although in the circumstances his death was a merciful release, had George lived even four months more, we would have saved some ten million in death duties which must now be found. Had he lived even longer, the savings would have been correspondingly greater. Nonetheless, the estate remains a sizeable one.

'Principally these dispositions were aimed at mitigating the substantial liabilities to tax that would otherwise be incurred, but also towards protecting the estate in the event of. . .' his jowls shook 'shall we say, adverse circumstances?

'I would not dream of troubling you with the details now, but broadly speaking under these arrangements, the house, the home farm, the surrounding four thousand acres and George's fifty-five percent holding in Rudlow Aircraft were placed in trust. The bulk of the income accruing is either to be applied to the estate or accumulated in a protective trust until such time as the eldest surviving son has a male heir . . .'

'Hold it.' Anthony stood up. His brain was spinning. His fist clenched and unclenched. 'Let me get this straight. "Accumulated until such time as the eldest surviving son has a male heir." Are you telling me that I inherit nothing? That only my son will inherit?'

'Not outright.' Sir Arthur pulled his red polka-dot handkerchief out of his pocket and wiped his brow. 'Of course, we had all hoped and expected that by the time George's life was drawing to a close, an heir would already have been born.'

'Yes, but that didn't happen, did it?' Anthony sighed. 'I'd just like to know where I stand.'

Sir Arthur scanned the papers before him. 'Yes, quite. Out of the income, you have an allowance which can be increased within certain limits at the discretion of the trustees to supplement your salary from the company. . .and, of course, you have the right to reside at Conningsby.'

'So, in effect, I'm treated like a minor, right? I'm thirty-six years old, I've been to hell and back again, and I'm treated like a twelve-year-old. Is that it?'

Sir Arthur sighed. He dabbed his forehead again with the handkerchief. 'Your father, dear boy, was naturally worried about your – your particular problem. You can understand that, surely? Although we all had confidence in your ability to overcome this – we hope and pray that it is now a thing of the past – certain steps had to be taken to protect the estate, certain amendments made to the terms of the trust, just in case. I admit that I raised the point a number of times with your father.'

'Thanks a lot,' Anthony slumped down again. 'And

who, may I ask, are these trustees to whom I must bow and scrape whenever anything needs to be done?'

'Well,' Sir Arthur puffed, 'that's rather an exaggeration. Provided everything runs smoothly — as I'm sure it will — I don't see why day to day matters can't be left in your own hands.'

'The trustees?' persisted Anthony. 'Who are they?'

'Myself and Hugh.'

Anthony glanced across at his brother. Hugh shrugged as if to say that this was none of his doing.

Anthony stared at Lady Rudlow. 'Mother, did you know about this?'

She looked back at him with sad, hurt eyes. 'Yes, I did, darling. George had to protect the estate, you must see that. And, remember, you were very ill at the time. There was no real alternative.'

'All that's behind me now . . .' But he could see the scepticism and disbelief in their faces. To them, this was just one more empty promise.

He shuddered at the chill in the room. They had warned him at the centre that old relationships would never be the same again; that he would have to work hard if he were ever to regain the trust of friends and family: but he had not prepared himself for this. He, a grown man, was to be treated as a minor. He felt like an outcast in his own home. He was alone. Totally alone.

And, perversely, as the feeling of isolation grew in him, the gnawing, the craving in his gut, returned.

He gazed on unseeing as Sir Arthur's morbid financial requiem took its course, as a dead man's money was apportioned and entailed, bequeathed and endowed.

The air seemed to fill with a mortuary stench. With each minute that passed, the pressure pounding on his temples grew more intense. He needed space. He needed to breathe again.

It seemed a long time before Sir Arthur finally drew his remarks to a close. Immediately he did so, Anthony sprang to his feet. He ignored Sir Arthur's and Lady Rudlow's calls to him and walked through the silent Great Hall, out on to the portico.

Beads of water bounced off the slippery stone steps on either side of him. The wind blew in his face and pushed back his hair. He gulped hungrily at the damp, fresh air.

The long shadows had faded into the stocking mask of twilight. Only the Palladian folly on the far side of the lake still glimmered in the solitary shaft of white light which somehow broke through the heavy black clouds.

He loved this place; its timelessness and tranquillity.

Hugh, he knew, had never felt about Conningsby as he had. As a younger son, he had always resented the fact that what would otherwise have been his own sizeable inheritance, would all go on the upkeep of the house, on maintaining and subsidising the estate.

To the businessman in him, the house was a white elephant with an insatiable thirst for money. In the same way that he had planned the dismemberment of the company, if ever he had the chance, Hugh would dismantle Conningsby.

The old tenants would go first, then some of the staff, then the land on the fringes of the estate would be sold for housing. Finally it would be the turn of the house itself. A school? A conference centre? 'Completely out of touch with the real world,' he could hear Hugh's easy words of justification. 'And it just eats money . . . wouldn't you feel much more comfortable in something more manageable?'

Anthony fought against the craving in his gut. His jaw tensed. His body raced. He must not, he knew, give in.

He only wished Loretta were with him now. She trusted him. She believed in him.

Somehow, she had the ability to claw him back into the real world. She led him on. She pulled him to her. She warmed the air before him. She hid the cracks in the tawdry scenery. She imbued the drab wasteland with the sparkle of her personality, made it vibrate and live.

It was not so much anything she said, it was because she understood. Somehow she seemed to know exactly what he was going through. He guessed that it must have been because of her years of living with a drunk for a father, and also, strangely, because of the pain – the sexual pain – which in her was like a raw nerve just beneath the surface of the cool, smooth skin. Pain made you sensitive. Pain opened doors to the heart, to understanding.

Loretta, somehow, was guiding him through to the real world on the back of her own pain.

In a way they were very alike, and he found the thought consoling.

Together, given time, given warmth, reassurance and love, he and Loretta could both win through.

An old American Airforce man had shuffled into the NA meeting last week. Anthony had wondered for a moment whether the man could possibly be Loretta's father. He had dismissed the thought, but had saluted the man anyway as proxy for a difficult old drunk with his head in the clouds who somehow had had it in him to sire such a creature.

Anthony tramped through the mud towards the church. Its grotesque gargoyles, which had scared him as a child, once more seemed almost threatening. The shadow of death had lent their crude carving an awesome vitality.

He skirted the flying buttresses and picked his way through the long wet grass to his father's grave. It had been filled now. A grid of fresh turf covered it in a bright green swathe.

His coat was heavy with the rain. The back of his collar was damp. A cold trickle of water ran down his spine.

He knelt down on the grass and closed his eyes. He mouthed a silent prayer.

# Chapter 29

The doorbell shrilled. Loretta looked up from her book and glanced at the bedside clock. One o'clock in the morning. What the hell . . .?

The bell rang again. Loretta threw back the quilt and swung her legs to the floor. She shrugged on her dressing gown and opened the window. 'Hello? That you, Shona? Forgotten your key?'

'Hi! It's me. Anthony.'

He moved back from under the porch and stood in the cone of blue light from the street lamp. She could see him now. Aside from his brilliant white shirt, he was dressed entirely in the colour of the night: black suit, black tie, black shoes. His hair was wind-blown and unkempt. 'Sorry. I saw the light on in your bedroom and couldn't believe it. Can I come up?'

'Er – sure.' She bit her lip. Her mind raced in confusion. 'Just give me a moment, will you?' She closed the window, then raced to the bathroom. She carefully tied the pink bow at the neck of the ivory satin night-dress and brushed her hair. Quickly, she made up her eyes. Only then did she press the answerphone to let him in. She still did not know what she was going to tell him.

'I'm sorry,' he panted as soon as she opened the door.

'I was just driving back from Conningsby. I never expected . . .' He shrugged. 'I missed you, really missed you.' He stepped forward, eyes glowing. His lips met hers. His arms went around her and he held her to him. His cold cheek rested against hers for a long moment. She felt his body trembling.

Finally he said, 'When did you get back?'

'O-only today,' she lied. 'For a meeting with André. And,' she sighed, 'it's back to the States again tomorrow.'

He groaned. 'Do you really have to go?'

''Fraid so.' She looked up at his soft hurt grey eyes, and swallowed. Gently she prised herself from his arms. 'Was it the funeral today?' she asked. 'I was very sorry to hear about your father.'

'A merciful release, really,' he replied dully.

'Look, you're soaking wet,' she said, suddenly brisk. 'Get those things off before you catch your. . .before you catch cold.'

'No, I'm fine, honestly.'

'No point in being a martyr.' She bit her lip. 'Could be a problem, though, finding you something to wear.'

She turned, wandered through to Shona's room and switched on the light.

When she came back, Anthony was still standing a foot from the door, in exactly the same place as she had left him. 'Here you are.' She tossed him a pair of blue jeans and a red-checked shirt. 'In case you're wondering, they belong to Shona's boyfriend.'

'Thanks.' He grinned.

'A drink? Something hot?' She moved over to the kitchen unit and filled the kettle. Behind her she could hear the swishing sounds as Anthony peeled off his wet clothes. 'There's a towel in the bathroom, if you want to dry yourself,' she called over her shoulder. 'Horlicks, cocoa, or rosehip tea?'

'Horlicks, please.'

She heard the bathroom door open and shut. She picked out the jar from the cupboard and made some Horlicks for him and some strong black coffee for herself.

She turned immediately as he re-entered the room. 'Now tell me, truthfully, while I've been away, have you . . .?' She stared hard into his eyes.

His palm curled outwards, then his fingers slowly clenched. 'Hell, everything was against me today.' He moved over to the sofa and slumped down on to its foam cushions. His breathing was short and fast. He ran trembling fingers through his hair. 'The family won't accept that I've changed. I'm still the petulant child who can't be trusted in the sweet shop. Seems you're the only one who has any confidence in me.'

'An-tho-ny, we agreed, no self-pity. Just tell me — did you?'

He shook his head vehemently. 'No. Absolutely not.'

'Good.'

He twisted round and looked up at her with pleading eyes. 'But I just had to talk to someone. I rang my sponsor — he was out. I tried a friend who was at the centre with me — she'd gone back on it a week ago. I never knew. Then on my way back to London, I thought it might help if I drove past your door.' He shrugged and smiled. 'Silly, really.'

She grinned back at him. She picked up the two mugs, handed one to him and sat down by his side. Back with him now, she felt the emptiness and anxiety of the last fortnight slip away.

'I'm very flattered,' she said softly, 'but I can't always be here to help you. Like they told you — just make up your mind to stay off it each hour. . .each hour. . .as it comes. You can do it. You'll see it off, I know it. With or without me.'

She sipped at her coffee and shuddered. She glanced across at him and watched as he hungrily gulped down the thick creamy liquid. His golden hair flopped down over his forehead. His shoulders were slightly hunched. Sitting there in the lumberjack shirt and jeans, he could have been half his age. She tapped his leg and laughed. 'Good, is it?'

His eyes swivelled upwards, looking at her above the rim of the mug. A small white moustache clung to his upper lip. 'Superb,' he grinned. 'Quite superb.'

'Some more?' she asked, laughing again. She leaned forward to wipe away the moustache, but Anthony intercepted her hand, squeezed it gently, then kissed it.

'Thank you, darling,' he said. He put down the mug on the coffee table and leaned towards her. He kissed her softly on the cheek. 'Thank you,' he said again. Then his head fell on to her shoulder like a child's might, nuzzling against the contours of her neck.

Already the aggression, the tension, was leaving him. He lifted his head off her shoulder and gently cradled her in his arms. Her heavy strands of chestnut hair tumbled across his knees. He brushed them with slow confident strokes with the palm of his hand. He smoothed the slight furrows on her brow.

She felt the warmth of his arms, his chest. She felt his lips on her forehead. She purred softly. She only wished that they could stay like this forever.

'Do you really have to go back to the States?' he asked again.

'Hmm,' she nodded. 'Sadly.'

'Funny, over this last fortnight, hardly a moment has passed when you haven't been in my thoughts.' His voice trembled. 'I love you, Loretta. You mean so very much to me. I want you to be with me always. I — '

'Anthony . . .' She felt the pain of longing in her gut. It was everything she had ever wanted to hear. . .but she could not risk Hugh telling him now. Not so soon after the shock of his father's death.

She put on her most business-like voice. 'I've got a very early flight tomorrow morning — well, this morning now. I really ought to get some sleep.'

His mouth twitched. She could see in his eyes how her brusque putdown had surprised and hurt him. His hand froze on her hair. 'Darling, I want to ask — '

'Please, Anthony. *Please*.' She sat up suddenly. 'Whatever you were going to say, please don't say it now.' She put her arms around him and squeezed him tight. 'You've just had a great shock. And I'm leaving in the morning.'

'But . . .' Then he shrugged and smiled. 'OK.'

She kissed him lightly on the lips one last time, then rose to her feet. With a heavy heart, she escorted him to the door. 'Take care,' she whispered. 'I'll ring you when I get back. And keep up the good work.'

His mournful eyes stared into hers. 'I love you,' he breathed.

'And I you.'

Then he quickly opened the door and stepped out into the darkness of the passage outside. She listened to his muffled footfalls on the stairs until they faded into the still sounds of the night. 'If only. . .' she mouthed. 'If only . . .'

With a sad, heavy tread, she made her way back to her single bed.

# Chapter 30

Shona's eyes opened wide. 'You did what?'

'I told him not to say anything then.'

'I don't believe this. I simply don't believe anyone could be so stupid.'

Blushing, Loretta glanced quickly behind her to where the other girls were standing. Sandy was polishing a silver money clip. Pauline was sorting through a pile of invoices. Zoe was attaching a small tag to a ruby and diamond ring. Their ears were finely tuned antennae. 'Please, Shona, keep your voice down. I don't want everyone to hear.'

Shona giggled uncontrollably. 'Oh, Loretta, you almost had me fooled for a second! Now stop teasing and tell me – '

'I'm not teasing,' she said emphatically. 'I promise you, that's what I said.'

'Oh, my God!' Shona's wide eyes stared straight at Loretta. She frowned. 'Treasure, we had better have a talk.' She turned to Zoe. 'Be a love and cover for us, will you? If André comes in, tell him that we'll only be five minutes. Loretta and I have some important business.'

Shona's outstretched arm went around Loretta's shoulders and propelled her towards the door.

Immediately Loretta was outside, the frigid air made her shudder. A large woman dressed in red blocked the pavement. She had a Yorkshire terrier with a diamanté collar in tow. Loretta nearly tripped over the dog's lead.

Shona hurried to her side. 'Christ, what got into you? I mean, I'd be the first one to tell you to stay cool and play hard to get, but not when he's about to offer a goddamn ring! Some rock, I bet, too.' She sighed. 'Dearest, isn't this taking things just a little too far? I can't bear to think of you blowing your chances like this. Hell, Anthony's some catch. Christ, if I go on thinking about it, I'll make myself positively ill! What more could you possibly want? You even love him!'

'I do. Yes, I do. Of course, I'm thrilled. Of course it's everything I've always dreamed of. More, really. It's just that. . .hell, if Hugh tells him all about us, Anthony's going to be so hurt. He trusts me now. He depends on me. I am his security. It would ruin *everything*.'

Shona stopped. Her hair swung from side to side as she shook her head. 'Look, if your little dalliance with Hugh is really going to put a spoke in the works – and I admit it might – then you might as well know now rather than later. It would be better coming from you anyway. You could make it all seem much more – well,' she shrugged, 'just one of those things.'

'And risk Anthony hating me? Risk him losing trust in me, in himself? Risk him going back on drugs? Especially now, so soon after the shock of his father's death.' She shuddered. 'I couldn't.'

Shona sighed. 'God, you've changed. Fine noble talk, treasure. Very impressive. Nevertheless, it's what you've got to do. I'm thinking of you now. What if he changes his mind? Even as we speak, he might be having second thoughts — I don't know — even proposing to someone else?'

'At ten-thirty in the morning?'

'Yeah, well, believe me, stranger things have happened. When a man makes up his mind to get married, he doesn't hang around.' She flourished one hand. 'I've seen it happen time and time again. It's always seemed to me — I know this seems ridiculous — but a lot of men seem to choose a wife like a car, really. They just go and pick the raciest model that's still unsold on the forecourt. Then — bingo!' She shrugged.

'You're not talking about mature men.'

'Maybe not.' Shona strode on along the pavement. 'But the chances are that if you let it drag on, he'll cool. Someone else will come along. Men hate indecision. And you'll be back in the shop stringing the price tags on to other girls' rings for the rest of your life. You'll have only yourself to blame then.'

Loretta bit her lip and sighed. She gazed beyond Shona at some half-clothed mannequins in a shop window. She shuddered. 'No, I can't do it to him,' she said in a small voice.

Shona clicked her tongue. 'Well, what are you going to do, then? Anthony might think it somewhat strange if he happens to breeze around again — '

'I know. I'm going to ask André for a few weeks' leave. Go back home for a while. Think things over.'

'You're being a damn' fool,' Shona sighed and shook her head, 'but if you think you know better. . .it's your life.'

'Exactly.' Loretta smiled, put her arm around Shona and they slowly walked back towards the shop.

353

# Chapter 31

The key turned in the lock. Hesitantly, Camilla put her head around the door. The rims of her tired eyes were red and slightly swollen. She blinked in the bright light of the midday sun pouring through the plate-glass windows, and listened very carefully.

'Hello?' she said quietly, then in a louder voice, 'Steve?'

There was no reply. She walked in. She still wore the black woollen dress and coat that she had worn to the funeral the day before, but now the shoulders sagged and the coat was flecked with mud.

She strode through the sparsely decorated room with its wide expanses of glass, large minimalist paintings and very low sofas.

The bedroom too had natural brick walls. She shrugged off her coat and dropped it over the unmade bed. She looked around for a chair, and not finding one, took hold of one of the bright green perspex and lacquer bedside tables and dragged it over the beige carpet to the base of the bright green wall-cupboards.

She flicked off her shoes, pulled up her skirt and climbed up on to the top of the table. The perspex squeaked. She balanced on tiptoe and pulled down three suitcases. They clattered to the floor.

She jumped down and lifted the largest of the three on to the bed. She opened the far right-hand cupboard, pulled the dresses off their hangers and bundled them in anyhow. The second case she lined with shoes, then laid more dresses on top. She went through into the small tiled bathroom, collected her things in a black plastic rubbish sack, and carted them back into the bedroom.

The telephone rang.

She let it ring ten, twelve times before finally she picked up the receiver. 'Hello.' Her voice was flat, expressionless.

'Hi, it's me. Loretta.'

'Oh, hi.'

'Look, I'm off to the States for a few weeks, maybe longer. Anthony is going to be all by himself. I'm sure he's going to be just fine, but I just thought you might like to know . . .'

Camilla sighed. 'I wish I could help, but I'm going away too. Switzerland.'

'Oh, that sounds fun. Is Steve going too?'

'Er – no.'

'Are you all right, Camilla? Maybe it's just a bad line but your voice sounds – I don't know – different somehow.'

There was a click as a key turned in the lock. 'That you, Cammy?' called a voice. Steve's.

Camilla raised a finger to her lips and bit the nail.

The receiver crackled. 'Hello?' Loretta called. 'You still there?'

His footsteps grew louder.

'I'm sorry, I really can't talk now. But keep in touch, OK?' Camilla dropped the receiver back into the cradle just as Steve walked into the room.

He stood in the doorway for a moment. His eyes were fixed on the suitcases on the bed. 'What the hell . . .?'

'Steve,' she said urgently, 'don't, whatever you do, make a scene. *Please*.' She moved towards him and looked up with anxious staring eyes. 'I'm sorry, but I just can't handle this.'

'Why, Cammy?' His fist beat against his leg. 'For God's sake, why?'

'Right now . . .' She bit her lip and began again. 'I'm sorry, I think it would be better for both of us if we call it a day. . .stop seeing one another.'

His lower lip trembled. He shook his head in disbelief. 'You're upset, I understand that. It's only natural. But, Christ, there's surely no need to walk out. . .after all your promises.'

'Right now, Steve, I don't know what I want. Honestly, I don't. I can't feel . . .' She blinked and shook her head. 'You've been very sweet and understanding. I can't have been easy to live with since — well, over the last week or so. I should never have moved these things in here in the first place.' She threw another blouse into the open suitcase. 'I think it's best if I go away for a while.'

'Go away?'

'Yes,' she said calmly. 'It's all arranged. I leave later today.'

'Where?'

'Oh, some cousins in Switzerland. Just now, I need my independence. I need to be alone, get away from everything. I need to think. I wish you'd understand. I'm sorry, it just doesn't feel right. Nothing feels right any more . . .' Her wide eyes pleaded for his understanding.

He moved towards her. 'Cammy, really.' His hand reached out and touched her lightly on the arm.

She shuddered and pulled her arm away. 'Don't touch me,' she remonstrated. '*Please.*'

She was still trembling as she paid off the taxi at Heathrow and boarded the plane. She saw the lights of Geneva through a haze of tears. A car awaited her there. It was eight o'clock when she arrived in Gstaad.

As they drove down the main street, dodging past other Range-Rovers, Toyota Landcruisers and a lone Rolls-Royce, Camilla barely gave a glance to the glittering displays of dresses and jewellery that shone out of the darkness like the windows of an Advent calendar.

They got caught in a traffic jam outside Charly's Tea Room, and again outside Oehrli, the chocolate shop, where a pack of lean girls in Lynx coats and fluffy fur boots were climbing out of a stretch Mercedes.

Above, on the side of a rock face dominating the village, stood the white mass of the Palace Hotel. Its turrets and towers were outlined with little fairy lights just like a Disney castle.

They turned left up a steep hill, then went along a winding road for a mile or so. They turned left again. All the time they were climbing.

The Range Rover drew to a halt outside a fine old chalet surrounded by pine trees plump with purple-tinged snow. Camilla looked up at the intricately carved eaves. The entire building, she knew, had been moved, beam by beam, from a neighbouring village to its present location.

The chauffeur leapt out and opened the passenger door. 'Thank you, Arthur,' she said quietly.

She stepped out and gazed down beyond the verandah to where the ground dipped and dropped precipitously into the thick milky mist of the valley. A purple glow rimmed the mountain tops. She breathed in great gulps of the cold fresh air and felt it soar through her head like smelling salts.

The door of the house swung inwards. A butler with greased-back hair and a deep tan bowed to her. 'Mrs Hardwicke is waiting for you in the drawing room, Miss Rudlow.'

She nodded and walked in. At another time, in different circumstances, this would have been an idyllic place to pass the bleak winter months: now it was just another prison.

'Camilla?' called a voice.

'Yes,' she answered automatically. She walked slowly down the narrow wooden stairs and into the drawing room.

A log fire blazed in an open hearth, giving the pine-panelled walls a reddish glow. The room was simply but expensively furnished. The base of the coffee table was made out of a gnarled root. On the walls were elaborate paper cut-outs of deer, trees and Swiss woodmen. The sweet scent of fresh flowers rose above the wood smoke.

A small, deeply tanned woman rose from her chair. She wore a shocking pink track-suit with a leaping leopard embroidered in gold thread across the front — Camilla's cousin, Sonia. 'Camilla! I'm so thrilled that you have come. We don't see nearly enough of you.' She leaned forward.

Camilla was expected to kiss her, of course. She did so. Formally. On both cheeks.

The woman squeezed her hand and fixed her with piercing brown eyes. 'Ridiculous. Nowadays Europe is so small, it is so easy. Two hours' flight, that's all. It's nothing — same as driving for a dinner party. What would you like to drink, my dear?'

'Wine, if you have some open?'

'But, of course.' Sonia signalled. Camilla heard some shuffling behind her, the pulling of a cork. 'Come here, and sit down. Elizabeth told me all about your — how shall I put it? — entanglement. How I envy you!'

'*You* envy *me*?'

'Yes, of course! It's wonderful to be in love. And it doesn't matter with whom — that is the least important thing — at least, at the beginning. Apart from anything else, it's so good for the complexion. Have you noticed? You sort of glow.'

Camilla stared at her, blank-faced.

Sonia flapped a hand dismissively. 'But that's a trivial point — don't get me wrong. Tell me about him. He's a musician of sorts, isn't he? Good-looking? I love musicians. They have what the Italians call — '

Camilla somehow mustered a smile and broke in, 'He's good-looking, I suppose, but not in the conventional sense.'

Sonia grinned. 'You mean he's short and squat with a long hooked nose?'

'No, quite tall actually,' she said vaguely. She sipped her wine.

'With beautiful hands?' Sonia prompted. 'As a musician, he must have beautiful hands.'

'Well, yes.'

'Hands that understand women?'

'I suppose so.'

Sonia nodded twice. 'That's enough for me. So important. And of course you're going to spend the rest of your life with him?'

'Up until now, that's what I had planned.'

'I detest prevarication above all things,' Sonia butted in cheerfully. 'It wastes so much time. You've got to get on with life. Long before Paolo proposed – you know, my first husband – I knew for certain that I would marry him. And five years later, I knew for certain that at the first possible opportunity, I would divorce him. Never once was I in any doubt. Your own life is too important to leave to others or the vagaries of chance.'

Sonia sipped her *tisane*. 'Same with Willie, you know – I was sure. And I regret none of it. I told Elizabeth that she shouldn't try to bulldoze you into leaving your musician – threaten you with the poor house. Not only is it extremely vulgar, it serves no useful purpose.'

Her eyes narrowed. 'From what little I know of you, I think you're a survivor, like me. Whatever happens, you'll land on your feet.' She frowned theatrically. 'Of course, there will be some bad times, we all have those, but you'll win through, richer for the experience. That's what matters in this life. The meek shall inherit the earth – what nonsense! My dear, just imagine the committee meetings.'

The beginnings of a smile crossed Camilla's face.

'Anyway, I hope you'll enjoy yourself for as long as you are here. For me, at least, if I'm not in love, I'd rather be skiing. And we have been very lucky with early snow this year. My son – you've met Max, haven't you? – is about your age and knows everybody.'

'Everybody, Cousin Sonia?'

'Everybody who counts. But enough of this. What you need now, my girl, after all that you've been through, is sleep. Lots of it. Griselda should have unpacked your things by now. Come along. To bed.'

361

# Chapter 32

At JFK there was the usual racetrack of luggage trolleys, the familiar lucky dip as suitcases circled on the carousels.

In the past she would have waited eagerly by the conveyor belt, stomaching her neighbour's overnight-flight breath, scrambling with the best of them to be first through Customs. Now Loretta waited calmly, away from the crush.

The Rudlows, she guessed, would not be subjected to any such indignities. They would come through the special way, reserved for private planes. Naturally, they would have access to the VIP lounge. Maybe even one of those little electric cars would drive up to meet them on the runway. They were Lords and Ladies, after all.

The customs officer made her open her luggage. He leafed through her blouses, her lingerie, her most private possessions, firing questions at her as he burrowed through the layers with meat-cleaver hands.

Just because she was a pretty girl?

He found nothing, of course. Finally he marked the case with a chalk cross, wished her a nice day without a trace of sincerity, and waved her on.

The damage had been done though. She would consign the whole lot to Stanley's laundromat the moment she arrived home.

A lady does not wear crumpled underwear. Hers comes out of a drawer scented with an embroidered lavender pomander . . .

From force of habit she walked, humping her luggage, in the direction of the bus queue. Then she stopped and shook her head. She turned and followed the arrow marked TAXIS.

'Where you going, lady?' asked the driver. She told him.

He made no move to help her with the suitcase, just sat and smoked and watched her in the mirror as she strained to lift it into the boot. 'Take a tip from me, lady,' he said as finally she climbed in, 'travel light.'

Or have a limousine waiting, she thought.

As they drove on through the sprawling suburbs, juddering and stopping as each fresh wave of traffic blocked them, the familiar harsh hooting filled her ears. She breathed in the familiar yellow-cab smell of road dust and warm leatherette, smouldering from the friction of a thousand backsides.

She found herself smiling. This, despite everything, was home. New York had taught her not to expect anything from anybody. It had groomed her and armed her. It had given her the drive to go out and cleave a place for herself, to go out and conquer. Now it might give her the courage to start again.

The house in Queens was exactly as she remembered. It was a low, two-storey house of yellow brick with a carport and a neat front garden. All around were identical buildings set back from a curving tarmac road. Only the style of the drapes varied.

Stanley, she guessed, had always loved Ma. When it had become clear that Pa was not coming back, and the mortgage company was just about to put their house up for sale to recover what was due to them, Stanley had stepped in and met the payments. It had been only a matter of time before he had moved in himself.

Ma, she suspected, had never really loved him, but he was a kind man and she seemed happy enough with him. Two years later, she had changed her name to his by deed poll.

Loretta paid the cab driver and pressed the doorbell. 'Just one second,' called a voice from inside.

The latch clicked. The chain rattled. The door swung outward. Her mother looked up, the habitual look of concern in her eyes, the habitual tea towel between her hands. Her eyes crinkled as she smiled. 'Oh, baby!' She quickly wiped her hands on the cloth, then hugged Loretta and stood on tiptoe to kiss her.

Mrs Wincheim, as she now called herself, was well preserved for her late fifties. Her hair was still auburn and bouffant. Despite her assiduous housework, her painted nails were still in cocktail party condition. Through stringent dieting, she still had the figure of a twenty-year-old. 'Don't just stand there. Come in, come in.'

'Great to be back home, Ma.' The house was as immaculate as ever. It had always been the best kept house on the street. Marsha Wincheim had a pathological hatred of dust, parasites, termites and cockroaches, and waged war on them weekly with an armoury of aerosols and proprietary powders. The fitted beige shag carpet was still fluffy and spotless after its latest shampoo. Loretta wiped her feet carefully on the mat before stepping inside.

'Flight OK, honey? You must be exhausted. Wait, I'll fix you some coffee — the kettle's only just boiled —

then you must tell me all your news.' Marsha turned and headed towards the kitchen. 'This is all so sudden, this trip, I mean. Nothing bad's happened, has it?'

Loretta grinned. 'No, Ma.'

'Thank God for that. Stanley's always such a pessimist. Immediately I told him that you were coming home, he thought you'd been fired.'

'No, work's going fine. André just gave me a few weeks off, that's all, and I thought why not go mad and fly home?'

Loretta shivered as she entered the kitchen. Ever since she had stopped living permanently in the house, she couldn't walk into the kitchen without imagining she could see her father there, as he had been on that last evening: eyes bloodshot and raw, slouching over the pine table, the whiskey bottle by his right arm, the broken glass on the floor; and Ma standing pressing a wet kitchen cloth to her face, pointing her finger at him, screaming.

'Thanks,' she said, and took the mug of instant coffee. 'So what's the big excitement here?'

'You knew Stanley had found a site for his fourth laundromat? Well, it's opened, finally.' Marsha scooped some powder into the dishwasher. 'I keep telling him he shouldn't work so hard, take things easy, but you know how he is. Nothing'll stop him. And he says we still owe too much to the bank. We couldn't afford to, not right now.'

She selected a program and switched on the dishwasher. 'Almost every cent we make goes to the bank. And the little bit we have left — where's that go, huh? Insurance. There was another break in at the 'mat in Dupont Street two nights ago, you know? They went off with the till, smashed two machines and blew the window out. Is it worth it, I ask you? Stanley promised me a new car just as soon as the new site begins paying for itself, but now. . .' she shrugged ' . . .who knows when that'll be?'

Loretta grinned at the familiar, unstoppable torrent of words. 'That'll be nice. What are you going to get?'

'Oh, nothing flashy, but you know, the Ford, it's four, five years old now. I take it out of the garage, I feel shamed, positively shamed. I'd park it a couple of blocks away if it weren't so awkward with the groceries . . .'

The warmth of the house after the cold outside was already making Loretta drowsy. She turned her head away slightly from her mother to conceal a yawn.

'You must be so tired, baby, and me thoughtlessly babbling on like this.' Her mother smiled. 'Why not take a shower and lie down for a while? You'll feel better for it.'

Loretta forced open her drooping eyes. 'Maybe you're right. . .but at least let me help you clear up these things first.'

'No, I won't hear of it,' her mother protested. 'You go ahead. The bed's aired.'

For all the familiarity of the house, for all the years she had lived there, Loretta felt like a stranger now. So much had happened to her in the last year, and so little here, that as she tramped up the stairs it seemed to her as if she were reliving a memory. The clock had stood still. Only biological time had been at work, softening Ma's fine features, deepening the lines.

Much as she loved her, her mother's way of life seemed alien, unreal now. It was as if she were listening to echoes from the past across a great chasm. Throughout her teens, Loretta had heard the saga of the laundromats, the problems with the bank, the endless discussions about new drapes, Stanley's cries for economy, her mother's promised new car.

Loretta threw off her clothes and slid the glass shower door shut. At a turn of a knob, strands of water as strong as wire thrashed and pounded her tired skin. She let out a little sigh and twisted her body, raised her hands.

This at least was something she had missed – a real shower.

# Chapter 33

'You sure you want to do this?'

Camilla nodded and shrugged. 'Yeah, I'm sure.'

The red chopper stood in a small clearing by the side of the road. She mounted the one small step and clambered inside. It seemed exceedingly light and flimsy: crowded, too, as Max and the guide climbed in next to her.

Only an inch or so of Max's golden hair was visible beneath his woollen hat. He patted her knee reassuringly, smiled at her.

The blades began to spin, the cabin to vibrate. Camilla swallowed twice. All around her the trees had lost their candy-floss hoard and danced wildly in the wind. The wind circled too, sending tiny crystals into a spiral above them.

And suddenly they were away, rising above the sunlit mountaintops. Camilla looked down at the crescents of icing sugar snow, the moon craters of rock, the glaciers of glistening ice, the strange surreal formations of the ever shifting, fluid landscape.

She thought she saw a chamois standing on a lone crag, but could not be sure. Just then the chopper dipped, leaving her stomach behind. It slowed and hovered above an icy peak. It rocked back and forth five times in the strong cross wind, then very slowly, very carefully, landed on the narrow shoulder.

Camilla opened the door and jumped out, crouching to stay well away from the blades. The noise was almost deafening. All around her snow rose up in the current of air to form a thick impenetrable mist that reduced the sun to a hazy white ball.

A foot away from the chopper the snow was very deep. Camilla ploughed through it as best she could. She crouched and covered her ears while the chopper took off in a cloud of snow, smoke and fumes, firing pellets of biting snow against her back.

When the noise had dropped away, Max passed her the skis. She shook off the snow and stepped into the bindings. She turned on the switch of the little red box which she wore on a string around her neck and listened for the whine. The avalanche bleeper was working. Everything was OK.

The mist cleared and there before her was mile upon mile of virgin snow. She breathed in great lungfuls of the thin, pure, cold air.

And then they were off, twisting down the mountain, carving little arcs at each turn. The mountain guide went first, then Camilla. There was something aggressive about her skiing at first, then the rhythm took hold. She unweighted and let the spring in the skis take her round. She was floating now, skimming across the surface of the soft white trampoline. A flurry of snow as light as talcum powder rose behind her.

Exhausted, Camilla loosened her boots and clambered up on to the terrace of the *bierstube*. She pulled off her blue mitts and fake fur hat. Her freed hair cascaded down the back of her turquoise suit. She pulled up a chair.

Heavy boots clattered behind her. 'Great, wasn't it?'

'Yeah.'

Max grinned. He placed a mug of steaming hot chocolate on the gingham-checked table cloth before her.

'Thanks,' she said. She sipped the drink and sighed.

When she looked up again she could not help noticing the two men sitting at the table at the other end of the balcony. The one on the left was tall, dark haired and very tanned. He had hooded brown eyes. The one on the right was also very tanned but shorter. Both of them were staring and grinning at her.

Camilla turned away. She gazed across the piste at the skiers parading their wares in a perpetual fashion show. There were walking duvets ornamented with studs, sequins, leather thongs, feathers and fur.

She felt the sun burning the skin of her face, parching her lips. She unzipped a pocket and took out a tube of sun cream and a small mirror. In the reflection there they were again, the two men, still ogling her.

The shorter one stood up and walked over to their table. Camilla did not look at him.

'Max, hi! Nice day.'

'Yes, Fabio.'

'Good. Good.' He pressed down on the back of a chair and leaned forward. 'And,' he grinned, 'your beautiful friend?'

'My cousin,' Max replied sharply. His jaw jerked forward. 'See you, eh?'

The man did not move. 'Hey, come on, Max! Doesn't she have a name?'

'Yeah, she has a name,' he replied cryptically, and glanced at his watch. 'We must go.' He rose, took

Camilla gently by the arm and hurried her out of the restaurant.

Just as they were about to descend the wooden steps, Camilla turned. The two men were still watching her. The taller one was laughing. She called to Max: 'Anything wrong?'

He shrugged. 'Just those two.'

'They seem harmless enough.'

For reply, Max merely shrugged again. He put his arm firmly around her and led her off in the direction of the waiting Range Rover.

'Who's calling?' asked Mrs Wincheim immediately she picked up the receiver. 'Right, I'll just see.' She nodded, put her hand over the mouthpiece and turned to Loretta who was sitting in the comfy chair by the fireplace. 'You wanna speak to someone called Camilla Rudlow, or shall I tell her you're out?'

Loretta leapt to her feet. 'No, Ma. I'll take it.'

She strode across the room and took the receiver eagerly from her mother.

'Camilla! Great to hear from you. I thought you were in Switzerland?'

'I am. Shona gave me your mother's number. Hope you don't mind.'

'Mind? I'm delighted.'

'You see there's no one I can talk to out here. Really talk to, if you know what I mean. And I want to find out what's going on between you and Anthony? This departure of yours is rather sudden, isn't it?'

Loretta swallowed. 'Well, it's all a bit complicated. I didn't know what else to do.'

Her mother was less than three feet away, spraying the

cut-glass vase on the hall table with a special crystal cleaner.

'Ma,' she called, 'I hate to ask you this, but do you think you could leave me alone for a little while? This is sort of private.'

Mrs Wincheim dropped the squeezy bottle and the duster inside the vase, then picked it up in her gloved hands. She straightened and turned hurt eyes to Loretta before retreating. 'I don't like secrets in my house, Lorie. You know that. Your Pa had secrets and look where that got him.'

'Sorry, Ma.' Loretta shuddered and bit her lip. She listened out for the sound of the kitchen door closing. 'Camilla, you still there? Sorry about that. Can I trust you? Really trust you?'

'Sure. I'm a brick wall.'

'You promise me that you will never breathe a word of what I say to anyone?'

'I promise.'

'Well. . .you know when we were jogging in the park and I asked you whether Hugh and Anthony had ever dated the same girl?'

'Yup. What of it?'

'It wasn't an entirely idle question.'

'Oh, Christ!' A deep sigh down the line. 'I hope you're not saying what I think you're saying?'

'Please,' Loretta pleaded, 'don't think badly of me.'

'And you don't mean just having a lamb chop and a glass of wine together, I suppose?'

'No. But it only happened once.'

'I know Hugh's quite attractive and all, but – '

'It was a mistake. The biggest mistake of my life.'

'You're telling me! Does Anthony know?'

'No.'

'Thank God for that! Whatever happens he must never ever find out, you hear?'

'That's the problem.' She explained about Hugh.

Camilla listened without interrupting as Loretta told her the full story. 'That's more than a problem,' she commented finally. 'I'm really sorry for you, Loretta. Truly I am. But I think you're doing the right thing. The only possible thing. And I respect you for that. It's a pity, seems we've both made a fair mess of things . . .'

Loretta put the receiver down with a heavy heart. Camilla had confirmed her worst fears.

The kitchen door opened. Her mother walked past her without even looking at her and carefully set down the vase on the hall table.

'Sorry about that, Ma.'

'Lorie, sometimes I don't know what to think,' Mrs Wincheim announced accusingly. 'You come back here giving us only a day's warning — hardly even time to get the bed made up — making Stanley and me all sick with worry in case you've been fired.

'Then this guy — Anthony what's-his-name — keeps on calling every day and you won't speak to him.

'And now you're taking secret phone calls.'

'Ma,' she sighed, 'it's a long, long story.'

'But you've been here ten days already. No story's that long.'

'Ma. Please trust me,' she pleaded. 'I wish I could explain, but it really wouldn't do any good.'

'Lorie dear, I hate to see you like this. You'd be surprised how many problems don't seem nearly so bad once you've thrashed them out over a hot cup of coffee. Why not give it a try?'

'It's just not that sort of problem. Thanks Ma, but I've got to work this one out on my own.'

Nothing much had changed in the old apartment she had shared with Julie.

She had almost forgotten quite how small her old bedroom was. 'Just room to swing a cockroach,' she remembered now was how Julie had first described it to her. The walls were still the same olive green. The small single bed with its orange quilted cover was the same. The posters on the wall, though, were different, as too were the jeans and sweat shirts which lay in a heap on the floor. It was some other girl's bedroom now.

Julie, as always, was dressed for comfort. She was wearing a man's woolly jumper, track suit bottoms and sneakers. Her moon face lit up in a broad smile.

'Hi.' Loretta kissed her. 'How you doing?'

'Oh, same as ever.' She shrugged. 'Great to see you. Really great. How's London? I want to hear everything, every tiny detail.'

'Oh, fine.'

Julie tilted her head and looked at her quizzically. 'Hmm? You don't seem sure?'

'Well, there are a few complications. Nothing to do with the job. I don't know, I might be coming back for a while.'

She bit her lip as Julie turned and walked along the bank of kitchen units. The flip-top bin was still overflowing with old cans and pizza cartons. 'If I did, is there any chance of my moving back in? I don't know how you're fixed for room — I suppose you're all settled now.'

Julie pulled an open bottle of wine out of the fridge.

She sighed. 'Well, of course it would be great having you around again, but Annie's sharing with me now and I can't very well throw her out, now can I?'

'Of course not.' Loretta swallowed. 'I quite understand.'

Behind the bow-fronted reception desk sat a redhead with a fixed, dead smile. Though it was past eight o'clock in the evening the offices of Wendheimer, Frink and Crindle were still humming, the telephones still ringing.

'Hi. I've come to see Mr Bob Slinger,' announced Loretta.

The redhead casually tossed back her mane. She stared at Loretta as if this were an extraordinary request. Her pencil tapped. 'May I ask,' she drawled, 'whether this is a professional or purely a social call?'

'You could call it social, or maybe dietetic,' Loretta replied curtly. 'You do allow your executives to eat, don't you?'

The dead smile twitched in its grave. 'Seventh office, on the right.'

Loretta padded along the thick beige carpet. She stopped outside the seventh office. She peered through the perpetual twilight of the smoked glass and watched Bob as he pushed back his chair with his strong legs and sweet-talked on the telephone.

She tapped on the glass. He looked up, beamed at her, signalled her through.

So this was the office that he had told her so much about soon after she arrived in London. It was about the size of a large double bed but, as Bob explained, it represented promotion. It was 1.63 cubic metres larger than his last office, which meant there was now room for a third chair. She sat on the second one, and waited.

'I'm sorry. The guy just would not stop talking,' he said at last. 'Loretta, hey, fantastic to see you!' He stood up and came round the desk. He glanced nervously at the smoked glass partition, then bent down and kissed her on the forehead.

'What do you think of the new office? Isn't it great?'

'Yeah, not bad!'

'Jeez, I'm glad you're here. I wanted to come over to England to see you so many times, but I just couldn't get away — you know how it is. Come on.' He grinned and shrugged on his coat. 'I thought we all might go and have some chilli and tortillas in SoHo. Pamela is dying to meet you.'

'Er — Pamela?'

'Didn't I tell you?' He smiled awkwardly. 'We've been going out now for six months or so. I'm sure you'll really love her.'

'Yeah.' She rose slowly, smoothed her skirt with her hand. 'I'm sure I will.'


New York, or at least the little corner of it that she had made her own, was a different place now, Loretta mused as she tucked herself into the small single bed in her mother's spare room. Her friends had moved on, formed new bonds. Of course, they would always remain friends, but it would never be quite the same again. She was different now and so were they.

Right now, despite being in her mother's house in a warm bed with the window closed against the vicious wind outside, she felt like a refugee. Her true being hovered somewhere over the Atlantic, vainly searching for a resting place. If she returned to New York for good, she knew that she would yearn for the glittering, magical life which she had found in London. Yet London without Anthony's smiles and warmth, without Conningsby, would be its own torture. Every street, every restaurant would remind her of him.

And if she were forced to make some final confession, and the pain of her betrayal was too deep for Anthony to bear, what then? If he went back to drugs, it would be her doing. The guilt, she knew, would haunt her for the rest of her life.

There was no way out. Whichever course she followed, she could not help but cause Anthony pain.

Loretta flinched as the wind outside roared and beat against the rattling panes.

After her father's addiction had become common knowledge in the neighbourhood, some of her classmates' mothers had forbidden their daughters from socialising with her. They seemed to think that in some way she was tainted too.

Maybe, it was true. Though she loved him still, her father had always brought pain to those closest to him. And she was the inheritor of his self-destructive genes.

Her teeth chattered and she was suddenly very cold.

In her mind's eye, she saw an image of her father. He was beckoning to her, calling out to her, pointing down to some dark space beneath him. And she, Loretta, was beckoning too. She was calling out to Anthony to follow.

Anthony picked up the receiver and stabbed out the long sequence of numbers on the keypad. He lodged the receiver in the crook of his shoulder and signed two letters while he waited for a reply.

'Hi. Who's calling?'

'Hello. Mrs Wincheim? This is Anthony Rudlow ringing from England. Any chance of talking to Loretta?'

''Fraid you've missed her again.'

'Don't seem to be having much luck, do I? She's been out every time I've rung, whatever the time of day. And not in André Swert's shop either.'

'She's a busy woman. We all are.'

'Too busy to return my calls?'

'Yup, well. . .guess she'll get back to you when she's good and ready.'

'And when do you think that that'll be?'

'How should I know? Lorie tells me nothing.'

'When is she planning to come back to England?'

'Dunno. All her plans seem to be up in the air at the moment. She might even be staying over here for a while yet. I know she's been back to her old apartment in Manhattan, but her old room has been re-let, of course. As far as I am concerned she can stay here with me for as long as she likes, but Queens. . .well, it's pretty far out – distance-wise, that is.'

'You mean . . .' Anthony swallowed, his pulse quickened, 'you mean that she might not be coming back to London at all?'

'Oh, she'll definitely be going back. Whatever she decides, she'll have to pick up her things, unless of course someone can pack them up for her, but who can you trust to do that for you nowadays? Anyway, I'll tell her you called again. Bye.'

The line went dead. He replaced the receiver in its cradle, then sat motionless in his chair for a full minute. A wave of self-loathing shook his body. He was, after all, an ex-junkie still tentatively coming to terms with the world. Who could blame her if she was running scared?

He stood slowly. His fists clenched and unclenched as he paced the room. On his third circuit Anthony stopped opposite his desk. He opened his diary and drew a line through his appointments for the next two days.

He pressed down the button on the intercom. 'Alice,' he called, 'reschedule my appointments for tomorrow and Friday, will you, please? I don't think that there's anything that can't wait until next week.'

'Very well. I'll get on to it right away.'

'Yes, and book me on to the first flight leaving tomorrow. New York.'

# Chapter 34

The foyer of the Palace Hotel was all wood and stone and slate in mock baronial style. Two very glamorous skinny blondes turned world-weary eyes towards the door as it opened, then shrugged and looked away.

Camilla followed Max past the displays of watches and jewellery and down the stairs to the entrance of The Green-Go. The concierge, a young woman with premature streaks of grey, took her coat. She rubbed the fake fur between her fingers and frowned.

Camilla bristled. She thought of giving the woman her lecture on real fur, but now was hardly the time. Max slipped the cloakroom ticket into his trouser pocket and they walked on.

Camilla was dressed entirely in black leather. The top of her white breasts bulged slightly over the tight bodice.

Although the air was warm, she shivered. The wall of sound beat against her. The little white fairy lights on the dance floor seemed intensely bright against the dim shaded candle-light of the rest of the club, but gradually her eyes grew accustomed.

She thought she recognised Roger Moore in one corner, but she could not be sure. For no particular reason she smiled across at him, but in the half-light he did not seem to notice.

Max, always the gentleman, cleared a path for her. All the banquettes were occupied so they wandered through into the overflow room next door. The ceilings were higher there and the walls either white or of tinted glass. There was a swimming pool to one side, smelling faintly of chlorine. It too was edged with fairy lights.

She looked up at Max and shook her head. The white walls made her feel naked and cold and empty. She wanted, needed, the dark.

She turned and moved back into the first room, closer to the disco. By chance two men in blazers were just vacating stools at the bar. She gestured to Max and with his excessive, very Swiss dedication to cleanliness, he brushed the perfectly clean leather stool with his handkerchief before he would let her sit down.

She liked the way the noise of the disco somehow blanked out all thought.

She liked the way the leather of the dress clung to the leather of the seat and rubbed against her thighs as she climbed on to the stool.

She sighed, then picked up the rum and diet coke the waiter had brought her and sucked a long draught through the bent straw.

Max was so kind, so considerate. He protected her like a brother. He got the barman to refill her drink three times. He danced with her himself, then got two of his friends to dance with her.

At first her muscles were sore and aching after the day's exertion, but then, in the heat and warmth, the stiffness left her and her limbs moved readily and easily. The other dancers swirled all around her, fencing her in, occasionally jolting against her. She felt still, though. Still and contained. She did not smile.

Then, across the other side of the room, to the left of the disc jockey's podium, there they were. . .the same two men who had been in the *bierstube*.

Both of them were ogling her with undisguised animal lust. The one on the left was short and dark with the kind of perpetual shadow on his chin which implied either a quirk in the evolutionary chain or the consistent use of a very blunt razor. He had heavy eyebrows and thick, dark hair which grew back in waves from his forehead. The other was slightly taller and thinner but he shared the same staring eyes, the same wide-mouthed grin.

At the end of the dance, Camilla did not go over and join Max's friends, but instead returned to the stool at the bar. Almost immediately, the shorter one came over. 'Hey!' He sat down beside her and mumbled something about star signs. There was something very provocative about the way he lowered himself on to the stool, his legs slightly apart. His jeans were very tight.

He got her star sign wrong twice before she told him what it was. Then, with a very direct look, he asked her to dance.

She nodded. As she suspected, his hands were all over her then. He smelled heavily of a rather pungent aftershave. Limes, she thought. She hated limes. He moved well, though. His feet that was. His hands moved – well – persistently. He laughed a lot at nothing in particular, baring a set of perfect white teeth.

'You like to dance?' he breathed in her ear.

'Yeah. 'S all right,' she shrugged.

'I like it, too,' he crooned, 'even if it's a game for children, huh? God, you are beautiful . . .God, if only you knew how I feel, dancing next to you. You feel it too, huh?'

Camilla danced with the taller one, too — Fabio had egged them on — though she never did quite catch his name. His hands proved equally persistent, his compliments equally extravagant.

She found out that they were both from Milan, but beyond that very little. Both were very fit, both were clearly confident, both were single.

Fabio glanced at his watch. 'Hey, why don't we continue this party somewhere else, huh? Somewhere where we can have more fun?' His eyes dropped from her face to her breasts and thighs.

Camilla stared at them blank-faced for a minute, then nodded slowly. 'What the hell? Just a minute. I'll get my coat.'

They both smiled back.

Max was chatting to his friends. She went over to him and kissed him. 'Thanks,' she whispered, 'for looking after me.' She lowered her eyes. 'If it's all right, I'm going now. Got the coat tag?'

'You want to go back?' he asked. 'I'll give you a lift.'

'No,' her hand covered his, 'it's OK. Fabio and his friend are looking after me.'

Max shook his head. 'Uh huh? They're not. *I* am.'

'That's really sweet of you, Max, but . . .'

'No. I said no.'

She flicked back her hair. Her fingers drummed on the back of his hand. 'Can I have the coat tag, *please*?'

Max sighed. 'Look, those two are animals. Scum. Believe me, I know them. I know girls who've been . . .

Women to them are nothing but . . . but bodies, machines for pleasure.'

'Good.' She nodded. 'As I thought. My view of them exactly. We all understand one another perfectly.'

'But Camilla . . .'

'Please, Max. Emotional complications I don't need. No one gets hurt. Everyone gets just what they ordered. Only, please, not one word to your mother. . .now, the coat tag?'

'No! For God's sake, Camilla!'

'Well,' she shrugged, 'I'll just have to pick it up in the morning, then.'

She turned and walked across the dance floor. As she did so, the two men leapt to their feet and filed out behind her.

As soon as they were out of the night-club and into the main body of the hotel, both the men put an arm around her waist and squeezed it tight.

Camilla took a deep breath. 'So where are we going?'

The two men exchanged glances. They nodded and smiled. Fabio stayed behind and waited with Camilla in the foyer while the other one collected the car. She climbed into the back of the blue Mercedes. Fabio climbed in beside her and even before the door had closed, his hand was on her crotch.

Camilla blinked at the early morning light coming through the window. Her hand fastened about the sheets. She looked up with bleary eyes at the white ceiling and wooden panelling.

At first she did not have the faintest idea of where she was. Then she smelt the stale sex on the sheets; heard the cackles of laughter coming from the shower. She tried to move and felt the rawness: her forehead was suddenly wet with sweat, her mouth filled with the bitter-sweet taste of bile.

All too clearly now she remembered what they had done to her, to each other, the incessant probing of every part of her in ways which she had always shied from before.

When they had both been inside her, she had expected to feel something — God, if not pleasure, at least *some* sensation — something that would have made her aware that she was alive, that she was a human being. But, no. Not really even pain. All the time that it had been happening, she had felt like a voyeur watching some squalid little peep show. That smooth-skinned body that was being prised open and defiled had had nothing to do with her.

Yet now the bed was damp with her sweat. The taste of bile was strong in her mouth. Her gut ached. She blinked, and found tears in her eyes.

This, she realised with a shudder, was the first time that her body had responded physically to anything since her father had died.

She heard the laughter from the shower again. Quickly she tossed back the sheets and lowered her feet to the floor. She dodged between the soiled tissues, picked up her dress and shoes and slipped them on. She rifled a pocket for enough francs for a taxi fare, borrowed a coat, and quietly crept out of the door.

Tears were trickling down her cheeks as she hurried along the passageway.

She could never tell Steve what she had done. She would never be able to look him in the eye again. In her imagination she saw his kind, gentle, trusting face. Vainly, she tried to dismiss it.

She was not worthy of him. Not now. Not ever. She had broken the bond of trust, and could never live with her own lies and deceit.

'Oh, Steve,' she moaned. 'Steve!'

# Chapter 35

Loretta was seated in her mother's living room restlessly flicking through the pages of *Vogue*.

'Lorie, dear,' her mother called above the wheezing of the vacuum cleaner, 'how many times have you read that magazine? It's four o'clock already and you haven't been out all day.'

Loretta looked up. 'Yeah, Ma, but I'm tired, OK? Didn't sleep well.'

Her mother pushed the Hoover further along the already spotless shag pile carpet. 'It's up to you, but I know that if I were on my precious vacation, I'd want to get out and do something, even if it were only hitting the shops downtown. Borrow the car, if you like.'

'Ma,' Loretta sighed, 'shops are my work.'

The doorbell chimed. 'I'll get it,' called Loretta, but her mother had already stripped off her dusting gloves and was on her way to the door.

She came back a moment later. 'It's someone for you, Lorie,' she said, slightly flustered. 'That man. The one who's always ringing you.'

Loretta's heart missed a beat. 'Ma, you're kidding. Here? Outside?' She jumped to her feet.

'You want me to tell him you're out, same as when he calls.'

389

'No, Ma. Show him in.'

'Lorie, you sure?' Her hands made a halting gesture. 'Just look at you! You're in jeans and a sweat shirt. Your hair's all over the place. Don't you want to fix yourself up first? I can stall him until you're ready.'

'No, Ma, I'm fine, and he'll be catching his death outside.'

Her mother frowned and shrugged. She returned to the door, and a moment later, Anthony was with them.

He took off his coat. He was wearing a blazer and jeans, just as he had been when she first visited him in Wilton Crescent. There were dark circles, like saucer marks on a table cloth, beneath his eyes.

'Hello, Loretta,' he said softly. He moved across the room to where she stood and kissed her gently on the cheek.

'Anthony,' she quavered. She bit her lip. 'This is a surprise.'

He turned and smiled shyly at her mother. 'I'm afraid it's very rude of me to intrude like this, Mrs Wincheim, but since Loretta is never available to answer my calls . . .'

'Doesn't matter at all, provided you don't mind the mess.' Mrs Wincheim shrugged awkwardly. 'Take a seat and we'll get acquainted. Make yourself comfortable. Now what would you like? Coffee?'

'Coffee would be excellent.' He glanced at Loretta, then lowered himself into the olive leatherette easy chair opposite her.

Loretta had very mixed feelings about his arrival. Her heart had yearned for him, yet seeing him there beside the hammered copper fire hood, one foot on the sheepskin rug, the other on the pale beige shag carpet, he looked so out of place. It seemed to emphasise the immense gulf between them, make her fantasies all the wilder and more unreal.

'My daughter tells me nothing,' announced Mrs Wincheim from the doorway. 'If it wasn't for your calls, I wouldn't even know that you exist. Let me get this straight – you're dating my daughter?'

'I have been, Mrs Wincheim.'

'You got a job?'

'Yes.' Anthony nodded. 'In the aircraft business.'

'Good prospects?'

'Ma,' Loretta interrupted, 'Anthony is an English Lord. A real one.'

Mrs Wincheim turned to her. 'Lorie, why didn't you tell me before that he was a Lord?'

'I'm sorry, Ma.'

'An English Lord, no kidding? This is quite something.' She gave Anthony a long hard stare, then disappeared to make the coffee. When she brought it in, it was in the best bone china cups.

'This, you know,' she announced proudly, 'is the first time we have ever had a real Lord in the place. Stanley's got a friend called Earl Ducas, works in the insurance business, but he's not a real Lord like you.' She nodded, pleased. 'So you've been dating my Lorie?'

'Yes, Mrs Wincheim.'

'Oh, call me Marsha. I hate formality.' She came towards them with coffee, milk and sugar on a laminated tray. 'You know, many of the mothers round here – in Queens, I mean – would be surprised to find their daughter dating a Lord. Not me. My baby has always had class, haven't you, Lorie?'

Her cheeks reddened. 'Ma, that's not really the kind of thing you say!'

'But it's the truth, you can't deny it.'

'Mrs Wincheim—'

'Marsha,' Loretta's mother corrected.

'I'm sorry. . .Marsha,' Anthony said with wry amusement, 'there is no doubt about it.'

'You see?' she exclaimed. 'Anthony agrees with me, and he should know, being a Lord and all.' She turned back to him. 'And I suppose you live in a great big house with lots of servants?'

'Well, yes. It is quite large.'

'Must be a headache to keep clean, but then again you don't have cockroaches over there, do you?'

'Mercifully, no.'

'Lucky. They're the worst.' She put down the tray on the glass-topped coffee table between them and gave Loretta a sidelong, knowing glance. 'Now if you'll excuse me, I've got a lot to do.'

'Right, Ma,' said Loretta.

Anthony stood. 'Thank you very much, Marsha.'

Loretta waited until she could hear her mother's footsteps upstairs before saying again, 'Well, this *is* a surprise. Over here on business?'

'I came to see you.'

'Well, here I am. And very flattered too.' She tried to make light of it, but her blood was racing so fast she could not sit still. She went to stand by the fireplace and turned her face away from him so that he could not see the anxious trembling of her mouth.

'Loretta,' he breathed from behind her, 'every time I've rung in the last fortnight, you've been out. Or so

I've been told. You never return my calls. I think you owe me some kind of explanation.'

'I needed time to think,' she said softly.

He sighed. 'I don't want to push you, but you've had two weeks now.' His fingers drummed against the fire hood. 'Isn't that enough?'

Her voice was very soft. 'But don't you see how impossible it all is? I'm glad you've come here. Look around you. I'm just an ordinary girl from Queens. I was never brought up to live somewhere like Conningsby. I would never be accepted.'

'I don't give a damn what the county set thinks!'

'But your mother, and Hugh!'

'You're frightened, that's all. Frightened of commitment. Any strong emotion is frightening. Especially love. It makes you so vulnerable. But that doesn't mean you can live your life in some kind of emotional twilight zone where nothing can touch you. We understand one another. Together, my darling, I know we can win through. Love is all that matters.'

'Yes,' she shuddered, 'but love can turn cold so suddenly, and I'm not strong enough for that. If you knew me, really knew me —'

'But, for goodness' sake, Loretta, we've been through so much.'

'Not the half of it.' She swung around suddenly, wild-eyed. 'I have made mistakes in my life. Big mistakes.'

'Haven't we all?'

'Yes, but what would you think, for instance. . .what would you think if you knew that — hell! — before I met you . . .' She shuddered. She could not go on.

'What, Loretta?' he demanded. 'Tell me.'

There seemed no way out now, she would have to

393

tell him. 'If I had been out with someone . . . Someone you knew very well?'

'Stranger things have happened.'

'Yes, but . . .' She took a deep breath, tried to quell the beating of her heart. 'Very, very well?'

Anthony shrugged. 'Loretta, honestly, I don't know what you're trying to tell me. There aren't all that many twenty-five-year-old virgins about these days. I wouldn't really expect − '

Her voice trembled. 'Yes, but what if that person happened to be a . . . a close relation?'

His fists clenched. 'Who, damn it? *Who*?' Then, suddenly, his face paled. His eyes turned cold and hard. 'Christ!' he spat. '*Christ!*'

'I should have told you right at the beginning . . .' The words came out fast now; her brain was spinning. 'Then it was too late. I never thought . . . I never dreamed that . . .' She swallowed and started again. 'You see that's why it's impossible. That's why I came here.'

Anthony slumped down into the chair. His trembling hands clutched the arm rest. He was very white and breathing fast. Then, as suddenly as he had sat down, he rose to his feet. His jaw set hard. The muscles around his neck were tense.

'Anthony,' she pleaded, 'whatever happens, I want you to know that I will love you always. I will never forget you . . . if you can find it in your heart to forgive me, I hope we might remain friends. I want that more than anything. It was the biggest mistake of my life.'

He turned on her. 'I would never have thought it of you, Loretta. I mean, *Hugh*! Anyone else in the whole world . . .' He shuddered. There was neither kindness nor forgiveness in his cold gaze. 'You made love to him, I suppose.' He made the word 'love' sound like an obscenity.

She felt numbness creep over her to the tips of her fingers. 'Only once. I'm sorry, Anthony.'

He shuddered again and walked towards the door, his feet dragging across the shag pile. He picked his blue overcoat off the chair, and shrugged it on. He fastened each of its four buttons with quick, cold precision. He put his hands deep into his pockets. She could see from the bulges they made they were still clenched into fists. 'Anything else you want to tell me?' he barked. 'Anything at all? You might as well let it all out now. Come on! Get your coat.'

'Is that an order?' she asked.

'Yes.'

She hesitated for a moment, then raced to the closet, tore her coat off the hanger and sped out of the open door after him.

When Loretta and Anthony returned to the house, it was past midnight. The blinds were drawn and only the hall light was on. The television, though, was still murmuring and flashing colours across the darkened living room. A short, thickset man with an olive skin and a dark shadow around his chin rose from the chair in front of the screen. 'Hey, we were worried about you. Didn't know where'd you got to.'

'Sorry, Stanley,' replied Loretta. She squeezed Anthony's hand and looked up at him. 'I'd like you to meet Stanley Wincheim, my step-father. Stanley, this is Anthony Rudlow.'

Anthony smiled and shook Stanley's hand. 'Delighted to meet you, Mr Wincheim.'

His eyes ranged over Anthony, across to Loretta, then back to their visitor. 'You the guy . . .?' he began, then swallowed his words.

'Stanley, where's Ma?' Loretta asked.

'Just gone to bed. Why?'

'We've got some news. News that can't wait.'

He looked hard at her. 'News, you say?' He pressed his palms together nervously. 'Now, you just sit down comfortably and collect yourself while I go get her.' He glanced quickly again at Anthony, then led Loretta to a chair, lowered her into it, patted her hand. 'You just stay there, you hear?'

He scampered upstairs. 'Marsha!' he called. 'Marsha! Lorie's got some news. Think it's important.'

There was rustling and creaking up there, a whispered conversation then muffled footsteps. All the time, Anthony was impatiently pacing the room.

Loretta's mother was wearing a pink nylon negligee. Her auburn hair was twisted around a mass of pink curlers. Her face, too, had been put to bed for the night. The face-cream made it a ghostly white. She raised one hand to her breast. 'What's this I hear, Lorie, about you got some news?'

'Throw this on or you'll catch your death of cold,' said Stanley, cocooning her in a bright quilted dressing gown.

'Yes, Ma. It's just . . .' Words failed her.

'Marsha,' Anthony announced in a firm, confident voice, 'I'd like to ask you for your daughter's hand in marriage.'

Mrs Wincheim clutched at Stanley for support. 'Marriage?'

'Yes, Ma,' Loretta repeated, standing now. 'Marriage.'

'If we have your approval?' added Anthony.

'But, of course.' Mrs Wincheim swallowed. 'If it's what Lorie wants?'

'More than anything in the world, Ma.'

Suddenly Stanley's arms were about her and he was squeezing her tightly to him. He could not stop hugging her. 'Lorie,' he croaked in her ear, 'you're a star, a star . . .'

'Stop making a fool of yourself, Stanley, and go get a bottle of that champagne,' Mrs Wincheim chided. She pulled him away and engulfed Loretta in the nylon warmth of her bosom. 'So exciting, baby! So exciting.' She patted Loretta's head and raised tearful eyes to Anthony. 'Promise to look after my baby? Look after her good, you hear?'

'Hey, what are we going to do about the wedding?' Stanley called from the kitchen. 'We'll need a hall. I could get a good deal on the gymnasium.'

'No!' Mrs Wincheim rebuked. 'We're talking class here. It'll have to be a hotel, somewhere real ritzy.'

'You know how much that costs?' Stanley appeared in the doorway with a bottle of a domestic brand in his hands. He shrugged and grinned. 'But what am I saying? Anthony, Lorie – we're so happy for you. Haven't I always told you, Lorie, you would go places? Haven't I always told you? I told you, didn't I?'

She looked up at Anthony and stood on tiptoe to kiss him on the lips.

She had not thought it possible but over dinner, tense and hurt though he had been, he had announced almost angrily that he was not going to let one damnfool mistake wreck their lives. That, she knew, was a very brave thing to have said. And she loved him all the more for it.

'Marriage,' she repeated, and linked her arm in his. 'I still can't believe it — marriage.'

# Chapter 36

Sonia Hardwicke leaned forward while the maid plumped up the pillows on the bed and piled them high behind her. She leaned back and waited. The maid carefully placed the breakfast tray on the bed. It had a wicker compartment to either side. On the left was the morning papers; on the right, the morning mail. On the tray itself were fresh orange juice, coffee, two hot croissants, a plate of muesli and a boiled egg.

The maid stood by the bed while Mrs Hardwicke checked the contents of the tray. 'Do you require anything else, Madam?'

'Perfect, Griselda. Oh, be a dear and bring me my address book, will you? It's on the hall table, I think. And the telephone.'

Mrs Hardwicke decapitated the egg and glanced through her mail, but immediately her maroon leather address book was handed to her, she put on her spectacles and quickly flicked through its wafer thin blue pages. 'Miss Camilla and Mr Max have gone out, haven't they?'

'Yes, Madam.'

'Good. Thank you, Griselda. That will be all.' She dialled the number of Conningsby and spoke to Gander. She spooned a mouthful of egg while she waited for him to find Lady Rudlow.

'Elizabeth darling, that you? . . . Yes, we adore Camilla. Absolutely no trouble at all . . . As I told you, she was a little reserved at first. Quiet, you know. Repetitive. She had that frightfully annoying habit of repeating back to you what you had just said . . . Stress? I know she's been under a lot of stress. But recently she seems to have been on a — how can I describe it? — very negative tack. Self-debasement, self-hatred — so destructive and so unnecessary, but so typical of the young . . .'

She spooned another mouthful of egg into her mouth, then dabbed the corners of her mouth with the linen napkin. 'But, my darling, I do think it's working. She hardly ever refers to that musician of hers. As far as we know Griselda, my maid, intercepted the only two letters the dear child sent to lover-boy. The first was all about her sorting herself out and not being ready for commitment — you know the kind of thing? — quite safe. And in the second, last week — I thought about ringing you, but I didn't want to raise false hopes . . . you know how the young are? — she actually broke the whole thing off. Pages and pages. A lot of rather touching, sentimental nonsense about breaking the bond of trust. I do so feel for her. Poor tormented heart! Just reading it made me feel quite young again. Anyway, we sealed them both up again and sent them on. I hope you approve . . .'

She sipped at the orange juice, wincing at the slightly sour taste. 'I wouldn't say he's quite out of sight, out of mind, but at least now she does seem to be able to look at other men . . . and, as far as I can read between the lines, sometimes rather more. Unfortunate, but there we are.

'Max tells me that they — yes, I'm afraid *they* — were

not exactly the companions he would have chosen. Rather louche, apparently. But anyway, *tant pis*, the important thing is that the live-in music maker has been given the heave-ho . . . and the hard school of experience is always the best one, isn't it? A few glamorous men later he'll be only a distant memory. She can get down then to the serious business of finding a suitable husband. I've dredged my address book for candidates. You must tell me your personal preference — extremely smart but penniless, or not *quite* so smart but stinking . . . I know, my dear, I know it's not the kind of choice one would ever wish to make, but these days where on earth do you expect me to find them? . . . My dear, it's not easy, really not easy. Anyway, it was a brainwave of yours to send her to me. And we love having her. No, no, I promise you it's been no trouble. No trouble at all. Now that's quite enough time spent on the children. I'm dying to hear all your news . . .'

Hugh walked into the Yellow Drawing Room.

'Good day?' asked Lady Rudlow, looking up from her seat by the fire.

He was still dressed in his hunting clothes and carried a whip in his right hand. His breeches were mudstained and smelled of horse sweat.

'Not bad. Five points. We killed two.'

'An awful lot has been going on while you've been out enjoying yourself,' Lady Rudlow said in a slightly strained, shrill voice, setting aside her canvas and frame. 'Anthony returned an hour ago direct from Heathrow. Apparently, he has proposed to that American girl.'

'Christ! He can't, he simply can't marry *her*! Mother, you told him not to be such a damn' fool?'

'Yes, of course, I did darling, but I doubt whether it will do any good. He is clearly besotted with her.' She sighed. 'I always feared that Anthony might do something reckless like this. I tried to explain to him that looks count for very little in the long term. If only he had a proper sense of family duty and responsibility − in his position, he shouldn't marry just *anybody*.'

'I need a drink. Can I get you anything, mother?'

'No, thank you, darling. I've had three already.'

Hugh poured himself a large neat malt, downed it in one, shuddered, sighed and refilled his glass.

'In the old days, of course, when parental control meant something,' Lady Rudlow announced, 'we would just have paid her off and sent Anthony for a spell in the Guards, but now everyone seems to choose their partners in such a haphazard manner. Except the Indians, of course. They're usually very happy, so I'm told. It's all much too serious a matter to be left to chance. If you think of how much trouble we all take when breeding racehorses . . .'

Hugh turned. 'Mother, please! We're talking about England in the late twentieth century. A little gold-digging trollop has just ensnared the son and heir and you're talking about Indians and racehorses.'

'Hugh, stop pacing, will you? You're making me quite giddy. Just say we were able to get rid of this little girl, then what? In my experience men almost always go for the same type. They never ever learn. Look at Archie Cottington − four wives, each one a lissom brunette, each one a disaster.'

She shrugged. 'If − and I say if − we were able to get rid of her, I bet you anything that within six months Anthony would return arm in arm with a carbon copy or maybe someone much worse. Maybe — I don't know — a drug crazed go-go dancer? Then where would we be?'

'Mother, I'm trying to be serious.'

'Darling, I *am* being serious. Very serious. Anthony was a very sick boy and as far as I can gather this girl has been extremely good at keeping him away from those beastly drugs. Very supportive. Very firm. And if she can keep on doing that, I really would not mind if she *were* a go-go dancer from. . .I don't know. Wherever it is that go-go dancers come from. He needs someone with mettle. You know, on reflection, mad though it sounds, she might even be the right choice for him.'

'But, for God's sake, the house, the history . . . Mother, are you seriously telling me we're going to stand by and let Ant marry that — '

'Darling, I know. It is a far from brilliant match, but in the eyes of the world Anthony is now a grown man. If the love birds are still cooing and flapping their wings in a month's time, then I think we'll just have to close ranks and put a brave face on it.'

'Not if I have anything to do with it. Mother, where is Anthony now?'

'Catching up on some papers, I think.'

Hugh drained his glass. He turned on his heels, slamming the drawing-room door behind him.

He found Anthony in the library seated in the leather chair by the fire.

'Ant, you can't be serious!' he announced as he crossed the room.

Anthony tossed aside the report he was reading and looked up casually. 'So you've heard, have you?'

Hugh looked down on his brother. 'Mother has just told me. You can't marry that . . . that little bitch!'

'You might speak civilly when you are referring to my future wife.'

The riding whip smacked on to the palm of Hugh's right hand. 'Don't be such a pompous arse, Ant. First you drag the family name through the mud with your pathetic drug addiction, and now you plan to marry an avaricious little whore. Sleep with her if you must, but why for God's sake do you have to marry her?'

'For the last time, Hugh, watch your language!'

'Painful though it may be, it's the truth, Ant. Thank God it hasn't been announced yet. There's still time to call the whole thing off.'

Hugh swung around suddenly and strode towards the Chippendale desk in the centre of the room. 'Don't be such a damn fool,' he called over his shoulder. 'Do you really think that she loves you?'

'Yes. I do.'

'In love with title, house and money. That I can believe.'

'I resent that, Hugh. You are in no position to judge. You've never been in love with anyone other than yourself.'

'Oh, aren't I?' Hugh perched on the edge of the desk and rolled the whip through his fingers. 'I think I am in a very good position to judge, considering Loretta and I are — such old friends. Has she ever told you about our time together?'

The colour drained from Anthony's cheeks. 'Yes, she did tell me that once — '

'I bet she didn't tell you the half of it.'

'Damn you!' Anthony rose and walked slowly

towards Hugh. 'All that happened some time before I met her.'

'Ant, I am only thinking of your future happiness,' he answered smoothly, 'as brother to brother. Divorce, as you know, is a very messy and expensive business. Your ridiculous infatuation with her has clouded your judgement. You can't see what's plain to all the world. She is after the house, your title and your money. You, I regret, just happen to be a necessary but incidental part of the package.'

'I love her and trust her,' Anthony replied firmly.

'Just ask yourself one question, Ant: If your sweet Loretta is such a saint, why did she make a dead set at me when she thought I was the heir to Conningsby? My charm? My rugged torso? My hairy chest?' he asked sardonically.

'Ant, she barely knew me! All it took was a few hot dinners before she was in bed with me – wanton, avaricious hussy. Honestly, is that the kind of girl you want to marry?'

Anthony bit his lip. His foot tapped nervously on the carpet. 'As I said before, all that happened before she met me.'

'So the leopard has changed its spots?'

'Let's get one thing straight. It was *me* who had to persuade *her* into marriage, not the other way around. I trust my feelings, Hugh. I feel sure that she loves me for myself, not my possessions, and she's anything but 'wanton'. She's very diffident about sex. Apart from that once with you, I'm not at all sure that she has ever – '

'And you believe that, do you?' Hugh chuckled and slowly shook his head.

'I don't see what's so funny.' Anthony was suddenly very pale.

Hugh sensed that finally he had found the way to undermine his brother's trust in Loretta. 'I am sorry, Ant, I just can't help finding it funny. She's really kept that act up all the time you have been going out with her, has she? What a prick-tease!'

Anthony stared at Hugh in silence. His lower lip trembled.

'No, my dear Ant, let me tell you about the *real* Loretta. She did not try her "almost-virgin" act with me. Pity really, it might have made it more of a challenge.

'I am sorry to have to tell you this, but with me, she was anything but inhibited . . . You can't really be serious about this girl. I mean, she wasn't even subtle about it. She was pawing at my clothes as we climbed the stairs, telling me how she couldn't wait to get me inside her, telling me exactly how she liked it.'

The fantasy was evolving in Hugh's mind. 'She was — how do I say it? — extremely imaginative when it came down to it. She had a few very special tricks which she certainly hadn't learned in a textbook — rather oriental in flavour.'

'Don't lie to me!' Anthony's face was flushed with anger. The veins around his neck were taut.

'But that's how it happened. Honestly, Ant. This *ingenue* act of hers is another of her tricks to trap you into buying some very shop-soiled goods. She came across as a very experienced little number. Like a call girl, really.'

'Bastard!'

Much too late, Hugh saw the fist coming towards him. He swerved to the left, but the fist followed and landed square on his jaw. He shuddered at the impact. His head spun. He tasted blood in his mouth. For a second his eyes lost their focus.

Hugh shook his head to clear it, pressed down on the desk behind him with the palm of his hand, and pushed himself back onto his feet.

Through a dull haze, he saw the outline of his brother weaving before him, like a boxer on guard. 'You had no right. . .!' he bellowed. He lunged forward blindly, lashing out with his hunting whip.

The whip whistled vainly through the air. 'Damn you!' he called, as Anthony danced backwards avoiding the blow.

His vision was clearing now. Anthony was in the space in front of the fireplace between the two sofas. As Hugh advanced, lashing out again with the whip, Anthony quickly sidestepped and tried to slide out between the end of the sofa and the wall.

Hugh ran forward, arms flailing. He swivelled around and brought down the whip in a side blow across Anthony's rump. He felt the handle of the whip reverberating in his hand.

Anthony bared his teeth, wincing at the pain, but he made no sound. Suddenly he lunged forward. Hugh felt his legs snap together, the pressure of Anthony's shoulder on his calves. He was falling forward, then his lips and chin were on the carpet and his nose was clogged with dust. Anthony was crawling up his back, pulling back his arms, locking them into his.

Hugh spun around and suddenly the two of them were rolling along the floor. One moment, the glass dome in the ceiling was spinning before him; the next, his mouth was forced against the weave of the carpet. A tripod table fell and a lamp shattered before finally they came to rest against the side of the sofa.

'You should learn some manners,' Anthony barked in his ear, tightening his hold. 'I know it's all lies. Admit it! Admit it, damn you!'

Hugh gave the barest nod.

'Pax!' Anthony called out triumphantly. He released his hold and lifted his weight off Hugh's back.

Hugh, freed now, twisted around on his haunches. 'That brings back memories, doesn't it, Ant?' he called as soon as he had regained his breath. He wiped the sweat from his brow. 'Just like old times in the nursery. I was only trying to do what any brother would do, old boy – save you from yourself. You must see that? Love makes fools of us all.'

'You're wasting your time, Hugh. I'm going to marry Loretta, and nothing you might say is going to persuade me otherwise.'

Hugh dabbed his swollen lip with the back of his hand. 'That's final, I suppose?'

'Yes.' Anthony grinned, 'You know if it hadn't been for you, I probably would never have even met Loretta. In a perverse sort of way, you've acted Cupid.' He rose unsteadily to his feet. 'A drink?'

'Why not?'

'What'll you have?'

Hugh shrugged. 'Oh, I don't know. Whatever Cupids usually have.'

# Chapter 37

'Madam?' The butler rose to his full height, and sniffed disdainfully. 'There is a person at the door.'

Mrs Hardwicke was dressed in a powder blue tracksuit. An appliqué-work rattlesnake rose up her left trouser leg, encircled her body three times and ended with its long curling tongue just below her right breast. '

She put down the copy of *Paris Match*. ' "Person"? By that, Geoffrey, I gather that you disapprove. What particular species of "person" is this?' She smiled as if sharing a private joke.

The butler bowed and grinned. 'All that I was trying to convey, Madam, was the fact that the person in question was a stranger and, as far as I could ascertain, a stranger without an appointment . . . He is seeking an interview with Miss Camilla.'

At that moment Steve walked in. 'Mrs Hardwicke?' He smiled. 'Sorry to impose, but — well, sorry . . .'

Mrs Hardwicke looked him up and down and nodded. 'Yes, come in, whoever you are.'

'Thank you.' He shook the snow from his hair.

Sonia observed him carefully as he crossed over to the fireplace. As he warmed himself, the snow on his leather jacket melted and ran down on to the carpet in little streams.

'I hope,' she said, 'you would not think I was prying unduly if I were to ask who you are?'

'No, of course not. The name's Bristow. Steve Bristow.'

'Of course.' She smiled and rose from the sofa. '*The* Steve Bristow. Coffee, Mr Bristow?'

'Yes, please. Thank you. That would be very civil. Very civil indeed.'

Mrs Hardwicke nodded to Geoffrey, then turned back to Steve. 'I've heard so much about you from Camilla.' She shook his hand. 'Forgive my surprise but, absent-mindedly, Camilla did not tell me you were coming.'

'She didn't know I was coming.'

'She didn't know?'

'Yeah, well − I just thought it was strange. I hadn't heard anything for a while, so as I happened not to be doing anything special this weekend − the album in the can and all − I thought, why not surprise her?'

'Yes, but more to the point. . .did she say that she wanted to see you?'

'Well, she didn't say she didn't, if that's any help. Nothing either way.'

'But I thought you two had − as they say − broken up?'

'Well. . .yes.'

The coffee arrived. Steve took a cup.

Mrs Hardwicke watched him. 'You know, Mr Bristow, I have been in a position to observe Camilla carefully over the last month, and understandably she has been very much affected by what happened to her father. I don't know the full story − I don't think any of us will ever know the full story − but certainly it was most unfortunate that Camilla went to see her father when she did. If I understand right, she was there at the end. Thoroughly morbid the whole thing, but there we are. Coffee how you like it?'

'Yes, thank you, Mrs Hardwicke.'

'Good. Without question, it has greatly affected her. That's why she's here.' She shook her head sadly. 'I'm just not at all sure what seeing you now will do to her.'

Steve's legs crossed and uncrossed. 'Er, like what?'

'Well, I know that it will upset her – that's for certain. Unhinge her, maybe. Her mind is in a very delicate state.'

'You think so?'

Mrs Hardwicke nodded and took a sip of coffee herself. 'I know so.'

'That bad, is it?'

'Afraid so,' she said gravely. 'I know it's a great sacrifice to ask of you, but if you love her – really love her – the kindest thing would be for you to stay away. Go back to England. Wait until she's ready, emotionally prepared.'

Steve sighed with a heavy heart. 'You sure, Mrs Hardwicke? Really sure? Last thing I would ever want to do is hurt Cammy.'

Mrs Hardwicke nodded again. 'Absolutely sure. Most understanding of you, Steve. I am sorry that you've had a wasted journey, but I know it's for the best. Now, all it would do is damage. Later, who knows? When you've finished your coffee, we'll check the flight times. I would have got the chauffeur to drive you to Geneva, but I've given him the day off. There is, however, a very good train.'

'I know,' said Steve, 'I've just come on it. Shame. Apart from seeing Cammy – Camilla, I mean – I was rather looking forward to a bit of skiing. Not that I'm an expert of course. Might try a few runs before heading back.'

'Yes, why not? Do you know Gstaad?'

'Nope. Where do you recommend?'

'Oh, the Eggli, or maybe the Wispile.' Geoffrey handed her a card. She examined it through a magnifying glass. 'Now let me see, there's a flight leaving Geneva at twenty-one thirteen and a train which gets you in at nineteen twenty-seven which would allow you − I never can work these things out − yes, well, nearly two hours to do all those tiresome things you always have to do at airports and time to do a couple of runs before you leave. Perfect!'

'Bullshit!' mouthed Steve to himself the moment he had left the chalet, and then again as he kitted himself out at the ski shop. He would find out the truth for himself. Loretta had rung him twice in the last week and told him that she was worried about Camilla. She had told him that he ought to get over there, and fast.

He checked a map. There were three main ski areas in Gstaad. He decided to pass on the two mountains which Mrs Hardwicke had mentioned. She would hardly direct him to the one where Camilla was, he reasoned. He would try the third: the Wasserngrat.

Gentle flurries of snow which seemed like nothing on the ground felt like gales while he was suspended on the open chair-lift some sixty feet in the air. He tried not to look up at the single length of piano wire which was all that was supporting him, and instead concentrated on the view: the forest of snowclad Christmas trees running down the mountainside; the undulations of hidden rocks and streams. He saw a lone ski-pole half-buried in the snow with a single glove resting on it. He swallowed.

He went up twice without finding her. He was not unduly bothered. He had all weekend and it would be easy as pie to track her down – all he had to do was make a few enquiries, find out which tearoom served the richest chocolate cake and stake it out. Failing that, he would wait for her to leave the chalet tomorrow morning . . .

Then, on the third descent, he saw her.

Hell, he had seen the girl in the turquoise and white overall twice already without realising it was her.

He blinked.

Yes, it was her all right. She had taken off the fake fur hat that had been her camouflage before, and now her long black hair ran in tangled snow-caked curls down her back.

He had watched, amazed, as she had jet-turned over a dozen moguls, shot down between the lift pylons, then stopped just below him and looked back up the mountain. He had not expected her to be an expert skier.

The muscles in his legs ached. Cold, melting snow trickled down the back of his neck. His Ray-Bans were all steamed up and slipping off his nose.

Steady, he thought. Carefully does it. Shoulders perpendicular, weight down the hill.

He quickly repositioned his sunglasses and brushed the snow out of his hair with gloved hands. He pointed the skis at a gentle angle to the slope and skied over, swishing through the wet snow. He stopped short of her. Just.

Still she had not noticed him. Still she stared up the hill, turning her head this way and that, as if she were looking for someone.

He sidestepped closer. A lump formed in his throat. He cleared it, leaned on his pole and said in a relaxed voice, 'Hi.'

She turned. 'My God,' she cried. 'Steve! What in hell are you doing here?'

'Oh,' he smiled toothily and shrugged, 'just thought I'd surprise you.'

'You most certainly have. I . . . I don't know quite what to say,' she replied, suddenly turning away. 'Didn't . . . didn't you get my letter?'

'Yeah, I did. That's why I've come.'

A shout came from further down the hill. Steve saw a lean blond man below, waving ski-poles at Camilla and hollering at her. She shouted and waved back in reply.

'Oh, Steve.' She frowned. Her sad eyes were only just visible behind the tinted glasses. 'I wish you hadn't come. It doesn't make it any easier . . . I'm afraid that I've got to go now. Enjoy your skiing.' At that, she headed straight over the shelf and into the moguls. She manoeuvred through them at speed, never changing her rhythm.

'Cammy, wait!' he called.

She skied on.


Panting and puffing, Steve finally skidded to a halt outside the mid-station. He sighed. He winced. His left ankle was throbbing after his last fall.

He blinked, trying to clear his vision. Steam was coming off his ski suit, his face, gloves and hair, like dry ice in a stage routine.

The queue outside the *télécabine* wound back and forth through a series of metal gates and railings. There must have been seventy to a hundred people waiting. A jaunty accordion tune was hammering in his ears.

He quickly snapped off his skis, winced again, then hobbled towards the entrance. He climbed on to the bottom rung of the metal barrier and craned over the heads of the queue, dodging the moving skis. She must be there. She must be!

'Cammy!' he shouted. 'Cammy!'

He blinked again and saw something turquoise and white at the head of the queue. He saw the lean blond man next to her holding two pairs of skis. A second later they had passed through a turnstile into the dark interior of the station and were gone.

'Wait, Cammy! Wait!' He tried to vault over the metal barrier, but the thick mass of moving sunburnt skiers pushed back at him. He jumped off the railings and raced around the side of the wood-framed building. Just beyond the *caisse*, he found a door marked *PRIVAT*. He pushed it open.

'Hey,' shouted a man in a donkey jacket.

Something glinted at him out of the darkness. Steve ducked, narrowly avoiding the approaching bubble car which had just swung round the corner. There was a heavy mechanical sound as the supporting strut of the car engaged on the track.

'Halt!' the man shouted again.

Steve ignored him, dodged a second car and ran along the narrow passageway beside the moving cars.

She was there on the platform not twenty feet away, climbing inside a waiting car. The lean blond man and two tall dark-skinned men were loading their skis on to the rack outside.

Steve rushed forward. 'Emergency, sorry.' He pulled

a pair of skis from the rack at random, pushed aside the man who was just trying to climb into the bubble, and clambered in himself. He sighed with relief when the doors wheezed shut.

Camilla watched Steve in silence as he took his seat opposite her. The sunglasses hid her eyes. Her mouth curled slightly downwards.

Steve bent forward. 'Cammy, please . . . we've got to talk.'

She did not reply, merely pulled out a lipstick holder and smoothed white salve over her already white lips.

'Cammy, this is ridiculous. I thought — I mean, we've been apart now six whole weeks. In my book that's quite long enough a break for anybody.'

'And what,' said Camilla finally, 'makes you think that I have the slightest desire to return to England? I happen to be enjoying myself.'

'As I said, you've been away quite long enough. And as a matter of fact,' he adjusted the Ray-Bans on his nose, 'I happen to be missing you. The place just doesn't feel right without you.'

'Nice of you to say so, Steve, but I thought I'd made myself plain.'

'It's not doing you any good being out here, I know it. Look, Cammy, I love you, I really do. Come back,' he pleaded. 'I beg you, come back.'

Very slowly, very deliberately, she shook her head. Then she said: 'Steve, may I introduce you to my *friend*, Max Cantozani.'

The man nodded to him. He grinned and started firing questions at Steve about who he was, what he did, what his flight had been like, how the weather was in England.

Camilla turned her head and stared out of the window.

She stayed like that without uttering another word until the *télécabine* entered the dark chamber of the top station.

Immediately they were outside, Camilla and the lean blond man snapped on their skis and headed off down the black run.

'Wait for me,' called Steve, but already they were away. 'Wait,' he cried again vainly. '*Wait*!' He angled his skis, and snowploughed down the gully after them.

They were only distant specks now, but he was sure that he saw them dodge under a red cordon that marked the edge of the piste some half mile away.

When finally he reached the same spot, he pushed down hard with his legs, strained, and dug the edges of the skis into the snow. He slid slowly to a halt.

He wiped his brow, gasped for breath and blinked into the light across the wide deep bowl of unpisted snow on the other side of the cordon. He looked down at the clear, deep groves left by two pairs of skis in the soft snow. He thought he heard — he was sure he heard — Camilla's 'Whoopee' from somewhere below.

He swallowed, sighed, 'What the hell?' and ducked under the cordon.

Almost immediately he found himself gaining speed. The snow was thick, crusty, and ridged like the furrows in a ploughed field. His knees were vibrating like worn shock absorbers. At each bump the pain in his ankle grew more intense. He leaned back, he leaned forward, but whatever he did only seemed to make the skis go faster still.

The wind rushed through his hair, pressed the skin against his face, froze the sweat almost before it formed. On and on he went, traversing the great white candyfloss bowl, up and over into a second gully.

He looked down then and swallowed. This slope was steeper still. He jerked his body around, trying to turn, pressing down hard with his ankles.

Suddenly something hard smacked into his shoulder. The snow was all around him, in his mouth, trousers, jacket, boots. His Ray-Bans and skis had gone. He took four deep, cold breaths and sat up. He squinted down the mountain and sighed.

At the bottom of the valley, far beneath him, he could see Camilla and the lean blond man turning through this thick porridge with the grace of swans gliding on a perfectly still pond. He saw her stop. She seemed to be waving at him.

Excited now, he stood and waved back at her. She was shouting something. He cupped his gloved hand to his ear, but all he could hear was the diffuse echo.

He spat the snow out of his mouth. 'Hang on. Down in a mo!' he shouted back, then brushed his suit and turned to search for his skis.

A great wall of glistening snow hung above the rock face immediately above him, casting a deep shadow across the top of the gully.

He walked three paces up the mountainside. On the fourth step, the ground seemed to rock beneath him. A pebble rolled past him, puckering the snow.

He looked up. The rock was bare. The snow had turned into a steaming liquid mass like a dense fog. The whole mountain seemed to be rolling down towards him.

It happened so quickly he did not even have time to cry out. The moving mass lapped at his knees. His arms flailed and he fell. He was swept along for a moment, along with the rock and the moving sea, then the second wave came, the deeper snow.

'Oh my God!' he cried. 'My God.' It struck him like a body punch. Suddenly it was dark. He was cocooned. He knew he was moving only from the lurching in his stomach and the sense of everything shaking. He gasped for breath, but all he seemed to inhale was snow. It was in his nostrils, his mouth, his ears. And it was cold, very cold. He flailed again, trying to clear a space around him, but this pressure that pushed down on him out of the darkness, punched out at him again . . .

She had seen it all from where she stood: the lone figure momentarily riding high like a surfer on a wave, the fall, then nothing but moving, sliding snow.

'Steve!' she yelled. 'Steve!' though she knew he could not hear.

The ground moved beneath her as she watched the snow sweep past her, some fifty yards to her right. The wind roared too. Along with the rock and the dirt, she thought she saw the red plastic top of a ski-pole half way along but she could not be sure.

It was all over very quickly. At the bottom of the gully, the mass of snow settled in the well of the bowl. There was nowhere else for it to go.

Camilla skied down. 'Steve!' she called again. 'Steve, where are you?' She took hold of her ski-pole and dragged it through the snow.

'Can you hear me, Steve?' she yelled. 'If you can, start digging, but spit first, you hear? Spit first to find out where's up and where's down.'

She stabbed at the ground, tears welling in her eyes. Max was digging too. 'Faster, faster!' she cried. She hit something hard. A stone. Seconds later, she found a pole. 'Please God,' she cried, 'please, please . . .'

She could hardly see in front of her now. Tears blurred her vision as she stabbed at the snow, trawling it for some sign . . .

Something hard again.

She bent down. She scooped away the snow with her hands in sharp frantic movements.

The sleeve of an anorak.

She dug deeper. She felt a vibration, a movement beneath her. At first she could not be sure.

When finally she saw him, caked in ice and snow, skin tinged green; when finally he spluttered out 'Thanks', all she could do was laugh and grin and touch him and rub his icy hands in hers.

'Don't you dare go doing anything like that again,' she said with genuine savagery. 'You hear? Never, never, never . . .'

She rubbed his frozen cheek. ''Fraid we haven't got any brandy. Try this.' She bent forward and kissed his cold lips, breathing her warmth into him. She kissed him on the neck, the chin. 'Oh, Steve, I've been such a fool . . .'

He slowly opened his eyes. He shrugged and smiled. 'What do you think I've been?'

She scooped away more snow and laid her head against him. 'I need you, Steve. I don't care what happens. From now on we'll stay together, right?'

The rapid heaving of his chest was the best reply she could have looked for. His frozen arms reached out and hugged her to him.

'Right, right, right,' he whispered again and again.

# Chapter 38

'Stanley, tell the driver to slow down.'

'Jeez, any slower and the car will stall.'

'But we're so early,' Loretta insisted. The bodice of her ivory satin wedding dress was embroidered with little seed pearls. It was very tight down to the hips from where it flowed into a full skirt.

'OK.' Mr Wincheim pushed a button and the glass partition between them and the uniformed chauffeur slid down silently. 'Driver,' he called, 'once more around the block.'

'There aren't any blocks in the countryside,' Loretta corrected.

'Hell, he knows what I mean.'

The indicators flashed and the huge black Daimler turned and wheeled down the narrow country lane. Hawthorn bushes, snowberries and wild privet lined the road on either side. The crocuses were out and a few brave daffodils were just coming through.

'My hair all right?' she asked for the second time in so many minutes. 'Nothing out of place?'

He glanced across. Loretta's hair was swept up into a chignon with whispers of loose curls at the nape of her neck. The veil of Brussels lace was crowned with a diamond and pearl tiara. 'Yeah, great,' he nodded. 'Don't touch it.'

Loretta pressed the bouquet of large creamy lilies to her veil and breathed in their rich scent to check that she was not dreaming. The three months since Anthony had proposed to her had passed in a whirl of wedding lists, engagement parties and dress fittings. She could hardly believe that now she was actually on her way to church. 'So, Stanley,' she asked distractedly, 'what do you think of the house?'

'What do I think? Jeez, what do I think! It's like . . . like San Simeon.'

'Only more tasteful.'

'Yeah, you're right. Have you seen the laundry room?'

'No, I haven't seen the laundry room. Now, Stanley,' she asked warily, 'you didn't embarrass me by asking Elizabeth to show you the laundry room, did you? *Did you*?'

''Course I asked.' He shrugged. 'What's wrong with that? It interests me. As I always say, once a professional, always a professional. I suggested some changes too. A couple of new industrial machines — Rex or Bendix — would save a fortune.'

'Stanley!'

'No, I promise you, Elizabeth was *really* grateful.'

'Stanley, please, I just don't want to hear about it. Not now.'

'Sorry, Lorie. I was forgetting myself again. Can't think straight.' His eyes were misty. He patted her hand and sighed. 'Look OK, do I? Not going to embarrass you, am I?'

'Tie's a bit crooked, otherwise great. Hey, how about me? In case you've forgotten, *I'm* the one who happens to be getting married. *I'm* the one who's meant to be getting the nerves.'

'Sorry. I just . . . feel so proud of you. Almost as if you were my own daughter. When you told us I thought that maybe – just maybe – you were exaggerating a teensy bit. But, Jeez, you were playing it down. And Elizabeth has been so charming, such a lady to your ma and me . . . and Anthony,' he added, 'he's a true gentleman. Matthew got along with him real well.' Stanley shook his head. 'You know, I still can't get used to the idea of you living in that heap. You're not going to get all high and mighty with us, are you, Lorie?'

'Oh, Stanley, don't be ridiculous,' she soothed. 'I'm still the same old Queens girl. Nothing's going to change that. Got a little extra living space, but it's only a house after all.'

The car navigated the corner and the church came into view. The sunlight danced over the flying buttresses casting interlocking shadows on the grass beneath. Already the sounds of the organ swelled above the voices of the huge crowd jostling and milling outside.

'Oh, my God!' he exclaimed. 'I thought you said you were having a quiet family wedding. Only half the world's *paparazzi* are here, that's all.'

Loretta grinned. 'Yeah, well, a quiet wedding is what we wanted . . . but these things are relative, you know.'

The car stopped. The door swung open. Shona, the chief bridesmaid, stepped forward and winked at Loretta.

She took a deep breath and climbed out. She blinked and smiled as flashlights popped all around her. A cheer rose up from the tenants. The Bishop came forward. He spoke to her in hushed tones. She tried to concentrate on what he was saying, but her eyes were on his gold-threaded cream cope. Now that was something! She had expected some minor competition from the women, but from the men?

'Are you ready?' he repeated.

'Er . . . yes.' She turned around. The six foot train stretched out evenly behind her. She nodded to Shona and together they advanced towards the porch, bathed in the brilliance of the *paparazzi*'s ever flashing lights.

The soft afternoon light shone through the stained glass window high above her, sending great patches of colour over the stone-flagged floor. The damp, dusty air was thick with the scent of the roses, cyclamen and hyacinths entwined about the columns.

Straight ahead of her was the family vault. Behind gilt railings surmounted by ornate tooled spears, the Elizabethan Rudlows, in bonnets and frills, doublets and hose, stared out at her from the bas-relief on the wall.

She felt a tug at her hem. She looked down and saw a ring of flowers on golden hair. A bridesmaid dressed in pale yellow spotted organdie gazed up at her, wide-eyed. 'Where are we going?' she whispered. 'To heaven?'

'No, my dear.' She could not help smiling. 'Just up the aisle. For now.'

There was much swooshing of dresses and clattering of feet as they lined up. In front of Loretta was the verger with his rod of office and the Bishop in his gold-threaded cope; behind her, the six bridesmaids, four pages, and maid of honour.

'Shona,' she called jokingly, 'don't look so nervous. Smile!' Then the bishop nodded gravely. Loretta lowered her palm over Stanley's shaking hand. The great organ wheezed and sounded a long low note. The murmur of conversation ahead of them stopped.

The verger and the Bishop were advancing now. Loretta took a deep breath. Immediately she stepped forward, she felt the weight of the train on her back. She steadied herself and passed through the Victorian arch into the aisle. Suddenly the light from the window fell on her veil: the figures around her were nothing but flashes of light and broad blocks of colour.

One pace forward and the dusty wedge of light was above her now. Brightly painted faces stared at her from beneath rows of coloured hats: pill box; cloche; wide-brimmed straw; netted boaters. Spring colours everywhere.

Anthony's side of the church was crammed with people she had never seen before. The Rudlows, apparently, were related to everybody, and the few they were not related to were intimate friends. There were three Dukes, a Marquis, five Earls, the French, Spanish, Greek and Belgian Ambassadors, and the Home Secretary.

Loretta's side of the church looked embarrassingly sparse by comparison. There was André in a grey morning coat so light it was nearly cream. Around his neck was a vast silk cravat held in place by a two-carat diamond. He was smiling and beaming at her, almost in tears. Lady Wellingham, standing next to him, had her eyes rather obviously on the diamond and not the bride. There was Bob who had gamely come over for the ceremony. She winked at him, though he probably missed it through her veil. Julie was next to him in a kind of sequinned tent.

Despite the organ and the commotion, her high heels seemed to click very loudly against the floor.

On the groom's side, she saw Jane Chalmers looking

425

dignified but rather sad, as if putting a brave face on a gross infringement of the person; then Marie-Louise, always ridiculously theatrical, dressed in black Armani of all things. Directly behind the family pew she saw Steve. He was leaning forward, whispering something to Camilla. Lady Rudlow was very formal and correct in a raspberry red wool Chanel suit with matching hat. She wore a very convincing smile.

On the other side of the church stood Loretta's step-brother Matthew, the scholar, in a hired Moss Bros suit which – alas – didn't quite fit. She had told him not to leave it until the last moment. He was comforting Ma who was almost completely obscured by a handkerchief and a huge Bill Blass straw hat.

Then, as the aisle opened up beyond the pews, she could see them: Anthony, immaculate and smiling, his blond hair swept back, standing proud and erect; and by his side Hugh, watching her every movement, expressionless.

She climbed the single step up to the altar rail. She winked at Anthony who grinned back.

Suddenly the church filled with the sound of fifty soprano and contralto voices in perfect pitch. Loretta tried to hold it back but could not: a single tear ran down her powdered cheek.

The service seemed somehow to flash by in a haze of light and colour and waves of sound. She wanted to turn and look at all her friends, eavesdrop on what they were saying, but she stared ahead rigidly at the altar and the cross. Anthony answered 'I will' in such a deep resounding voice she hardly recognised it. She, to her surprise, was only just audible.

Then the Bishop said: ' "I pronounce that they be Man

and Wife together. . ." ' and suddenly she felt a kind of glow fill her whole body. A smile of triumph danced about her lips.

A chopper was waiting for them on the grass just beyond the main portico of the house. They boarded it immediately the reception was over. Loretta's cheeks still burned from the congratulatory kisses and compliments; her ears still reverberated with the laughter and the cheers.

She threw her bouquet to Camilla. She smiled as she saw the tears fill her sister-in-law's eyes. Camilla hugged Steve and pressed her head against his chest.

Loretta was still waving when the figures below were only matchsticks. She thought, though, that she could just make out her mother down there, who in the excitement of their departure had forgotten to hold on to her hat and was now searching for it in the rhododendrons with Stanley.

Anthony had not told her where they were going for the first night. From the direction in which they were travelling, she suspected that it might be somewhere on the south coast; but the helicopter continued over the grey-blue mass of the Channel, and landed just outside Paris from where a cream Rolls-Royce Corniche took them to the Place Vendôme.

The bed-chamber of the *Suite Imperiale* in the Ritz Hotel had pale silk damask on the walls. Antique furniture with fine marquetry work and ormolu mountings studded the room. An Empire chandelier headed with gilt feathers hung from the ceiling. The bed had a plumed gilt wood half-tester above it, from which hung silk damask in fringed scallops. By the side of the high windows stood a faux-marble column with a huge arrangement of spring flowers.

They dined lightly off foie gras and salad, hot mousselines of langoustine and petits four which were brought to the room by a uniformed waiter and set out on a table by the window. Then it was time to retire for the night.

She still did not know quite how she would react when Anthony came to her. Her limbs were tense, her head still spinning from the champagne, but immediately she felt the touch of his fingers as they began to smooth her skin, she found that for once she felt no apprehension, no fear.

All her life she had been striving for the security that her father had denied her. All her life she had felt like a victim waiting for something to happen. Now, at last, she felt these fears being soothed away with each gentle movement of Anthony's hands.

He leaned slightly towards her. His lips trembled. She kissed him lightly once, eyes half-closed, then playfully retreated. His lips returned, lingering for a second, barely touching the soft membrane of her own, then he kissed her hard.

In that kiss, she sensed the sensitivity of him. While before this sensitivity had frightened her because she had feared its demands on her, now she basked in it.

She saw what a fool she had been. What she had interpreted as strength in a man, more often than not had been nothing but stubbornness. Men like Hugh had seemed strong and imperturbable only because they did not feel, only because they did not see, only because they did not understand.

She shuddered as she felt the waves of tension leaving

her body, and it occurred to her that never before in her whole life had she really truly relaxed. She had never let herself go.

She gazed up at the moving shadows on the plasterwork ceiling, at the tassels and plumes of the half-tester above the bed, and she sighed.

Her body was tingling all over yet she felt a kind of peace, a calm she had never experienced before.

There was nothing selfish or hurried about any of his movements. There was a confidence about him. All the anguish in him had gone.

As he went lower, his hands and mouth teasing her, she felt her body cry out for him. She closed her eyes, steadying herself. 'Yes,' she whispered. 'Yes.'

But still he did not come to her. His hands and mouth kept on driving her on, making her bubble up inside until the tension was like a coiled spring that would snap at the slightest pressure.

Just as she thought she would scream, he entered her.

She raised her body very slightly and let him slide in deeper until she felt the tip of him against her. She breathed in sharply and tightened. She wanted him to stay like that forever. Never before had she felt so complete, so fulfilled. But slowly he moved back and she felt him sliding away from her. She gripped his back and waited for his return.

He was very gentle, very slow. His movements were as smooth and supple as a dolphin sliding into water, and he was playing with her, taking her up into the skies and keeping her there until she could bear the tension of it no more.

There was an intensity about his movements. It was as if his whole mind and body had been transmuted into this one act. She was a goddess, mother earth, giver of all things. He was crawling back into the womb. He was losing himself in her.

His pace quickened. The stars and heavens raced in a furious dance. Her body melted with the heat of him. She held on tight, nails biting into his skin, and screamed: 'Yes . . . yes . . . *yes*.'

# Chapter 39

April, a year later: London was bitterly cold. Inside The Retreat, however, it was perpetual tropical summer.

A blue and white light came off the pool and dappled the walls of the huge arched atrium. A red and yellow parakeet squawked overhead and flapped its wings listlessly. Mynah birds sang too. The palm trees rustled gently in the air-conditioned, dehumidified air. Bach played softly in the background.

Loretta slicked back her hair. She tugged gently at the sides of the green scalloped swimsuit, then, lazily, she swam one more length of the pool.

Two girls with perfectly honed bodies chatted and trod water, side by side. The one on Loretta's far left was white-skinned and dark-haired; the other, blonde with a deep tan. As if to steady herself, the blonde reached out. Her hand touched the other girl's white breast just above the nipple. The dark one laughed, then playfully pushed the other girl away.

Loretta shuddered. As she climbed out of the pool, she sensed the two girls watching her. She shook her hair then bent down and plucked a towel off the pile. She quickly wrapped it around her and sauntered through the tiny tropical rain forest over to the Turkish Steam Room.

A mosaic of brilliant blue, black and gold, covered the

431

walls. She laid down a second towel on the cold marble slab, peeled off her costume and lay on her back, letting the heat and the moisture open and cleanse her pores.

The high humidity reminded her of those first days of her honeymoon before the cooler weather had come. Strangely, neither Anthony nor Hugh had ever mentioned the holiday house in Nassau to which they had gone. Neither had they mentioned the twenty-five-foot Sorrento Sundancer moored in the harbour there.

Those had been languorous days. Loretta had never seen Anthony more content than when out in the boat in pursuit of blue marlin and sail fish. He had sat for hours on the swivel chair in the cockpit while she had lain stretched out on the foredeck, perfecting an even golden tan. She had read a bit, slept a bit, waiting for Anthony's whoops of pleasure at the sudden screech of the reel.

In the evenings they had either danced at The Club or had gone to one of the countless parties. She was glad that she had brought her jewels. The simplicity of island life during the day had given way at nightfall to a very cosmopolitan sophistication. Faces from New York which had featured monthly in the pages of *Town and Country* and *Interview*, or which she had glimpsed from afar at openings, were now those of constant dinner companions, friends and acquaintances.

She had deflected the gentle probing about her upbringing from the older, more conservative strain. She was an aristocrat now with youth, beauty and money – credentials which even the most conservative of East Coast coteries could not ignore. The Rudlows were a golden couple, and had been fêted for their glamour, for their extravagant parties, and strangely enough for the convenience of hitching a lift on their little Rudlow Moth biplane for shopping trips to Miami.

At one of the parties they attended their host had circulated, along with the liqueurs and the pre-Castro cigars, a silver-gilt box which, he had claimed, contained the purest possible cocaine, especially imported for him by his own private mule. Connoisseur's stuff. But to Loretta's delight, Anthony had shaken his head and passed it untouched along the table without even a moment's hesitation.

The steam clogged her breath and made her body glow. The two girls who had been in the pool now lay side by side on a slab a few feet from her. Each was rubbing and smoothing the other's back.

As Loretta rose, both girls turned. Their eyes flicked over her body. One of the girls smiled. Loretta shook her head, tightened the towel about her and walked out, back into the covered leafy atrium. It was cooler there and she felt the slightest of breezes on her warm skin.

'Are you ready, Lady Rudlow?' asked the tall dark girl in a white overall.

Loretta nodded and followed the girl through into an adjoining room. There were rows of ferns and pot plants there too and a Rousseauesque mural on the walls. From between the trees, a black leopard stared out with bright yellow eyes.

Next to the day bed was a low table containing dozens of little glass jars. The smell of jasmine and spices rose from the pan on the small electric burner.

Loretta lay down on a fresh towel on the bed. The girl scooped up a little oil. Loretta sighed as she felt the warmth of the oil on her stomach, and again as the expert fingers smoothed the muscles around her neck.

She would never forget her homecoming to Conningsby. When they had landed at the helipad beyond the lake, an open carriage — a black victoria — had been there to meet them. The coachwork had shone like satin in sunlight. Two footmen in powdered wigs had stood pillion. Two behatted coachmen in the olive green and grey Rudlow livery had sat behind two matching dappled greys.

She remembered the way the carriage had rocked and creaked as she had mounted; the smell of the old leather and coach wax; above all, the men's smiles. It was the tradition, Anthony had told her. She had felt very proud, very regal as the carriage had bounced along the drive. The estate workers had lined the way to welcome them home and as Loretta and Anthony passed, had shouted and cheered. The women had thrown flowers; the men their hats.

Loretta had waved back until she felt her arm go numb. She had swallowed hard and tried not to cry.

In front of the house, dwarfed by the huge Palladian portico above them, the inside staff had waited in line. All had worn black and white or shades of grey. Gander the butler had stood closest to the door, then Mrs Dauney, the housekeeper, Mrs Grundy the cook, two footmen, the two ladies maids, the four house maids, and last of all Peter, the odd job man.

As soon as the carriage had drawn to a halt, Gander had walked towards them, very erect, very self-important. He had opened the carriage door and bellowed in his master-of-ceremonies operatic bass: 'Welcome to Conningsby, Your Ladyship.'

As she had dismounted, the men had bowed and the women had curtsied, like a wave passing down the line.

Anthony had kissed her, then to the sound of cheers he had scooped her up and carried her all the way up the steps and across the threshold into the hall.

Soon afterwards, there had been the launch of the Condor at the Paris Airshow. From the outside, the Rudlow chalet had looked much the same as all the others with a prefabricated sloping roof and dirty blue and white awnings. Inside, though, it had been carnival time.

For the campaign Ken Slipper had transformed the interior into a little slice of England. Between two huge photographs of the Condor, the bird, and the Condor, the plane, had stood an illuminated cardboard cut-out of Big Ben with a working clock. Girls in tight Union-Jack mini-skirts, like something out of Carnaby Street in the sixties, had squeezed between guests dispensing champagne and smoked salmon canapés.

Even Loretta, who previously had had no real interest in planes, had felt a tingle down her spine when the Condor finally swooshed overhead. The underbelly was a buffed pewter against the light. The Red Rudlow emblem shimmered on the plane's tail fin.

She had stood beside Anthony and hugged him as he glowed with pride. The orders had come rolling in. The first two years' production had been sold within a fortnight of the launch.

'There we are, Lady Rudlow.'

'Thanks. That was just what I needed.' Loretta blinked up at the light and sighed. 'Maybe if you could do my stomach again? Very, very lightly.'

The girl in the white overall smiled. 'Yes, of course. We don't want any stretch marks, do we? How long to go now?'

'Only six weeks.'

Loretta closed her eyes. She breathed in the smell of the scented oils. Once more, the strong supple fingers came down and ever so gently smoothed the tender stretched skin.

Her mouth opened slightly. 'Yes,' she purred. She sighed. 'Yes. Just there.'

# Chapter 40

It had all been like a dream: the rattling of the trolley beneath her, the fluorescent lights on the hospital ceiling flashing by before her eyes. Her hands had clutched her belly through the thick cotton robe. It had been as numb and as hard as the shell of an egg.

She had heard the tread of Anthony's and her mother-in-law's footsteps following behind. 'There, there,' Elizabeth had said. 'Absolutely nothing to worry about. Nothing at all. They're so good at these things nowadays. Quite unlike my day. The trouble I had with Anthony, you know, quite beastly. He was enormous . . .'

The white-coated orderlies had wheeled the trolley round, making Loretta's head spin. The corridor had become a cell of polished steel. Anthony had planted one last kiss on her forehead and Elizabeth had waved goodbye just before the lift gates had wheezed shut behind her. 'With you in spirit, my dear,' had been her mother-in-law's parting words.

Through the swing doors, she remembered, the air had been heavy with the smell of antiseptic. She had heard the squeak of yellow Wellington boots on tiles. There had been bright signs everywhere, a flashing light, then she had been wheeled through another door into a white-tiled room. The interrogation lamps had made her eyes water.

'Easy now,' someone had said. Kindly eyes sandwiched between masks and white caps had stared down at her. She had floated up in strong arms on to the white disinfected slab.

'This won't take long,' a disembodied, muffled voice had said and already her lower abdomen had been stripped bare and someone had painted crosses and lines upon it with a felt tip pen. Wires, needles, tapes had shuddered on her skin. Then she had seen the glinting steel of the surgeon's scalpel.

The air had broken with a cry. For a second she had been confused. She had thought it was her own voice, or, foolishly, the surgeon's. The room had danced around her. She had struggled to keep her eyes open. Tears had misted them and clogged her vision. She had squinted up through the bright lights and seen in the surgeon's rubber-gloved hands the soft hazy outline of a miniature body. Tiny doll-like waving arms. Tiny clenched toes . . .

'Oh God,' she had cried. 'Oh God!'

The tears had started streaming, then. She had felt a profound peace, a sense that she had just witnessed a miracle. All she had wanted to do was take her baby to her and clutch it to her breast.

As they had brought it to her, it had kicked and flailed, eager for life. She had felt the warmth of its slippery body against hers. She had closed her eyes.

'Thank you, God. Thank you for a boy.'

Back in the nursery at Conningsby, the tiny figure lay asleep in its cradle. Very thin blond hair covered the baby's head. His minute, perfect hands clutched the blanket. The bed clothes rose very slightly at each breath.

Loretta had left the nursery just as it was. The frieze of playing bunny rabbits still ran around the top of the pink and blue striped walls. The old dappled grey rocking horse still stood in the centre of the room.

She sat there, quiet and content, gently rocking the cradle. She thought back to the pain of her own childhood, to her father's drunken outbursts, to that dark night when she had been attacked in the elevator. None of these memories now held any fear. In a way she was even glad that had been the course upon which chance had taken her. Painful though it had been, it had given her the means of helping Anthony when he had needed it. Now, in return, he had given her the love and security for which she had craved.

She glanced across to the painted dresser on the far wall and there on the top shelf was the doll in the burgundy velvet cloak trimmed with speckled fur. 'Yes,' she remembered with a smile, 'the Lady of the Court.'

*More Compulsive Fiction from Headline:*

# BUTTERFLY

## THE DELICIOUSLY PROVOCATIVE NEW NOVEL

# KATHRYN HARVEY

'Glamour, wickedness and passion spark this
highly commercial novel, which builds to a
dramatic and unexpected conclusion.'
*Publishers Weekly*

What is the secret of Butterfly – the most
discreet, the most luxurious, the most
exclusive club in Beverly Hills? Masquerading
behind the facade of a chic Rodeo Drive men's
store, it offers its all-female clientele a chance
to fulfil their wildest sexual fantasies. Who is
the genius behind this magical dream palace?
Whose brilliant idea was it to create a fantasy
world of sensuality, where women would find
total discretion, total safety in which to act
out their most secret desires? Where they
would find elaborately opulent settings in
which to enjoy the partner of their choice?

If they only knew it, Butterfly's members have
much in common with each other – and with
the club's mysterious founder. Each has a
hidden past, a broken heart and a desire for
sexual and emotional fulfilment in a modern
woman's world . . .

' . . . a gilded extravaganza of sexual revenge'
*Company*

' . . . a great read, raunchy and cleverly
concluded' *Today*

FICTION/GENERAL    0 7472 3220 2

# A selection of bestsellers from Headline

**FICTION**

| | | |
|---|---|---|
| ONE GOLDEN NIGHT | Elizabeth Villars | £4.99 □ |
| HELL HATH NO FURY | M R O'Donnell | £4.99 □ |
| CONQUEST | Elizabeth Walker | £4.99 □ |
| HANNAH | Christine Thomas | £4.99 □ |
| A WOMAN TO BE LOVED | James Mitchell | £4.99 □ |
| GRACE | Jan Butlin | £4.99 □ |
| THE STAKE | Richard Laymon | £4.99 □ |
| THE RED DEFECTOR | Martin L Gross | £4.99 □ |
| LIE TO ME | David Martin | £4.99 □ |
| THE HORN OF ROLAND | Ellis Peters | £3.99 □ |

**NON-FICTION**

| | | |
|---|---|---|
| LITTLE GREGORY | Charles Penwarden | £4.99 □ |
| PACIFIC DESTINY | Robert Elegant | £5.99 □ |

**SCIENCE FICTION AND FANTASY**

| | | |
|---|---|---|
| HERMETECH | Storm Constantine | £4.99 □ |
| TARRA KHASH: HROSSAK! | Brian Lumley | £3.99 □ |
| DEATH'S GREY LAND | Mike Shupp | £4.50 □ |
| The Destiny Makers 4 | | |

*All Headline books are available at your local bookshop or newsagent, or can be ordered direct from the publisher. Just tick the titles you want and fill in the form below. Prices and availability subject to change without notice.*

Headline Book Publishing PLC, Cash Sales Department, PO Box 11, Falmouth, Cornwall, TR10 9EN, England.

Please enclose a cheque or postal order to the value of the cover price and allow the following for postage and packing:
UK: 80p for the first book and 20p for each additional book ordered up to a maximum charge of £2.00
BFPO: 80p for the first book and 20p for each additional book
OVERSEAS & EIRE: £1.50 for the first book, £1.00 for the second book and 30p for each subsequent book.

Name .................................................................................

Address .............................................................................

.............................................................................

.............................................................................